The Emperor of China in a House of Ill Repute

The Emperor of China in a House of Ill Repute

Songs of the Imperial Visit to Datong

幸雲曲

Pu Songling

蒲松齡

Translated by
Wilt L. Idema

OXFORD
UNIVERSITY PRESS

Oxford University Press is a department of the University of Oxford.
It furthers the University's objective of excellence in research, scholarship,
and education by publishing worldwide. Oxford is a registered trade mark of
Oxford University Press in the UK and in certain other countries.

Published in the United States of America by Oxford University Press
198 Madison Avenue, New York, NY 10016, United States of America.

Library of Congress Cataloging-in-Publication Data
2023915081

ISBN 978-0-19-760630-8

Printed by Sheridan Books, Inc., United States of America.

Contents

Acknowledgments

Rummaging through the backyard of Chinese literature, I have always re-lied on the unstinting cooperation and assistance of the library staffs at the institutions where I have worked. It is a pleasure for me to once again express my gratitude to the staff of the Asian Library at Leiden University and also that of the Harvard-Yenching Library at Harvard.

While Pu Songling is an extremely well-studied author, most scholars have focused on the classical tales of his *Strange Stories from a Chinese Studio*. One of the rare exceptions in the Anglophone world in recent years has been Lu Zhenzhen, whose thesis "The Vernacular World of Pu Songling" helped to rekindle my own interest in Pu Songling's works in his own local dialect. Whenever I consulted her over the course of the present translation project, Zhenzhen happily shared the materials she had collected during her dissertation research with me. These materials proved to be very helpful, and I am deeply grateful for her generosity.

I also want to express my gratitude to the numerous Chinese colleagues I have never met who spent their careers in collecting, editing, and study-ing the rustic songs of Pu Songling. Without the availability of the superb research of Zhang Shuzheng on the language of Pu Songling's vernacular works, I would not have dared to tackle *Songs of the Imperial Visit to Datong*.

I thank the editors of the Hsu-T'ang Library for their decision to include this relatively little-known work in the series. I also thank them and the staff at Oxford University Press for their many suggestions for improving my English and for all the care with which they have seen this volume through the press.

April 2023
Leiden
Wilt L. Idema

Chinese Dynasties

XIA 20th–15th century BCE

SHANG 15th century–ca. 1046 BCE

ZHOU ca. 1046 BCE–256 BCE

QIN 221–207 BCE

HAN 206 BCE–220 CE

THREE KINGDOMS 220–280
    Wei 220–265   Wu 220–280   Shu-Han 221–265

JIN 265–420

NORTHERN AND SOUTHERN DYNASTIES 420–589

SUI 581–618

TANG 618–907

FIVE DYNASTIES 907–960

SONG 960–1279
    Northern Song 960–1127
    Southern Song 1127–1279

LIAO 907–1125

JIN 1115–1234

YUAN 1271–1368

MING 1368–1644

QING 1644–1911

Introduction

Songs of the Imperial Visit to Datong (*Xingyun qu* 幸雲曲) tells the fictional story of an incognito trip of the Zhengde 正德 emperor (Emperor Right Virtue;[1] r. 1506–1521) of the Ming dynasty (1368–1644) to Datong in northern Shanxi Province, a border area that is also broadly referred to as "within the clouds" (Yunzhong 雲中).[2] In the guise of a common soldier, the emperor visits the red-light district of that major garrison city and meets with the young courtesan Buddha's Lust (Fodongxin 佛動心), who has been led to believe that it is her destiny to marry the emperor. Having been forced to share the lowly soldier's bed, she comes to realize his true identity as the Son of Heaven. Eventually, the emperor takes her back with him to Beijing, but only after he has had his revenge on all those who aroused his displeasure while in disguise. This story of a philandering emperor and a virtuous courtesan is told as a "rustic song" (*liqu* 俚曲), one of the many genres of prosimetric narrative that flourished in late-imperial China.[3] In this case, it means that each of the twenty-eight chapters of our text is made up of alternating passages in prose and in verse, the latter to be sung to the tune of "Having Fun with the Child" (*Shuahai'er* 耍孩兒).

Songs of the Imperial Visit to Datong is one collection of the many rustic songs written by Pu Songling 蒲松齡 (1640–1715). Today Pu Songling is one of the best-known authors of premodern China, but in his own day he at best enjoyed only some local fame in his home province of Shandong. His modern fame is due to his *Strange Stories of Make-do Studio* (*Liaozhai zhiyi* 聊齋志異), a collection of nearly five hundred short stories and anecdotes in Literary Chinese. These tales of love affairs of young men with seductive vixen or winsome ghosts (and much more) are distinguished by exceptional fantasy, a sharp wit, and mordant satire. Pu mostly composed

---

1   More correctly, *zhengde* should be translated as "correcting the virtue [of the people]" in view of the classical source from which the term derives (Geiss 1988, 403, n. 1), but I believe that the term will more commonly have been understood as "right virtue." Moreover, calling the emperor by that name created an ironic contrast with his actual behavior.

2   Several manuscripts of this text have the title as *Xingyun qu* 行雲曲, meaning "Songs of a Roving Cloud."

3   In modern Chinese, stressing not the form but the performance, such texts are collectively designated as "chantefable literature," or literature for telling and singing (*shuochang wenxue* 說唱文學 or *jiangchang wenxue* 講唱文學).

them in the difficult middle years of his life (his preface to the collection is dated 1679). They had already attracted some attention during his lifetime, but were first printed more than fifty years after his death in 1766. Ever since then, these tales have remained extremely popular, both in their original form and in their rewritings as plays, vernacular tales, and ballads in many genres. Later on, these tales would also reach mass audiences in their adaptations for the silver screen and digital media. Pu Songling's enduring fame earned him his own museum in his original hometown of Zibo, called Zichuan at the time.[4]

The Author

The Pu family in Zibo traced its descend to a certain Pu Luhun 蒲魯渾 (or Puluhun), who was stationed at Zibo at some time during the Mongol Yuan dynasty (1260–1378). The name suggests that Pu Luhun may have been of non-Chinese (or at least non-Han) descent. One legend tells that his descendants had to hide with the local Yang 楊 family when the Yuan dynasty collapsed and the Mongols were chased from China proper by the founder of the Ming dynasty, the Hongwu 洪武 emperor (r. 1368–1398), only to resume the Pu family name at some later time. The Pu Songling Museum at Zibo prides itself on asserting that the Pu family is and always has been Han Chinese. Throughout the Ming, the Pu family would appear to have maintained its status among the local educated elite—one grand-uncle of Pu Songling even achieved the presented scholar (*jinshi* 進士) status in 1592 by passing the highest metropolitan examinations, and served for a while as a magistrate.[5]

Pu Songling's father at one time abandoned his studies to engage in trade, but returned to teaching once he had sufficiently restored the family fortunes through his commercial ventures. Pu Songling elicited high hopes for a brilliant career in the imperial bureaucracy when at an early age he passed all elements of the lowest examination (at the prefectural level) with top rankings. Throughout his life, he would continue to participate in the triannual provincial examination but never succeeded to pass and obtain the degree that would have allowed him to sit for the metropolitan

---

4 Stories from *Strange Stories of Make-do Studio* have been widely and repeatedly translated. For an introduction to this collection, see Zeitlin 1993.

5 Throughout the Ming and Qing dynasties, the examination system was the most prestigious entryway into the imperial bureaucracy. The extremely competitive examinations were conducted on three levels (prefectural, provincial, and metropolitan) and were held once every three years. The participants were tested on their knowledge of the Classics and had to answer questions on statecraft.

examinations.[6] To make a living, he in 1670 joined the staff of the official Sun Hui 孫蕙 (1632–1686) when the latter served in Baoying and later in Gaoyou, but he could not get used to "the music of whips" that accompanied his work as a secretary. Upon his return to his hometown, he eked out a living as a teacher and is credited with several texts on the deplorable existence of school masters.[7] During the 1670s, his short stories found their first readers, and by the end of 1679 he was hired by Bi Jiyou 畢際有 (1623–1693), then the head of the wealthy Bi clan, renowned for its large library. For the next thirty years Pu Songling continued in the employment in the Bi family, where he also became good friends with some of its members.[8]

Pu Songling was an extremely prolific writer. The most recent edition of his collected works consumes three fat volumes and runs to more than 3,400 pages.[9] Like any literatus of his time who participated in social life and tried his luck in the examinations, he wrote a staggering amount of prose (such as essays and biographies) as well as poetry (both poems [shi 詩] and song lyrics [ci 詞]). As a teacher, he compiled a fair number of textbooks and compendia for his students. Like many other scholars, he kept a record of anomalous events and local gossip, which in his case developed into his *Strange Stories of Make-do Studio*. The intellectual Hu Shi 胡適 (1891–1962), a champion of the modern vernacular language and a pioneering scholar of traditional vernacular fiction, argued in the 1930s that Pu Songling also must have been the author of the 100-chapter vernacular novel *A Marriage to Awaken the World* (*Xingshi yinyuan zhuan* 醒世姻緣傳).[10] But that claim has not been universally accepted, not that Hu Shi's claim was inherently implausible. Other Shandong authors of the seventeenth century (for instance, Jia Fuxi 賈鳧西 and Ding Yaokang 丁耀亢) also showed an active interest in vernacular literature. If Pu Songling stands out among them, it is because of the large corpus of performance texts that he authored. These texts are nowadays commonly referred to as *Rustic Songs of Make-do Studio* (*Liaozhai liqu* 聊齋俚曲), and with their 800 pages make up almost one

---

6   For an analysis of the impact of the examination on the life of Pu Songling and its reflection in his works, see Barr 1986 and Weightman 2004.

7   See, for instance, his *Scrounging for a School* (*Naoguan* 鬧館). This short play is translated in Lu 2014.

8   For an account of Pu Songling's life and works, see Chang and Chang 1998, 11–70. For more detailed accounts in Chinese, see Lu Dahuang 1980; Yang Hairu 1994; Yuan Shishuo 1988; Yuan Shishuo 2009, 9–80.

9   Pu Songling 1998.

10 Hu Shi 1953.

quarter of his collected works.[11] Whereas the classical tales of *Strange Stories of Make-do Studio* found favor throughout the Chinese-reading world, the rustic songs, employing local tunes and drawing on the resources of the local dialect, circulated exclusively in central Shandong, where the texts survived in manuscript and through oral transmission.[12] As the reputation of Pu Songling increased in the eighteenth and nineteenth centuries, more and more vernacular works that circulated in central Shandong were ascribed to him, and when manuscripts of his writings started to be collected by aficionados in the 1920s, many anonymous works may have been deliberately passed off as works by Pu Songling to meet the demand.[13] More manuscripts of works by Pu Songling or locally credited to his authorship emerged in the 1950s.[14]

The Genre

A list of fourteen (there were actually fifteen) titles of "popular rustic songs" (*tongsu liqu* 通俗俚曲) is engraved on the back side of the tomb stele at Pu Songling's grave. While the tomb stele (destroyed during the Cultural Revolution) was erected in 1725 to carry a formal tomb inscription written by Pu Songling's fellow townsman Zhang Yuan 張元 on its front side, it is not clear when this list of titles was carved on the back side and by whom. But despite some misgivings about its authenticity, most scholars would appear to take the list as reliable, even if incomplete.[15] While Zhang Yuan does not mention the rustic songs in his discussion of Pu's literary works, Pu Songling's eldest son Pu Ruo 蒲箬 had done so in a more extensive description of his father's life, which he composed in 1716:

> For his eight scrolls of *Strange Stories*, he hunted down and collected events he had heard or read about, and through them he expressed his innermost feelings. It took him several years to complete this work.

11   Most of the rustic songs are narrative in nature and were intended, it seems, to be performed by a single person. But three of the rustic songs are plays: *On Top of the Wall* (*Qiangtou ji* 牆頭記); *The Spell against Jealousy* (*Rangdu zhou* 禳妒咒), and *Song of Tribulations* (*Monan qu* 磨難曲). While the first is a relatively short play in four scenes (*hui* 回), the two other plays amount to thirty-three and thirty-six scenes, respectively. For an English translation of *The Wall*, see Pu Songling, Chang and Mair, trans., 1986. Pu Songling is also credited with some short plays that are not listed as rustic songs.

12   The overwhelming majority of studies on rustic songs of the last few decades have been devoted to the grammar and vocabulary of these texts. For a brief survey of these studies, see Lin Xiaoshuang 2015. I have relied primarily on Zhang Shuzheng 2018.

13   Lu 2017. Zou Zongliang (2021, 116–120) identifies one Wang Fengzhi 王豐之 as an active purveyor of fake Pu Songling manuscripts.

14   Miao Huaiming 2021, 17, 21–22, 31, 46, 66.

15   Liu Jieping (1970, 7–8) draws attention to the problematical aspects of this inscription.

In all, it served as needle and awl for learned gentlemen and high dignitaries. But he still regretted that it could not be like a morning bell and evening drum, and dispel the delusions of the simple and boorish, and greatly awaken market women from their dreams. So he developed some classical tales into popular mixed songs (*tongsu zaqu* 通俗雜曲) in order that on streets and in lanes, those who saw them might sing them and those who heard them might cry. His compassionate desire to save the world was such that he would portray the most elegant and vulgar of men and the most fierce and jealous of women all in the same piece.[16]

When he stressed that while the moral message of Pu Songling's classical tales could be perceived only by highly educated readers, his rustic songs were intended to move everyone, literate and illiterate, to virtue performed, his filial son Pu Ruo may have been thinking especially of those rustic songs that were adaptations of materials that Pu Songling treated earlier in his *Strange Stories of Make-do Studio,* and that most likely date from the later decades of his life. Compared to their companion pieces in the *Strange Stories,* these much longer versions as rustic songs tend to be far more outspoken in their moralism.[17] But Pu Songling most likely already started to write rustic songs in his early thirties, and in these earlier works he first of all wanted to entertain.[18] While some scholars also date *Songs of the Imperial Visit to Datong* to the last years of Pu Songling's life, most, in view of its subject matter, consider it a work of his middle years.

16 Lu Dahuang 1980, 76
17 An example is provided by *The Cold and the Dark* (*Hansen qu* 寒森曲), which is an adaptation of two tales, "Shang Sanguan" 商三官 and "Xi Fangping" 席芳平. For a partial translation of this rustic song ballad, see Pu Songling, Bailey and McDougall, trans., 2008. For a systematic comparison of Pu Songling's classical tales and rustic songs, see Shao Jizhi 2008.
18 Guan Dedong 1980, 1–5; Cai Zaomin 2003. Rustic songs commonly assigned to Pu's middle period are *The Union of the Beast and the Beauty* (*Choujunba* 醜俊巴) and *A Pleasant Song* (*Kuaiqu* 快曲). *The Union of the Beast and the Beauty* is devoted to the passion of the deified Pigsy (Zhu Bajie 朱八戒) for the ghost of Pan Jinlian 潘金蓮 (only the first chapter of this work has been preserved). (For an English translation, see Pu Songling, Idema, trans., 2022b.) *A Pleasant Song* narrates how, after the battle at Red Cliff, Zhang Fei 張飛 kills Cao Cao 曹操 after Guan Yu 關羽 has failed in his assignment to do so. (For an English translation, see Pu Songling, Idema, trans., 2022a.) Both of these texts place a new interpretation on characters and events well known from vernacular fiction and drama. Many scholars also place the composition of *Marital Harmony* (*Qinse le* 琴瑟樂) in this period, but it is unlikely that the text that nowadays circulates under that title is indeed by Pu Songling (Idema 2021; Zou Zongliang 2021).

The Story

Whereas later Chinese novels and plays about emperors traveling through the empire in disguise, such as the Kangxi emperor (r. 1662–1722) and the Qianlong emperor (r. 1736–1795), may stress how they come to the aid of the poor and suppressed by uncovering corruption and punishing local bullies, such episodes, while present, play a less dominant role in *Songs of the Imperial Visit to Datong*.[19] Rather, Pu Songling's work represents the culmination of a somewhat different tradition of tales, one about emperors who sneak out of the palace and visit incognito the most famous courtesans of the capital, such as Emperor Chengdi (r. 32–7 BCE) of the Han dynasty and Emperor Huizong (r. 1101–1125) of the Song dynasty. In *Songs of the Imperial Visit to Datong*, however, the Zhengde emperor does not limit himself to raiding the best bordellos of Beijing, but extends his excursions even to Datong after his evil genius Jiang Bin 江彬 (d. 1521) tells him about the beauty of the three thousand courtesans in the Displaying Martiality Ward (Xuanwuyuan 宣武院), the red-light district of this garrison town.

In imperial China, where upper-class culture insisted on the separation of sexes and marriages were arranged by families, courtesan houses were a government-regulated enterprise of all major cities and towns. The registered courtesans could not only be summoned to provide musical and other entertainment at official functions, but also receive individual patrons at home. These patrons, preferably, would stay at their homes for a longer period, showering the objects of their affections (and the other members of their households) with gifts. Patrons were aware that most courtesans had been sold into prostitution, but the institution was commonly accepted in traditional China. Men were warned in many ways of the dangers of falling into the clutches of these seductive women, who would turn them out on the streets once they had fleeced them (or would betray them if they were foolish enough to marry them), but highly popular stories of the Tang dynasty (617–907) and later also told tales of men who had found true love in these dens of inequity, and of former courtesans who made perfect wives once they had been freed from their vile condition. Since such stories of rapacious prostitutes and bawds, as well as tales of innocent and loving courtesans, circulated widely, not only in manuscript and print but also as

19 In the story "Fourteenth Lady Xin (*Xin Shisiniang* 辛十四娘) in Pu Songling's *Strange Stories of Make-do Studio*, a tale of a student who marries a fox with the aid of a ghost, the Zhengde emperor, while visiting the red light district of Datong, saves the life of this outspoken student, who has been framed for murder by an offended rich fellow student. The emperor does so when he is informed of the facts of the case by the student's servant girl, who has taken on the guise of a local courtesan (as instructed by the student's wife, the vixen Xin Shisiniang).

ballads and plays, the author and audiences of *Songs of the Imperial Visit to Datong* were very well acquainted with these stereotypes. In most of the stories on loving courtesans, the male hero is a handsome and bright (but impecunious) student. He may have to compete for her favors with a rich but boorish merchant who has the full support of the bawd, but in one of the most popular vernacular stories of the Ming, a simple oil peddler manages to marry Hangzhou's most beautiful and sophisticated courtesan because of his sincere devotion, once she has been confronted with the callous cruelty of her rich patrons.[20]

Despite his reign title meaning Right Virtue, the historical Zhengde emperor was a dismal failure as a human being and a ruler. As a young prince, Zhu Houzhao 朱厚照 (1491–1521) had been an intelligent boy, but one who loved ease and pleasure. Once he ascended the throne in 1505, he was in a position to indulge his passions in the Leopard Ward, a pleasure park outside the palace. Pampered by eunuchs since his infancy, he was happy to leave most of the daily administration during his early years on the throne to the eunuch Liu Jin 劉瑾 (d. 1510).[21] The emperor loved to spend time with military types rather than with moralizing civil officials, and as his reign was plagued by wide-spread banditry and rebellions, some modern scholars eager to save his reputation have suggested that he may have wanted to reinstall something of the martial spirit of the founders of the dynasty into his reign. The emperor's long-term favorite Jiang Bin had first impressed him in 1512 with the scars of the battle wounds he had suffered the previous year during the suppression of a local rebellion.[22] He went on to stimulate the emperor in his military pretensions and build him a major palace in his own hometown Xuanfu, north of the Great Wall. It is also said that he greatly praised the beauty of the courtesans there. At Jiang Bin's suggestion, the emperor made long elaborate trips outside

---

20 For general surveys of the literature on courtesans (and their own contributions to it), see, for instance, Gong Bin 2001 and Tao Muning 2006. For a translation of "The Oil-Peddler Wins the Queen of Flowers," see, for example, Feng Menglong, comp., and Yang and Yang, trans., 2009, 38–77. From the final century of the Qing dynasty, we have a large number of courtesan novels. Starr (2007, 29–40) discusses Ming vernacular stories of courtesans. The best-known courtesan quarters of the final century of the Ming are those of Nanjing and Suzhou (see Ōki 2002 and Ōki 2017). For a study of the career of a courtesan (based mostly on late-Qing fiction), see Zamperini 2010. For a work largely focused on the interactions of courtesans and literati in the last century of the Ming, see Liu Shiyi 2018.
21 Goodrich and Fang 1976, 941–945. On eunuch power in the Ming dynasty, see Tsai 1996.
22 Goodrich and Fang 1976, 230–233.

the capital, first to Xuanfu in 1517–1518;[23] then to Xuanfu, Datong, and Taiyuan in Shanxi Province in 1518–1519; and later also south to Nanjing and Yangzhou in 1519–1520. During these trips he assumed the persona of supreme commander Zhu Shou 朱壽, but his personal contributions to the suppression of foreign invaders and internal rebels remained minimal despite his self-aggrandizing titles.[24]

Already during his lifetime, the Zhengde emperor's antics had become the subject matter of storytellers. The popular imagination turned the imperial journeys into incognito trips in search of women. In view of the universal condemnation of the Zhengde emperor in later ages, it is difficult to determine the trustworthiness of the many anecdotes, following his early death, that recount this predatory behavior toward women. In the early seventeenth century, Shen Defu 沈德符 (1578–1642) summarized the most scandalous liaisons of the emperor in the following:

> When the Martial Ancestor visited Yulin, he took the daughter of Regional Commander Dai Qin 戴欽 and made her a concubine. When he visited Taiyuan, he took the wife of Yang Teng 楊騰, a professional musician in the household of the Prince of Jin and the daughter of one Liu Liang 劉良. He greatly loved and favored her and took her with him on his rambling progression. Jiang Bin and the Eight Cronies all served her as the mother of the nation, [i.e., the empress].[25] When the emperor went on his Southern Progress, the woman Liu gave him a hairpin as a token, but he later lost it while galloping. When he arrived at Linqing and summoned her, she refused to go because the token was lacking. The emperor hurried back as far as Luhe by light conveyance and brought her along on his trip to the south.

23 Traveling from Beijing to Xuanfu, the emperor had to pass through Juyongguan (Juyong Pass), a heavily fortified gate in the Great Wall. When he arrived there, the commander did not let him pass, since he had not been properly informed of the emperor's arrival. The emperor could only return to the capital. When sometime later he arrived again at Juyong Pass, he had made sure that the commander had been replaced by a more pliable type.

24 Geiss 1987; Geiss 1988; Goodrich and Fang 1976, 307–315; Robinson 2001. In its account of the Zhengde reign, the History of the Ming (Mingshi 明史), the dynastic history of the Ming dynasty published after several revisions in 1739, provides a rather bland picture of the emperor, relegating most of the scandalous episodes of his reign to its biography of Jiang Bin. But already before its completion, the famous scholar Mao Qiling 毛奇齡 (1623–1716) had excerpted the descriptions of such incidents from the Factual Records (Shilu 實錄) of the Zhengde reign and compiled them as An Unofficial Account of the Martial Ancestor (Wuzong waiji 武宗外紀), first printed in 1699.

25 Other sources specify that they addressed her by the title niangniang 娘娘, which was reserved for the empress.

Also, when he visited Xuanfu, he took the younger sister of Regional Commander and Assistant Commissioner-in-Chief Ma Ang 馬昂 into his harem. Married to Commander Bi 畢, she was already pregnant at the time. She excelled in horseback shooting and mastered Mongolian. The emperor took a fancy to her and raised Ang's rank to that of Right Commander-in-Chief, so all his servants called him Imperial Brother-in-Law Ma.

Furthermore, he also requisitioned Korean girls, Central Asian girls, and Uyghur dancing girls. When he came to Yangzhou, he rounded up all virgins and widows. In Yizhen he selected courtesans, again, too many to count. . . .

Then there was Wang Mantang 王滿堂, the daughter of Wang Zhi 王智, a citizen of Bazhou. She participated in a selection for the imperial harem, but was rejected. When she came home, she was ashamed of her exceptional beauty, fell into depression and refused to marry. She also said that she repeatedly dreamed that only a certain Zhao Wanxing 趙萬興 would be her husband.[26] The devilish priest Duan Chang 段錩 learned of this, so he changed his name to marry her and lived with her family as a son-in-law. Chang assembled troops and rose in rebellion in Yixian in Shandong Province. He even proclaimed his own dynasty. . . . He made Mantang his empress. When he was subsequently defeated and taken to the capital as a captive, she as an accomplice was to suffer decapitation with him, but her life was spared by a Palace edict, and she was assigned to the Washing Office. Later she enjoyed the emperor's favor in the Leopard Ward, to be released again when the emperor had passed away.[27]

While the story of the courtesan Buddha's Lust in *Songs of the Imperial Visit to Datong* is probably inspired by twisted memories of the spectacular life of the woman Liu, Buddha's Lust's dream of a predestined meeting with the emperor may well be derived from the tale of Wang Mantang.

The full title of *Songs of the Imperial Visit to Datong*, as listed on the backside of the 1725 stele, is *The Expanded and Completed Songs of the Imperial Visit to Datong* (*Zengbu Xingyun qu* 增補幸雲曲), which thus advertises that this text is an expanded version of an earlier work of the same title. Early manuscript copies do not include these two characters in their titles. Pu Songling also calls his text *Right Virtue Goes Whoring in the Ward* (*Zhengde piaoyuan* 正德嫖院), which closely echoes the two alternative titles (*Whoring in the Ward* [*Piaoyuan ji* 嫖院記] and *Right Virtue* [*Zhengde ji* 正德記])

26 Zhao was the surname of the ruling house of the Song dynasty (960–1278).
27 Shen Defu 1980, 544–545.

XX   THE EMPEROR OF CHINA IN A HOUSE OF ILL REPUTE

of an anonymous play that circulated by the end of the sixteenth century, two acts of which have been preserved in *Selected Brocade and Exceptional Sounds* (*Zhaijin qiyin* 摘錦奇音), a drama anthology first published in 1611. The contents of these two acts closely correspond to Chapter 5 of *Songs of the Imperial Visit to Datong* and tell how the incognito emperor, during his trip from Beijing to Datong, arranges a wedding to a rich girl on behalf of the poor woodcutter Zhou Yuan 周元 who provided him hospitality during the night.[28] The play must also have featured Buddha's Lust's fellow courtesan Guanyin's Equal 賽觀音 and the latter's patron Wang Long 王籠. This Wang Long is an evil local bully who tries to profit from the emperor but is frustrated in his attempts and eventually tries to murder him, only to be cruelly punished instead. That Guanyin's Equal and Wang Long had a large role in the play becomes clear from a song to the tune of "Splitting Jade" (*Pipoyu* 劈破玉) also included in *Selected Brocades and Exceptional Sounds*, which provides the following summary of the play:

Guanyin's Equal
And Buddha's Lust
Were from birth as beautiful as flowers.
When young master Wang learned about them
He also cavorted with these two whores,
And when the Zhu emperor heard the tale, he arrived in person.
Lord and vassal competed in treasures,
Not ceding half a pace to each other.
Down on his luck, that Wang Long,
Down on his luck, that Wang Long
Was flayed and his skin was filled with straw![29]

Short as it is, the song proves that the main plot of this play corresponded to that of Pu Songling's *Songs of the Imperial Visit to Datong*. While it is possible that Pu Songling based his work on this play, he also may have based his rustic song on some other, now lost vernacular work on the same theme, whether a play, a novel, or a prosimetric narrative.

In adapting the tale of the affair of Right Virtue and Buddha's Lust, Pu Songling provides detailed descriptions of life in the courtesan houses of

28 Guan Dedong 1997, 1–4. The story of Zhou Yuan's encounter with the emperor remained popular in later times. By the nineteenth century, Zhou Yuan had become Zhou Xuewen 周學文, the main protagonist of the popular prosimetric narrative (*tanci* 彈詞) *The Dropped Golden Fan* (*Luo jinshan* 落金扇). See also Jin Xia 2019.

29 The founder of the Ming dynasty, Zhu Yuanzhang, had instituted flaying (and subsequently stuffing the skin with straw for exhibition) as a punishment for extreme cases of corruption. See Luo Dianhong and Tian Cuiying 2006; Zhang Ningbo 2015.

the licensed prostitution quarters, but is rather reticent when it comes
to the erotic aspects of the relationship. Pu would appear to be most interested in the relation between appearance and reality, spoken words
and their real intention, disguise and intrinsic identity. The emperor is
described as loving to dress up to assume different personae. Throughout
his stay in the prostitution quarter, he takes pains to maintain his disguise
even as he repeatedly hints at his true identity as the emperor. When he
finds it insufficient to present himself as a common soldier, he deliberately
plays a fool. But when his antagonists suggest that he himself may have a
vile status and be a pimp or even a catamite, he feels deeply offended. But
even if the emperor had wanted to escape his true identity, it would have
been impossible, as he, whether deliberately or inadvertently, continuously
betrays it, and is rescued by gods and ghosts whenever he is threatened
by physical harm.

While most of the action of Pu Songling's *Songs of the Imperial Visit to
Datong* is set away from the capital in Datong, the opening chapters and
the penultimate one take place at the imperial court in Beijing, and so we
encounter some of the other famous personalities of the Zhengde era and its
immediate aftermath. None of Jiang Bin's partisans are mentioned by name,
but we encounter some of the persons instrumental in Jiang Bin's downfall
following the death of the emperor. The first of these is Empress Zhang
張, who is portrayed by Pu Songling in Chapter 2 as the emperor's wife.
(The historical Empress Zhang was the emperor's mother.) The eunuch
she relies on to imprison Jiang Bin during the emperor's absence is Zhang
Yong 張永 (1465–1529). One of the rare regular bureaucrats mentioned by
name is Mao Ji 毛紀 (1463–1545), who had been a tutor of the Zhengde emperor and who rose to high position during his reign to become one of the
engineers of Jiang Bin's downfall. We also encounter the State-Stabilizing
Duke (Dingguo gong 定國公), who, as the descendant of the fourth son
of Zhu Yuanzhang's trusted general Xu Da 徐達 (1332–1385), is one of the
highest ranking members of the court aristocracy. Legend held that the
State-Stabilizing Duke had been charged by Zhu Yuanzhang to strike down
any dysfunctional emperor or traitorous minister with the bronze mallet he
entrusted to him and his heirs. While the State-Stabilizing Duke eventually
forces Jiang Bin to disclose the whereabouts of the missing emperor, the
emperor himself apparently never becomes dysfunctional enough to be
struck down by the bronze mallet. Wang Long's father, Minister of War
Wang, is not given a personal name in *Songs of the Imperial Visit to Datong*,
but this figure may have been inspired by Wang Qiong 王瓊 (1459–1532).
Wang Qiong hailed from Taiyuan in Shanxi Province and competently
served during the Zhengde reign as Minister of Revenue (1513–1515), Minister of War (1515–1520), and Minister of Personnel (1520–1521). He was

dismissed upon the emperor's death, but was reinstated after a number of years owing to his capabilities.

Pu Songling was not the only Qing author attracted to the theme of the erotic adventures of the Zhengde emperor.[30] The famous playwright Li Yu 李漁 (1611–1679) composed a play titled *The Jade Hairpin* (*Yusaotou* 玉搔頭) about the relationship of the emperor and the woman Liu from beginning to end, turning the emperor very much into a romantic lover in search of true passion.[31] Over the course of the dynasty many playwrights would follow his example.[32] As centuries passed, the background shifted from the emperor's northern trip to Datong and Taiyuan to his southern trip to Nanjing and Yangzhou, while the woman Liu from the eighteenth century on had to share her place as the emperor's love interest with Li Feng 李鳳 (Phoenix Li), the daughter of an innkeeper. When the incognito emperor visits Li Feng's establishment, he is smitten by her beauty and, thinking her to be a common courtesan, makes a pass at her. She protests her innocence, and when the emperor eventually sleeps with her, he finds to his pleasure that she is indeed a virgin. Many varieties of prosimetric narrative employed this story. From the nineteenth century, we also have several novels that develop the tale. One of these, *The Visit by Right Virtue of the Great Ming to the Jiangnan Area* (*Da Ming Zhengde you Jiangnan* 大明正德遊江南), by He Mengmei 何夢梅, was translated into English shortly after its first known printing of 1842 by Tkin Shen (under the supervision of the famous missionary James Legge) as *The Rambles of the Emperor Ching Tĭh in Këang Nan: A Chinese Tale* (1843).[33]

The Text

In view of the enduring popularity of tales about the propensity of the Zhengde emperor to raise humble girls to high status, it should come as no surprise that *Songs of the Imperial Visit to Datong* was one of Pu Songling's most popular collections of rustic songs. By the early decades of communist China, the genre was on the verge of extinction, as most of the original tunes had been forgotten.[34] But when the famous musicologist Wu Zhao

---

30 Li Wanying 2016.

31 Hanan 1988, 17, 138–184.

32 Hua Wei 2019, 71–111.

33 He Mengmei, Shen and Legge, trans., 1843. In view of the date of publication of the English translation, it is likely that He Mengmei's novel had already circulated before 1842 either in manuscript or in print. The English translation was also quickly translated into German and Dutch.

34 Since the 1980s, great efforts have been made to revive the performance tradition of the genre, with a strong emphasis on Pu Songling's plays. Chen Yuchen stands out for his efforts to recover the melodies that had been forgotten in Zibo.

吳釗 conducted his pioneering research on the genre's performance in 1963,[35] he reported that the local blind singer Liu Wengao 劉文鎬 used to perform the complete *Songs of the Imperial Visit to Datong*, and that Liu's pupil Han Bingxiang 韓秉祥 was still able to do so. This would mean that the tune of "Having Fun with the Child" might be one of the very few rustic song tunes that could boast of a continuous tradition from Pu Songling's lifetime down to the twentieth century.[36]

The text of *Songs of the Imperial Visit to Datong* survived not only in manuscript, but may also have been one of the rare rustic songs to be printed before the appearance of Pu Songling's collected works in 1936. In 1963 Wu Zhao was told by the blind performer Zhao Ziqin 趙子欽 that before he had lost his eyesight, he had seen an edition of *Songs of the Imperial Visit to Datong* in the possession of a certain Mr. Song 宋 that had been printed in 1749 with full musical notation.[37] We have no further information on this edition, if it ever existed.[38] Several publications mention a lithographic printing of *Songs of the Imperial Visit to Datong* produced in 1919 in Shanghai for a Zibo bookshop, together with a lithographic printing of yet another rustic song titled *Songs of Tribulations* (*Monan qu* 磨難曲).[39]

Unfortunately, we lack a comprehensive survey of the surviving manuscripts of *Songs of the Imperial Visit to Datong*. Writing in 1947, the Pu Songling scholar Liu Jieping 劉階平 states that apart from the lithographic edition, he had also seen two manuscripts of the text, one of which belonged to his fellow Pu Songling aficionado Lu Dahuang 路大荒.[40] That manuscript, which most likely served as the basis for the printed edition of *Songs of the Imperial Visit to Datong* in the Shijie shuju edition, may perhaps be identified with the manuscript now in the library of the Shandong Provincial Museum at Jinan and reprinted in volume 48 of the third installment of *A Complete Collection of Shandong Documents* (2006–2011) (*Shandong wenxian jicheng* 山東文獻集成).[41] The Capital Library in Beijing also houses a manuscript of *Songs of the Imperial Visit to Datong*. The Liaozhai Collection in the library of Keio University in Tokyo, based on

---

35 Wu Zhao's original report was at the time distributed only as an internal publication. For a summary of its contents, see Liu Xiurong and Liu Tingting 2016, 86–97. Also see Wu Zhao 1983.

36 Liu Xiaojing 2002, 26–27.

37 Liu Xiaojing 2002, 26–27.

38 Yang Hairu 1991, 136.

39 Lu 2017, 199, n. 542. The catalog of the Jilin University library records a copy including both *Songs of Tribulation* (*Monan qu*) and *Songs of the Imperial Visit to Datong* (*Xingyun qu*), but the copy held by the University of Michigan Library includes only *Songs of Tribulation*.

40 Liu Jieping 1950, 22a–b.

41 Pu Songling 2009.

the materials collected in the 1930s in Zibo by the Japanese physician Hirai Masao, includes three manuscripts of *Songs of the Imperial Visit to Datong*, two of which most likely had been made for him by copying manuscripts in local collections.[42] The Pu Songling Museum at Zibo also holds several manuscript copies of the text. One is the copy made in the 1950s for display purposes. Yet another manuscript at the museum titled *An Addition to "Strange Stories of Make-do Studio"—The Song of a Roaming Cloud: Right Virtue Goes Whoring in the Ward* (*Liaozhai zhiyi bubian Xingyun qu Zhengde piaoyuan* 聊齋志異補編行雲曲正德嫖院) has its first page reproduced in *The Collected Rustic Songs of Make-do Studio* (*Liaozhai liqu ji* 聊齋俚曲集), edited by the Museum and published in 2018. The Pu Songling Museum has so far not published a catalog of its holdings of manuscripts related to Pu Songling, but we can safely assume it holds more copies. During field work in Pu Songling's hometown in 1956, students of Guan Dedong 關德棟 (1920–2005) copied out a manuscript of *Songs of the Imperial Visit to Datong* that had been copied out by an eighth-generation descendant of Pu in 1939. This text was later made available to selected scholars in mimeographed format.[43]

To the extent that the available printed editions of *Songs of the Imperial Visit to Datong* discuss the sources of their texts, they tend to be frustratingly vague. The collective edition of Pu Songling's rustic songs edited by the Pu Songling Museum, claims to "have fully made use of the Museum's holdings," and to "have edited and collated these texts by consulting Lu Dahuang's *Pu Songling ji* and Sheng Wei's *Pu Songling quanji*,"[44] but this edition does not include any critical apparatus.[45] Zhang Tai himself based his "critical and annotated" edition of Pu Songling's rustic songs on the texts as included in the 1986 reprint of Lu Dahuang's *Pu Songling ji* of 1962. And he collated this text against the editions in Sheng Wei's *Pu Songling quanji*, Lu Dahuang's *Liaozhai quanji* (1936), Pu Xianming and Zou Zongliang's annotated edition of Pu Songling's rustic songs (1999), and "manuscripts of surviving works [of Pu Songling] in the collection of the Pu Songling Museum."[46] Zhang Tai's critical notes for *Songs of the Imperial Visit to Datong*

---

42 Fujita 1988, 132.

43 In its modern edition (Pu Songling 2020), this text has been collated against the edition in Pu Songling, Sheng Wei, ed., 1998. Guan Dedong had been teaching oral literature at Shandong University since 1954.

44 Pu Songling 2018, 930. Pu Songling, Lu Dahuang, ed., 1986. Pu Songling, Sheng Wei, ed., 1998.

45 The editors note major differences between the manuscripts at their disposal and the earlier printed versions for only one title, *Rustic Songs* (Pu Songling 2018, 931), not *Songs of the Imperial Visit*.

46 Zhang Tai 2019, 1.

are very limited in number and mostly concern matters of orthography for dialect words and expressions. Only in three cases does he refer to a manuscript he consulted.[47]

This translation of *Songs of the Imperial Visit to Datong* is based on Zhang Tai's critical edition.[48] For understanding the text, I have greatly benefited from Zou Zongliang's extensive annotations in *Liaozhai liqu ji*.[49] Zhang Shuzheng (2018), in his encyclopedic study of the language of Pu Songling's vernacular works, provided an indispensable tool to tackle the many problems and enigmas the text provides to anyone not acquainted with the Zibo dialect.

Formal Features

For the arias in his rustic songs, Pu Songling employs some fifty popular local tunes. By far the most frequently used tune is "Having Fun with the Child," partly because it is the only tune used in *Songs of the Imperial Visit to Datong*. Songs to the tune of "Having Fun with the Child" have eight lines, divided in three groups of three, three, and two lines, respectively.[50] In the first group, the first two lines consist of two groups of three syllables (separated by a caesura); these two lines are followed by a seven-syllable line (with a caesura following the fourth syllable). The second group is made up of three seven-syllable lines. And the last two lines each consist of four syllables (often preceded by groups of three syllables). Lines four and five are expected to have a parallel structure, and likewise the last two lines. All lines rhyme, except lines four and seven.[51] As an example I here present the Chinese text of the final "Having Fun with the Child" song of the first chapter, in which Jiang Bin praises the beauties of Datong to the emperor. For each line of text, I present the Chinese text in Chinese

---

47 Zhang Tai (2019, 649–650) notes that in the "Opening Scene," the expression *angbang* 昂 邦 is written as *angcang* 昂臧 (of tall and strong built) in the manuscript at his disposal. This is an important variant because some scholars consider *angbang* to be a borrowing from the Manchu *amban* and on the basis of this loanword argue for a late dating of the text. The two other cases (pp. 656, 696) are of minor importance.

48 Zhang Tai 2019, 649–756.

49 Pu Songling, Pu Xianming, ed., Zou Zongliang, ann., 1999, 898–1040.

50 A standard eight-line poem would be made up of four two-line couplets, with even lines rhyming and the caesura falling in the same place in each line.

51 This tune has been discussed repeatedly by musicologists. See, for instance, Chen Yuchen 2004, 214–224; Chen Yuchen 2019, 2–17; Liu Xiaojing 2002, 181–212. Its history can be traced back to as early as the twelfth century. Pu Songling notes the quick turnover of popular tunes at the opening of Chapter 1 of the present work. This phenomenon had also been discussed earlier, for instance, by Shen Defu (1980, 647). In Ming and Qing times the tune was also quite popular in Daoist prosimetric storytelling (*daoqing* 道情).

characters, in transcription, and in word-for-word glosses. In the Chinese character text, two slashes (//) mark a strong caesura and a single slash (/) a weaker caesura. In the transcription, the rhyming words are underlined.

微臣奏 // 主得知

Weichen zou zhu de zhi:
Minor minister reports lord may know

十三省 // 數山西

Shisan sheng shu Shanxi,
Ten three provinces count mountains west

大同城裡 / 好景致

Datongcheng li hao jingzhi.
Great Together city inside fine scene situation

　男人清秀 / 真無比

　Nanren qingxiu zhen wu bi;
　Male person clear outstanding true no comparison

女人風流 / 更出奇

Nüren fengliu geng chu qi:
Female person wind stream even-more stand-out exceptional

人才出色 / 多標致

Rencai chuse duo biaozhi.
People talent stand-out beauty many topmost situation

　宣武院 // 三千粉黛

　Xuanwuyuan sanqian fendai
　Display martiality ward three thousand powder black

一個個 // 亞賽仙姬

Yi gege yasai xianji
One piece piece nearly surpass immortal maiden

In translation this becomes,

　　Your humble servant reports to Your Majesty as follows:
　　Of the thirteen provinces, Shanxi is counted first by far;

The city of Datong priding itself on the finest scenery of all.
    The men there, handsome and graceful, are beyond compare;
The women, fine and charming, are even more exceptional.
Its people are extraordinarily talented and all very beautiful.
    The three thousand courtesans of the Displaying Martiality
    Ward
Are each and every one the near-equal of immortal maidens.

As the genre of rustic songs was intended to appeal to a large, and pre-sumably largely illiterate, audience, the songs are written in a simple, and at times even prosaic, style, freely employing the local dialect. I would have loved to use rhyme in my renditions of these versified passages, but unfortunately my linguistic abilities fall short of such a task.[52]

In *Songs of the Imperial Visit to Datong*, the number of "Having Fun with the Child" songs in each chapter can vary widely. Chapter 24 contains nineteen such songs, while Chapter 19 has only four, but then this latter chapter is made up largely of elaborate word games that will have provided the performer with ample opportunity to display his vocal skills. As a rule, each song is followed by a passage in prose, but songs to the tune of "Having Fun with the Child" can also be organized as suites, and at various places we encounter sets of two or three songs without intervening prose. The longest suite in *Songs of the Imperial Visit to Datong* amounts to five arias.

While the textual format of "Having Fun with the Child" songs in Pu Songling's rustic songs conforms to the format of such songs encountered in *zaju* plays and *sanqu* songs of the second half of the thirteenth century and beyond, Pu repeatedly stresses that his "Having Fun with the Child" songs are performed to a new tune. The first chapter of *Songs of the Imperial Visit to Datong* starts, for instance, in the following way:

Now let me tell you that I have composed this work about this strange
affair to the tune of "Having Fun with the Child." Even though this
tune has been popular for a long time, everybody sings it differently.
So when you hear me sing it, my dear audience, don't complain that
I sully your ears!
    The affairs of this world seem to follow a circle;
    People of today are not like those of the past:
    Each year a new tune is replaced by another.
        "Threads of a Silver Knot" was barely abandoned,

---

52 As a vehicle for narrative, "Having Fun with the Child" songs may well be compared to
    ottava rima.

When later on "Beat the Jujube Branch" appeared;
"Lock Southern Twig" is half inserted in "Luo River Grudge."[53]
  Now we have here *Right Virtue Goes Whoring*.
Its "Having Fun with the Child" is quite original!

Yet another rustic song, *The Beautiful Yaksha* (*Jun yecha* 俊夜叉), about a woman who saves her husband from his gambling addiction, starts in the following manner:

These songs have been composed to the fashionable tune of "Having Fun with the Child." They can make gentlemen collapse with laughter and cause common folks to raise their spirits. So let me start singing, and listen!

Unfortunately, we do not know how this new tune would have sounded differently from the old tune.[54]

Some chapters, especially in the first half of the text, may also contain rhymed sections intended for declamation, further contributing to the variety of delivery in performance.[55] These sections have been set off from the surrounding prose by typographical means.

Each chapter is headed by a title made up of a parallel couplet of two seven-syllable lines or two eight-syllable lines, and the whole text is opened and concluded by a lyric to the tune of "West River Moon" (*Xijiangyue* 西江月), each made up of two four-line stanzas. Lyrics to the tune of "West River Moon" are used like poems: they are intended to be recited, not sung. They are made up of two four-line stanzas, and the lines in each stanza are made up of six syllables, except for the third line, which is longer with seven syllables. Perhaps in memory of its prior existence as a play, *Songs of the Imperial Visit to Datong* begins with an "Opening Scene" (*kaichang* 開場).

Readers primarily interested in the relation between the emperor and Buddha's Lust need some patience. *Songs of the Imperial Visit to Datong* appears to be composed in four sections of seven chapters each. The first seven chapters are made up of a string of episodes, narrating the adventures of the emperor as he travels alone and in disguise from Beijing by way of Juyong Pass to Datong and as he arrives in the city and finds an inn. In the second set of seven chapters, the emperor proceeds from the inn to the private bedroom of Buddha's Lust at her establishment in the red light

---

53 These three lines mention several popular song tunes of the Ming dynasty.
54 Zhou Yibai 1986, 650.
55 For a brief discussion of such rhymed declamation pieces in Pu's rustic songs, see Liu Shuiyun and Che Xilun 2003.

quarter. To arrive there, he relies on the assistance of Brother Six (Liuge 六哥), a young servant at the inn who sings the praises of Buddha's Lust's charms. He also establishes contacts with her bawd, who then visits the inn to inspect the prospective customer/patron. Once the bawd has been persuaded of the emperor's eligibility by his cash, she forces her wayward adopted daughter (who has been allowed to preserve her virginity as she waits for the emperor) to visit him in his room at the inn. Her servants fail to fool the emperor, and as a last resort Buddha's Lust persuades him to accompany her to the red light district. The second part of *Songs of the Imperial Visit to Datong* is set there. During the first seven chapters, Buddha's Lust becomes more and more convinced that her moronic patron is indeed the emperor. After a further attempt to fool her patron has failed, Buddha's Lust is finally deflowered. Staying in her room, the emperor becomes acquainted with Wang Long, the rich patron of Guanyin's Equal, Buddha's Lust's elder sister in the trade. Wang Long hopes to profit from the emperor, whom he takes for a gullible fool, but the emperor easily wins in every game and pastime. In Chapter 21 we find the emperor and Buddha's Lust in the apartment of Guanyin's Equal and Wang Long, where the emperor cleans Wang Long out while gambling and then disrobes to take a bath. At the opening of Chapter 22, the emperor discloses his true identity to Buddha's Lust. When later an enraged Wang Long and Guanyin's Equal attempt to murder the emperor, the latter is saved through the intervention of Millionaire Hu (Hu Baiwan 胡百萬), a dirt-poor student who survives as a sponger in the red light district. Meanwhile, back at the capital Jiang Bin is forced to confess that he had urged the emperor to visit Datong's red light district and savor its pleasures, whereupon all the court officials travel to Datong to bring the emperor back to the palace. He agrees to follow them back to Beijing, but only after he has punished Wang Long and Guanyin's Equal, rewarded Brother Six and Millionaire Hu, and burned Datong's famous red light district to the ground. When Buddha's Lust arrives at the palace, she is treated with great kindness by the empress.

Critical Evaluation

The enduring popularity of *Songs of the Imperial Visit to Datong* has not endeared it to Marxist critics in the People's Republic. If one wants literature to present poor peasants or sincere students rising against oppression and corruption, or young men and women in patriarchal families suffering in their unfulfilled search for freely given love (that is, marital unions unconstrained by parental authority), our text has little to offer. Moreover, it is largely devoted to the daily activities inside a bordello and even mentions sex—topics abhorrent to Marxist critics, who tend to be quite Victorian when it comes to the physical aspects of love. While critics in the People's

Republic have usually praised Pu Songling for his clear compassion for the poor and downtrodden, his frank portrayal of bureaucratic corruption, and his warm sympathy for young people in love, they have long continued to characterize *Songs of the Imperial Visit to Datong* as an exception in his oeuvre because of its poor taste. This dismissal of the text is still encountered in reference works of the 1980s.

Only around the turn of the century did some articles appear that sought to assert the literary quality of this work. These critics not only stressed elements of social criticism in the work in its portrayal of an irresponsible emperor, official corruption, and wide-spread social misery; they might even stress the work's originality and humor, ranging from irony to sarcasm.[56] The most original article in defense of *Songs of the Imperial Visit to Datong* may well be the long article by Liu Yuansheng, who reads the irresponsible and amoral behavior of the Zhengde emperor as a rebellion against the rigid and stultifying rules and rites governing the lives of Ming emperors.[57]

All critics, of course, draw attention to the miserable fate of Buddha's Lust, who had been sold into prostitution at an early age, and who is forced by her madam to sleep with a lowly soldier because he spends gold like water. More recently Che Zhenhua has relativized this appreciation of *Songs of the Imperial Visit to Datong* as a work of incisive social criticism. He treats it as a work of satire and fun, writing,

> As far as its listeners are concerned, it is difficult to imagine that after their grueling labor they, like gentry and high officials, would be able to summarize the experiences of history and vent their feelings in poems on historical subjects. Instead of saying that this is Pu Songling's criticism of imperial rule, it may be better to say that he turns the secret history of the highest ruler into a vehicle for country folks' entertainment and amusement. Whether the Zhengde emperor leaves a fragrance for a hundred generations or a stench for all eternity may be not for the history books to determine, but for country folks to freely determine in the process of telling stories.[58]

Perhaps the enduring popularity of *Songs of the Imperial Visit to Datong* may indeed be due to the perennial interest of people at large in the love lives of the high and mighty, the rich and powerful. Our story, of course, tells a tale of the blatant abuse of patriarchal power, but only too many

---

56 Li Xianfang 1999. Also see Liu Ruiming 2006.
57 Liu Yuansheng 2001.
58 Che Zhenhua 2015.

people seem willing to suspend their moral verdict in their fascination with the bedroom adventures of a Henry VIII or J. F. Kennedy. Chinese audiences were no different. The persistent attempts to read the famous eighteenth-century novel *Dream of the Red Chamber* (*Honglou meng* 紅樓夢) as a coded account of love affairs at the Manchu court show that many readers are inventive enough to find such "secret histories" in unexpected places. In the case of *Songs of the Imperial Visit to Datong,* no such forced interpretations are needed. Even though he has the character of a playful and lascivious monkey, the Zhengde emperor remains at all times a true dragon.[59]

---

59 Abe 2020, 254–255.

增補幸雲曲

The Emperor of China in a
House of Ill Repute

開場

[西江月] 一自元朝失政，天生火德臨凡。洪武晏駕許多年，傳流正德登殿。天下太平無事，朝廷戲耍民間。風流話柄萬人傳，呀，名爲正德嫖院。

　　西江月既畢，待在下把這椿故事略表幾句：

　　好玩耍的天子，嫖了個絕妙的嬌娃。

　　極貧賤的小子，得了個異樣的榮華。

　　兵部堂的公子，遭了個無情的橫死。

　　宣政院的婊子，從了個昂邦的良家。

1　The Mongol Yuan dynasty ruled from 1260 to 1368. During its final decades the regime witnessed many rebellions and increasingly lost the grip on power. Its successor, the Ming dynasty, was proclaimed in Nanjing in 1368 by Zhu Yuanzhang 朱元章, one of the many competing warlords at the time. Each dynasty was associated with one of the Five Phases (Metal, Wood, Water, Fire and Earth). As the family name Zhu also means "red," it was natural to associate the Ming (bright) with the phase of Fire. Zhu adopted as his first (and only) reign-period title the phrase "Grand Martiality" (Hongwu 洪武, 1368–1398), and became known to posterity as the Hongwu emperor. His successors followed his example and all used only one reign-period title. When the young Zhu Houzhao (1491–1521) succeeded to the throne in late 1505, the reign-period title adopted was Right Virtue (Zhengde 正德). According to the classical source from which the term was borrowed, *zhengde* should be understood as a verb-object combination and is more correctly translated as "correcting the virtue [of the people]." The word "virtue" here should be understood as "inherent power."

Opening Scene

To the tune of "West River Moon"

Once the Yuan dynasty had failed in its rule,
The heavenly virtue of Fire descended to earth.
And after Grand Martiality had ruled in peace for many years,
His distant heir Right Virtue ascended the throne.[1]

The whole world being at peace, without any war,
This emperor amused himself among the people.
A tale of romance has been transmitted by the masses
Known as "Right Virtue Goes Whoring."

Now that this lyric to the tune of "West River Moon" is finished, let me summarize our story in a few lines:

A Son of Heaven who loves to play patronizes a most beautiful maiden,
And nobodies who live in extreme poverty achieve extraordinary glory.
While the noble son of the minister of war suffers a pitiless execution,
A common whore of Displaying Martiality ward[2] marries a
    herrlichen man.[3]

---

2   Throughout the text, the courtesan quarter in Datong is called the Displaying Martiality Ward 宣武院. Here the text uses "displaying authority ward" 宣政院, which must be a mistake, as it was the name of the Commission for Buddhist and Tibetan Affairs of the Yuan dynasty (1260–1368). Upon the establishment of the Ming dynasty, the Hongwu emperor assigned the registered courtesans of Nanjing to the Rich Pleasure Ward (富樂院), so it is likely that in other major towns too, courtesans were assigned to their own ward. We have no information on the Displaying Martiality Ward outside this text, but Datong was a major garrison town on the northern border, so most of the intended customers of the local courtesans would have been military personnel. Perhaps we should also remember that sexual intercourse was often described in terms of battle.

3   I translate *angbang* 昂邦 as *herrlichen* a resplendent man. *Angbang*, according to some commentators (including Zhang Shuzheng 2018, 422), is a transcription of the Manchu word *amban* (lord, prince). For these commentators, the use of this loanword from the Manchu also suggests a relatively late date for the composition of this text. Pu Songling 1999 (900) explains *angbang* as meaning "hard; here referring to a status different from the crowd."

你說這正德嫖院，不大之緊，弄出了幾件故事，甚是出
奇。是那幾件呢？

朝廷賭博又宿娼，光棍　　打柴漢子做新郎；美對
酒保做了乾殿下，胡混　　趕著姐姐叫娘娘。奇事

"Bare stick" is the common designation for unattached poor men who travel around looking for work, money, and sex. In the eyes of established communities, these "bare sticks" were dangerous vagrants.

Though you may say that this "Right Virtue Goes Whoring in the Ward" is of no importance, it nevertheless produces some stories that are quite remarkable indeed. Which stories?

His Majesty engages in gambling and cavorts with a harlot: just like a bare stick![4]
A guy who survives by carrying firewood becomes a husband: what a great match!
A wine shop servant ends up the adopted son of the emperor: what a total mess!
When meeting with one of the girls, he calls her Your Majesty: what a strange affair!

第一回 坐北京正德臨朝 誇大同江彬獻諂

話說只爲這件奇事，編了一部要孩兒，雖則傳流已久，
各人唱的不同。待在下唱來，尊客休嫌污耳。

[耍孩兒] 世事兒若循環，如今人不似前，新曲一年一遭換。
銀紐絲兒才丟下，後來興起打棗桿，鎖南枝半插羅江怨，又
興起正德嫖院，耍孩兒異樣的新鮮。

自從洪武立世，傳流九輩君王，改天年，立帝號：改天
年，是正德元年；立帝號，是武宗即位。這萬歲是按上
方觜火猴臨凡，光好貪耍。聽我道來：

武宗爺正德年，觜火猴來臨凡，性情只像個猴兒變。無心料
理朝綱事，只想天下去遊玩，生來坐不住金鑾殿。自即位北
京三出，一遭遭四海哄傳。

---

1 These three lines mention several popular song tunes of the Ming dynasty.
2 "Martial Ancestor" actually was the posthumous title of the Zhengde emperor, but it is
   quite common in later texts to designate deceased emperors also while still alive by their
   posthumous title.
3 "Beak" is one of the twenty-eight constellations known as the "lunar lodges." These
   constellations mark the point due south at the moment of sunrise throughout the year.
   Each of these lodges was later also associated with a directional element and an animal.
   Beak was associated with the West and fire and the monkey. The lodges were each also
   conceived of as a divinity.

1   Enthroned in Beijing, Right Virtue receives his officials;

Vaunting Datong, Jiang Bin offers duplicitous advice.

Let me tell you, I have composed this work about this strange affair to the tune of "Having Fun with the Child." Even though this tune has been popular for a long time, everybody sings it differently. So when you hear me sing it, dear audience, don't complain that I sully your ears!

> The affairs of this world seem to follow a circle;
> People of today are not like those of the past:
> Each year a new tune is replaced by another.
>   "Threads of a Silver Knot" was barely abandoned
> When later on "Beat the Jujube Branch" appeared;
> "Lock Southern Twig" is half inserted in "Luo River Grudge."[1]
>   Now we have here *Right Virtue Goes Whoring*.
> Its "Having Fun with the Child" is quite original!

After Grand Martiality had established the dynasty, the throne had passed through nine generations when the reign period was changed again and a new imperial title established. When they changed the reign period, it became the first year of Right Virtue. When the title had been established, the emperor ascended the throne as Martial Ancestor.[2] This emperor was the Beak's Fire Monkey from up above who had descended to earth: he wanted only to play. Listen to me as I tell you,

> The Martial Ancestor of the Right Virtue years
> Was an incarnation of Beak's Fire Monkey:
> By nature he seemed the manifestation of a simian.[3]
>   He had no desire to manage the affairs of the court,
> He only wanted to roam through the world for fun.
> From birth he couldn't sit still in the Golden Bells Hall.[4]
>   After his accession to the throne, he left Beijing three times,
> And each time it caused a stir throughout the world!

---

4   The Golden Bells Hall is the throne hall in which the emperor is seated during the court audiences at dawn.

這萬歲頭次出京，到了臨清州，收了江彬，現任威南道。這奸黨內欺天子，外壓群臣，他後來被定國公打死。二次出北京，山西嫖院，收了佛動心，帶進皇宮，另蓋一座黑瓦殿給他居住。三出北京，揚州遊玩，十月打春，誰人不知，那個不曉。頭回不說，三回不表，單表二次出京。恐君不信，有西江月爲證。好耍武宗皇爺，出朝離京散心。路遇周元提成親，六哥交了好運。萬歲山西取樂，朝中苦煞江彬。只爲一個佛動心，可惜王龍命盡。

那正德爺非等閒，天生下只好玩，貪花戀酒偏能慣。上殿嬾整君王事，

5   It is not clear to me which function or title of Jiang Bin may be intended by the phrase *weinandao* 威南道 (overawing the southern circuits?).

6   Jiang Bin first met the emperor in 1512 in Beijing, when he was received in audience. He greatly impressed the emperor by his war scars and his views on the military. He quickly became one of the emperor's most trusted advisers and was accordingly promoted to higher and higher positions. Following the emperor's death, he was quickly arrested at the orders of the new power-holders. After the accession of the Jiajing emperor (r. 1522–1566), he was condemned to death for rebellion and executed.

The historical sources do not mention an early trip by the emperor to Linqing, a rich commercial town in Shandong on the Grand Canal. On his southern tour of 1519–1520, however, the imperial entourage was held up at Linqing for a month while the emperor traveled back to Beijing to fetch his favorite concubine. As suggested here, there may have been an earlier trip of the emperor to Linqing. One late Qing novel on the southern

When the emperor first left the capital, he came to Linqing, where he met with Jiang Bin, who at that moment had been appointed as *weinandao*.[5] Inside the palace, this traitor bamboozled the emperor, and outside the palace, he oppressed the ministers. Later he would be beaten to death by the State-Stabilizing Duke.[6] The second time the emperor left Beijing, he went whoring in Shanxi, where he married Buddha's Lust. He took her back with him to the imperial palace, and there built a black-tiled palace hall especially for her to live in. The third time he left Beijing, for fun he traveled through Yangzhou, where he celebrated New Year in October. Who doesn't know this? I will not talk about the first time, nor will I narrate the third time; I will only tell how he left the capital the second time. If you don't believe me, there is a lyric to the tune of "West River Moon" that gives a description:

The pleasure-seeking emperor Martial Ancestor
Abandoned the court and the capital for some fun.
On the way he met with Zhou Yuan and arranged his marriage,
While Brother Six had a stroke of good fortune.

As His Majesty was enjoying himself in Shanxi,
Back at court Jiang Bin suffered great misery.
Now if it had not been for that endearing Buddha's Lust,
The royal dragon, alas! would have lost his life!

His Majesty Right Virtue was not the common sort:
From the day of his birth he only wanted to play.
The man was an outstanding expert on women and wine!
    Too lazy on his throne to tend to for the business of kings,

---

tour of the Zhengde emperor indeed includes an account of an earlier trip by the emperor to Shandong.

"State-Stabilizing Duke" (Dingguo gong 定國公) was the title of the fourth son of Xu Da 許達 (1332–1385) and his heirs. Xu Da had been one of the most important generals of Zhu Yuanzhang, the Hongwu (Grand Martiality) emperor. One of Xu Da's daughters became the wife of Zhu Yuanzhang's fourth son Zhu Di 茱棣 (1360–1424). When Zhu Di rebelled against his nephew, the Jianwen emperor (r. 1399–1402), Xu Da's eldest son sided with the Jianwen emperor, while his fourth son sided with Zhu Di, providing him with secret information, for which he was executed by the Jianwen emperor. Following his victory, Zhu Di, now the Yongle emperor, posthumously awarded this son the title of State-Stabilizing Duke to be inherited by his heirs. These heirs continued to occupy important military positions throughout the Ming dynasty. On the Peking Opera stage, the title is also given to Xu Da. He and his heirs are said to carry bronze mallets and to have been charged by the founding emperor to strike to death any befuddled ruler or traitorous minister.

諸般技藝都學全，萬里江山他不戀。萬歲爺山西嫖院，有江
彬苦楚難言。

　　話說那萬歲自從臨清回京，常想天下景致，心中不足。

　　這日早朝登殿。

聖天子下龍牀，一枝花侍君王，玉芙蓉打板高聲唱。三千粉
黛紅娘子，步步嬌送出朝陽。萬歲離了銷金帳，前後走宮娥
彩女，混江龍駕出朝綱。

　　詩曰：金殿龍樓早早開，靜鞭三下響如雷；

　　　　　飄飄一簇看烟過，萬歲皇爺出殿來。

萬歲爺設早朝，景陽鐘三下敲，靜鞭響罷文武到。二十四拜
山呼罷，曲背躬身貓伏着腰。聖王傳下皇宣詔，

問文武班齊不齊，當駕官前來跪倒。

　　萬歲早朝升殿，文武齊集，皇上開金口露銀牙問道：
　　「文武班齊不齊？」當駕官叩頭稟道：「文武列班已齊，
　　都在金闕伺候御駕。」聖主曰：「既是文武班齊，天下
　　寧靜不寧靜？八方太平不太平？」

7　Beautiful girls.

8　Chaoyang 朝陽 was the name of the eastern palace gate in Ming times. Most likely, this
　is a mistake for Zhaoyang 昭陽, in Han-dynasty times the name of the main hall in the
　rear palace where the empress dwelt.

9　They assembled outside in the courtyard in front of the throne hall.

He was fully adept at arts and skills of all kinds,
But neglected the myriad miles of rivers and mountains!
    And when His Majesty went whoring in Shanxi,
The sufferings of Jiang Bin were unspeakable!

Let me tell you, ever since His Majesty returned from Linqing, he felt unsatisfied, longing for the scenery of the wider world. That day at dawn he ascended the throne hall.

As the Sagely Son of Heaven stepped down from his bed,
A girl like a sprig of flowers was waiting on her lord
    and king,
While jade hibiscus[7] beat their clappers and sang their song.
    Three thousand powdered and rouged servant girls
Gracefully accompanied him out of Chaoyang Gate.[8]
His Majesty emerged from gold-spangled bed-curtains.
    Surrounded on all sides by palace maids and elegant
    ladies—
A dragon disturbing the river, His Majesty left to hold court.

A poem reads,

The golden halls and dragon towers have been opened quite early.
The Whip of Silence, cracked three times, resounds like thunder.
Surging and drifting in thick clouds, one sees the incense waft by.
The Imperial Lord of Ten Thousand Years emerges from the hall.

When His Imperial Majesty holds court at dawn,
The Jingyang Bell is beaten three times.
When the Whip has sounded, officials and officers arrive.
    After they have bowed down twenty-four times and cheered
    thrice,
They bend their backs and fold their bodies, crouching down like
    cats.
Whereupon the Sagely King sends down his imperial summons.
    When asked whether all the officials and officers have
    assembled,
The reporting official comes forward and falls to his knees.

When His Majesty had ascended the hall at dawn and the officials and officers had assembled,[9] he opened his golden mouth, displayed his silver teeth, and asked, "Have the officials and officers all assembled in

跪倒了眾官員，奏我主放心寬，天下豐收民不亂。風調雨順
人安樂，五穀豐登太平年，像堯王重坐金鑾殿。普天下太平
無事，十三省處處安然。

　　聖上曰：「朕乃末世之君，怎比的古聖先皇？一來是朕
　　的洪福，二來是群臣的造化。有事者出班早奏，無事卷
　　簾散朝。」

散去了眾官員，萬歲爺把旨傳，獨把江彬傳上殿。江彬忙跪
金闕下，雙膝跪在品級山，朝參已畢旁邊站。萬歲爺即開金
口，叫愛卿你靠跟前。

　　文武散朝，獨留下江彬，江彬叩頭在地，說：「用臣那
　　邊使用？」

萬歲爺吐龍言，叫愛卿一事煩，坐在宮中真悶倦。欲待出朝
去玩耍，背著群臣離順天，

10 King Yao is one of the sage rulers of the mythical past.
11 The territory of the Ming dynasty was divided into thirteen provinces.
12 The topmost mountain is the mountain-shaped marker for the position of the highest
    officials during audiences at court.
13 Shuntian was the metropolitan prefecture in which Beijing was located.

their ranks?" The reporting official beat his head against the ground and reported, "The civil officials and military officers are arrayed in their ranks. At the golden pillars, they all await Your Majesty's presence." The Sagely Ruler then asked, "So the officials and officers are all assembled. Is all-under-Heaven quiet? Are the eight directions at peace?"

> The government officials all bowed to the ground
> And reported, "Our Lord, please set your mind at rest:
> The harvests are rich, and the people not rebellious.
>   The winds and rains are timely and mild, and the people happy.
> The five grains grow abundantly in these years of
>   great peace,
> As if King Yao occupied the throne in the Golden
>   Bells Hall.[10]
>   The whole wide world enjoys peace without any warfare;
> Every place in the thirteen provinces feels at ease."[11]

The Sagely Ruler replied, "We are the lord of a degenerate age, so how can We be compared to the sages of old and former rulers? This is due, first of all, to our huge good fortune and second to the good luck of you, my ministers. Those with business may step forward to report. If there is no business, the screen shall be rolled up, and you are dismissed."

> When all government officials had dispersed,
> His Majesty sent down an imperial edict,
> Summoning Jiang Bin alone to ascend the hall.
>   Hastily Jiang Bin kneeled down below the golden steps.
> And on both knees he knelt down at the topmost mountain.[12]
> Having paid his respects, he stood down to one side.
>   His Majesty thereupon opened his golden mouth,
> Saying, "My beloved minister, please come closer."

When the officials and officers had dispersed, he kept behind only Jiang Bin, who prostrated himself on the floor and asked, "What is your command?"

> His Majesty pronounced these dragon words:
> "My beloved minister, I have to bother you.
> Sitting here in the palace, I'm just so bored.
>   I want to leave the court and go have some fun,
> And leave Shuntian without telling the officials,[13]

那裏好景我看一看。多待上十朝半月，散散心即早回還。

江彬聽說，心中大喜：「我正要圖謀天下，這昏君待要出去看景，我哄他向那險要去處，路途駕崩，何愁江山不到我手！」這奸黨才待開口，吃了一大驚，說：「錯了！我若說出地方，昏君離朝，萬一日子久了，掌印的張皇后甚是伶俐，廣有計謀，若犯疑忌，便問他串宮太監，遂說萬歲出朝那裏去了，知道的就說江彬。知道那水性潑賤，素不喜我，聽了江彬二字，越發生氣，雪上加霜，那張太監合我不睦，只落的求榮反辱了。」那江彬口內不言，心中暗想，低頭不語。聖上曰：「景在何處？據實奏來。」江彬叩頭說道：「有景臣不敢說。」聖上曰：「你怎麼不敢說？」江彬說：「臣若說出地方，萬一有奸臣得知，安排下刺客，路途有失，可不是臣的罪麼！」聖上曰：「不好說，怎麼處？」江彬說：「臣有本奏給皇爺看罷。」聖上曰：「本在那裏？」這江彬即忙回府，把本做的停當，遂即轉身入朝，叩首丹墀。萬歲說：「景在何處？」江彬說：「盡在本上。」萬歲接來從頭觀看。

微臣奏主得知：十三省數山西，

---

14 The Zhengde emperor's formal wife was surnamed Xia 夏. Empress Zhang 張 was actually his mother. She was to play a major role in the downfall of Jiang Bin and his associates following the death of her son. This text has transferred her name and her strong character to the emperor's wife.

To enjoy the scenery wherever it's finest.
At most, it will be ten days or half a month.
Once I've cleared my mind, I will surely return."

When Jiang Bin heard this, he felt quite elated: "Right now when I have designs on all-under-Heaven, this stupid lord wants to go on a trip. I will trick him into going to some strategic location, and if His Majesty passes away while on the road, I won't have to worry about not being able to lay my hands on these rivers and mountains!" But just when he wanted to open his mouth, this fiend was frightened and said to himself, "No, that would be a mistake. If I tell him the place and this stupid ruler abandons the court, and if by chance he's gone for quite some time, and if Empress Zhang—who is in charge of the seal[14] and is extremely intelligent and devious—harbors any suspicions, she will question the eunuchs that go in and out of the palace. She will say, 'Where did His Majesty go when he left the court?' and those in the know will mention my name. I know that that fickle woman is a mean shrew who never liked me. Once she hears the name 'Jiang Bin,' she will become even more enraged, adding frost to snow. That eunuch Zhang[15] doesn't see eye to eye with me either, so in the end my search for glory would end in shame." So Jiang Bin did not say a word; mulling it over in his heart, he stayed silent. The Sage Ruler said, "Where do I find the scenery? Tell me the truth!" Jiang Bin kowtowed and said, "There's plenty of scenery, but I don't dare mention it." The Sage Ruler said, "Why don't you dare tell me?" Jiang Bin replied, "If I told you the place and by some chance a traitor learned about it and set up an ambush, something untoward might happen to you while out on the road. Wouldn't that then be my crime?" The Sage Ruler said, "If you cannot tell me, then what can be done?" Jiang Bin replied, "I will submit a report to Your Majesty to read." When the Sage Ruler asked, "Where is this report?" Jiang Bin hurried back home to his mansion and prepared a proper report, whereupon he immediately turned around and entered the court, kowtowing before the red steps. When the emperor asked, "Where is the finest scenery?" Jiang Bin told him, "It is all in my report." The emperor took it and read it through from the beginning:

Your humble servant reports to Your Majesty as follows:
Of the thirteen provinces, Shanxi is counted first by far;

---

15   The eunuch Zhang Yong 張永 (1465–1529) was one of the most powerful persons at the court of the Zhengde emperor. His ample military experience made him a rival of Jiang Bin.

大同城裏好景致。男人清秀眞無比，女人風流更出奇，人才出色多標緻。宣武院三千粉黛，一個個亞賽仙姬。

萬歲看罷，喜之不勝，說道：「江愛卿，你暫回府，明晨早來，送朕出京。」江彬回府，萬歲回宮。未知後事如何，且聽下回分解。

The city of Datong priding itself on the finest scenery of all.
    The men there, handsome and graceful, are beyond compare;
The women, fine and charming, are even to more exceptional.
Its people are extraordinarily talented and all very beautiful.
    The three thousand courtesans of the Displaying Martiality
    Ward
Are each and every one the near-equal of immortal maidens.

When the emperor had read this, his joy knew no bounds, and he said, "Beloved Minister Jiang, go back to your mansion and be here tomorrow at dawn to accompany me when I leave the capital." Jiang Bin returned to his mansion, and the emperor returned to the inner palace. If you don't know what happened next, please listen to the following chapter.

第二回 張皇后苦諫天子 武宗爺喜扮軍裝

話說那萬歲御駕回宮，國母接至坤寧宮，擺開御筵，君妃對飲。

坤寧宮擺御筵，接皇爺共成歡，宮娥彩女兩邊站。萬歲山西去的盛，那裏有心共笑談，美酒到口也難咽。萬歲爺把杯放下，叫御妻你聽我言。

萬歲說：「御妻，朕有一句話待說，不知你意下何如？」國母說：「朝中有事君臣論，家中有事父子商。似這宮中無人，有話君妻不說，還合誰說？」萬歲說：「正是。寡人上朝，文武奏本，天下寧靜，朕欲遊玩私行看景。」國母說：「不可！萬歲與天爲子，與民爲父，黎民不可一日無主。萬歲若要私行，可有三件太掛心的事。」萬歲說：「那三件？」國母說：「萬歲離京，朝內空虛，怕有奸臣篡朝，這是一件；或有奸臣下一封反書，勾引胡人困了北京，那時萬歲有家難奔，有國難投，這是二件；再者路途怕有刺客，眞假不辨，恐有不測，

---

1   "Mother of the nation" here is used in reference to the emperor's wife. The emperor consistently addresses her as imperial wife (*yuqi* 御妻), here rendered as "my empress." Kunning Hall was the private quarters of the empress during the Ming dynasty.

2 Her Majesty Zhang sternly admonishes the Son of Heaven;
The Martial Ancestor enjoys dressing up in military garb.

Let me tell you, the emperor returned to the inner palace, and here the mother of the nation welcomed him in the Kunning Hall.[1] When an imperial banquet had been spread out, the lord and his spouse, facing each other, had a drink.

> An imperial banquet was laid out in the Kunning Hall
> Where the empress received the emperor to enjoy it together.
> Palace maids and ladies of elegance stood on both sides.
>   The emperor, preoccupied with his journey to Shanxi,
> Had no desire to engage in any laughter or banter.
> Nor could he swallow the finest wine in his mouth.
>   His Majesty the emperor put down his cup
> And said, "My empress, please listen to me."

The emperor said, "My empress, there is something We want to tell you. What do you think about that?" The mother of the nation replied, "Any business at court is discussed by lord and ministers; any business in the family is discussed by father and son. As it seems there is no one in the palace if you did not talk to me, whom would you talk to?" The emperor said, "You are right. When We held audience, the officials and officers all reported that the whole world is at peace, so We would like to roam for pleasure and enjoy the scenery, traveling incognito." The mother of the nation replied, "Impossible! Your Majesty, you are the Son of Heaven and father to the people, and the people cannot be a single day without a ruler. If you were to travel incognito, Your Majesty, there are three things that worry me too much!" When the emperor asked her what three things, she replied, "Your Majesty, if you leave the capital, the court will be left empty, and I fear that traitors might usurp the court. This is the first thing. A traitor might send out a traitorous letter, inviting the barbarians to lay siege to Beijing. Your Majesty would have no family he could flee to and no country he could appeal to. This is the second thing. And when out on the road, you might be ambushed. As you might be easily misled, I fear something untoward might happen.

這是三件。」皇爺說：「御妻多慮了。眞天子百靈相助，朕洪福齊天，邪不侵正，怕他怎的！」國母說：「你領多少人馬？」皇爺說：「我若領著人馬，扎住行營，那黎民驚慌，都躲著皇帝走，怎麼得見好景？我只單人獨馬，自己私行便了。」國母說：「萬歲，你記的那幾句俗語麼？」皇帝說：「那幾句俗語？」國母說：「鳳不離巢，龍不離海，虎不離山，天子不離金闕。萬歲不信，聽小妃道來。」

雙膝跪叫主公，俗語好你是聽：百鳥不尊離巢鳳，龍離大海遭蝦戲，虎離深山被犬輕。天子離朝人不重，我勸你休要看景，惜江山且在北京。

萬歲爺叫御妻，鳳離巢百鳥依，虎離深山走平地，龍離大海還有水，君出深宮誰敢欺？遊行遊玩何妨事，我憑著齊天洪福，到處裏有甚差遲。

國母說：「你曉的那輩古人麼？」萬歲說：「你不出三宮六院，曉的甚麼古人？」國母說：「聽小妃道來。」

尊萬歲聽小妃，公子光原姓姬，

This is the third thing." The emperor said, "My empress, you worry too much. The true Son of Heaven is assisted by a hundred gods, Our huge good fortune equals heaven, and evil cannot harm right, so what should I fear?" The mother of the nation then asked, "How many infantry and cavalry will you lead?" "If I lead infantry and cavalry and set up camp," the emperor replied, "the common people will be scared witless and hide themselves, so how can I see any good sights? Better that I go by myself on a single horse, traveling incognito." The mother of the nation said, "Your Majesty, do you remember those few common sayings?" When the emperor asked which ones, the mother of the nation replied, "The phoenix does not leave its nest; the dragon does not leave the sea; the tiger does not leave the mountains, and the Son of Heaven does not leave his golden palace. Your Majesty, if you don't believe these sayings, please listen to your humble spouse!"

> Kneeling down on both knees, she said, "My lord,
> You should listen to these good common sayings:
> The birds don't honor a phoenix away from its nest.
>   When a dragon leaves the ocean, it gets toyed with by
>   shrimps.
> When a tiger leaves the hills, it is despised by dogs.
> A Son of Heaven without court commands no respect!
>   I urge you not to go out in search of fine scenery,
> But to cherish your rivers and mountains here in Beijing."

> His Majesty the emperor answered, "My empress,
> Away from its nest the phoenix is followed by all birds.
> Away from the mountains a tiger walks on a level plain.
>   Away from the ocean the dragon still has its streams.
> Who dares cheat a lord who has left his deep palace?
> What is the harm in rambling and roaming for pleasure?
>   When I rely on my huge good fortune equal to heaven,
> What can possibly go wrong wherever I go?"

The mother of the nation said, "Do you know about those people of antiquity?" The emperor retorted, "You never left the three palaces and six courtyards! What do you know about the people of antiquity?" The mother of the nation replied, "Please listen to your humble spouse!

> Your Majesty, listen to your humble spouse:
> Prince Guang was originally surnamed Ji,

王僚也是親兄弟，只因要爭王子做，千金聘了老專諸，刀藏魚腹真奇計。天地間人情難料，好萬歲休要執迷。

萬歲爺笑開言，叫御妻休胡猜，放心穩坐何妨礙？天下寧靜無兵馬，八方太平那裏的災？處處有人把我拜。放寬心不要多慮，我散散心即早回來。

　　國母雙垂淚，再三苦叮嚀，莫要出朝去，恐防有災星。

　　天子龍眉豎，御面赤通紅，拔出龍泉劍，亮開雪練鋒，

　　拿過黃金箸，一剎兩分平，誰人敢擋我，依律定不輕！

有國母跪當前，非是我把你攔，恐防失體人輕慢。萬歲既然主意定，憑君走上焰摩天，誰敢再把君王諫。有句話叮嚀囑咐，看看景即早回還。

　　萬歲說：「御妻這話早在那裏來！朕也不吃酒了。」駕回寢宮，身臥龍牀。玉兔東升，龍樓起鼓，

2　These events took place in the sixth century BCE in the southern state of Wu: Prince Guang 光 had his full brother King Liao 王僚 murdered by one Zhuan Zhu 專諸 to become king in his place.

3　The jade hare inhabits the moon.

4　The night was divided in five watches, marked by beating drums.

And King Liao of Wu was his own full brother,
    But because the prince wanted to replace him as king,
He hired old Zhuan Zhu for plenty of gold,
And hid a dagger inside a fish—a nice trick![2]
    Feelings between heaven and earth are unfathomable.
So my good emperor, don't hold on to your delusion!"

His Majesty the emperor replied with a smile:
"My dear empress, don't be suspicious!
I occupy the throne without worry. What's the big deal?
    All-under-Heaven is quiet, without any military activity;
The eight directions are at peace, without any disaster.
I am venerated by the people throughout the world.
    Set your worries aside, and don't fret too much.
Once I've cleared my mind, I'll quickly return."

The mother of the nation dissolved into tears
As she repeatedly tried to change his mind:
"On no account should you leave the court,
I fear that you may meet a star of disaster."
The Son of Heaven knit his dragon brow,
His imperial face suffused with crimson.
He drew from its sheath his dragon-source sword
Brightly disclosing its blade, white like silk.
Having grasped some chopsticks of yellow gold,
He cleaved the bundle into two equal halves:
"Whoever dares oppose me and block my plans
Will be treated harshly according to the rules!"

The mother of the nation knelt down before him:
"I would not dare block your plans,
But I fear you may lose your life or be maligned.
    As Your Majesty has already made up your mind,
It's up to you to ascend the flame-scorched sky.
Who would dare warn you against it again?
    There's only one thing that I want to repeat once more:
Having seen your fill, return as quickly as you can."

    The emperor said, "My empress, there's no need to say so. Now We are done drinking wine!" The emperor returned to his sleeping quarters and stretched himself out on his dragon couch. As the jade hare rose in the east,[3] the drum was struck on the dragon towers.[4]

只聽的更鼓齊忙，皇爺心緒撩亂。

一更裏心緒焦，想山西睡不著，大同幾時才能到？怎麼樣的一座宣武院，好歹私行瞧一瞧，人人說好想是妙。看一看果然齊整，住些時嫖上一嫖。

二更裏睡不濃，龍樓上鼓咚咚，翻來覆去心不定。總有龍牀睡不穩，恨不能插翅出北京，一心無二去的盛。想山西連夢顛倒，眼前里就是大同。

> 那萬歲翻來覆去，睡臥不安，強捱到三更，果然夢境隨邪，合眼就到了山西。牽著馬進的城來，見人烟湊集，男女清秀，景致無窮。到了宣武院，果然妓女出色，人物標緻，亞賽仙姬，俊如嫦娥。那萬歲心猿意馬，難鎖難拴，遂共樂一處。

三更裏盹睡迷，夢陽臺到山西。果然院中好景致，三千姐妹都齊整，一似仙姬下瑤池，溫柔典雅多和氣。誇不盡妖嬈俊美，俊多嬌賽過御妻。

---

5 Chang'e 嫦娥 is the beautiful goddess of the moon, filled with amorous thoughts.
6 A common designation for courtesans.

Hearing only the equally fast pace of the watch drums, the emperor's head was filled with all kinds of confused thoughts.

> During the first watch, his thoughts were tangled.
> Thinking of Shanxi, he could not sleep:
> When would he be able to arrive in Datong?
> What would the Ward for Displaying Martiality be like?
> For better or worse, he'd travel incognito and have a peek!
> If everyone said it was so great, is must be marvelous.
> He would have a look to see if it was indeed so perfect,
> And stay for a while, and maybe cavort there with a whore.
>
> During the second watch, his sleep was not heavy
> While the drums resounded on the dragon towers.
> He tossed and turned, his heart in a mess.
> Even on his dragon couch, he couldn't sleep soundly.
> Too bad that he lacked the wings to flee the capital!
> His heart was undividedly set on departing.
> His longing for Shanxi overturned even his dreams
> And before his eyes, Datong had already appeared.

The emperor tossed and turned, unable to sleep. But when he had made it to the third watch, his dream visions followed his sinful thoughts. When he closed his eyes, he had arrived in Shanxi! Leading his horse, he entered the city and saw that the place was quite populous, that the men and women were handsome and graceful, and that the scenery was inexhaustible. When he arrived at the Displaying Martiality Ward, the courtesans were indeed exceptional and their figures were beautiful. They nearly equaled immortal maidens and were as outstanding as Chang'e.[5] The emperor could not restrain the monkey of his mind and the horse of his desire, and so he took his pleasure with them.

> During the third watch, he dozed off in an illusion.
> Dreaming of sex, he arrived in Datong,
> And there the ward indeed offered a sight:
> Those three thousand sisters[6] were all perfect.
> Like immortal maidens having descended from Jasper Pond,
> They were agreeable, impeccable, and mild-mannered.
> Their charming beauty couldn't be vaunted enough,
> And in their artful grace, they surpassed his empress!

衆姊妹陪君王，觀不盡好風光。龍樓畫鼓催三撞，醒來卻是
南柯夢，搗枕捶牀恨夜長，天交四鼓雞初唱。萬歲爺抖衣扒
起，驚動了掌印的娘娘。

　　那萬歲強捱了一夜，天交四鼓，抖衣扒起。國母說：
「天尚未明，萬歲那裏去？」萬歲說：「趁著此時，正
好出京；天若明了，不好。」國母說：「可知路麼？」
萬歲說：「江彬引路。」國母聽說，懷恨在心，已知留
他不住，叫宮官看膳來。萬歲說：「不用膳，看我那衣
服來。」這皇帝家除了穿龍衣，可別穿甚麼？這萬歲是
個馬上皇帝，最好私行游玩，有江彬做就的行衣：青布
衫，黃罩甲，綁腿，鞥鞋，簷邊氈帽，皮鞓帶，椰瓢，
鬧龍褡包。宮官將衣服拿來，萬歲爺可扎挂起來了。

萬歲爺巧扎點，穿上件青布衫，龍袍緊蓋防人見。腰間束上
皮鞓帶，鬧龍褡包掛胸前，綁腿鞥鞋穿的慣。帶上簷氈大
帽，打扮起像一個軍漢。

萬歲爺要起程，趁未明好出京，天子動了閒遊興。白銀金錢
不算賬，赤金豆子帶一升，

7　In "An Account of the Governor of the Southern Branch" (*Nanke taishou zhuan*), a well-
known classical tale of the Tang dynasty, a man falls asleep and has a marvelous career as
the prefect of Southern Bough, only to realize on waking up and seeing an anthill below
the southern bough of the huge acacia tree in his courtyard, that it all had been only a
drunken dream. For an English translation, see for instance Nienhauser 2010, 131–188.

The many sisters thronged around their lord and king.
He could not take his eyes off the thrilling sight!
When the painted drums of the dragon towers resounded three
    times,
   He woke up—it had been a Southern Bough dream![7]
Beating cushion and couch, he hated the night for its length.
As soon as the rooster crowed and the fourth watch began,
   His Majesty the emperor grabbed his clothes and got up,
Disturbing Her Majesty, the empress in charge of the seal.

When the emperor had made it through the night and the fourth watch
of the night was sounded, he grabbed his clothes and got up. The mother
of the nation asked, "The sky is not yet light. Where do you want to go,
Your Majesty?" The emperor replied, "I want to avail myself of this hour
to leave the capital. Once the sky has brightened, it won't be so easy."
The mother of the nation asked, "Do you know your way?" The emperor
replied, "Jiang Bin will guide me." When the mother of the nation heard
this, she was filled with hatred [toward that man] and realized that she
could not keep the emperor back, so she called a palace official to prepare
food. But the emperor said, "I won't have food, just bring me my clothes."
Now what else would this emperor wear apart from his dragon gown? This
emperor was a horseback emperor. What he loved to do most was to roam
about incognito, and for that he had a set of clothes that had been made by
Jiang Bin: a blue linen gown, a yellow mail-covering, shin wraps, boots,
a brimmed felt hat, a leather belt, a coconut gourd, and a double satchel.
When the palace official had brought his clothes, the emperor could start
dressing himself.

His Majesty the emperor started to dress himself.
He put on his blue linen gown, which tightly covered
His dragon robe so no one could see it.
   He tied the leather belt around his waist,
The double satchel he hung on his breast;
He was comfortable wearing shin wraps and boots.
   And with his brimmed felt hat on his head,
He was dressed exactly like a common soldier.

His Majesty the emperor wanted to start on his trip
And slip out of the capital before it turned bright.
The Son of Heaven wanted to roam at will.
   He kept no count of the pure silver and gold coins,
And carried a liter of beans of red gold

路上隨便零星用。多拿些金銀財寶，宣武院好去嫖風。

萬歲爺扎點停當，叫宮官：「你看我像一個甚麼人？」宮官叩頭道：「奴婢不敢說。」萬歲說：「但說不妨。」宮官說：「赦奴婢不死，我才敢說。」皇爺說：「赦你無罪。」宮官說：「萬歲像一個軍漢。」萬歲說：「我不像個皇帝了？」宮官說：「龍蛇難辨，誰可認的。」萬歲大喜：「牽我的馬來。」這匹馬是外國進來的日月驌驦駒，金鞍玉轡，外面使羊皮遮了。遂把馬牽到分宮樓下。那國母攜手攬腕，送出萬歲前到分宮樓。主上說：「御妻不可遠送了。」

有國母跪埃塵，尊萬歲要小心，路途凡事加謹慎。醉後休說朝裏話，防備刺客有歹人，走漏了消息無投奔。到晚來早早宿下，休要住野店荒村。

萬歲說：「我曉的了，御妻請回宮去罷。」

有國母回了宮，萬歲爺便起程，自己把馬牢牽定。私出正陽門一座，江彬跪下叫主公，倒把皇爺諕了個掙。萬歲爺低言悄語，江愛卿不要高聲。

To use along the way for small expenses.
   He also took some extra precious baubles of gold and silver
To play the patron in the Displaying Martiality Ward.

When His Majesty the emperor had dressed himself up to perfection, he asked a palace official, "What do I look like?" That palace official kowtowed and said, "Your slave doesn't dare say." When the emperor said, "Just tell me, it's all right," the palace official said, "Your slave will only dare say if you pardon me from the death penalty." When the emperor had said that he would pardon him for any crime, the palace official said, "Your Majesty looks like a common soldier." When the emperor asked, "So I do not look like the emperor?" the palace official replied, "Dragon and snake are indistinguishable: who could recognize you?" The emperor was greatly pleased, "Bring me my horse!" This horse was a sun and moon thoroughbred colt that a foreign country had offered in tribute: it wore a golden saddle and silver bridle and was covered with a sheepskin. When the horse had been led to the Tower for Leaving the Palace, the mother of the nation held the emperor's hand and grasped his arm as she accompanied him to the palace gate. There he said, "My empress, there's no need to accompany me any further!"

   The mother of the nation knelt down in the dust,
   "Your Majesty, please make sure to be careful!
   While on the road be circumspect in all things!
      Don't talk about court affairs while drinking;
   Be on your guard against ambushes and evil men.
   If your secret gets out, you'll have nowhere to run.
      When evening falls, hasten to seek lodging for the night.
   Don't stay at inns in the wilds or in derelict villages."

   The emperor replied, "I know, my empress. Now please go back to the inner palace."

   While the mother of the nation returned to the palace,
   His Majesty the emperor promptly set out on his trip,
   Leading his horse himself with a firm hand.
      When he had slipped through the Zhengyang Gate,
   Jiang Bin knelt down and called, "My Lord!"
   Scaring his imperial master out of his mind.
      His Majesty the emperor whispered softly,
   "Beloved Minister Jiang, don't shout so loudly!"

　　江彬說：「臣候了多時了。」皇爺說：「愛卿謹言，有人
　　聽見怎了！」江彬說：「萬歲請上馬走罷。」

萬歲爺上了馬，鞭子打腿又夾，江彬跟隨在步下。一心只上
大同去，夾馬搖鞭興致佳，朝裏軍情全不掛。出城來走了數
里，有江彬前來跪下。

　　「臣有句話不敢說。」萬歲說：「但說不妨。」江彬說：「萬
　　歲上山西，那黎民肉眼凡胎，誰認的是皇帝，但恐路途
　　阻隔，臣有一個行票給萬歲拿著。」萬歲自思：果然人
　　離鄉賤，物離鄉貴。我出了門子，倒還不如江彬這小子
　　的體面。「行票在那裏？」江彬取出，遞與萬歲，收拾
　　停當，君臣作別，那萬歲爺奔上大路。未知後事如何，
　　且聽下回分解。

8　Chinese riders did not use spurs, but urged their horses on by pressing the horses' sides
with their knees.

Jiang Bin replied, "I have been waiting here for so long!" But the emperor said, "Beloved minister, be careful of your words! What if we're noticed?" Jiang Bin said, "Your Majesty, please mount your horse so we can go!"

> His Majesty the emperor, having mounted his horse,
> Struck it with his whip and pressed it with his knees,[8]
> And Jiang Bin followed, walking all the way.
>   The emperor's one desire was to travel to Datong.
> Pressing the horse and wielding the whip, he was happy,
> Not caring at all about court business or the military.
>   When they reached several miles outside the city,
> Jiang Bin stepped forward and knelt down.

"There is something I don't dare say." The emperor said, "Just say it; it's all right." Jiang Bin said, "Your Majesty is going to Shanxi, but the people there are common mortals with limited sight, so who will recognize you as the emperor? I am afraid that you may run into trouble while on the road, so I have prepared for you an official passport, which I hereby present to you." The emperor thought to himself, "Indeed: 'Outside their own village, people lose their status; outside their own village, goods get expensive.' Once I've gone out the gate, I don't even have the status of a nobody like Jiang Bin." Then he said, "Where is that passport?" Jiang Bin took it out and handed it to the emperor. When the emperor had carefully tucked it away, lord and minister separated, and His Majesty the emperor hurried forward on the main road.

If you don't know what happened next, please listen to the following chapter.

第三回 使金錢鄉人拿響馬 拜御駕巡檢受天恩

　　話說江彬回京，皇爺心忙意急，策馬加鞭。
萬歲爺去私行，駕離朝上大同，文武百官如做夢。一心山西
去嫖院，酒店收了東斗星。有榮有苦前生命：時來了賣酒的
六哥，苦煞了倒運的王龍。
　　卻說那國母在宮中暗想：江彬哄駕出京，定要圖謀江
　　山。遂叫：「張永何在？」那張永在龍簾以外叩頭，口
　　稱：「國母喚奴婢那邊使用？」國母說：「我想江彬這
　　廝，定有篡朝的心腸。你領我這道密旨，把江彬拿來，
　　打在刑部監裏。萬歲爺一日回朝，一日放他出監。違旨
　　者項上一刀！
張公公心裏焦，領密旨出了朝，江彬做夢不知道。指望興心
做皇帝，不想國母識破了，這場大禍從天掉。進府去不由分
訴，把江彬即時綁了。

1　The Eastern Dipper is a constellation of three stars that shines brightly in the eastern sky
　before dawn. All stars are divinities and may be reborn on earth. The wine-seller Brother
　Six, whom the emperor while traveling incognito will adopt as his son, is said to be an
　incarnation of the Eastern Dipper Star.

3   A mounted bandit is arrested by villagers for spending gold cash;
Celestial grace descends on a police chief who bows to His Majesty.

Now let me tell you, Jiang Bin returned to the capital, but the emperor, in a hurry, whipped his horse on.

> His Majesty the emperor left on an incognito trip:
> The Ruler left the capital on a trip to Datong,
> While his officials and officers had no clue at all.
>   His mind was set on whoring in Shanxi.
> At a wine shop he'll adopt an Eastern Dipper Star.[1]
> Glory or suffering depend on one's former life.
>   The opportunity arrived for wine-seller Brother Six;
> Down on his luck, Wang Long suffered greatly.

Let me tell you, the mother of the nation in the inner palace thought to herself, "Now that Jiang Bin has tricked the emperor into leaving the capital, he must be scheming to lay his hands on our rivers and mountains." Then she called, "Zhang Yong, where are you?" Zhang Yong kowtowed outside the dragon screen and said, "Your Majesty, how do you want to employ your slave?" The mother of the nation said, "That scoundrel Jiang Bin, I'm afraid, definitely intends to usurp the nation. You hereby receive my secret edict to arrest Jiang Bin and lock him in the prison of the Ministry of Justice. The day His Majesty the emperor returns to court is the day he will be released. Anyone who disobeys this edict will be beheaded!"

> Eunuch Zhang was worried stiff.
> Upon receiving this secret edict, he left the court,
> But Jiang Bin remained ignorant and had no idea.
>   He hoped to achieve his aim and become emperor,
> But had no idea that the empress already knew,
> So this major misfortune descended out of the blue.
>   When his mansion was entered, no protest was allowed.
> Jiang Bin was arrested and promptly shackled.

這張永領了密旨，拿了江彬，送在刑部監裏，回朝交
旨，不在話下。單表的是萬歲出了北京，一路上景致無
窮：草芊芊，柳綿綿，荼蘼架，牡丹顏，鶯燕啼林外，
蜂蝶舞花前，爭翠的芍藥舞，迎風的海棠翻，荒村無火
桃噴火，野店無烟柳帶煙，雁飛不到處，人被利名牽。
萬歲爺離順天，心裏焦不耐煩，閒花野草無心戀。兩程並做
一程走，頓斷絲韁又加鞭，恨不能插翅飛進宣武院。一路上
心忙意急，前來到居庸高關。

　　萬歲來到居庸關口，磕馬徑過。那把關的攔住道：「長
官那裏去？」萬歲說：「過關。」那人道：「誰不知你
過關哩。你家裏的門麼，你走的這等大意？」萬歲自
思：「這狗頭瞎了眼了！真正是俺家裏的門，竟不要我
走！」遂說道：「你不要我過去，有甚麼話說？」那人
道：「俺不是私意，俺有朝廷的明文，把守關口，留下
稅銀，才叫你過去。」皇爺說：「我那裏的銀子？」那
人道：「你沒有銀子，你是奉差的，該有牌票。」皇爺
說：「也沒有。」那人大怒道：

2   The rising smoke of cooking fires is a sign of human habitation. Accordingly, the lack of
smoke indicates that the inn has been abandoned.

3   Juyong Pass to the northwest of Beijing is one of the major gates in the Great Wall, and
as such was a place of great strategic importance.

Having received this secret edict, Zhang Yong arrested Jiang Bin, delivered him to the prison of the Ministry of Justice, and reported back to the palace—but no more about this. I will only narrate how the emperor had left Beijing and encountered endless scenery along the road:

> The grasses were exuberant;
> The willows were stretching on.
> Here were the trellises for roses;
> There were the colors of tree peonies.
> Orioles and swallows twittered beyond the groves;
> Bees and butterflies were dancing amidst the flowers.
> Competing in halcyon green, herbaceous peonies danced,
> And welcoming the breeze, crab apples were turning around.
> In overgrown villages without cooking fires, peaches spat their flames;
> Near inns in the wilds without smoke, willows were
> encircled by mists.[2]
> To places no goose reaches while flying,
> People are pulled by profit and fame.

His Majesty the emperor, having left Shuntian,
Was anxious in heart and filled with vexation,
With no desire for idle flowers or wild grasses.
   He combined two stretches of the road into one.
When the silk cord broke, he took another whip.
Alas, he lacked wings to fly to the Displaying Martiality
   Ward!
   Throughout the trip he was impatient and hurried,
And so he arrived at the high Juyong Pass.[3]

When the emperor arrived at the entrance to Juyong Pass, he spurred on his horse to pass quickly. But the man guarding the pass blocked his way, saying, "Sir, where are you going?" The emperor replied, "Through the Pass!" "Obviously you want to go through the Pass," the man said, "but why are you so arrogant, as if this were the gate to your own house?" The emperor thought to himself, "The bastard is blind in both eyes! This really is the gate of my own house, and he won't let me through!" But he said, "Why won't you allow me to pass?" The man replied, "It isn't up to me. I have a clear appointment from the emperor to guard this pass. I can only let you go on if you pay the toll." The emperor said, "Where would I have money?" "If you don't have money," the man said, "you must be traveling on official business and have a chit." The emperor replied, "I don't have that either." At that, the man exploded in rage,

「你的牌票、銀子全無，你莫非是一個響馬？這兩日關前短了皇杠，一個也還沒拿著哩。關上要緊，誰敢放你過去！你同我見見俺那官何如？」萬歲自思：「江彬曾說路上要緊，我且不信，果然是實。給了我那行票，未知他體面何如。既到危急之處，少不的撒一個謊了。」說道：「你不知我是江都督差來的，要上甯西查邊，軍情緊急，來的慌速，沒帶牌票；銀子到有，迭不的拆封。你放我過去，銀子也有，牌票也有。」那人陪笑道：「何不早說！早知道是江老爺的差官，只該遠接。」萬歲道：「你倒不怕皇帝，倒怕江老爺？」那人道：「怎麼不怕皇帝？那皇帝罷，他在京裏；江老爺差官往來常走，得罪著他，着叫俺有死無活！」萬歲說：「你講的有理！我不怪你。」把馬催開上的關來。那萬歲自從四更天起身，無曾吃飯，肚中飢餓，欲待下馬吃飯。那路南裏有一個人就叫：「老客，要吃飯來咱家。」萬歲聽說，下馬進店。店家說：「老客待吃甚麼？」萬歲說：「你有甚麼，盡數拿來罷。」

乾燒餅拾一盤，鹹菓子黑菜籃，盛上一碗溫水麵。萬歲嘗嘗不美口，少油缺醋又精鹹，這樣東西吃不慣。店主說想是你盤費短少，待要吃恐怕沒錢。

那萬歲聽說，羞的那面紅過耳。

4　Probably Ningxia is intended.

5　In Ming dynasty China, silver was a common means of exchange, but it was not minted. Large amounts were paid in ingots of a fixed weight, while small amounts were paid in small pieces of silver weighed on payment.

6　The fourth watch of the night corresponds to roughly 1 a.m. to 3 a.m.

"If you don't have a chit or money, you must be a mounted bandit! A few days ago, an imperial transport was robbed before the pass, and we haven't yet arrested a single person! Security is tight at this Pass, so who would dare let you through? How about you and I pay a visit to my officer?"

The emperor thought to himself, "When Jiang Bin told me that security was tight along this road, I didn't believe him, but it's indeed true. He gave me that passport, but I don't know what his status is. Now that I've arrived at this critical spot, I'll have to try a lie." He said, "You don't know this, but I have been sent on a mission by Commissioner-in-Chief Jiang to Ningxi to inspect the borders.[4] Because of the urgency of the military situation, I came here in great haste and didn't bring a chit. I have plenty of silver, but I haven't yet had time to break up an ingot.[5] Just allow me to pass, and you'll have your money and your chit." Now the man said with an unctuous smile, "Why didn't you say so earlier? If I had known right away that you were an emissary of His Excellency Jiang, I should have gone out of my way to welcome you!" "So you fear His Excellency Jiang more than the emperor?" the emperor asked. The man replied, "The emperor lives far way in the capital, but the emissaries of His Excellency Jiang pass through here all the time, and if I displease them, it will mean my death!" The emperor said, "You are right. I don't blame you." He urged his horse forward and passed through the Pass.

Now, the emperor had started out in the fourth watch and hadn't eaten anything since, so he felt quite hungry.[6] When he wanted to dismount and have some food, someone on the southern side of the road called to him, "Guest, if you're looking for some food, please come to my place." When the emperor heard this, he dismounted from his horse and entered the shop. The shopkeeper said, "What would you like to eat, dear guest?" The emperor replied, "What do you have? Bring out everything!"

> A full plate of dried-sesame-seed cakes,
> Salted fruits, and a basket of black greens.
> He also filled a bowl of hot water.
>   But when the emperor had a taste, he didn't like it:
> Too little oil, no vinegar, and far too much salt!
> He was not used to eating such stuff.
>   The shopkeeper said, "I'm afraid you're short of cash,
> You want to eat, but I fear you lack the money."

When the emperor heard this, he blushed even behind his ears for shame!

萬歲爺面帶嚚，伸龍爪解開包，取出金銀桌上料，五個好錢你拿去。王小拾起睜眼瞧，看見金錢諕一跳，渾身走了三魂號，靈山點卯一遭。

那王小急跑到後房，叫聲老婆子：「大禍臨門，可了不的了！」婆子道：「怎麼來？」王小說：「每日拿響馬拿不著，響馬來了咱家裏了！」婆子道：「你認的麼？」王小說：「古怪！進店來吃飯，嫌寒道冷，我造次他幾句，他給我五個金錢。這小人家誰敢使？不是短了皇杠，就是打劫了王子，不是響馬是甚麼！」婆子道：「賊不咬恩人，你將這錢還給他拿去罷。」王小出來說：「老客呀，拿著錢走罷。你虧了撞著我，你犯了法了。你這錢民間沒有，是皇爺家東西。」萬歲說：「祖祖輩輩都使的是這錢，沒犯一遭法。」他二人爭嚷，驚動了街房都來大叫：「王小，客的錢皮些收著罷，嚷的是甚麼，看壞了鋪子！」萬歲道：「我這錢是人家那錢的祖宗，他還不要哩。」眾人說：「錢在那裏？」王小用手一指：「桌子上不是。」眾人都掙了。

街市人把眼睜，起黃色不像銅，霞光萬道寶色重，兩條小龍上邊戲。眾人看見諕一驚，湯著送了殘生命。眾人說真正響馬，拿了他咱去請功。

7 Small amounts were paid using copper coins. Such coins were round and had a square in the middle. On one side they carried a four-character inscription.
8 Traditionally, one was said to have three souls (*hun* 魂) and seven spirits (*po* 魄). On death, the three souls disperse, while the seven spirits stay and decay with the body.
9 A traditional Chinese copper coin is round with a square hole in the middle. On one side the coin carries four characters usually stating the reign period of production. The back side of the coin will be smooth and empty. These gold coins from inside the imperial palace have been decorated with imperial dragons.

The emperor's displeasure showed on his face.
Stretching his dragon claws, he opened his bag
And threw down gold and silver on the table.
  "Go ahead and choose the five finest coins!"[7]
Little Wang picked them up and had a close look.
Seeing the gold coins, he jumped up in fright.
  His three souls fled from his body
As if reporting for duty in the other world![8]

In a panic, Little Wang ran into the backroom and shouted, "Great disaster stands at the gate! We're doomed!" When his wife asked what was going on, he told her, "For days they've been hunting down those mounted bandits without catching anyone, and now one of them has come to our place!" When his wife asked him how he had recognized the bandit, Little Wang said, "It's really weird! When he entered the shop to have some food, he complained that this was too cold and that was too hot, but when I chided him, he gave me five golden coins. Who among us ordinary folks dares to use them? If he hasn't robbed the imperial transport, he must have stolen them from some prince! What can he be but a mounted bandit?" His wife replied, "Bandits don't bite their benefactors. Return the coins to him, and let him take them back."

So when Little Wang came out of the backroom, he said, "Dear guest, please take these coins with you. You're lucky that you ran into me, since you must have broken the law. These coins have no use among us common folks. They are playthings from the imperial palace." The emperor replied, "My ancestors have used these coins for generations, and we have never broken the law!" Their shouting attracted the attention of the neighbors, who gathered and cried, "Little Wang, don't fleece your customers! What are you shouting about? It's bad for business." The emperor said, "My coins are the ancestors of everybody else's coins, but he still doesn't want them!" When the neighbors said, "Where are these coins?" Little Wang pointed with his hand, "There on the table!" Everyone gaped at them.

The neighbors gaped at them with wide eyes.
The golden glare they gave off was nothing like copper.
The myriad flashes of colored light proved their value.
  Two little dragons played on both sides of the hole.[9]
When the neighbors saw them, they were terrified,
As though to touch them would cost them their lives!
  So the neighbors said, "He's a bandit for sure.
We'll arrest him and go and collect our reward!"

那萬歲見勢不好，牽馬就走。眾人道：「漢子那裏走！這兩日關前響馬短了皇杠，正拿不著。你使出這金錢來，莫不是響馬？」萬歲說：「我怎麼就是響馬？」眾人道：「是與不是，你見見俺那老爺。」眾人圍繞，萬歲在危急之處，不能走脫。城隍、土地著忙，有那巡檢張敖，正在那涼牀上盹睡，夢中神靈顯聖。

有巡檢是張敖，涼牀上才睡著，城隍土地高聲叫。休推睡里合夢裏，不是怪來不是妖，北京聖駕前來到。醒來快忙救主，免的你項上一刀。

張巡檢忽的醒來，吃一大驚，疑惑不定。忽然街裏來報：「老爺，有了響馬了！」張敖說：「怎麼見的響馬？」眾人遂從頭說了一遍。

張巡檢把頭低，口不言心裏思，翻來覆去無主意。有心拿他當響馬，適才一夢好蹺蹊。這椿事兒非輕易，若還是朝廷老子，叫小官溺在磬裏。

那張敖同眾人來到街前，看那人打扮的像個軍漢行持。合該那張敖的時來，遂大喝一聲：「眾人休得無禮！只怕是老爺的差官。那響馬短了皇杠，他還敢在這裏買飯吃？」那萬歲被那巡檢一句話提醒了，遂說：「我是江都督的差官。」張敖說：「你就沒個

---

10   The lowest representatives of the celestial bureaucracy on earth, the divine counterparts to district magistrates and village heads.

11   The intended meaning of this sentence must be something like "Then I will be in a tight spot." The stones of a chime have a small hole for the strings by which they are tied to a frame.

When the emperor saw that the situation had taken a bad turn, he wanted to leave and began leading his horse. But the neighbors said, "Hey, where are you going? A few days ago, mounted bandits robbed an imperial transport before the pass, and so far they haven't been arrested. You're spending golden coins, so you must be a bandit." The emperor said, "How can you say that I'm a bandit?" But the people said, "Whether you're a bandit or not, you're going to pay a visit to our boss." Surrounded by the crowd, the emperor was in a tight spot with no way to escape. So the city god and the god of the soil[10] panicked and manifested themselves in a dream to Police Chief Zhang Ao, who was taking a nap on his shaded couch.

> There was a police chief named Zhang Ao.
> He had just fallen asleep on his shaded couch
> When the city god and the god of the soil shouted,
>   "Don't claim that this is only a dream in your sleep.
> We are no monsters, nor are we demons.
> His Majesty from Beijing has arrived here.
>   Wake up and hurry to save your lord.
> Otherwise, you will be beheaded!"

Police Chief Zhang awoke with a start. He was greatly frightened, but beset by doubt. Suddenly he heard the neighbors report, "Boss, we've caught a bandit!" When he asked them how they knew the man was a bandit, they explained the whole story from the beginning.

> Police Chief Zhang lowered his head.
> Not saying a word, he pondered the matter.
> Looking at it from all sides, he couldn't make up his mind.
>   He was tempted to arrest the man as a mounted bandit,
> But his dream of a moment ago had been quite weird.
> This case was something out of the ordinary!
>   "But if it really is the old guy from the palace,
> He will have me peeing through a chime!"[11]

When Zhang Ao followed the crowd into the street, he saw that the man was dressed like a common soldier. Zhang Ao's moment had arrived. He shouted, "Good people, don't mistreat him. He must be the emissary of some higher-up. Would a mounted bandit still dare come here and buy food after robbing an imperial transport?" That one sentence of the police chief gave the emperor an idea. He said, "I am an emissary of Commissioner-in-Chief Jiang." Zhang Ao asked, "But don't you have

牌票麼？」萬歲說：「你是甚麼人？」張敖說：「我是這居庸關的巡檢。」萬歲說：「有牌票。你不來，我不給人看。」張敖說：「拿來我看無妨。」

取行票與張敖，一張紙紅筆標，上邊寫著都督票。張敖看罷雙膝跪，許多街里都告饒：老爺來時不知道。這些人肉眼凡胎，不認的休要計較。

萬歲自思：「他們有眼無珠，怎知我是皇帝。我有心待給他個利害，恐上不的山西了。」說道：「你都是些小人，我不怪你。休說我是個差官，就是北京城裏御駕降臨，你得罪著，大人不見小人過，也都饒了你。」衆人叩頭，俱各散去。張敖說：「長官到我衙門裏吃杯茶何如？」那萬歲肚中飢餓，將機就計，跟著他進了衙門，把門封了，讓的萬歲官廳坐下，細瞧了瞧，雙膝跪下。

張巡檢跪案前，叫萬歲將臣憐，肉眼不識君王面。萬歲聞言諕一跳，森森的恐怕露機關，登時就把容顏變。平白的呼皇道寡，這巡檢好像風顛。

萬歲說：「你虧了撞著我，若是那樣人，回朝對都督說了，那江都督是朝廷近臣，駕前一本，就說居庸關巡檢呼皇道寡，聖上惱了，發一路人馬

a chit?" "Who are you?" the emperor asked. Zhang Ao replied, "I am the police chief for Juyong Pass." The emperor said, "Of course I have a chit. But I will show it only to you." Zhang Ao said, "There's no harm in letting me have a look."

> He took out the passport and handed it to Zhang Ao.
> It was one sheet of paper with writing in red ink.
> On top it stated, "Issued by the commissioner-in-chief."
>   Having seen it, Zhang Ao knelt down on both knees,
> And all the many neighbors begged for forgiveness.
> "Your Excellency, we didn't know it was you!"
>   "These people are common mortals with limited sight!
> They didn't recognize you. Don't hold it against them!"

The emperor thought to himself, "These people have eyes, but lack sight. How could they know that I am the emperor? I'd like to teach them a lesson, but if I did, I'm afraid I wouldn't make it to Shanxi." So he said, "You are all ordinary folks, so I will not blame you. Let's forget that I am an emissary. Even if His Majesty the emperor from Beijing passed through this place and you offended him, such a great man would not notice the faults of ordinary folks. So I too forgive you all." Those people all kowtowed and dispersed. Police Chief Zhang said, "How about coming to my office for a cup of tea?" The emperor was still very hungry, so he changed his plans and followed Zhang Ao into his office. After Zhang locked the gate, he invited the emperor to take his seat in the main hall, and looking around carefully, he knelt down on both knees.

> Police Chief Zhang knelt down before the table
> And shouted, "Your Majesty, take pity on me!
> My poor eyes failed to recognize your features."
>   When the emperor heard this, he was frightened;
> Shaking, he feared that his secret was exposed,
> So he immediately changed his facial expression.
>   "Without reason he addresses me as His Majesty!
> This police chief seems to me to be raving mad!"

The emperor said, "It's a good thing you met with me! If it had been someone else, he would have informed the commissioner-in-chief upon his return to the court. Commissioner-in-Chief Jiang is a trusted minister of the emperor, and if he had submitted a report stating that the police chief at Juyong Pass addresses people as His Majesty, the Sage Ruler would be annoyed and dispatch a battalion of infantry and cavalry to

抄了滿門，可不是弄假成眞？」張敖叩頭說：「莫要哄臣，有神靈警夢與臣，才知聖駕降臨。」萬歲說：「眞果是實？」巡檢說：「不敢撒謊。」萬歲道：「你既認的我，不可走漏消息，若洩漏一字，全家聽斬！你若謹慎，待我回來之時，好好帶你進朝，封你個坐京的都巡檢。」張敖聽說，叩頭謝恩。

張巡檢謝龍恩，雙膝跪拜至尊，駕臨時俺有緣分。小臣見了皇帝面，免我三層地獄門，不受陰司閻君恨。萬歲說：你不要胡言亂語，只要你謹慎小心。

張敖說：「臣曉的了。」皇爺說：「有甚麼飯拿來我吃。」張敖慌忙上膳來。皇爺用膳已避，即時起身。張敖牽馬送下關來，前到了密松林來，君臣作別。未之後事若何，且聽下回分解。

12 King Yama is the ruler of the underworld where sinners are tortured in punishment for the sins they committed while alive.

seize your whole family. Wouldn't that turn fake into fact?" But Zhang Ao kowtowed and said, "Don't fool me! Divinities forewarned me in a dream, and that's how I knew that Your Majesty was visiting." When the emperor asked, "Is that so?" Zhang Ao replied, "I wouldn't dare lie." The emperor said, "You may have recognized me, but you cannot let the secret out. If a single word leaks out, I'll have your whole family beheaded! But if you're careful, I will take you back with me to the capital on my return and appoint you Executive Police Chief for the capital." Hearing this, Zhang Ao kowtowed to express his gratitude.

> Police Chief Zhang thanked the dragon's grace;
> Kneeling on both knees, he bowed to the Most High:
> "Karma determined my meeting with Your Majesty!
>   Now that I've been allowed to see the emperor's features,
> I'll be spared from the triple layers of the prisons of hell
> And be free from the wrath of King Yama down below!"[12]
>   His Majesty said, "Don't blabber such nonsense,
> Just make sure that you be careful, and watch your words!"

Zhang Ao replied, "Understood." The emperor said, "Now if you have some food for me, please bring it out." In all haste Zhang Ao provided him with a meal. After the emperor had finished, he immediately got up. Leading the emperor's horse, Zhang Ao accompanied him down the Pass, and when they had arrived at a dense pine forest, lord and minister parted.

If you don't know what happened next, please listen to the following chapter.

第四回 武宗爺過山遭渴難 雲魔女送水動君心

不說巡檢回衙，單表萬歲急奔大路。

萬歲爺奔紅塵，風陣陣熱難禁，千辛萬苦言不盡。馬踏河沙如鐵烙，小橋流水似鍋溫，苦煞朕當誰來問？一路上心如烈火，前來到曠野山林。

萬歲爺飢餐渴飲，夜住曉行，一路無辭，前來到梅嶺山下，擡頭觀看，山勢險峻。

萬歲爺進了山，睜龍眼四下觀：百鳥乘涼枝頭串，隱隱怪石如虎坐，彎彎枯木似龍蟠，左右都是深溝澗。看不盡山中的野景，巧丹青畫不周全。

4   Crossing the mountains, His Majesty the
Martial Ancestor experiences thirst;

Bringing him water, the Māra Maiden of
the Clouds arouses the emperor's lust.

I won't tell you how the police chief returned to his office, but will only
narrate how the emperor hastily pursued the main road.

> His Majesty the emperor hurried on through the red dust.
> With gust upon gust of wind, the heat was unbearable.
> His myriad sufferings were unspeakable.
>> When his horse stepped on the riverbank sand, it felt like a
>> branding iron;
> The stream flowing below the bridge resembled a pan of seething
> water.
> "To whom can We direct Our complaints?"
>> Throughout the trip, his heart felt like a burning fire;
> Advancing, he came to an open field and a mountain forest.

His Majesty the emperor ate when hungry and drank when thirsty, rested
for the night and departed at dawn, and shirked no exertion all along the
way. Advancing thus, he arrived at the foot of Plum Ridge Mountains. When
he looked up, the mountains were steep and inaccessible.

> When His Majesty the emperor had entered the mountains,
> He widened his dragon eyes to look all around him.
> All kinds of birds, enjoying the shade, were strung on branches.
>> The vaguely visible weird-shaped rocks resembled crouching
>> tigers;
> The curved and bent withered trees looked like curled-up
> dragons.
> To his left and his right were only deep gullies and ravines.
>> The wild scenery of these mountains was more than his eyes
>> could take in.
> Not even an accomplished painter could depict it all in full
> detail!

萬歲爺帶著那全副的撒袋，山路崎嶇，木石交雜，不覺
的渾身是汗，呼呼的氣喘，火燒心內，無計可奈。
受不盡熱熬煎，口又澀舌又乾，渾身遍體流香汗。五臟廟裏
失了火，熱焰騰騰燒肺肝，眼前乾的黃花亂。萬歲爺思水解
渴，驚動了玉帝不安。

玉帝正坐，見一股紅氣升天，便叫千里眼、順風耳：
「你去打探一遭，看是何人受難，即速報來。」
千里眼順風耳，看了看是武宗，懨懨害的難掙扎。慌忙回到
靈霄殿，前後說知就裏情。玉帝就把慈心動，叫一聲雲魔天
女，要你去顯顯神通。

玉帝說：「他也是輩人王帝主，須周濟他才是。雲魔
女，差你去下邊送水一遭。」仙女領旨，出了南天門，
急駕祥雲照梅嶺來了。

1   In late imperial times, the Jade Emperor was the highest divinity in the popular celestial
    bureaucracy.

His Majesty the emperor was wearing full gear, and the mountain road was steep and rocky, with jumbled trees and rocks. Before he'd noticed, his body was covered in sweat and he was panting heavily. A fire burned inside his heart, and there was nothing he could do about it.

> The boiling, roasting heat was utterly unbearable:
> His mouth and tongue were dry as dust,
> While fragrant sweat coursed down his whole body.
>   In the temple of his five innards, a fire had started;
> Soaring and climbing, hot flames burned his organs.
> Heat caused yellow flowers to dance before his eyes.
>   His Majesty the emperor longed for water to quench his thirst
> And this disturbed the Jade Emperor, making him feel upset.[1]

Seated on his throne, the Jade Emperor observed a red ether that rose to heaven, so he ordered Thousand Mile Eyes and Sharp Ears, "Go and find out who is in trouble, and report back immediately."

> His spies Thousand Mile Eyes and Sharp Ears
> Saw right away that it was the Martial Ancestor,
> Who had suffered so much that he could barely go on.
>   They returned as fast as they could to the Divine Welkin Hall
> And delivered a full report on the facts from beginning to end,
> Stirring the merciful heart of the Jade Emperor
>   Who called out, "Māra Maiden of the Clouds,[2]
> We need you to go down and show your powers!"[3]

The Jade Emperor said, "Since he is the current King of Humans and Imperial Ruler, we must come to his assistance. Māra Maiden of the Clouds, I send you to the world below to bring him some water." Having received this order, the immortal maiden left heaven through its Southern Gate and, riding a colored cloud, quickly came shining down on Plum Ridge.

2 In Buddhism, Māra is the divine ruler of the sensuous realm. When the Buddha was about to achieve enlightenment, Māra tried to distract him in various ways. His final attempt was to send his three beautiful daughters who tried to seduce the Buddha with their voluptuous dances. Here Māra means little more than "seductively beautiful."
3 This song is printed as prose in Pu Songling 1999.

雲魔女下九天，一條擔壓香肩，打水三娘重出現。金蓮動處腰肢軟，擔上山坡步步難，搖搖眞似楊柳線。武宗爺堪堪渴死，看見水喜動龍顏。

那萬歲正然思水解渴，忽聽那打水女子，心中自思，我正要思水解渴，又不好叫他甚麼。勒馬站在路旁，總不言語。仙女說：「待我問他一聲。行路的君子，你莫非待吃水麼？」萬歲說：「正是緊用著了。」仙女說：「有水。只是無甚麼奉客，下馬來，就這筲裏吃些罷。」萬歲說：「潑婦！這不是戲起我來了麼？」那萬歲跳下馬來，把椰瓢摘下遞與仙女，盛一瓢來，那萬歲一氣飲乾。這皇帝是個酒色之徒，吃了水不肯走，站在路旁，不轉睛的上下前後看起那女子來了。

萬歲擡頭看，心裏暗掂挓：雖是莊家女，卻也似天仙。烏雲蟠龍髻，斜插鳳頭簪；秋波如綠水，兩道柳眉彎；一點櫻桃口，含笑不開言；袖中籠玉腕，

---

4 Li Sanniang 李三娘 was the daughter of a rich farmer. When she saw how snakes appeared from the bodily openings of the sleeping farmhand Liu Zhiyuan 劉智遠, she realized that he was destined to become emperor. When she told her father, he had her marry him. Following her father's death, however, her elder brothers chased Liu Zhiyuan from the farm, even though their sister was three months pregnant. She remained steadfastly loyal to her husband, while her brothers imposed heavy and demeaning chores on her, such as hauling water. Eventually the couple was reunited, and Liu Zhiyuan became the founding emperor of the Posterior Han dynasty (947–950). The story was widely popular in all genres of early vernacular literature from as early as the twelfth century. See Doleželová-Velingerová, Crump, trans., 1971.

The Māra Maiden of the Clouds descended from Ninth Heaven,
A carrying pole weighing heavily on her fragrant shoulders.
Li Sanniang, hauling water, again appeared on earth![4]
    When her golden lotuses moved,[5] her waist was pliant;
As she carried her load up the mountain, each step was hard.
She resembled a willow strand as she moved back and forth.
    The Martial Emperor was about to die of thirst,
So upon seeing her water, his dragon face showed joy.

Just when the emperor was longing for water to quench his thirst, he suddenly heard a girl carrying water, but he thought to himself, "Right now I am longing for water to quench my thirst, but it is also not proper to call out to her." He halted his horse and stood by the side of the road, not saying a word. The immortal maiden said, "Let me ask him! Traveling gentleman, could it be that you would like some water?" The emperor replied, "Yes, I need water urgently." The immortal maiden then said, "I have plenty, but nothing in which to serve it to you. If you come down from your horse, you can drink from this bucket." The emperor replied, "You impudent slut. Are you making a pass at me?" The emperor jumped down from his horse, got out his coconut gourd, and handed it to the immortal maiden. When she had filled it, the emperor gulped it down all at once. Now, this emperor was an alcoholic and a sex fiend, and when he had drunk the water, he refused to leave. Standing by the roadside, he stared at the girl from head to toe, front and behind.

The emperor lifted his head to have a look,
Secretly evaluating her in his heart:
"Even though she is only a country girl,
She somehow resembles an immortal maiden!
Raven-black clouds curling up into a dragon bun
Are held in place by phoenix hairpins.
Her autumn waves resemble green streams,[6]
And her willowy eyebrows are curved.[7]
Her little mouth is a single red cherry dot;
Her smiling lips utter not a word.
Her sleeves embrace her jade-white arms,

5   A woman's small bound feet. These bound feet held great attraction for men. If a woman
    allowed a man to touch her bound feet, it signaled her willingness to have sex with him.
6   "Autumn waves" is a common metaphor for beautiful eyes.
7   Curved eyebrows are commonly compared to willow leaves.

裙底罩金蓮。仙姬更無二，女中奪狀元。萬歲心迷了，
難把意馬拴，下腰推盛水，伸手捏脚尖。仙女只一躲，
罵聲村長官。萬歲陪笑臉：大姐，我是合你玩。

雲魔女不耐煩，罵一聲村長官，欺心你把律條犯。旣讀孔孟
詩書字，不達周公禮半篇，涎皮涎臉把奴看。不看你是過路
的行客，小廝來把你毛揎！

萬歲自思：「他不認的我是皇帝；他若知道，跪前跪後，
央我封他一宮，還不能勾。我把那漏八分的話，說與他
聽聽。」

紅了臉氣昂昂，叫村女休裝腔，誰著你來這井邊撞？分明也
不是個乾淨貨。看上你眼就拿糖，誰沒見你那喬模樣！自估
著容顏俊俏，還不如俺那掃地梅香。

---

8 The Top of the List is the person who passes the triennial metropolitan examinations,
   including the final palace exam, with the highest grade and whose name therefore is
   listed first on the poster of the names of successful candidates.
9 In late imperial times, the content of a formal education was made up of the Four Books
   and the Five Classics. The Four Books included the *Analects* (*Lunyu* 論語), which recorded the sayings of Confucius and his conversations with his students, and *Mencius*
   (*Mengzi* 孟子), which recorded the conversations between Mencius and rulers of his

And her skirt's hem covers her golden lotuses.
Among immortals she is without compare,
Amid women she is Top of the List!"[8]
The emperor's mind was entranced,
Unable to rein in his horse of desire.
Bending down as if to take some water,
He stretched his hands to grasp her feet!
The immortal maiden evaded him
And cursed him as a scoundrel!
But the emperor showed a smile,
"Sister, you and I will have some fun!"

> The Māra Maiden of the Clouds lost her temper
> And cursed him out as a lout and worse,
> "You transgress all laws and regulations unconscionably!
>   Haven't you read Confucius, Mencius, and the classics?
> You don't understand half a chapter of the Duke of Zhou:
> Drooling down your chin as you stare at me![9]
>   If you weren't a traveler passing by on the road,
> I would pull out all of your hair, little boy!"

"She does not understand that I am the emperor," the emperor thought to himself. "But if she knew, she would kneel down in front of me and behind me and implore me to apportion her a palace—and still that would not be enough! Let me say a few words that will disclose two-thirds of the truth!"

> With his face all red and his energy ablaze,
> He shouted, "Village girl, don't put on airs!
> Who told you to meet me by the side of this well?
>   It's obvious that you are not clean goods;
> As soon as you're attracted, you fetch the sugar—
> Who wouldn't see that you're playing hard to get?[10]
>   You may be thinking that you're charming and pretty,
> But you don't even match the maids who sweep my floor!"

---

day. The Duke of Zhou was credited with the authorship of some of the Five Classics, which formulated the rules for the proper relation between the sexes. The aim of this education was moral perfection.

10 "To fetch the sugar" is glossed as "putting on airs," but I suspect that it rather means "taking on a seductive pose."

仙女暗說：「好昏君！他連這話都說出來了。誰不知你是皇帝哩？我自有道理。」

雲魔女惡狠狠，罵一聲賊強人，這等無禮不幫寸！青天白日山溝裏，調戲人家良婦人。少死的村夫，該打一頓！饒了你流水快走，等來人打斷你那嬾筋！

萬歲說：「不知你打手何如，光支架子。」一行說著，不覺的意亂心迷，一陣心慌。

正德爺跑過來，把仙姬摟在懷，慌忙要解羅裙帶。三生有幸今朝遇，看上眼了你拿甚麼歪？人到了著急不怕你怪。雲魔女使個手段，把萬歲閃在那塵埃。

那萬歲撲了一把，只聽的耳邊風響，眼前發花，忽的一跌，倒在塵埃。甦醒半晌，扒將起來，把眼摸了摸，也不見那女子了，也沒有莊村了，左右都是坍塌了的無主孤墳。馬尋野草，那椰瓢摔在路旁。萬歲驚疑：這荒草野坡，多是妖精，假裝人形來戲弄寡人。我若不是皇帝，就被他吃了。那萬歲牽馬逃命，方才待走，忽聽的空中有人大叫：「正德爺休走呀！」

雲魔女起在空，在雲端罵一聲，

---

11 The "three lives" refer to one's past life, present life, and future life.

The immortal maiden thought to herself, "What a deluded ruler! He'll even say such things! Who doesn't know you're the emperor? I have my way of handling this."

> The Māra Maiden of the Clouds was fierce,
> And cursed him out as a violent bandit,
> "This rude language won't help you one bit!
>   Under a clear sky in broad daylight, in a mountain gully
> You try to rape the lawfully wedded wife of a commoner:
> You damn lout, you deserve a sound beating!
>   I'll let you run off like flowing water—
> If anyone shows up, he'll break your bones!"

The emperor said, "I don't know why your henchmen are so slow to arrive. You're all talk." As he spoke, he suddenly lost all self-restraint in a bout of insanity.

> His Majesty Right Virtue ran over to her,
> Clasped the immortal maiden in his arms
> And hastily tried to undo the sash of her skirt.
>   "This day is the happiest day of my three lives![11]
> I am smitten by you—how can you fault me?
> If they catch us in the act, I don't fear your blame!"
>   The Māra Maiden of the Clouds used her tricks
> And threw the emperor down in the dust.

The emperor was smacked in the face and only heard ringing his ears. Stars danced before his eyes, and suddenly stumbling, he fell down in the dust. When he finally came to, he crawled to his feet, and after rubbing his eyes, he noticed that the girl was gone—and so was the entire village! All around him there were only ruined masterless graves. His horse was grazing on the wild grass, and his coconut gourd had been thrown down by the side of the road. The emperor was startled and wondered, "This overgrown wild slope must be a place where monsters and demons take on a human shape to abuse people. If I weren't the emperor, I too would have been devoured!" The emperor grabbed his horse to flee for his life. But the moment he wanted to run off, he suddenly heard someone in the sky calling to him, "Your Majesty Right Virtue, don't run!"

> The Māra Maiden of the Clouds appeared in the sky
> And from her cloud she reviled him at length:

你今錯把心兒用。我是上方雲魔女，領了敕旨下天宮，梅嶺
山下把水送。吃了水胡思亂想，你是個混帳朝廷！

　　萬歲聽說著，忙捻土焚香，望空禱告；小王有甚德能，
敢勞仙女送水？異日回朝傳旨，着天下蓋下廟宇，塑下
金身。那萬歲拜罷，上了龍駒，大路前行。仙女上天交
旨，不在話下。未知後事如何，且聽下回分解。

"You've guessed completely wrong!
  I am the Māra Maiden of the Clouds from up above.
Receiving an order, I descended from the sky
To bring you some water near Mt. Plum Ridge.
  On drinking the water, you got crazy desires:
You are one muddle-headed Son of Heaven!"

When the emperor heard these words, he hastily rolled earth into incense and prayed to heaven, "Who am I, a little king, to bother you, immortal maiden, to bring me water? When I return to court, I will issue an edict ordering all-under-Heaven to build temples in your honor and erect golden statues." When the emperor had finished his bows, he mounted his dragon colt and pursued his journey. The immortal maiden ascended to heaven and reported on her mission, but no more about that.

  If you don't know what happened next, please listen to the following chapter.

第五回 私行主投宿問更 打柴兒殺雞換妻

話說萬歲過了梅嶺山，山下有個周家莊，莊裏曾有個周員外，仗義疏財，極其好善。他的夫人姓劉，生下一個兒子，名喚周元，字宗寶。自從員外故去，家業飄零，終日靠兒子打柴度日。也是天向好人，合該他時來運轉。這日天色將晚，周元不見歸家，劉夫人放心不下，巴著板門凝睛懸望。恰好萬歲來到近前，擡頭見個老婆婆，便說：「夫人，你家有閒房，借宿一晚何如？」那夫人道：「俺不是開坊子的人家，我是幼兒寡婦，自己吃的沒有，怎留下你？」一言未了，天降大雨。皇爺說：「你不留我，如何避的這雨？」婦人道：「不嫌我家裏寒苦，就請進來罷。」

牽著馬進門來，睜龍睛把頭擡，屋牆倒塌門窗壞，坑上少席三寸土，爐內無煙又無柴。萬歲一見沒計奈，乍離了三宮六院，這去處叫人怎捱！

萬歲看罷，無計所奈。夫人把馬拴下，萬歲只得

---

1   A raised brick platform inside the main room of a house in northern China. It is heated from below by the smoke of the cooking stove. As the warmest place of the house in winter, it is the place where the family gathers and where they sleep.

5   The incognito lord seeks lodging and asks about the watches;

The woodcutter son gains a wife by slaughtering a chicken.

Let me tell you, after the emperor had crossed Mt. Plum Ridge, at the foot of the mountain he came to the Zhou Family Village. Once upon a time, a certain magnate named Zhou lived in the village. He distributed his wealth according to righteousness and loved to do good deeds. His wife was surnamed Liu and had given him one son, whose name was Zhou Yuan and whose social name was Zongbao. When the magnate passed away, the family was reduced to poverty, and his widow relied entirely on her son, who cut firewood to make a living. But, in truth, Heaven smiles on good people. Fittingly, his time had come, and his fortune was about to change.

This day, as evening was falling, Lady Liu had not yet seen Zhou Yuan return, so she could not set her worries aside. She stared out the wooden gate, filled with anticipation. Just then the emperor passed by and saw the old woman. He said, "Lady, would your house perhaps have an empty room I could rent for the night?" The lady replied, "We are not a public house. I am a widow with a young son. We don't have anything to eat for ourselves, so how could we offer hospitality to you?" But before she had finished speaking, a heavy rain came down, so the emperor said, "Where can I avoid this heavy rain if you don't take me in?" So the lady said, "If you don't think our place too cold and shabby, please come inside."

> Leading his horse, he entered the gate.
> Opening his dragon eyes wide, he looked around:
> The walls had collapsed, the windows were broken.
> On the *kang*[1] no mat covered the three inches of earth;
> There was no fire in the burner, firewood was lacking.
> When the emperor saw this, he was at a loss!
> "I've just left my three palaces and six courtyards,
> How can a man spend the night in such a place?"

The emperor saw the situation, but there was nothing he could do. The lady hitched up his horse, so the emperor could only sit down on

在那土坑上就坐。不一時，劉氏提了一壺茶來，說道：
「長官，你吃了一杯茶，暫且解乏。等俺那兒來，買些
甚麼來你吃。」皇爺說：「你那兒那裏去了？」劉氏說：
「山上打柴去了。」這也是君臣該會的日子，道猶未了，
這周元擔著擔子，就闖進門來。

放下擔往裏瞧，見個人甚蹊蹺，頭上帶著個簷氈帽。撒腳不
敢回頭看，口中只說不好了，要軍錢的漢子又到了。扯腿走
像個烏鴉閃蛋，回頭看似鯉魚打漂。

這周元喘息未定，正撞著母親劉氏道：「周元，你來了
麼？前頭有客哩。」周元道：「諕殺我！我只當是要軍
錢的。是那裏的客？」劉氏道：「是過路的長官，被雨
截在咱家裏。你去會他一會。」周元來到前路，說道：
「長官，作揖了。」萬歲說：「免禮罷。」周元說：「長官，
天黑了，你走不的了。宿是小事，只是我可給你甚麼吃
呢？俺逐日打一擔柴來，糶一升米，俺母子共用。夜來
打的那擔柴誤了趕集，還沒有後响飯哩。」皇爺說：「隨
便罷了。」周元說：「還有一擔柴錢哩，我去買幾個饞
饞來你吃罷。」皇爺說：「正好。」周元聽說，回家拿錢，
到了街上，買了幾個饞饞，見了萬歲說道：「長官，有
了饞饞還沒有菜，我有一個媳婦，殺給你吃了罷。」萬
歲說：「諕我，怎麼忍的殺人吃？」周元說：「是媳婦，
可還沒變過來哩。」皇爺說：「怎麼沒變過來？」周元說：
「是我餵的一個母雞，下了蛋來抱一窩小雞，出息著掙
個私囊，尋個媳婦。今日殺給你吃了，可不是殺了媳婦
你吃了麼？」皇爺說：「你殺了給我吃了，我還你個

---

2   Some other texts that adapt this story explain that Zhou Yuan had hoped to sell the hen and the pullets she produced, and then buy a piglet. When the piglet grew into a pig, he would sell that animal, hoping that by then he would have enough money to acquire a wife.

the earthen *kang*. After a while Lady Liu brought him a jug of tea, saying, "Please, sir, have a cup of tea to help you recover from your tiring trip. When my son arrives, we will buy something for you to eat." The emperor asked, "Where is your son?" She replied, "He is on the mountain cutting firewood." This was the day that lord and minister were destined to meet: before she had finished speaking, Zhou Yuan barged through the gate, carrying his load of firewood.

> When he put down his load and peeked inside,
> He saw a man who looked quite strange:
> On his head he was wearing a brimmed felt hat.
>> He ran off and didn't dare look back,
> As he muttered to himself, "This doesn't bode well,
> That guy collecting military taxes has come again!"
>> He ran with big strides like a crow stealing an egg;
> Looking back, he resembled a jumping carp.

Still panting, Zhou Yuan bumped into his mother. Lady Liu said, "Zhou Yuan, is that you? We have a guest in the front room." Zhou Yuan replied, "I was scared witless. I thought he had come to collect military taxes. Where is he from?" Lady Liu said, "He passed by our house while traveling and was stopped by the rain. Go and keep him company for a while." Zhou Yuan came to the front and said, "Sir, my respects!" The emperor replied, "No need for ceremony!" Zhou Yuan said, "It's pitch dark now, you can't travel on. It's fine if you stay for the night, but what can we give you to eat? Each day I go and cut one load of firewood that I sell for one cup of rice. That feeds my mother and me. I was too late to make the market last night with my load of firewood, so we don't even have an evening meal." The emperor replied, "Whatever suits you." Zhou Yuan said, "I still have one load's worth of money, so let me go and buy you some buns." The emperor said, "Great!" Hearing this, Zhou Yuan went back into the house, got the money, and went out to buy some buns.

Greeting the emperor he said, "I have some buns, but still no side dishes. But I have a wife, and I will kill her for you." "Nonsense!" the emperor replied, "How could I let you kill a human being for food?" Zhou Yuan said, "It's my wife, but she hasn't yet changed into that shape." When the emperor asked, "What do you mean, 'She hasn't yet changed into that shape'?" Zhou Yuan replied, "I'm talking about the hen we keep. She has laid eggs and is breeding out some chicks. From the money to be made from them I had hoped to scrape together the funds to find me a wife.[2] If I kill her to feed you today, then I'd be killing my wife, wouldn't I?" The emperor said, "If you kill her for me, I can provide you with

媳婦不難。」那周元疾忙來到後房，從頭至尾說了一遍。劉氏把雞做了，周元送至前頭。萬歲用飯已畢，就說：「我乏了，收拾我睡覺罷。」坑上沒有蘆席，周元拿了個桿草來鋪上，那萬歲渾衣歆倒。不覺的夜靜更深，恰才合眼，忽聽的那梆鈴一派響亮，萬歲醒來，頓足捶胸。恐君不信，後有小詞爲証：

一更裏月朦朧，合煞眼睡正濃，梆鈴驚醒了南柯夢。沒有宮娥來打扇，小屋無風熱似籠，扇兒搖著似千斤重。也是我爲君的不正，原不該私出了北京。

二更裏月兒高，合煞眼睡不著，虼蚤咬的心焦燥。乍離龍牀鴛鴦枕，土坑上無蓆鋪桿草，半頭甎又墊上簷氈帽。這是我爲君的不正，尋思起自己錯了。

三更裏月正圓，在外人好孤單，蟲聲叫的人心亂。剛才夢在龍牀上，佳人倒鳳又顛鸞，醒來却在荒村店。也是我爲君的不正，原不該私出了順天。

四更裏月兒歪，聽簷前鐵馬篩，

3   Having sex.

another wife." Zhou Yuan hurried to the backroom and told his mother the whole story from beginning to end. When Lady Liu had prepared the chicken, Zhou Yuan brought it to the front room.

When the emperor had finished his meal, he said, "I'm tired. Please clean up so I can go to sleep." There was no reed mat to cover the *kang*, so Zhou Yuan got some straw to cover it, and the emperor lay down fully dressed. It was the dead of night before he knew it, but he had barely closed his eyes when he suddenly heard clappers and bells sounding loudly. The emperor woke up, stamped his feet, and beat his breast. You may not believe me, but later there were some short lyrics that offer a description.

> In the first watch of the night, the moon was vaguely visible.
> He had firmly closed his eyes and had sunk into a deep sleep,
> When rattles and bells woke him up from his dream with a start.
>   There were no palace maids to come and wave their fans—
> The little room, without fresh air, was as hot as a steamer.
> When he waved a fan, it seemed to weigh a thousand pounds.
>   "This is all because of my own faults as a lord:
> I should never have left Beijing in secret!"

> In the second watch of the night, the little moon had risen high.
> He firmly closed his eyes, but couldn't catch any sleep,
> Because to his great vexation he was bitten by fleas.
>   He had left his dragon couch and mandarin-duck cushion
> For this earthen *kang* lacking a mat and covered with straw.
> Half a brick propped up his brimmed hat as his headrest.
>   "This is all because of my own faults as a lord:
> I should never have left Beijing in secret!"

> In the third watch of the night, the moon was fully round.
> As a man traveling far from home, he felt alone and lonely,
> And the chirping cicadas plunged his heart into confusion.
>   Just as he was dreaming how on his dragon couch
> He was overturning the phoenix with one of his beauties,[3]
> He woke up to find himself in an inn in a desolate village.
>   "This is all because of my own faults as a lord:
> I should never have left Beijing in secret!"

> In the fourth watch of the night, the moon was sinking.
> As he listened to the tinkling chimes below the eaves

聲聲聒的魂不在。白日裏奔波還好受，黑夜淒涼好難捱，前生少下孤單債。這是我爲君的不正，失主意走出京來。

五更裏雞報曉，星兒稀天明了。周元起來把爺叫：我今要上長街去，不得送你休計較，老客請起登古道。想是你軍情緊急，你的事休要誤了。

周元自思：「今日給那長官甚麼吃？不如我早著些叫他走了，我好上山打柴。」周元說：「長官，你起來罷。天明了，你還不走，等甚麼哩？誤了我早去打柴。」那萬歲起的身來，取出一錠銀子來，說道：「周元，你拿去當飯錢罷。」周元道：「長官差了。俺不是做買賣的人家，不要銀子。」皇爺說：「我自來不好乾吃人的東西，你既不要，我有道理。你這裏隔著甚麼城近？」周元說：「沒有城。」皇爺說：「今夜怎麼梆鈴幾乎聒殺人？」周元說：「你不知道，那是後莊裏曹老爺家打更。」皇爺說：「那個曹老爺？」周元說：「就是那做三邊總督的。」皇爺說：「哦！是曹重麼？」周元說：「你風麼！曹老爺知道，拿了你去，豁口子加牆板。」皇爺說：「怎麼講？」周元說：「可就打殺了！」

曹老爺還體情，那別爺更不通，縣官拿著當奴才用。耳軟光聽下人的話，

4　It was considered highly disrespectful to pronounce someone's personal name. Gentlemen had a social name, by which they expected to be addressed by their equals, while their underlings had to address them by their title or an appropriate status term.
5　In the popular legend of Meng Jiangnü 孟姜女, Meng's husband is a corvée worker employed in the construction of the Great Wall. After he has been worked to death, his corpse is buried in the body of the wall.
6　A person is said to have "soft ears" if he is easily persuaded.

Their incessant sounds made such a clamor that he lost his mind.
  "Hurrying on in broad daylight is still tolerable,
But the loneliness of darkest night is truly unbearable.
I must still owe a debt of solitude from a former life!
  This is all because of my own faults as a lord:
I should never have left Beijing in secret!"

In the fifth watch of the night, roosters announced dawn.
As the stars grew scarce, the sky became bright,
And Zhou Yuan got up and called to the emperor,
  "I have to leave for the market right now,
So I hope you don't mind that I can't show you out.
Dear guest, please get up and continue your trip.
  I take it that the military situation is very urgent,
So make sure you don't fail in your mission."

Zhou Yuan thought to himself, "What food do I have now to give to our guest? The best thing is to urge him to leave as early as possible, so I also can go into the mountains to cut firewood." So Zhou Yuan said, "Sir, please get up! The day has begun, and you haven't moved. What are you waiting for? You're keeping me from setting out early to cut firewood." When the emperor got up, he took out an ingot of silver and said, "Zhou Yuan, please take this as payment for a meal." Zhou Yuan replied, "You are mistaken, sir. This isn't our trade, and we don't need your silver." But the emperor said, "Of course, I cannot eat people's food for free! If you don't want it, I have another solution. What city is nearby?" Zhou Yuan replied, "There is no city nearby." The emperor asked, "Then why did rattles and bells make such a ruckus last night?" Zhou Yuan replied, "You would not know, but that is the mansion of His Excellency Cao in the back village sounding the watches." The emperor asked, "Which Excellency Cao?" Zhou Yuan replied, "He is the commissioner-in-chief for the three border regions!" The emperor then asked, "You mean Cao Zhong?" Zhou Yuan reacted, "Are you mad? If His Excellency Cao knows you've spoken his name,[4] he will have you arrested and use you to fill a breach in the wall!"[5] "What do you mean by that?" the emperor asked. Zhou Yuan replied, "He will beat you to death!

  His Excellency Cao is still a decent sort,
But the other bosses are even less reasonable.
If the magistrate arrests you, he treats you like a slave.
  His soft ears[6] only listen to the talk of his underlings,

眞是一個糊突蟲。管家還比主人勝，一個鷹頭鱉耳，酷像是做了朝廷。

皇爺說：「這廝恁麼利害！我且問你：他家有多少人口？」周元說：「曹老爺，曹奶奶，曹小姑。」皇爺說：「那曹小姑不知多大年紀？出了閣不曾？」周元說：「還沒哩。」皇爺說：「我把曹小姑來給你做個媳婦，何如？」周元說：「不敢，不敢！曹老爺利害，昨日上山打了一擔柴來，他說是割了他的山場了，把我拿去弔了一夜，虧了俺娘跪前跪後的，才饒了我，誰敢惹他！」皇爺說：「有我不妨，那是我家支使的小廝。」周元說：「我不信，我不信，他是一個大官，倒給你這長官支使？」皇爺說：「我哄你呀，我合他是個朋友。我寫個帖子給你，拿去給他，量他幾石糧食來給你娘們吃，好呀不好？」周元道：「只怕你那帖子不準呀。」皇爺說：「你拿筆硯來使使。」周元聽說，把筆硯墨紙拿來。萬歲自思：我寫書給他甚麼是顯驗？萬歲脫了那鞝鞋，把那裏腳裂下一幅來。周元看見，吃了一驚。周元說：「長官，你這裏腳上不是蛇麼？」萬歲說：「這是故事。」把書來寫的停當，遂說道：「我若去了，你可送給曹重，他自然看顧你。」周元說：「他發作了著呢？」皇爺說：「我教你兩句話給你，到他門上，你可吆喝著說。你就說：我有一封信，曉諭曹重知：北京一長官，宿在我家裏，吃了一頓飯，用了一隻雞。你家曹金定，配與我爲妻。你若不依允，就是造化低；

---

7   The dragon nature of a true emperor often manifests itself in the shape of a snake.

He truly is one muddle-headed critter!
The major-domo is even worse than his master:
    With his eagle head and turtle ears,
He looks just like the emperor!"

The emperor said, "So this fellow is terrible! Let me ask you, how many people are there in his family?" Zhou Yuan replied, "There's His Excellency Cao, Lady Cao, and Miss Cao." The emperor then asked, "How old is the young lady? Is she already engaged?" When Zhou Yuan replied that she wasn't, the emperor said, "What would you think if I made Miss Cao your wife?" But Zhou Yuan said, "I wouldn't dare! His Excellency Cao is terrible. A few days ago, I cut a load of firewood in the mountains, and he said that I had invaded his section of the mountains and had me strung up for a whole night. He only pardoned me after my mother knelt down in front of him and behind him. I wouldn't dare raise his ire!" The emperor said, "I can make it happen. He's only some nobody in my employ." But Zhou Yuan replied, "I don't believe you! He's a high official, so how could he be in your employ?"

The emperor said, "I'm just joking. He and I are friends. I will write a note, and if you take it to him, I reckon he will give you some sacks of grain to provide for your mother and you. How about that?" Zhou Yuan replied, "I'm afraid only that your note won't work." The emperor said, "Bring me a brush and an inkstone." When Zhou Yuan heard this, he brought him a brush, an inkstone, ink, and paper. The emperor thought to himself, "What will be clear evidence when I write a letter to him?" The emperor took off a boot and tore a piece of his foot-swaddling cloth. When Zhou Yuan saw this, he was quite frightened and asked, "Isn't that a snake on that cloth?"[7] The emperor replied, "It's only a decoration." Zhou Yuan said, "And what will I do when he flies into a rage?" The emperor said, "I will teach you a few words that you must declaim loudly when you arrive at his gate. You must say:

I have come to deliver a letter
And hereby inform Cao Zhong
That a high official from Beijing
Stayed at my house for the night.
He there had one meal of rice
And also enjoyed a chicken.
Your daughter Cao Jinding
Is to be given to me as a wife.
If you do not obey his order,
Your fortune will steeply decline,

你若從下了，賞你一領大大的面皮。」
萬歲爺把話教，小周元諕掙了，三魂七魄出了竅。面上土色
瞪著眼，手腳猖狂身子搖，聲聲只把長官叫，是俺達復生跳
起，活活的把我送了！

周元說：「不好不好！你不送了我了麼？」皇爺說：「有
我哩。」周元說：「怕的有你沒有我了！」皇爺說：「不
妨，我有一點薄體面。」周元把書收了，皇爺就要起身。
萬歲爺要登程，子母們來送行，周元把馬牢牽定。囑咐那周
元休當戲，千金難買書一封，小小體面頗堪用。早早的將書
投上，子母們無限崢嶸。

萬歲催馬去了，周元母子商議。劉氏道：「我兒你去，
他若是朋友，他不打你，替他問安。」那周元果然依著
那長官的話，拿著書戰戰兢兢的來到後莊，站在大門首
便說：「門上的替我傳傳，有老爺的個朋友，留得一封
書在此，還有許多面話要說的。」那看門的聽的說是
老爺的朋友，不敢怠慢，即忙稟於曹重。曹重說：「蹺
蹊！今夜夢見聖旨到來，這事有些古怪，快把屏門開
了。」那周元見開了屏門，慌忙進去，見了曹重，磕了
一個扁頭。那萬歲教他的話，也不敢說，只把書來遞與
曹重，心裏戰兢的，

8   This line is ironic. Zhou Yuan states that unlike certain types of shamans, he is unable to go down to the underworld in a trance and come back to life.

9   Under normal circumstances, the family of the groom would be expected to pay a hefty dowry.

10   The "screen gate" is the gate between the front courtyard and the back courtyard in an official's home that is only opened for major events.

But if you do as I tell you,
Your status will be greatly increased!"

> When the emperor had taught him these words,
> Little Zhou Yuan was extremely frightened;
> The three souls and seven spirits left his body!
>   His face had a ghastly color, his eyes bulged out,
> His arms and legs and whole body were shaking.
> Again and again he called out to his guest,
>   "Sure I'm able to come back to life and jump about![8]
> You are sending me off, healthy and hale, to my death!"

Zhou Yuan shouted, "No way! You're sending me off to my death!" The emperor said: "Leave it to me." But Zhou Yuan said, "I'm just afraid that you'll be left and I'll be gone!" The emperor repeated, "There's no harm; I have a certain status." When Zhou Yuan took the letter, the emperor was ready to set out.

> The emperor was ready to pursue his journey,
> And mother and son saw him off as he left,
> With Zhou Yuan firmly leading his horse.
>   He urged Zhou Yuan repeatedly not to treat this as a joke:
> "To get a nice girl with only a letter is a rare chance![9]
> My status may be minimal, but it still has its use.
>   Deliver that letter as quickly as possible,
> And mother and son will see a spectacular rise!"

When the emperor had urged on his horse and left, Zhou Yuan and his mother deliberated. Lady Liu said, "My son, you must go. If they are friends, he will not give you a beating, but ask how his friend is doing." So Zhou Yuan did as the guest had told him. His whole body shaking, he took the letter to the back village, and when he stood in front of the imposing gate, he said, "Dear doorman, please report on my behalf that a friend of His Excellency left a letter with me, and that there is a lot I have tell him in person." When that doorman heard that it concerned a friend of His Excellency, he didn't dare tarry, but in all haste reported it to Cao Zhong, who said, "How strange! Last night I dreamed that an imperial edict arrived, so there is something weird about this. Open the screen gate!"[10] When the screen gate was opened, Zhou Yuan hurried inside, greeted Cao Zhong, and kowtowed until his head was pounded flat. He didn't dare pronounce the words the emperor had taught him, but only handed the letter to Cao Zhong—his heart was racing, fearing

恐怕發作起來，那眼不住的瞰那路徑，若有動靜，好跑他娘的。只見那曹重急忙把書接下，仔細觀看。有詩半篇：「聞的你家女兒好，提他嫁與周宗寶；若問月老是何人，北京皇帝朝廷老。」曹重看罷，將書懸起，倒身下拜。

曹老爺拜聖言，喜壞了小周元，休說長官無體面，一塊裹脚嘎要緊，見了磕頭禮拜參，跪在地下如搗蒜。曹老爺官職不小，倒怕這一個軍漢。

曹重拜罷道：「你給誰下的書？」周元道：「是北京一個長官。」曹重道：「你認的他麼？」周元說：「不認的。」曹重說：「那是北京皇帝。」周元說：「錯了，早知他是個皇帝，我留他在俺家裏，一輩子不怕人。」曹重說；「他封了你官了。我家曹金定與你爲妻。」周元說：「不敢，不敢！給我二斗糧食吃著打柴罷。」曹重說：「你以後不用打柴了。」吩咐左右：「給他把衣裳換了罷。」

還是那舊周元，換新衣另一看，村頭窮腦登時變。乍穿著尺頭不大緊，

---

11 The Man in the Moon creates couples by tying men and women together with a red string.
12 This quatrain is called "half a poem" in comparison with the eight lines of a regulated poem.

that Cao Zhong would explode in a rage, and his eyes darted about, looking for an escape if something went wrong. He only saw how Cao Zhong
hastily took the letter and carefully perused it. It contained half a poem:

I've learned that your family has a fine daughter
And propose that she be married to Zhou Zongyu.
If you wonder who this Man in the Moon[11] might be,
I am the emperor in Beijing, His Imperial Majesty![12]

When Cao Zhong had finished reading the letter, he hung the letter on the
wall and fell on his knees to bow before it.[13]

> His Excellency Cao bowed before the Sage Words,
> While little Zhou Yuan was overcome by joy:
> "You couldn't say that this guest had no status at all!
>   How could one piece of a foot wrapping be so important?
> As soon as he saw it, he kowtowed and bowed by the rules,
> Kneeling down on the floor, kowtowing as if beating garlic to a
>   pulp.[14]
>   His Excellency Cao isn't a minor official,
> But he's still quite afraid of that common soldier!"

When Cao Zhong had finished his bows, he asked, "Who left this letter
with you?" Zhou Yuan replied, "A guest from Beijing." Cao Zhong asked,
"Did you recognize him?" When Zhou Yuan replied that he hadn't, Cao
Zhong said, "That was the emperor from Beijing!" But Zhou Yuan replied,
"No! If I had known that he was the emperor, would I have been so brave
as to have him at my place?" Cao Zhong then said, "He has appointed
you to office, and our Cao Jinding will be your wife." Zhou Yuan replied,
"I wouldn't dare! Just give me two pecks of grain to live on while I cut
firewood." But Cao Zhong replied, "There shall be no need for you to cut
firewood anymore!" And he ordered his underlings to give him a new set
of clothes.

> It was still the old Zhou Yuan,
> But in a new outfit he looked different:
> That poverty-stricken rustic oaf was suddenly changed.
>   When he still wore rags, he was fine,

---

13 That is, he treats the poem as an authentic imperial edict.
14 A common image for kowtowing often and rapidly.

身下悶癢似蟲鑽，霎時拿把的通身汗。新學著作揖唱喏，好一似猢猻鑽圈。

　　周元前廳坐下，那曹重來到後邊，合馬夫人商議。夫人道：「我這麼一個女兒，就給了周元！」曹重說：「婦人家你曉的甚麼！違背聖旨，全家該斬！」那夫人聽說，即速上了繡樓，將小姐打扮。曹重分付擡下香案。

小周元起拜著，看小姐賽嫦娥，頭暈似在船中坐。他是天上的神仙女，湯他一湯就造化多，頭皮薄敢說將他摸？餓老鴟時來運轉，一把兒抓住天鵝。

　　二人拜完天地回房，曹重差了兩個家人，去給劉氏道喜。却說劉氏在家，見他兒子去了，多時不回來，心中甚是掛念，說道：「想是俺那冤家不會說話，得罪著那曹老爺家。沒影的下了一位客，宿了一宿，吃了一頓飯，見沒問他要錢，他就沒的揪作揪作，就寫了個帖子，給那曹老爺，著他給俺兩石糧食吃。我就短了一句話，沒囑咐他到那裏略問他要要，他若不給，就流水回來罷；俺那冤家指著個帖子，合聖旨呀是的，仔管問他要，想是要的發作了，打他哩！我出去看看的。」劉氏正走到大門邊，手扶著那門，叫了一聲小周元，「這麼晚還不來，必定是吃了虧了！

15　Zhou Yuan has to learn how to behave in an upper-class manner. In a formal greeting, one raises the folded hands before one's breast and makes a light bow. The expression translated as "saying yes" is *changnuo* 唱喏, the formal way of replying to superior.

16　An "embroidery room" is the common term for the private room of a grown-up girl or wife.

But now he was itching all over, as if bitten by lice;
Suddenly he felt so constricted that he was sweating.
    When first learning to raise his hands and shout yes,[15]
He resembled a monkey jumping through a hoop.

While Zhou Yuan was seated in the front hall, Cao Zhong went inside to deliberate with his wife, Lady Ma, who cried, "You have given this fine child of mine to Zhou Yuan!" But Cao Zhong said, "Woman, you don't understand a thing! If we disobey the imperial edict, our whole family will be beheaded!" When his wife heard those words, she immediately went up to the embroidery room and dressed her daughter for marriage.[16] Cao Zhong gave orders to set out the incense table.

When little Zhou Yuan rose upon bowing,
He saw that the young lady rivaled Chang'e.
His head swirled as if he were sitting in a boat.
    She was an immortal maiden from highest heaven,
To caress her only once would be the peak of good fortune;
The skin of her face was so thin he would never dare touch it!
    The hungry old owl had a stroke of good fortune:
Its claws were now full of a heavenly swan.[17]

After the two had bowed to Heaven and Earth, they retired to the bridal room. Cao Zhong dispatched two servants to tell Lady Liu the happy news.
    But let me first tell you that Lady Liu was at home and filled with worry when she saw that her son had not come back after such a long time. She said, "My darling son must have not expressed himself well and offended His Excellency Cao. Out of the blue we had a guest, and he slept here for a night and had a meal. We didn't ask for money, and he didn't have much of anything, but he wrote a note to His Excellency Cao, telling him to give us two stone-weights of grain.[18] But I forgot to instruct my son not to insist on too much when asking, and to come back like running water if he would not give anything. My darling son considered that little note an imperial edict and must have demanded the grain, so His Excellency Cao must have exploded in rage and given him a beating! Let me go have a look." Right then Lady Liu walked to the main gate, and with her hand on it, she called, "Little Zhou Yuan, if you still haven't come back, you must have met with misfortune!

17 In a common phrase, a hungry owl is said to rejoice over a rotting rat.
18 A stone (*dan* 石) is equivalent to 120 pounds.

甕裏米沒一升，打一頓來家中，吃著甚麼去養疼？心下躊躕
還未了，來了二人跑的凶，倒把婆兒諕了一個掙。多管是打
了兒子，拿我去還要找零。

只見二人跑將進來，看見劉氏雙膝跪下。劉氏慌忙拉起
說：「大哥們折罪殺我了！」那人道：「奶奶喜事臨門！
你家里宿的是皇帝，封了你那兒一個官，合俺家小姑娘
配爲夫婦了。叫俺來報喜，還嘱咐不要走漏了消息。」
劉氏聽說，又驚又喜，又是著忙。二人去了。劉氏回
家，滿斗焚香，拜謝天地。

謝天地滿斗香，又是喜又是慌，渾身也不知是怎麼樣。我兒
模樣也不醜，只是手腳太村幫，咱合小姐配不上。叫姑娘還
怕不理，做個夢敢著他叫娘。

劉氏拜謝天地已畢，曹老爺差著小廝丫頭，把劉夫人擡
進府來，母子們享受榮華，不在話下。再說萬歲登程，
未知後事如何，且聽下回分解。

19 In a sedan chair, as befitting her new status.

"We don't have a cup of rice in the vat,
So whenever you come home,
What can you eat to recover from your pain?"
    While she was in doubt, unable to calm herself,
Two men came charging toward her,
Scaring the old woman out of her wits.
    "This must mean they have given him a beating,
And are arresting me too to get more cash."

But those two men, on seeing Lady Liu, knelt down on both knees. Lady Liu hastily pulled them up and said, "Dear brothers, you do me too much honor!" But the men said, "Your Ladyship, good fortune visits your house! The guest who stayed at your place was the emperor. He has appointed your son to an office, and your son has married our young lady as his wife. We have been told to tell you the happy news, and to instruct you not to say a word about this." When Lady Liu heard this, she was both scared and happy, and also felt a great urgency. After the two men left, Lady Liu went inside and burned a peck of incense to express her thanks to Heaven and Earth.

She thanked Heaven and Earth with a peck of incense.
On the one hand she was happy, on the other flustered,
And her whole body felt out of sorts.
    "My son really isn't that ugly,
But his hands and feet are much too coarse.
We cannot be a match for the young lady!
    I'm afraid it isn't suitable for me to call her 'daughter';
Even in dreams, would I dare let her call me 'mother'?"

After Lady Liu had expressed her gratitude to Heaven and Earth, His Excellency Cao sent some boys and maids to carry her[19] to his mansion, where mother and son enjoyed riches and glory. But no more about that. Let me tell you again how the emperor pursued his journey.

If you don't know what happened next, please listen to the following chapter.

第六回 十字街閑游子弟 孤老院戲賺君王

話說萬歲離了周元，走了多時，來到一道山嶺，見了許多的人，拿著枚鑹修路。那萬歲不知是做甚麼的，遂問道：「你這些人修路爲何？」衆人說：「長官，你不知道麼？我說與你聽罷。」

修路的官票是老江。北京城裏浪蕩皇，聽說他要出來撞。三宮六院嬌娥女，陪著自在何等強。這個朝廷精混帳，只管他閒游閒，那知道百姓遭殃！」

萬歲說：「你好大膽，敢罵皇帝！」衆人道：「隔著這麼些路，他那裏有驢耳朵怎麼樣長，他伸過來聽聽，就知道是俺罵他。」萬歲自思：好沒要緊，問了他問，就惹的他罵了這麼些。我待加罪與他，他乃是鄉民無知。自古道：背地裏皇帝也得罵。這也是我自惹其禍，好沒要緊。便笑著問道：「那是往大同去的路徑？」衆人說：「山下頭有一座石橋，橋西頭有兩條路，南股正沖著大同府的去路，到東門還有三十五里。」萬歲聽說，提轡就走。

萬歲爺沒打撒，待問他做甚麼，好好惹了一場罵。

1   A *li* measures roughly one-third of a mile.

6 Playboys are enjoying themselves at the crossroads;
The emperor is tricked into going to the almshouse.

Let me tell you, the emperor, having taken his leave from Zhou Yuan and having traveled for quite some time, arrived at a mountain range, where he saw quite a lot of people with shovels and pickaxes repairing the road. The emperor didn't understand what they were doing, so he asked them, "Why are you all repairing this road?" The workers replied, "Don't you know, sir? Let us tell you!

> "The order to repair the road came from old Jiang:
> That ne'er-do-well emperor from Beijing
> Wants to travel, we have been told, in this direction.
>   Three palaces and six courtyards full of pretty girls—
> What a pleasure it must be to spend time with them!
> This emperor must be muddle-headed in the extreme:
>   He only cares about rambling and roaming for pleasure,
> With no idea how the common people suffer disaster!"

The emperor said, "You are quite brave to revile the emperor like that!" But the workers replied, "There's a long road in between us. Can he have donkey ears so long that he'd hear us cursing him out if he stretched them?" The emperor thought, "This is all nonsense! I ask them a question and they revile me like this. But even if I want to punish them, they are just unknowing villagers. Since ancient times it has been said, 'Behind his back you can curse even the emperor.' This is a misfortune I've called down on myself. How stupid!"

Thereupon he asked them with a smile, "What is the shortest road to Datong?" They told him, "At the foot of this mountain you will come to a stone bridge. To the west are two roads. The southern one goes straight to Datong. You still have thirty-five *li* to the east gate."[1] Hearing this, the emperor took the reins and pursued his journey.

> His Excellency the emperor looked downcast:
> What had he done by asking them that question?
> He only had provoked them to soundly curse him!

下的山來往西走，看見大同城裏塔，十里聽的人說話。勒住馬撾頭遠望，躊躕道問問不差。

　　那萬歲正走，看見了城池，勒住馬問那行路的人：「這是大同府麼？」衆人道：「正是了。」萬歲聽說，打馬進城來了。

行走著來到了，城牆下好深壕，紅蓮綠水重楊罩。心忙不看城外景，闖進城來四下瞧，三街六市人煙鬧。果然是男清女秀，一個個異樣風標。

　　萬歲進的城來，見男清女秀，人煙湊集，果然好景。按下萬歲不表，却說這大同府有兩家鄉宦，生下兩個兒子，喚做張王二舍。先人故後，撇下無限產業，不安分讀書，光好結交光棍，狐群狗黨，專好吃酒賭博。一日在酒樓上飲酒中間，王舍說：「張大哥，咱在這酒樓上吃酒，好不悶的慌！依著我說，咱上那十字街前，打掃乾淨，擺下桌酒，或扶骨牌，或打雙陸，引的好耍的子弟上了咱的當，哄他幾兩銀子，咱好花費花費，好不好？」張舍說：「妙妙妙！」

二子弟下樓來，前來到十字街，排下一桌酒合菜。二人拍手哈哈笑，

Having descended the mountain, he traveled west
And saw the pagodas inside the walls of Datong.
From ten *li* he heard the hubbub of its inhabitants.
    Halting his horse, he took a look,
But still in doubt he asked around to make sure.

As the emperor was traveling, he saw the wall and its moat, so he halted his horse and asked the pedestrians on the road, "Is this Datong Prefecture?" They all replied, "Indeed it is." Hearing this, the emperor urged his horse on and entered the city.

Pursuing his journey, he arrived
At that very deep moat below the city wall,
A green stream with red lotuses shaded by weeping willows.
    In his haste he didn't watch the scenery outside the walls,
But rushed into the city to look around
At the busy crowds on the three streets and six markets.
    Indeed, the men were handsome, the women charming;
Each and every one displayed an exceptional beauty.

When the emperor had entered the city, he saw that the men were handsome and the women charming, and that they congregated in crowds. It was indeed a grand sight! But let's forget for the moment about the emperor and mention that in Datong there were two families of local officials that both had one son. These two men were known as young master Zhang and young master Wang. When their parents passed away, they left behind unlimited wealth, but these young men did not devote themselves to study as their status required. Rather, they teamed up with bare sticks, foxlike friends, and doglike companions, and all they liked to do was drink and gamble. One day when they were drinking in the upper room of a wine shop, young master Wang said, "Brother Zhang, isn't it way too boring to sit here in this room drinking? I think we should clean up a spot in front of the crossroads, set out some wine and food, and try to entice those fun-loving playboys to fall into our trap with dice or backgammon, and relieve them of their silver so we can spend it. What do you think?" Young master Zhang replied, "Great! Let's do it!"

The two playboys descended the stairs
And walked over to the crossroads,
Where they set down a table with wine and food.
    The two clapped their hands, laughing loudly,

咱今吃個大開懷，巡盃換蓋流星快。他兩個輕狂賣弄，行酒令又把枚猜。

按下二人飲酒，話說那萬歲來到十字街前，看見張王二舍在那裏打雙陸，遂下馬來站在旁裏觀看。本府城隍恐怕萬歲有失，叫大小鬼使，快去十字街前，保護聖駕。不一時，那五花琉璃鬼、青頭赤髮鬼、沒要緊的賭仗鬼、門後頭的壁牆鬼、不幹好事的促狹鬼，衆小鬼們直到街前。那張舍拿起骰子來要一個六，却擲了一個么。那萬歲看饞了，不覺的說出來了個六。大小鬼聽的萬歲叫六，就翻過來了。張舍遂贏了十兩銀子。張舍道：「這長官帽破衣殘，到是極好的口才。分明是個么，說六就過來了。長官休走，等著我給你二錢，你買頓飯吃。」那萬歲是一朝人王帝主，眼中可那裏有這二錢銀子，萬歲不答。王舍道：「你這個花子，放著路不走，來這裏溜和溜和的！你只等溜頓皮捶，你才息了心！」萬歲道：「你待打誰？只怕石頭鑽的鼓子不中打，糴的二升秕芝蔴打了沒油水。」那張舍滿臉陪笑，說道：「這個兄弟不知道甚麼，得罪著你，萬望長官容恕，我管陪情。」萬歲被張舍撫恤了幾句，也就漸漸的消了怒。王舍道：「張大哥，只是便宜了那花子，若是小廝們湊集挑挑嘴，就把他毛來撏一個淨！」張舍道：「休惹禍。」王舍道：「他除非是個皇帝。」張舍拉著王舍上酒樓去了。

萬歲爺發玉言，那朋友請回還，

2　When talking about silver, a *qian* 錢 is one tenth of an ounce.

"Today we will drink to our hearts' content,
Passing the beakers and cups faster than shooting stars!"
  The two of them showed off their mad bravado,
Engaging in drinking games and finger guessing.

Let's forget about those two guys drinking so that I can tell you how the emperor arrived at the crossroads. When he saw the young masters Zhang and Wang engaged in a game of backgammon, he dismounted and watched from one side. The city god of this prefecture was afraid that something might happen to the emperor, so he ordered his big and small ghostly underlings to hasten to the crossroads to protect His Majesty. In a moment, all the many small ghosts—the five-colored glazed-glass ghost, the blue-faced red-haired ghost, the unimportant blind-stick ghost, the ghost of the wall behind the gate, and the ghost of narrow lanes up to no good—had all assembled at the crossroads. When young master Zhang took up the dice and wanted to throw a six, he threw a one instead. The emperor was fascinated by the sight and involuntarily shouted "Six!" When those big and small ghosts heard the emperor shout "Six!" they turned the dice over so that young master Zhang won ten ounces of silver. Young master Zhang said, "His hat may be torn and his clothes may be worn, but this guy has exceptionally persuasive powers. That was clearly a one, but when he said 'six,' it turned over. Sir, don't leave. Let me give you two *qian*² so you can buy some food."

Now the emperor was the king of men and the imperial lord, so what were two *qian* of silver to him? When the emperor did not answer, young master Wang said, "A beggar like you interrupted your journey to mess with something that's none of your business. You're asking for a sound beating. That'll teach you not to meddle!" The emperor replied, "Who do you want to give a beating? I'm afraid there's no point in beating a drum made of stone. Even if you bought two cups of sesame seed, you couldn't press oil out of them." Young master Zhang said, "My brother has stupidly offended you, please forgive him. I will make it up to you." The emperor was comforted by these few words of young master Zhang, and he slowly let go of his rage. But young master Wang said, "Brother Zhang, you are too easy on that beggar. If we meet him again by chance and he's still angry, I'll pull out all his hair!" Young master Zhang said, "Don't call down calamity!" And young master Wang replied, "As if he were the emperor!" Young master Zhang pulled young master Wang along as they went to the upper room in the wine house.

His Majesty the emperor spoke these words of jade,
"Dear friends, I propose to come back again.

搗盅寡酒也沒的幹。我雖人家不大大，生平賭博不疼錢，一半兩銀子也看的見。咱不過閑暇無事，我合你玩上一玩。

皇爺說：「二位，我合你玩玩。」張舍說：「你那裏的銀子，敢說合俺玩玩？」王舍道：「張大哥，這花子不知好歹，叫咱合他賭，咱回去合他賭賭，贏他幾兩銀子添梢。」張舍道：「好眼色！披著蓑衣吃蔴籸，不看吃的看穿的，渾身衣服不值一個低操，贏他命麼？」王舍道：「你沒眼色，他那一匹馬不值好幾十兩銀子麼？」張舍道：「也是。」二人回來，望著皇帝唱了一個大喏，說道：「長官，你待玩玩，俺可玩的大，方才沒見一帖是十兩？沒的長官就玩不起百十兩銀子麼？只怕你輸了沒甚盤費，每帖三錢何如？」皇帝說：「在你隨便。」三人坐下打雙陸，兩人是一個心，要賺萬歲的龍駒。

忙端過骰子盆，雙陸馬兩下分，二人點子總不順。萬歲呼嘎就是嘎，兩帖贏了六錢銀。張王二舍心不忿，往常時顯著你我，把雙陸輸與別人。

萬歲贏了兩帖，張舍道：「我說你不要合他玩，這不是被他贏了？」王舍道：「賭錢避不的輸贏，光贏人誰合咱賭？」張舍道：「輸給個好人罷了，被這花子贏了，怎麼見人？」王舍道：

> There's no point in pouring wine and just drinking.
>   Though my family is not the highest of the high,
> All my life I have happily risked my money in gambling
> And half an ounce of silver isn't something I'd notice.
>   As we are only wasting our time doing nothing,
>   Why don't we amuse ourselves with a game?"

The emperor said, "Gentlemen, let's have a game." Young master Zhang said, "With what money do you dare challenge us in a game?" But young master Wang said, "This beggar doesn't know what is good for him. He tells us to gamble with him. So let's go back and play a game. If we win a few ounces of silver, at least it's something." Young master Zhang retorted, "You must be blind. He's wearing a straw cape and eats chaff buns. If you don't want to look at what he's eating, then look at what he's wearing. All the clothes on his back aren't worth a cropped coin. Are we trying to win his life?" But young master Wang said, "It's you who are blind! Isn't his horse worth several dozen ounces of silver?" Young master Zhang replied, "That's true."

The two men returned and said to the emperor, "Sir, you want to have a game, but we play for high stakes. Didn't you see a moment ago that the prize was ten ounces? If you don't have that, Sir, you can't play for hundreds of ounces. We're afraid that you'll have nothing left to live on if you lose. So what about three *qian* a game?" The emperor replied, "That's up to you. Whatever you like." The three men sat down for a game of backgammon, two united in their desire to gain the emperor's dragon colt.

> Quickly they set out the bowl for the dice,
> The backgammon stones were evenly divided,
> But none of the moves of the two was right.
>   When the emperor called "I win," he won,
> And in two games he gained six *qian* of silver
> To the frustration of the masters Zhang and Wang.
>   "In the past it was always only you and me,
>   But now we're losing to this stranger."

After the emperor had won two games of backgammon, young master Zhang said, "I told you not to play against him! Haven't we lost?" But young master Wang replied, "In gambling you can't avoid winning and losing. If you always win, who'd gamble with you?" Young master Zhang said, "But one should lose to a decent person. How can I face others now that I've lost to this beggar?" Young master Wang replied,

「南京城裏沈萬山，泊頭北裏枯樹皮，人的名，樹的
影，誰不知你我？發一個慈悲，著他拿了去買酒買飯，
濟他受用；沒有我的口號，他若是動動我這銀子，鉤子
匠不鑽眼，生釘這狗頭！」張舍道：「長官原來是玩，
休動這銀子。」

二子弟氣狠狠，說長官你不認人，你來大同捎捎信，宣化府
裏數著俺，俺是大老爺家二代孫，吃酒賭錢打光棍。叫長官
把銀子留下，動一動這拳頭無親！

萬歲說：「沒見你那打手何如，先說你那不出門子的奸
漢嚇人。我要說出我那家鄉居住，你只是搬了罷。」王
舍道：「你在雲霧裏往來，你說的都是雲彩眼裏的話。」

皇帝說：「人不說不知，你且站住，我說與你聽聽。」

武宗爺怒生嗔，罵二位太欺心，你去北京問一問，莊上主管
無其數，出名的總管一大群，我是天下頭一條好光棍。不是
我誇句海口，惱了時抄你的滿門！

二人道：「哈！你是皇帝麼，能抄人？」萬歲說：「雖不
是皇帝，卻也合那皇帝鄰牆。我往常時，上無片瓦蓋
頂，下無寸土立足。那一日

---

3   Shen Wanshan 沈萬山 (also known as Shen Wansan 沈萬三) was a contemporary of
    Zhu Yuanzhang. He is said to have been so rich that he paid for the construction of the
    huge city walls of Nanjing.

4   This sentence probably means: No one will be able to tell from the silver that it has been
    won from us, and if this common soldier uses it, he will only call down disaster upon
    himself. Killing someone by driving a nail into his skull is a common motif in premodern
    Chinese crime fiction.

"Millionaire Shen from Nanjing,[3] the bark of the barren tree north of the wharf: the name of that person, the shade of that tree—who doesn't know you and me? Show some compassion, and let him take the money to buy the food and wine he needs. The silver doesn't carry our name, so if he uses it, the clamper won't inspect it carefully and drive a nail into the shithead!"[4] But young master Zhang said, "Sir, this was only a game. Don't touch that silver!"

> The two playboys were overcome by rage
> And said, "You, dear sir, do not know us.
> On arriving in Datong, you should have asked.
>   In Xuanhua Prefecture[5] we are counted first.
> We're second generation grandsons of prefects.
> In drinking and gambling we beat all bare sticks.
>   So we tell you, Sir, leave this silver behind,
> As soon as you touch it, you'll be tasting our fists!"

The emperor said, "I haven't seen how well you fight, but first let me talk about the way you traitors who have never left home try to scare people. As soon as I tell you my home village and where I live, your only option will be to pack up and move far away." Young master Wang said, "You are wandering in the clouds and what you say is all talk inside clouds!" The emperor replied, "If I don't tell you, you'll never know. So stay over there and listen to me."

> His Majesty the Martial Ancestor was overcome by rage,
> He cursed out those two men like bullying hoodlums,
> "Just go to Beijing and ask around there, for a change!
>   The managers at my estate are without number,
> The famous chief managers are one large crowd:
> I am the number one bare stick of all-under-Heaven!
>   It's not that I want to brag beyond measure,
> But if you anger me, I'll confiscate your homes."

The two said, "Oh, are you the emperor? You can confiscate homes?" The emperor replied, "I may not be the emperor, but I live next door to the emperor. In the past I didn't have a single tile over my head, and I didn't have an inch of land on which to place my feet. Then one day I

5 Xuanhua Prefecture was located in contemporary northern Vietnam in Ming dynasty times, so Zhang and Wang are claiming they are famous throughout the known world.

撞著正德，他說，你這麼一個人，就無棲身之所，跟我來給你一間屋住。他那皇城西裏給了我一間住著。那皇帝他每日裏抄人，我就學會了。」王舍道：「張大哥，這長官說話有些京腔，風裏言風裏語的，都說萬歲爺待來看景呀，咱兩個福分淺薄，也會不著那皇帝，只怕是出來私行的官員，今日得罪著他，回朝上本，可不抄了咱麼？」張舍道：「不是就是響馬，若得罪著他，咱就休出門了。設或路上撞著，可成了冤家路窄了，漫窪中夾夾馬趕下咱去，颼的一箭，嗤的一聲，一刀可就殺了咱了。拿著細絲紋銀合他惹仇家哩！」張舍道：「怎麼處？」王舍道：「我有道理。」遂秉手當胸叫道：「老客，你不要惱，俺兩個相處朋友，不論生熟，好調寡嘴。那六錢銀子你拿了去罷。你的雙陸擲的高妙，有心待請你到舍下來求教一二，天又晚了，來日相會罷，請了。」二子弟打下躬，叫長官你是聽：你的雙陸比俺勝。白銀贏了六錢整，當與長官來接風，權當寫了奉申敬。萬歲說有勞二位，陪我到宣武院中。

二人聽說，那鼻子裏就嗤了：「這花子這麼不識擡舉，咱混他一混。長官，你待上院裏投親去麼？」萬歲說：「好剁鮓的戲弄我寡人麼！該死狗頭！」遂沒好氣的說道：「沒有親。」王舍道：「沒有親，去做甚麼？」萬歲說：

---

6 Probably a reference to the Leopard Ward.

7 Courtesans belonged to the despised classes. To suggest that a man has relatives in the courtesans' ward implies that that person himself is of vile status and makes his living as a pimp.

ran into Right Virtue and he said to me, 'Does a man like you not have a place to rest? Come with me, and I'll give you a house.' And he gave me a place to the west of the imperial city.[6] Now the emperor confiscates homes every day, and I've learned how, too." Young master Wang said, "Brother Zhang, this guy's accent sounds like he's from the capital. It's all idle gossip, but people say that His Majesty the emperor wants to come here to enjoy the scenery. Now, our fortune may be too poor to meet with the emperor, but I fear that this is an official who has come from the capital traveling incognito. If we now offend him and he submits a report upon his return, won't they confiscate our possessions?" Young master Zhang said, "Or he must be a mounted bandit. If we offend him, we won't be able to leave our houses. If we run into him on the open road, we'd be like enemies meeting in a narrow lane! If he pursued us on horseback into the marsh, and shot an arrow, gave a shout, or struck us with his sword, we'd be killed. Just for some fine-grained silver, we had to make him our enemy!" Young master Zhang asked, "What do we do now?" Young master Wang said, "I have a plan." With his hands folded on his breast he said, "Respected guest, don't be angry. We two are friends who live together and enjoy making fun of people, be they strangers or acquaintances. Take the six *qian* of silver with you. You are a master backgammon player, and we would love to invite you to our home for some instruction. But it is already late, so let's meet again tomorrow. Farewell."

> The two playboys bowed deeply
> And said, "Dear sir, please listen:
> Your skill at backgammon surpasses ours.
>   You have won these six *qian* of silver.
> We should invite you to our home;
> Please consider this our humble invitation."
>   The emperor replied, "I have to bother you two
> To take me to the Displaying Martiality Ward."

Hearing this, they snorted, "This beggar truly doesn't realize how well he is being treated! Let's fool him." [And they said,] "Sir, do you want to go to the ward to see a relative?"[7] The emperor said to himself, "These assholes! You want to make fun of the emperor? You shitheads deserve to die!" Thereupon he said sharply, "I have no relatives there." Young master Wang asked, "What do you plan to do there if you have no relatives there?" The emperor replied,

住家鄉在順天，我是個窮長官，閒來山西把心散。外聞貴處
姐兒好，尋個婊子玩一玩，不知那是宣武院？你二位陪我走
走，窮軍家自然不乾。

　　王舍道：「這花子除贏了咱的銀子，還著咱陪他，我嗤
　　他往孤老院裏走走何如？」張舍道：「極妙！」王舍拱
　　手道：
不攏過陪你嫖，叫老客休計較，我今對你說院裏的道。俺倆
明日攜盒酒，敬上院裏望一遭，旁人看著才榮耀，都說是長
官體面，張王舍都合他相交。

　　皇爺說：「多蒙厚意。那裏是去徑？」王舍道：「順大街
　　往北走，轉過隅頭向東一座木牌坊，路北裏新蓋的大門
　　樓，那門上有匾，匾上有字，字字寫的明白，那就是宣
　　武院。」萬歲聽說，心中大喜，上馬去了。未知後事如
　　何，且聽下回分解。

"My home village is in Shuntian Prefecture.
I may be only a poor officer,
But I've come to Shanxi to have some fun.
    I've learned long ago that the sisters here are fine,
So I wanted to find a whore to amuse me.
Tell me, where is the Displaying Martiality Ward?
    If the two of you will accompany me there,
I will, of course, make it worth your while."

Young master Wang said, "This beggar not only has won our money, but also wants us to accompany him. What if I deceive him into going to the almshouse?" When young master Zhang agreed, young master Wang folded his hands and said,

"We don't have time to accompany you there!
Respected guest, please don't hold that against us.
But let me now tell you the way to the ward.
    Tomorrow the two of us will bring a jug of wine
And come to the ward to pay you a visit—
In the eyes of others, that will be a great honor!
    Everyone will say that it enhances your status
When Zhang and Wang are your friends!"

The emperor said, "Many thanks for your kindness. But what is the shortest way?" Young master Wang replied, "Follow the main road to the north and turn east at the corner, and you come to a wooden memorial archway. On the northern side of the road is a large gate, and on that gate is a large plaque clearly inscribed with characters. That is the Displaying Martiality Ward." Greatly pleased on hearing this, the emperor mounted his horse and left.

If you don't know what happened next, please listen to the following chapter.

第七回 獃萬歲孤老院尋妓 乖六哥玉火巷逢君

　　話說張王二舍哄的萬歲去了，在那街前拍手大笑。
好計謀自家誇，自在的笑哈哈。這兩行子沒造化，朝廷在前
還不識，順著口子光瞎吧，頂著蒲笠似天那大。古丟丟死還
不覺，呲著牙喜的是甚麼？

　　那萬歲騎馬順大街前行，轉過街口，果然有座木牌坊，
　　路北里瓦門樓，上挂著牌匾，那牌上是「養濟院」三字。
　　萬歲進院的心盛，沒往上看，光見了一個院子。萬歲下
　　馬進去，他沒見那好姐兒，都是些蒼顏白髮，有紡棉花
　　的，有納鞋底的，有補補丁的，拿虱子的，洗鋪襯的。
　　萬歲暗罵：江彬砍頭的，哄了我來！你說三千名妓，亞
　　賽嫦娥，這就是樣子了麼？我曉的還在裏頭哩，恐怕風
　　吹日炙曬黑了，我進去看看。

進院來細端詳，見了些女娥皇，個個都有五十上。口裏沒牙
眵糊著眼，

1　In laughing. These two lines describe Zhang and Wang.
2　The text mentions Ehuang 娥皇, the wife of the sage king Shun 舜 of the mythic past.
　　Upon the death of her husband, she drowned herself and became the goddess of the
　　Xiang River in Hunan.

7   A stupid emperor seeks a courtesan in the almshouse;
Shrewd Brother Six meets his ruler in Jade-Fire Lane.

Let me tell you, young master Zhang and young master Wang, having sent off the emperor in the wrong direction, clapped their hands and were laughing loudly in the street.

> They prided themselves on their clever scheme
> And laughed loudly without any worry.
> But these two scoundrels lacked good luck.
> The emperor went on ahead, still uninformed.
> Following their instructions, he blindly continued.
> The cap covering his head was as wide as heaven!
> Floored and knocked out, unaware even in death,
> Showing their teeth[1]—why were they so happy?

Astride his horse, the emperor went on ahead on the main street, and when he turned a corner, he saw indeed a wooden memorial archway. On a tile-covered gateway on the northern side of the road hung a plaque, and on that plaque were clearly written the three characters "Nurturing Sustenance Ward." In his eagerness to enter the ward, he didn't look up to have a good look. Having only seen the one character "Ward," the emperor dismounted and went inside, but he didn't see any sisters! All he saw were men with sallow faces and white hair: some were spinning cotton, and some were filling shoe soles, while others were patching clothes, catching lice, or washing stuffing. The emperor cursed under his breath, "Damn you, Jiang Bin, you fooled me! You said that the three thousand famed courtesans nearly equaled Chang'e, and this is what it looks like? I understand: they must be staying inside, afraid that out in the wind and exposed to the sun they'll get a dark tan. Let me go inside and have a look."

> On entering the ward he had a close look,
> He saw indeed some beauties of ancient times:[2]
> Each and every one was over fifty years of age!
> With their toothless mouths and pus-covered eyes,

東倒西歪曬太陽，通然不像個人模樣。破衣服赤身露體，哼殺我好他那髒娘。

那萬歲正往裏走，從裏頭出來了一個老漢，說道：「長官，你來院裏做甚麼？」皇爺說：「我來耍耍。」老兒道：「你會刀呀，是耍槍？耍把戲，弄傀儡，說快書，唱道情，你去上那十字街前，耍給人看，掙幾百錢好買嗄吃，你來這裏耍，可給你甚麼？」皇爺說：「我來看看。」老兒說：「你來看親麼？」皇爺道：「沒有親。」老兒道：「可有朋友麼？」萬歲大怒道：「合你這忘八做甚麼朋友？我對你說，我來找個婊子玩玩。」老兒大怒道：「你鋪著扁擔蓋著帶子睡來麼？你這不識時務的貨！耍婊子可沒有，不棄嫌，有孤老哩，給你幾個耍耍罷！」萬歲說：「好哇！我來嫖婊子，不想撞著孤老窩裏 來了。」萬歲又道：「你是誰家的孤老？」老兒道：「誰家給俺飯吃，就是誰家的孤老。俺吃的是皇帝家的俸糧。」那萬歲聽說，才知道是孤老院，羞慚滿面，無言可答。低頭一計，便說道：「我是江老爺的差官，來這孤老院裏查查，年老的許他吃糧，若是年少的趕出院去。」老兒聽說，磕頭在地，說：「小的不認的是差來的老爺。」皇爺說：「我不怪你。我要進宣武院，坐落那裏？」老兒道：「出門向西走，轉過隅頭向北，那西巷裏坐北朝南，景致無窮，王孫子弟有錢者，往那裏去樂。」萬歲聽說，牽馬出院，羞愧難當。

---

3   *Daoqing* designates a seventeenth-century genre of prosimetric storytelling on Daoist themes, such as resurrection of a skeleton by Zhuangzi 莊子 or the conversion of the staunch Confucian Han Yu 韓愈 (768–824) by his nephew Han Xiangzi 韓湘子, one of the Eight Immortals. See Idema 2014.

Leaning to the left or right enjoying the sun,
They didn't even look like human beings anymore!
   Their torn clothes exposed their naked bodies.
"They give me the creeps, those dirty crones!"

Right when the emperor was walking around, an old man came outside and asked him, "Sir, what are you doing here in this ward?" The emperor replied, "I came here for entertainment." The old man said, "Can you handle a sword or a lance? Do you want to perform a play, perform with marionettes, tell a fast tale or sing *daoqing*?[3] If you go to the crossroads and perform before an audience, you can make a few hundred coins and buy some food. But what can we give you if you perform here?" The emperor said, "I came here to have a look!" The old man asked, "Did you come here to look for a relative?" The emperor replied, "I don't have any relatives here." The old man asked, "Then perhaps a friend?" The emperor flew into a rage and said, "How could I be friends with a pimp! I'll tell you, I came here to find a whore to have some fun with." Now the old man exploded in rage and said, "Are you asleep on your carrying-pole bed with your belt covering your eyes? You must not know anything! If you want whores, we don't have them here. What we have here, if you don't disdain us, are orphans and elderly people. I'll give you some of them to have your fun with!" "Fine and dandy!" the emperor said, "I wanted to find a whore but ended up in the poorhouse instead!"

The emperor then asked, "So whose orphans and elderly are you?" The old man replied, "If anyone provides us with food, we are his orphans and elderly. Our food comes from the emperor's tax grain." Only on hearing this did the emperor realize that he was in the almshouse, and with his face covered with shame, he knew not what to say. But when he lowered his head, he came up with a scheme and said, "I am an emissary of His Excellency Jiang. I have come to this almshouse for an inspection. People of an advanced age are entitled to food, but younger people have to be expelled." When the old man heard this, he beat his head against the floor and said, "Sir, I didn't realize you were an emissary." The emperor replied, "I don't blame you. Where is the Displaying Martiality Ward located, if I want to go there?" The old man said, "Go out of the gate, head west, then you turn a corner and go north, and you will find it in a western lane on the northern side, facing south. There the beautiful scenery has no limit. It's where princes and playboys with money go to have their fun." When the emperor heard this, he led his horse out of the ward, overcome by shame.

一時覺著身體乏困，尋思道：「我暫且找一店房歇息半日，叫店主送我進院，有何不可。」那萬歲尋找店房，且說這玉火巷店家李小泉，有個走堂的六哥兒，他是東斗星臨凡，合該他時來運至，這大同城裏不知有多少酒肆飯店，萬歲爺正眼不理，一騎馬竟進了玉火巷來了。

牽著馬尋店家，吃酒飯解解乏。走堂的高叫來咱家罷，暖閣樓房高大廈，圈椅方桌仔細茶，酒果飯食都減價。北京城官員過往，那一個不來咱家！

那六哥正在店房，忽聽的鑾鈴響亮，跑到門前，看見萬歲，慌忙籠住龍駒，就說：「老客裏邊下何如？」六哥他：

一見皇帝面，和顏悅色添，向前攏著馬，話兒比蜜甜，老客咱家住，三生結下緣。不是小飯店，東西盡皆全：肉包蘸著蒜，碗哪大食團，雪白稻米飯，火燒是水煎，雞汁水花麵，只要八個錢。若要候朋友，擺酒不費難，南菜咱都有，海味件件鮮，

---

4   The stars of the Northern Dipper (Ursa Major) are widely venerated as powerful deities. In due time they became accompanied by the gods of the Southern Dipper, Eastern Dipper, Western Dipper, and Central Dipper, collectively known as the Five Dippers.

Suddenly he felt tired and thought, "Let me find a room and rest there for half a day, and then I can tell the innkeeper to take me to the ward. Wouldn't that be better?" So the emperor went looking for an inn. Now let me tell you, Li Xiaoquan, an innkeeper in Jade-Fire Lane, had a servant, Brother Six. He was an Eastern Dipper star[4] who had descended to earth. It was destined that his time had come and his fortunes would change. Inside the walls of Datong there were endless wine houses and inns, but His Majesty the emperor paid them no heed. Rather, he rode his horse straight into Jade-Fire Lane.

> Leading his horse he looked for an inn
> To have some food and wine and recover his strength.
> A servant shouted, "Come to our place!
>   Warm chambers, upstairs rooms, a high and large hall,
> Round chairs and square tables, high-quality tea;
> Wine and snacks and all foods at lowered prices!
>   All officials on their way to and from Beijing
> Come and stay here with us!"

Brother Six was inside the inn when he suddenly heard the sound of a horse bell, so he ran outside. When he saw the emperor, he hastily grabbed hold of his horse, and said, "Respected guest, how about dismounting here?"

When Brother Six saw the emperor's features,
His friendly face became suffused with pleasure,
And as he stepped forward to halt the horse,
His words were sweeter even than honey:
  "Respected guest, please stay at our place:
We have a bond dating back three generations.
Our place here is not some small restaurant.
Everything is perfectly prepared.
  Pork dumplings are seasoned with garlic.
The bowls are made for large portions.
The rice here is always white as snow,
Whether fire-baked or water-steamed.
  Water-froth noodles in chicken broth
Will cost you as little as eight *qian* here.
If you want to entertain your friends,
It's no problem to lay out a banquet.
  We have all the southern vegetables;
The seafood is as fresh as can be.

燒酒壺又大，黃酒苦又甜，雙陸合棋子，悶了有絲絃。
錢不論好歹，銀子九二三，無錢且上賬，過日隨心還。
高房又大廈，馬棚數十間。萬歲心裏喜，牽馬到裏邊。
六哥拴下馬，向前問事端，掃地只一躬：「長官是那
邊？」皇爺說：「你是問的我，北京藍旗官，家鄉也不
遠，居住在順天。自小油滑無能幹，江都督手下做差
官。今日路過大同府，專到寧夏去查邊。」

那六哥道：「早知是江老爺的差官，就該遠接，接的遲
了，萬望恕罪！路遠山遙，鞍馬勞困，多有辛苦了。」
這六哥也是福至心靈，神差鬼使，使的着他奉承了幾
句話。那萬歲大喜，暗暗稱獎道：「人不在大，馬不在
小，果然是實。我自離了北京，一路見了多少人，沒人
問我個辛苦；這小廝不上十五六歲，偏知道我的辛苦。
我自不虧人，問他問是甚麼姓名，久後回京，封他一官
半職，也是他問我辛苦一場。」皇爺說：「小夥貴姓？」
六哥說：

5　Silver with a purity as low as 92 or 93 percent.
6　"Blue banner," when written as 藍旗 as here in the text, refers to a section of the Manchu army during the Qing dynasty and would be an anachronism in this text (Zhang Shuzheng 2018, 864). But written as 藍旂, the term refers in vernacular literature of the Qing to army scouts who, on fast horses, precede marching troops and alert the commander to any obstacle they may be approaching. This second meaning fits the context very well and should be preferred.

The distilled spirits come in a big jug;
The yellow wine is bitter and sweet.
   Backgammon boards and go games,
And if you're bored, there's string music!
We take all coins, both good and bad;
As for silver, it's nine-two or three.[5]
   Without cash, you can stay on credit
And pay later when it suits you better.
We have high rooms and large halls,
And the stables hold dozens of horses."
   The emperor was very pleased by this
And he led his horse into the courtyard.
After tethering the horse, Brother Six
Stepped forward to ask for information.
   Sweeping the floor, he bowed from the waist,
"Sir, whereabouts are you from?

The emperor replied,

"Are you asking about my background?
I'm a blue-banner soldier[6] from Beijing.
My home village is not far from there,
As I live in Shuntian Prefecture.
   From an early age, I've been a slippery sort without abilities.
I'm an emissary under the command of Commissioner-in-Chief Jiang.
I'm passing through Datong Prefecture today only because
I'm on my way to Ningxia to inspect the local border conditions."

   Brother Six exclaimed, "Had I known that you were an emissary of Commissioner-in-Chief Jiang, I would have gone out to welcome you. Please forgive me for being so slow! Your road is long and the mountains stretch far, so you must be exhausted riding on horseback. You must have suffered a lot." This Brother Six was richly blessed with a smart mind, but he too was sent and commanded by gods and ghosts, who made him flatter the emperor with these few words. The emperor was greatly pleased, and deep inside praised him: "It doesn't matter whether a man is big or a horse is small. That saying turns out to be quite true. Since I left Beijing I have met with quite a few people on the road, but no one has asked about my sufferings. This boy isn't even fifteen or sixteen, but he knows I must have suffered. I will not treat people unfairly, so I'll ask him his name, so when I eventually return to the capital, I can appoint him to an office of some kind, because he asked me about my sufferings." So the emperor said, "Young man, what is your surname?" Brother Six replied,

「不敢，愚下姓尹。」萬歲說：「城裏人家孩，讀了二年
書，就會說愚下。你的尊諱？」六哥說：「我沒有名字，
家父養活了俺兄弟六個，我是個老生子，排行叫六哥。
　　長官路上困乏了，我燒些水來，你淨淨面好吃茶呀。」
淨面湯一銅盆，獻過來花手中，細軟肥皂多清潤。老客一路
多辛苦，鋪下牀兒放放身，休歇休歇眼不困。小六哥乖滑伶
俐，萬歲爺件件隨心。
　　那萬歲吃茶已畢，六哥將樓房掃除乾淨，拿了一個坐
來，說道：「老客請坐，我取飯來你用。」
小六哥笑顏生，叫老客你從容，待吃好物我管奉。又有合汁
又有麵，新出爐的熱燒餅，肉包火燒隨心用。一路來千辛萬
苦，拿酒來先吃幾盅。
　　六哥道：「你會吃酒麼？」萬歲說：「我才是天下吃酒的
祖宗頭。」六哥說：「你是吃酒的那頭，我就是賣酒的
那頭。」萬歲說：「你這小廝賣了多少酒？」六哥說：
「老客，我說這話你休怪俺，這一年拋撒的那酒，也勾
你吃一輩子的。」皇爺說：「你有甚麼好酒？」六哥說：
「休問我那好酒，你來霎就沒見我那酒望上寫的那對子
麼？」皇爺說：「你拿來我看看。」六哥把酒望取來，
遞與萬歲。萬歲接來觀看，上寫著：

7　The flag hung up outside a wine shop, advertising its wares.

"Your humble servant's surname is Yin." The emperor said, "When kids in the city have been to school for two years, they already know to call themselves 'your humble servant'! And what is your personal name?" Brother Six replied, "I don't have one. Our father sired us six brothers, and I am a son of his later years. Because of my rank, I'm called Brother Six. Sire, you must be dead-tired from your trip. Let me heat some water for you so that you can clean your face and have some tea."

A bronze bowl was filled for washing one's face.
He also presented the emperor with flowery towels,
While the fine, soft soap was pure and mild.
　"Respected guest, you must have suffered on the road,
So I'll make a bed on the couch so that you can lie down
And take a rest for a while, even if you don't sleep."
　Little Brother Six was shrewd and smart,
In each aspect pleasing the emperor.

After the emperor had finished his tea, Brother Six cleaned the upstairs room, brought a chair, and said, "Dear guest, please sit down and I will bring you your food."

With a smile on his face, this little Brother Six
Said, "Respected guest, please take your ease.
If you want to eat something special, let me serve it.
　We have noodle soup, and we have plain noodles.
We also have hot cakes straight from the oven,
And fried pork dumplings, as many as you want.
　While on the road you must have suffered a lot.
Why not have a few drinks first? I'll get the wine."

Brother Six asked, "Can you drink wine?" The emperor replied, "I am the ancestor of all drinkers throughout the world!" Brother Six said, "If you are the champion of all drinkers, I am the champion of all wine sellers." The emperor then asked, "So how much wine do you sell each year, young man?" Brother Six replied, "Respected guest, don't blame me for what I will say, but in your whole lifetime you could never finish drinking the wine that I spill in one year." The emperor asked, "What kind of good wine do you have?" Brother Six replied, "If you're asking about our good wine, you probably didn't see the couplet written on our wine flag[7] when you arrived." The emperor said, "Get it so I can have a look." Brother Six fetched the wine flag and showed it to the emperor. The emperor took it from him to have a good look, and it read,

「隔壁三家醉，開罈十里香。酒高壺大，現錢不賒，霸
王吃酒要現錢，張飛沒錢剝下靴。」皇爺說：「這小廝
好利害！霸王平分天下，張飛是三國忠臣，要錢罷了，
就許你剝靴！待我耍他一耍。」遂說：「你這話頭不好，
我給你改了，情管生意大快。」六哥說：「你給我改了，
我掙了錢來孝敬你老人家。」萬歲說：「不難，拿筆來。」
萬歲爺一筆到底，六哥看了看，改的是：「也漫說那酒
高壺大」，第二句是「清香賽過屠蘇」。六哥說：「是怎
麼講？」萬歲道：「這屠蘇是古時美酒，你那酒比他還
強。」六哥大喜道：「好口才！好口才！」皇爺又題道：
「色比葡萄才半熟，插上楊梅同做。」六哥道：「這又
是怎麼講？」萬歲說：「這兩句是說你那酒的顏色好，
紅通通的，就像那半熟的葡萄，加上那楊梅一樣的嬌
嫩。」六哥說：「妙妙！」皇爺又寫道：「行人也不來飲，
鄰里也不來沽，一年只賣兩三壺。」六哥大怒道；「這
不壞了麼？休寫罷，賣不的還好哩！」萬歲說：「你休
要燥發，你看下句：剩下的却曬好醋。」

六哥兒心裏焦，叫老客你把我敲，幾般好酒你不知道。我有
七十二樣酒，見樣拿來你瞧瞧。品品不好往當街倒，從今後
不開酒店，

---

8   Following the death of the First Emperor in 210 BCE, rebellions broke out all over the
Qin empire. Of the many warlords, two emerged as most likely to conquer the Chinese
world. One was Xiang Yu 項羽 (232–202 BCE), an aristocratic young hero from southern
China who was undefeatable in personal combat. He had adopted the title of Hegemon
King of Easter Chu. Xiang Yu eventually lost out against the low-born Liu Bang 劉邦
(d. 195 BCE), who was surrounded by many capable generals and advisers and became
the founder of the Han dynasty (206 BCE–220 CE). Zhang Fei 張飛 (d. 221 CE) was one
of the sworn brothers of Liu Pei 劉備 (161–223), who in the final decades of the Han
dynasty carved out his own territory in modern-day Sichuan, where he became the

"At a distance of three houses, people are already drunk; when the jar is opened, ten miles share the fragrance. The wine is strong, the jug is large; one pays in cash, no credit allowed. Even when the Hegemon King drinks our wine, he has to pay in cash; and when a hero like Zhang Fei lacks money, we take his boots in payment."[8] The emperor said, "This young man is terrible! The Hegemon King took one half of all-under-Heaven, and Zhang Fei was a loyal vassal of the Three Kingdoms period. If you want your money, fine, but are you allowed to strip him of his boots? Let me have some fun with him."

And so the emperor said, "These phrases are no good. Let me change them for you, and I promise that your business will greatly improve." Brother Six replied, "If you change them and I make more money, I will respect and serve you as my parent!" The emperor said, "No problem, bring me a brush!" He wrote without any interruption down to the end, and when Brother Six had a look, he saw that the emperor had changed it to "Don't say, 'The wine is strong, the jug large." The second line was now "Its pure fragrance surpasses Tusu."[9] Brother Six asked, "What does that mean?" The emperor replied, "This Tusu is a fine brew from ancient times, your wine cannot surpass it." Brother Six said happily, "What rhetorical talent!" The emperor also wrote, "Its color compares to grapes halfway ripened; it is prepared by adding bayberries." When Brother Six asked what that meant, the emperor said, "These two lines explain that your wine has a fine color. It is red through and through, just like half-ripe grapes, to which has been added the sweet charm of bayberries." Brother Six said, "Wonderful!" The emperor continued to write: "Passers-by don't enter here to drink, / Neighbors do not come to buy the wine: / In one year's time, he only sells two jugs." Brother Six exploded in rage and said, "Wouldn't that kill me? Don't keep writing. What I can't sell is still good stuff." The emperor replied, "Don't get so angry. Just read the last line, 'But what is left in the sun becomes vinegar'!"

> Brother Six was extremely anxious
> And shouted, "Guest, please don't swindle me!
> You've no idea of my many brands of fine wine.
>   I have seventy-two kinds of wine here,
> And I'll bring out each kind for you to inspect.
> If anything doesn't taste good, pour it out on the street!
>   And from then on, I'll close up shop right then and there.

founder of the Shu-Han dynasty, one of the Three Kingdoms that ruled China for most of the third century.

9   Tusu 屠蘇 is a type of rice wine drunk in spring to ward off epidemics.

說聲薄把壺貶了！

皇爺說：「你有甚麼好酒，說來我聽。」六哥說：
時黃酒合春分，狀元紅蜜林檎，鎮江三白顏色俊；尋常就是
白乾酒，每瓶只要一錢銀。老客不必你多心問，我還有黃菊
高酒，每一瓶二錢紋銀。

皇爺說：「你拿黃菊高酒來我吃罷，那混帳酒我吃他不
慣，情願多給你價錢。」六哥說：「老客既要吃好酒，
我去拿的。」跑下樓去，叫掌櫃的把原封好酒裝上兩
壺，提到樓上，滿斟一盃，遞與萬歲吃了一口，果然好
酒。萬歲開懷暢飲。那六哥滿面悅色，無不奉承。六哥
道：「我賣酒這幾年來，再沒見個會吃酒的，你真是天
下吃酒的個祖宗頭。」萬歲說：「好酒！你拿那望布來，
給你另改了你好賣。」六哥說：「吃酒罷，不要改了。」
皇爺說：「不妨。」六哥把望布拿了來，萬歲提筆在手，
上面題西江月一首：

春夏秋冬好酒，清香美味堪誇。開罈十里似蓮花，八月
聞香下馬。洞賓留下寶劍，昭君當下琵琶；劉伶愛飲不
回家，好酒哇醉倒西江月下。

---

10 Lü Dongbin 呂洞賓 is one of the Eight Immortals. He is often depicted as a student
carrying a sword. One of the best-known stories about him tells of his visits to the wine
house at Yueyang Tower.
11 Wang Zhaojun 王昭君 was a palace lady during the reign of Emperor Yuan (r. 48–33
BCE) of the Han dynasty, who married her off as a Chinese princess to the khan of the
Xiongnu, his warlike northern neighbors. Ever since the third century, she has been
depicted as traveling on horseback and holding a lute while lamenting her fate.
12 Liu Ling 劉伶, one of the third-century Seven Sages of the Bamboo Grove, was renowned
for his addiction to alcohol.

Just call one kind weak and I'll flatten the jug!"

The emperor said, "If you have anything good, tell me—I'm listening."
Brother Liu replied,

> "Season's Yellow, a wine fit for mid-spring;
> Top-of-the-List Red and Honeyed Crabapple;
> Triple White from Zhenjiang, with its fine color.
>   The most common kind is our colorless liquor:
> A bottle will cost you only one *qian* of silver.
> Dear guest, you don't have to be too concerned.
>   I've also got Yellow Chrysanthemum Sorghum.
> Each bottle of that costs two *qian* of fine silver."

The emperor said, "Get out that Yellow Chrysanthemum Sorghum and
I'll have some. I'm not used to drinking those vile wines, so I'm happy to
pay your price." Brother Six said, "Sir, if you want to drink our best wine,
I'll get it." He ran downstairs and told the manager to prepare two jugs of
the finest wine straight from the unopened jar. He carried those upstairs,
filled a beaker to the brim and handed it to the emperor to have a taste.
It was indeed a fine brew, and the emperor drank to his heart's content.
Brother Six looked extremely pleased and unceasingly flattered the emperor, saying, "We have been selling this stuff for a number of years, but
I've never seen anyone who could drink it. You truly are the ancestor of
drinkers throughout the world." The emperor said, "This is great stuff. Get
me that flag once again, and I will change it again to enhance your sales!"
Brother Six replied, "Just drink your wine; don't change it again!" But the
emperor said, "Don't worry!" Brother Six fetched the flag, and the emperor
raised his brush to inscribe on it a lyric to the tune of "West River Moon":

The best wine for spring, summer, fall, and winter;
Its pure fragrance and perfect taste deserve praise.
When the jar is opened, the fragrance for ten miles resembles lotus
     flowers:
Smell that scent in the Eighth Month and dismount!

Lü Dongbin left behind his precious sword,[10]
And Wang Zhaojun even pawned her lute.[11]
Liu Ling loved to drink it so much that he never went home:[12]
Because of this wine, he collapsed in a stupor below the West River
     Moon.

萬歲爺笑顏開，叫六哥你過來，有了好酒要好菜。賣飯不怕大肚漢，好物濟數都拿來，除了要錢有何礙？小六哥滿心歡喜，這長官仗義疏財。

六哥說：「你待吃菜麼？」皇爺說：「寡酒難飲。只怕你店裏沒有好菜。」六哥道：「只怕你無錢。休說是你，就是北京城大駕降臨，俺擺個御筵也擺的來。」皇爺說：「你就拿著家當比那北京皇爺麼？我從來沒見御筵，你就擺一桌罷，我正不待吃那混賬東西。」也是他君臣意投，六哥急忙走下樓來，叫一聲掌櫃的：「樓上客吃了足色好酒，又要吃足頂好菜哩。咱給他吃不給他吃？」李小泉說：「我不管你。那闖江湖的調喉舌、弄寡嘴騙子極多，給他吃了有錢極好；若無錢，他吃了，有扒肚子的御史麼？待要的漫了，人折了本；待緊了，壞了咱店裏門市。吃與不吃我不管。」六哥說：「狗脂！他若無錢，我認著我這一年工價，也該二十兩多銀子，也還管的起他頓飯了。」

小六哥整攢盒，松子榛仁把皮剝，柑橘酥梨擺幾個；羊肚松傘沙魚翅，猴頭熊掌共燕窩，件件齊整看的過。休說道將這長官款待，皇帝老待吃甚麼？

六哥整了一桌酒菜，擡上樓來。萬歲一見，滿心歡喜。

13　A kind of mushroom.

His Majesty the emperor's face broke into a smile
And he called to Brother Six, "Come over here!
Now that I have this fine wine, I want some fine dishes!
    One selling food doesn't fear a big-bellied fellow:
Bring out the whole set of all the finest stuff you have.
What's there to stop you? Price is no object!"
    Little Brother Six was overcome with joy as he thought,
"This guest disperses wealth based on righteousness!"

Brother Six said, "Do you want something to eat?" The emperor replied, "Wine without food doesn't go down very well. I'm only afraid your inn doesn't provide any good dishes." Brother Six said, "You should only fear that you don't have the money. Let's forget about you—even if His Majesty in Beijing would deign to visit us, we could lay out an imperial spread." The emperor replied, "So you compare your own place to His Imperial Majesty's in Beijing? I have never seen an 'imperial spread,' so set it out before me. I really don't want to eat any vile stuff."

This was a case where the intent of lord and vassal converged. Brother Six hurried down the stairs and shouted, "Manager, now that the guest upstairs has enjoyed our very best wine, he also wants to eat some top-grade dishes. Shall we let him have them or not?" Li Xiaoquan replied, "That's up to you. Roaming the rivers and lakes are quite a few smart-talking, glib-tongued swindlers. It's fine to let him have the dishes if he has the cash. If he's already eaten them but doesn't have the cash, is there a censor who will open his stomach? If we don't get our money, we'll run a deficit, and in the worst case it could ruin our business. It's all up to you whether to let him have those dishes or not." Brother Six replied, "Bullshit! If he doesn't have the money, I'll put up my wages for this whole year. That's more than twenty ounces of silver, so that should be enough for a single meal for him."

    Little Brother Six prepared the boxes.
    Pine nuts and hazelnuts peeled and shelled;
    Oranges, tangerines, together with tender pears;
        Lamb bellies, pine-parasols,[13] and shark fins;
    Monkey brains, bear paws, and swallow nests—
    Each item neatly arranged; all a pleasure to view.
        Forget that it was treatment fit for this guest.
    Would His Majesty ever have enjoyed such a meal?

    When Brother Six had set out this table of dishes, he carried it upstairs, and as soon as the emperor saw it, he was overcome with joy.

安排的甚均勻，端上來香噴噴，盤碗鮮明顏色俊。肥豚笋雞天花菜，鰣魚鰒魚共海參，還有蘑菇合香蕈。萬歲爺滿心歡喜，缺少個作樂的佳人。

　　萬歲見那酒食美味，任意取樂，但少個佳人陪伴，遂把那六哥喚來，叫他往宣武院搬婊子。未知六哥去與不去，且聽下回分解。

Everything was arranged quite nicely;
When served, the dishes gave off a strong fragrance.
Plates and bowls were fresh and bright, in beautiful colors.
    Fat pork, bamboo shoot chicken, heaven-flower fungus,
Hilsa herring, abalone, as well as sea cucumber;
And then there were mushrooms and fragrant herbs.
    His Majesty the emperor was overcome with joy,
But now he still lacked a beauty to play a song.

When the emperor noticed how good the wine and food tasted, he enjoyed them to his heart's content, but he still lacked a beauty to keep him company, so he called Brother Six over and told him to go to the Displaying Martiality Ward to bring him a whore. If you don't know whether Brother Six went or not, please listen to the following chapter.

第八回 六哥筵前誇妓女 萬歲樓上認乾兒

話說那萬歲飲酒中間，叫道：「六哥靠前來！」六哥尋思道：「你這京花子無廉恥，哄我近前有甚麼話？」說道：「老客有甚話說罷。」萬歲笑道：「你知有三般景致麼？」六哥道：「那三般？」萬歲道：「羽州的城牆，大同的教場，宣武院的姑娘。」六哥道：「羽州的城牆聽的說，可沒曾見；大同的教場也不爲景致，只是大就是了，有九頃六十四畝，天下人馬聚集，一年兩操；只有宣武院的姑娘，果然艷色出奇。」萬歲說：「果然是實？你給我搬一個來陪我，何如？」六哥說：「你就是猴子扒竹竿，一節一節的來了。進店來住了好房子，吃了好酒，又吃好菜；好酒好菜都吃了，又格外生事，又要個作樂佳人陪伴。只怕你沒有錢，你搬婊子，可是要省錢的，要費錢的？」萬歲說：「省錢的不知要幾千？費錢的不知要幾萬？」六哥道：「省錢的店前有極好的招牌，只是底板沉些。」萬歲道：「你實說罷，我是個夯人。」六哥道：「模樣極好，就是腳大些。」皇爺說：「你把那好的搬一個來玩玩罷。」六哥道：「我先說說你聽聽著。」宣武院姐兒多，無名的數不著，有名略表個數個：金玉銀玉天生俊，

1   One *mu* measures about one sixth of a hectare, and one hundred *mu* make one *qing*.

8   Over a meal, Brother Six praises some courtesans;

In his room, the emperor adopts a boy as his son.

Let me tell you, while drinking his wine, the emperor called, "Brother Six, come over here!" Brother Six thought to himself, "This capital beggar has no shame at all! Why does he want me to come over?" So he said, "Sir, please tell me what you have to say." The emperor replied with a smile, "You know the three famous sights?" Brother Six asked, "Which three?" The emperor said, "Yuzhou's city walls, Datong's parade ground, and the girls of the Displaying Martiality Ward." Brother Six replied, "Yuzhou's city walls I've heard about but never seen, and Datong's parade ground is not a great sight. It's just big, that's all. At nine *qing* and sixty-four *mu*,[1] the infantry and cavalry from all-under-Heaven congregate there for drill exercises twice a year. Only the girls of the Displaying Martiality Ward present a truly gorgeous sight."

The emperor asked, "Is that so? How about you fetching one to keep me company?" Brother Six replied, "You're like a monkey climbing a bamboo stalk, advancing node by node. Entering this inn, you got the best room, drank the best wine, had the best food, and now that you're finished with the wine and food, you come up with something else! A beauty who can play a song to keep you company? I'm afraid you don't have the money. If you want to fetch a whore, do you want a cheap one or an expensive one?" The emperor asked, "How many thousands for a cheap one? And how many tens of thousands for an expensive one?" Brother Six replied, "A cheap one can be found outside the inn. Her shop front is quite fine, but her ground-slappers are on the heavy side." "Spell it out for me," the emperor said. "I'm pretty dense." So Brother Six replied, "Her looks are fine, but her feet are on the big side." The emperor said, "Then fetch me a better one to have some fun with." Brother Six replied, "Let me enumerate them for you:

> The sisters are many in the Displaying Martiality Ward
> And I cannot enumerate all those without renown.
> I will mention ten or so who have a reputation.
>   Golden Jade and Silver Jade display celestial charms.

愛愛憐憐都差不多，素娥月仙也看的過。這還是尋常的豔色，有兩個賽過嫦娥。

　　萬歲道：「甚麼名字？」六哥道：「一個是賽觀音，一個是佛動心。」萬歲道：「怎麼樣的兩個人兒，就敢起這個名字？」六哥道：「這賽觀音有說，這佛動心有講。賽觀音是老鴇子尋的，長到十二三，扎挂起來，甚是風流。子弟們看了，都說合觀音相似的，老鴇子綽號那點口氣，就叫做賽觀音。」萬歲道：「那佛動心呢？」六哥道：「他是揚州人氏，姓劉，父母雙亡，從七八歲他姑娘賣在他院里，溫柔典雅，體態輕盈。眾人誇獎，就說老鴇於你的時來了，你家二姐，活佛見了他動心，就叫起來了。若見了他時，就像那二月二的煎餅。」皇爺道：「怎麼講？」六哥道：「就攤了呢！」皇爺說：「怎麼樣的豔色，說來我聽聽。」

單表起佛動心，滿院裏他超羣，金蓮小小剛三寸。彎的是眉兒，乖的是眼，俊的是模樣，俏的是心。尋常不肯合人混，這妮子拿糖捏醋，看不上公子王孫。

　　皇爺說：「一身難嫖兩個，你把那賽觀音搬來我嫖嫖罷。」六哥說：「你來的晚了，接了客了。說起那客來，有他坐的去處，還沒有你站的去處。」皇爺說：「瞎話！你說是那裏的客？」六哥道：「是王尚書的公子王三爺，名喚王龍。你敢叫他的婊子！他若惱了，送到你縣裏，打你頓板，還給你個

2　The bodhisattva Guanyin (Avalokiteśvara) was widely venerated in late-imperial China in a female manifestation that was considered the acme of beauty.

3　The word for "flattened" (*tan* 攤) has the same pronunciation as the word meaning "an itch/itching all over" (*tan* 癱). An itch is the common designation of an irrepressible desire or an addiction.

4　Her bound feet.

5　When spoken aloud, the name Wang Long 王龍 can also be understood as "royal dragon" or "fake dragon."

Ai'ai and Lianlian are of about the same class,
While Su'e and Moon Fairy are a pleasure to look at.
　　They may be gorgeous, but are still quite common.
　　There are only two who outshine even Chang'e!"

The emperor asked, "And what are their names?" Brother Six replied,
"One of them is called Guanyin's Equal, and the other is Buddha's Lust." The
emperor said, "Who are they that someone dared give them such names?"
Brother Six replied, "There's an explanation for Guanyin's Equal and for
Buddha's Lust. Guanyin's Equal was found by the old bawd. When she'd
grown up to be twelve or thirteen, they started to dress her up, and she
turned out to be extremely seductive. When the playboys saw her, they
all said that she resembled Guanyin,[2] so the old bawd turned that into an
advertisement and called her Guanyin's Equal." The emperor asked, "And
what about Buddha's Lust?" Brother Six replied, "She hails from Yangzhou
and is surnamed Liu. When her parents both died, she was sold at the age
of seven or eight into the ward by her aunt. She is gentle and handsome,
and has a gracious appearance. Everyone praised her, saying to the old
bawd, 'Your time has come! Seeing that second daughter of yours, even
the Buddha would be stirred to lust!' That's how she got her name. If you
see her, you'll resemble the baked cakes of the second day of the Second
Month!" The emperor said, "What do you mean?" Brother Six said, "You'll
be flattened."[3] The emperor said, "What are her charms? Tell me about
them—I'm listening."

　　"Let me tell you only about Buddha's Lust:
　　She surpasses all other sisters in the ward.
　　Her golden lotuses[4] barely measure three inches.
　　　Her eyebrows are curved, her eyes sparkle;
　　Her features are pretty, and her heart is soft.
　　Ordinarily she refuses to mingle with people.
　　　The wench plays sweet but pisses vinegar,
　　Looking down on all noblemen and princes."

The emperor said, "As one man, I cannot patronize two whores, so
fetch me Guanyin's Equal so that I can fool around with her." Brother
Six replied, "You're too late. She already has a patron. Speaking of that
patron, there's no place for you to stand where he's sitting." The emper-
or replied, "Nonsense! Tell me, what kind of patron he is." Brother Six
replied, "He is Third Lord Wang, son of Minister Wang, and his name is
Wang Long.[5] If you dare choose his whore and he gets angry, he'll send
you over to the magistrate to administer you a beating, and he'll have

作道哩。」皇爺笑道：「只有我打的人，人再治不的我。但只是賽觀音旣接了他，我也不合他爭，你搬那佛動心來陪我罷。」六哥說：「六月六的豆腐，陪不的了。」皇爺說：「怎麼陪不的我了？」六哥道：「你不知佛動心不接凡人。當初有個逼退給他算卦，丫頭先合他說，俺二姐姐極愛奉承，到那裏哄他二兩銀子，咱倆好分。那逼退果然有天沒日頭的，說他有一宮皇后的命。那瞎刀子扎的哄了銀子去了，那皇帝那狗頭也不來了，哄著二姐今日等皇帝，明日等皇帝，到如今還守寡哩。」皇爺說：「你這小廝反了麼！你敢罵皇帝！」六哥道：「他在北京，他就知道我罵他哩。」皇爺說：「不必多嘴，你快去搬了他來。我不肯空支使你，我給你十來個錢，你做身衣服穿。」六哥說：「休說做衣服，就買幾張剛連紙來也不勾糊一身衣服的。」皇爺道：「一個錢還用不了的。你不信，我先給你看看。」

萬歲爺龍心歡，褡包裏取出錢，十個就是二兩半。若是搬的二姐到，給你做領紅布衫，冷天穿著好跌麵。常言道天不支使空人情，管我打發你個喜歡。

那六哥接著金錢，跑下樓來，誤誤掙掙的叫掌櫃的拿戥子來使使：「長官叫我去搬佛動心，給了我十個錢，我稱稱。」小泉道：「你幾輩子沒使錢了，拿著幾個錢這麼親？十個錢還要戥子稱著使。」六哥道：「你枉做買賣一輩子，

---

6   In the hot summer months, tofu easily spoils and cannot be stored (*dui* 堆). This words rhymes with *pei* 陪 (to keep company).

7   Two and a half ounces of silver.

you punished." The emperor said with a smile. "Only I can have people beaten, and there's no one who can discipline me. But as Guanyin's Equal is already seeing him, I won't fight over her with him. Fetch me Buddha's Lust." Brother Six replied, "That's like tofu on the sixth day of the Six Month—you can't be her companion."[6]

So the emperor asked, "Why can't I be her companion?" Brother Six replied, "You wouldn't know this, but Buddha's Lust doesn't see ordinary people. Once upon a time, a blind fortune-teller was going to read her future, and her servant girl told him in advance, 'Our second sister greatly loves to be flattered. If you cheat her out off of two ounces of silver, you and I can share them.' That fortune-teller couldn't recognize the sun in the sky and told her that she was destined to become an empress. The damned blind crook disappeared after taking her silver, but the shithead emperor never showed up, so that deluded second sister is still waiting for her emperor today—and she'll still be waiting tomorrow. To this day she lives the chaste life of a widow." The emperor cried, "You nobody, do you rise in rebellion? You dare revile the emperor!" But Brother Six said, "He lives in Beijing, so how would he know I'm cursing him?" The emperor said, "There's no need to blabber on. Go fetch her for me. I wouldn't make you go for nothing at all, so I'll give you a dozen coins. Go have a full set of clothes made for yourself." Brother Six replied, "Forget about a set of clothes. With that, I can't even buy a few sheets of paper to paste together an outfit!" The emperor said, "Even one coin would be more than enough! If you don't believe me, I'll let you have a look first."

> His Majesty the emperor's dragon heart was pleased,
> And from his satchel he took out some coins:
> Ten of them were as good as two and a half ounces.[7]
> "If you fetch Buddha's Lust and bring her here,
> I will have a red linen gown made for you.
> You'll look great wearing it on cold days!
> The proverb says 'Heaven doesn't employ people without pay,'
> I promise that I will send you off to your satisfaction."

Upon receiving the golden coins, Brother Six ran down the stairs. He was delirious with excitement and shouted, "Manager, get out your scales! That guest ordered me to fetch Buddha's Lust. He gave me these ten coins, and I want to weigh them." Xiaoquan replied, "For generations on end you haven't had any money, so how come you love coins so much now that you have them? Ten coins, and you want my scales?" Brother Six replied, "You have been in business all your life, but in vain.

老的牙都白了，曾見這樣錢來麼？你看看何如？」掌櫃
的接過錢來，看了一看，霞光萬道，瑞氣千條，嚇的半
晌無言。接過來耀眼明，掌櫃的諕一驚，這人不是小百
姓；不然是個真強盜，寶藏庫裏剜窟窿，或是短了天朝
的貢。若是你使了發了，葬送你小小殘生！

六哥說：「只怕不給我哩，若給我幾千，我化成金子，
換成銀子，可不財主了麼？」六哥提著酒上的樓來，
滿斟一杯，遞於萬歲，就深深的唱了一個大喏，謝了
又謝。一霎叫大叔，一霎叫爺爺，喜的前跑踢、後跑
踢的。萬歲說：「你愛那錢麼？」六哥道：「誰是背財
生的！我每日賣酒，也見銀子來，也見銅錢來，可沒
見這金錢。」萬歲道：「你既愛我這金錢，我合你認門
親戚罷。等我那小廝們來時，多給你幾串，強似你起
五更、睡半夜的賣酒。」六哥道：「金不好使，親戚難
認。不棄嫌，合你拜個兄弟何如？」皇爺說：「折的你
慌了！」六哥說：「你待嘎是個皇帝，叫人兄弟就折殺
了？」皇爺說：「你若愛我金錢，斟上三杯酒，跪在樓
上磕二十四個頭，叫我三聲乾爺，我認你做乾兒罷。」
六哥道：「羞人答答的，看人笑話。」萬歲說：「你若不
從，難得我這寶貝。」六哥說：「也罷，這樓上無人見，
就叫他三聲爺，哄他幾串金錢，誰待爺長爺短的跌歇著
口子常叫他哩。沒有金錢出上，我就不叫他；若是有金
錢，還有叫人祖、叫人宗的哩。」

8　Copper coins (round, with a square hole in the middle) were strung together on strings
　of nominally a thousand coppers.

You're so old that your teeth are gray, but have you ever seen coins like these? Have a look! What do you think?" When the manager took the coins from him to have a good look, he saw a myriad multicolored flashes and a thousand-fold auspicious aura. He was so startled that he was speechless for quite some time.

> When he took the coins, they dazzled his eyes:
> The manager was startled into a fright:
> "This guest is no ordinary fellow!
>   If he's not some professional thief
> Who bored his way into a treasure vault,
> He must have robbed a tribute mission.
>   If you use these coins and are discovered,
> That will be the end of your miserable life!"

But Brother Six said, "My only fear is that he won't give them to me! If he gives me a few thousand, I will turn them into gold, and when I exchange that for silver, I'll be rich!" Brother Six went up the stairs with some wine, and poured out a full cup to give to the emperor. He loudly thanked him again and again. One moment he called him "dear uncle," the next moment "Your Excellency," and in his joy he ran around kicking left and right. The emperor said, "You love those coins?" Brother Six replied, "Who turns his back on a rich man? Day in and day out, I sell wine, so I have seen silver and bronze coins, but I've never seen gold coins." The emperor said, "Since you love my gold coins, let me recognize you as a relative. When my underlings arrive, I will give you even more strings.[8] That's a better life than selling wine: getting up in the fifth watch and catching sleep only after midnight." Brother Six replied, "Gold is not easy to spend, and kinship is not easily feigned. Unless you reject me, how about we become sworn brothers?" The emperor replied, "That would be your undoing!" Brother Six said, "As long as you're not the emperor, how can it be my death to call you my brother?" The emperor said, "If you love my golden coins, pour out three cups of wine, kneel down on the floor, kowtow twenty-four times, and call me your adoptive father three times. Then I will accept you as my adoptive son." Brother Six said, "I'd be ashamed to do that. You're joking!" But the emperor said, "If you don't do as I say, you won't get these treasures." So Brother Six said to himself, "In this upstairs room, there's no one to see us. I'll call him 'father' three times and relieve him of a few strings of golden coins. Who's going to call him 'father' all the time like a panting puppy? If I weren't going to get gold coins, I wouldn't call him that even if he were my elder. But to get gold coins, I'd call any man granddad or ancestor!"

那六哥斟上了三杯酒，跪在樓上，口稱：「乾爺，我認
了你了。」

小六哥斟上酒，跪下去磕個頭。也是前生緣法湊，萬歲一見
心歡喜，叫了一聲我兒流，爺們說不的尋常厚。只要你用心
孝順，我分給你頃地犋牛。

萬歲心中大喜，說道：「好個龍虎山張天師，他算朕當
乏嗣，半路裏拾了一個乾殿下，果如其言。」

萬歲爺笑顏開，我的兒你起來，前生有福把我拜。咱門戶不
在人以上，體面也還撐的來，說聲做親還有人愛。我給你尋
個媳婦，治幾件霞帔金釵。

萬歲道：「六哥兒你耐心，等待我給你做領紅布衫。」

六哥自思：可出了醜了。俺乾爺不是個轎夫，就是個鼓
手。遂說：「乾爺，你給我做別的罷，我不要紅布衫。
我曉的乾爺，你是一名軍，你回京著說六哥兒跟我去看
看，你乾娘去這麼遠，我待不跟你去一趟哩。到了北
京，初一十五的就說，小六哥，跟我去點點卯，穿著那
紅

---

9   "Conventional" here would seem to have the meaning of "feigned." So the sentence
seems to mean that Brother Six called the emperor "father" with true sincerity.

Brother Six poured out three cups, knelt down on the floor, and said, "I acknowledge you as my adoptive father."

> Once little Brother Six had poured out the wine,
> He knelt down on the floor and kowtowed to him.
> This was a karmic bond from their earlier lives.
>   On seeing this, the emperor was filled with joy
> And cried out, "My son! Now when saying 'father,'
> What you show is not just conventional sincerity![9]
>   If you exert yourself and serve me filially as my son,
> I will apportion you a *qing* of land and a team of oxen."

The emperor was overcome with joy and said, "So much for that Heavenly Master Zhang from Mt. Dragon-Tiger![10] He foretold Us that We would lack an heir, but on the road I've picked up an adoptive prince—just as he said!"

> His Majesty the emperor was all smiles:
> "My darling son, please rise!
> It was your luck from a former life to bow to me!
>   Even though our family may not rank above all others,
> We still have managed to acquire some status.
> So when it comes to marriage, people love us.
>   I will make sure to find a fitting wife for you,
> And prepare colored capes and golden hairpins."

The emperor said, "Little Six, just wait patiently, and I will have a red linen gown made for you!" Brother Six thought to himself, "That would be a disgrace! My father is either a sedan chair carrier or a drummer!" So he said, "Adoptive father, please have something else made for me. I don't want a red linen shirt. I understand that you are a soldier. When you return to the capital, you'll say, 'Little Six, come with me to meet with your adoptive mother.' Wouldn't I go with you, despite the distance? Once we're in the capital, on the first and fifteenth of each month you'll say, 'Little Six, come with me as I report for duty and wear that red mail

---

10 Heavenly Master Zhang 張天師 is the title of the hereditary head of the Zhengyi 正一 sect of Daoism headquartered at Mt. Longhu 龍虎 (Dragon-Tiger mountain) in Jiangxi Province. The Heavenly Masters enjoyed great prestige during the Ming dynasty and had their own establishment at the capital to facilitate their frequent contact with the emperors. In scholarship of the first half of the twentieth century, the Heavenly Masters are often designated as the "Daoist Pope." See Goossaert 2022.

罩甲子。這也是小事。只是如今人合那脆草哇似的，打
起你死了著，那左隣右舍說：有小六哥，不是他兒麼？
俺祖輩有軍。這兩名軍，可就送了我這命了！」皇爺
說：「你放心。我這軍好著哩。我家裏有兩條帶，捎根
來給你扎腰。一條白的，一條黃的，你待要那一條？」
六哥道：「年小小的，扎著根黃帶子醜醜的，給我那條
白的罷。」皇爺說：「這小子造化不小，把一條白玉帶
討在腰裏了。」又說：「我還給你一頂帽，你要不要
呢？」六哥道：「甚麼帽？」皇爺說：「是半邊帽。」六
哥說：「給我就給我頂圓圓的，那半邊帽子怎麼戴？」
皇爺說：「要一個四趁，戴著那半邊帽，穿着那紅布
衫，扎著那白玉帶子，就支極好的架子。」六哥說：「無
功受祿，寢食不安。搬了二姐來，任憑乾爺給我甚麼不
遲。」皇爺說：「正是。若搬不了來，跌咱爺們的架子
了。」

小六哥賣巧言，叫乾爺你放心寬，我今就上宣武院。蜜口糖
舌將他請，他若不來將毛撏，見了咱磕頭如搗蒜。叫乾爺樓
上待等，這椿事在我不難。

　　六哥下了樓，向宣武院去搬佛動心。不知搬了來搬不了
　　來，且聽下回分解。

11　In modern Chinese, "half a hat" is a hat with a rim on only one side, so a cap. Throughout
　　this paragraph and the preceding one, however, the emperor appears to hint that he will
　　eventually appoint Brother Six to high office. In the Ming dynasty, the officials of the
　　highest ranks in the bureaucracy wore red gowns (of silk), with large decorated belts.
　　"Half a hat" would therefore refer to the caps worn by officials that sported "wings" on
　　both sides but had no rim in front or in back.

cover.' That's all unimportant. But people these days are just like a field of brittle grass. When you die in battle, won't your neighbors on both sides say, 'Isn't that little Six his son?' Among my ancestors there's also a soldier. These two soldiers are going to be my death!"

The emperor said, "Don't worry! This military status of mine is safe. At home I have two belts. Choose one to wear. One is white, and one is yellow. Which do you want?" Brother Six said, "A yellow belt looks bad on someone so young, so please give me the white one!" The emperor said, "This young man's good fortune is not minor! He has asked for a white jade belt around his waist." He said, "I will also give you a hat. How about it?" Brother Six asked, "What kind of hat?" The emperor said, "It is half a hat."[11] Brother Six said, "If you want to give me a hat, give me a full hat. How could I wear half a hat?" But the emperor said, "You need a fitting combination. Wearing half a hat, in your red linen shirt, girded with a white jade belt, you will cut quite a figure." Brother Six replied, "'Receiving a salary without having established any merit, one feels ill at ease while sleeping and eating.' I will first fetch second sister, and afterward it won't be too late for you to give me whatever you want." The emperor said, "You're right. You dishonor your father if you don't fetch her."

> Little Brother Six bragged of his smart words
> And then said, "Adoptive father, please don't worry,
> I am off to the Displaying Martiality Ward.
> I'll invite her with honeyed words and sweet language,
> And if she refuses to come, I'll pull out her hair.
> Seeing me, she will kowtow as if smashing garlic!
> Adoptive father, please wait here in your room,
> Leave this business to me. It's no problem at all!"

Brother Six went downstairs and left straight for the Displaying Martiality Ward to fetch Buddha's Lust. If you don't know whether he succeeded in fetching her, please listen to the following chapter.

第九回 說虔婆六哥進院 相嫖客老鴇登樓

　　話說那六哥下的樓來，李小泉道：「六哥，你在樓上合長官說的是甚麼？」六哥笑道：「有一句話不好說，我認了長官做了乾爺了。」眾人拱手說：「大喜了！」六哥說：「少笑俺。乾爺著我給他上宣武院搬婊子去。他吃用的嘎都算我的，休要慢待了他。」小泉說：「你說的是那里話！你的乾爺就是我的朋友，你放心罷。」

六哥兒滿面歡，你休要不耐煩，莫要將我胡瞞怨。千萬只是托著你，茶水酒飯要周全，休把乾爺來輕慢。在店中住上幾日，吃了飯算我的工錢。

　　六哥道：「我上宣武院去，夥裏的買賣耽誤了工夫，叫夥計們說嘎？把那舊營生做起來罷。」遂把那瓜子、嬌梨拾了一盤，抗將起來，出了店門，一聲吆喝，可就賣起來了。

　　六哥出店把口誇，東西地高南北窪，幾畝窪地種蜀秫，幾畝高地種棉花；剩下幾畝沒嘎種，種了許多大西瓜。王孫子弟來找我，

Brother Six enters the ward to persuade
the madam;
The old bawd ascends the stairs to inspect
a patron.

Let me tell you, Brother Six descended the stairs, and Li Xiaoquan said,
"Brother Six, what did you discuss upstairs with that guest?" Brother Six
replied with a smile, "It's somewhat awkward to tell: I acknowledged him
as my adoptive father." The others all folded their hands and said, "Congratulations!" Brother Six said, "Don't laugh at me! My adoptive father
ordered me to go to the Displaying Martiality Ward to fetch him a whore.
Put whatever he eats or drinks on my tab, and don't treat him with disre-
spect!" Li Xiaoquan replied, "What are you saying! Your adoptive father
is my close friend! Don't worry!"

> Little Brother Six put on a happy expression,
> "Don't be irritated by my behavior,
> And please don't carry a grudge against me.
>   No matter what, I implore you,
> Provide him with tea and water, wine and food.
> Don't treat my adoptive father with disrespect.
>   As long as he will be staying in this inn,
> Deduct all he drinks and eats from my wages!"

Brother Six said, "I'm off to the Displaying Martiality Ward. We all share
this business, and if I don't make my hours, my colleagues may complain,
so I will take up my former business again."[1] He then collected a plate of
melon seeds and tender pears and, carrying the plate on his shoulder, left
the inn, calling and shouting all the time that these were for sale.

As Brother Six left the inn, he loudly praised his wares:
"East and west the land is high; north and south a marsh.
On a few plots of marshy fields, tall sorghum is grown;
On a few plots of high fields, cotton flowers are grown.
  On the few plots that remain, where nothing is grown,
I've planted lots of big watermelons.
The noblest princes and richest playboys seek me out

買些瓜子閑嗑牙。早來提名姓，晚來剩自家。吾乃不是
別人，賣瓜子的小六哥又來了耶。

瓜子盤端起來，宣武院說裙衩，吆喝一聲把瓜子賣。院中許
多嬌娥女，見了罵聲小乖乖，點點人兒真作怪。沿門子磨牙
鬪嘴，誰知他別有安排。

按下六哥進院。且說那老鴇子見連日沒客，悶悶不足，
叫了聲丫頭說道：「玉火巷您尹六叔，往常時三朝兩日
的就送客來，如何這一向絕不來走走？你去找著他說，
俺娘請你，你怎麼不去玩玩。你若是閑著，把那瓜子、
梨兒拿些來院中走走。」丫頭聽說，出的門來，看見六
哥，即回後房道：「媽娘，俺六叔來了。」媽兒聽說，
走出門來，接著六哥，拜了又拜：「您六叔賊天殺的！
誰惱著你來，許久不來玩玩？」

老虔婆話兒甜，假捏虛長笑顏。許久不進宣武院，只說那個
得罪你，今日來時我放心寬。失迎就是好幾遍，多揀著拜了
又拜，假奉承說了些虛言。

六哥說：「你老人家好麼？」鴇兒道：「甚麼好！跳起來
只是生氣。」六哥道：「誰氣著你來？」鴇兒道：「只小
二妮子那奴才就氣殺我了！我又不值錢，

---

1 Before Brother Six became a servant in the inn, he made his living, it would appear, as
   a peddler of fruits in the courtesan quarter.
2 A pretty woman.

To buy my melon seeds to snack on as they chatter.
    Early in the morning I call my name;
Late at night it still remains the same.
I'm none other than the melon seed seller,
Brother Six, and here I am again!"

He carried before him his plate of melon seeds
To persuade 'a skirt and hairpins'[2] in the ward.
Calling and shouting all the while, he sold his melon seeds.
    Inside the ward, many pretty wenches
Saw him and insulted him by calling him a baby:
"Such a tiny fellow is truly a monster, for sure!"
    Door by door they teased him, vying with each other with their
        jokes,
But who knew that he had quite a different purpose?

Let's not talk about Brother Six entering the ward. Let me tell you, the old bawd was despondent over not having any customers for a number of days. She called over a servant girl and said, "Your uncle Yin Six from Jade-Fire Lane used to send us customers every few days, so how come he hasn't been here for so long? Go find him and tell him, 'Our madam invites you. Why don't you come and have some fun? If you have the time, take some of your melon seeds and tender pears to the ward for a visit.'" So the serving girl went outside, and when she saw Brother Six, she promptly went back inside, saying, "Madam, our uncle Six is here!" When the madam heard this, she went out to welcome him, and as she did, bowed and bowed again. "You damned uncle Six! Who made you so mad that you haven't come here to have fun in so long?"

The old madam's words were sweet,
And in putting on a show, she grew a smile.
"You haven't been in the ward for quite a while!
    I've been wondering who might have displeased you.
Now that today you've come, I can set my worries aside.
And again I've failed to welcome you properly!"
    All atremble, she bowed to him and bowed yet again,
Falsely flattering him as she spoke many empty words.

Brother Six said, "How are you doing, madam?" The bawd replied, "How I am doing? As soon as I jump up, I fly into a rage!" Brother Six asked, "Who's annoying you?" The bawd replied, "It's my second little girl, that slave, who drives me mad. 'I'm not worth any money' and

沒人要了；他又不接客，著那瞎子哄著他，每日接皇帝。若依著我，等甚麼皇帝，趁著年小，接客掙錢我使才好。」六哥道：「正是，還是你見的明。若等不著時，可不耽誤了他麼？」鴇兒道：「你給我說著使大錢的客，接了他罷。」六哥道：「我店裏就下了個使大錢的，叫二姐去陪了他罷。」鴇兒道：「是那處人？」六哥道：

那個人好怪哉，從北京問了來，一心要會你令愛。渾身不上眼不上眼，誰知手裏有錢財。那人行事好大待，搬婊子吃酒玩耍，爲這個今日才來。

鴇兒說：「你怎麼知道他大待？」六哥說：「支使了我一遭，就給了我十個錢。」鴇兒說：「十個錢就看在眼裏，似俺這煙花巷里，十數兩銀子也曾見過。」六哥說：「你空這麼大年紀，吃緊的就沒見這錢也是有的。」鴇兒問道：「甚麼錢？拿來我看看。」六哥取出金錢，遞與虔婆。鴇兒一見就慌了心說：「您六叔，他這東西有多少？」六哥道：「誰知道他的哩。」

六哥兒叫老媽，你休笑那軍家，仗義疏財手段大。鴇兒聽說財神到，心裏癢癢沒處去抓，科上摘下那齊整話。說我去相他一相，我看是怎麼樣的一個軍家。

鴇兒道：「我先合你去看看。」六哥道：「正是。眼見是實，耳聽是虛，我就說的那龍吱吱的，叫你也不信。」鴇兒道：

3 "Misty flowers" is a common euphemism for courtesans and prostitutes.

'Nobody wants me,' while she won't receive any customers! She let that blind fool deceive her into waiting each day for the emperor. If it were up to me, she wouldn't wait for any emperor. Let her use her youth to see customers and make money, so I have something to spend." Brother Six said, "Indeed, you're right. If she waits to no purpose, won't that ruin her life?" The bawd said, "You should persuade some big-spending patron to take her in." Brother Six replied, "A big-spender is staying at our inn right now, and he wants second sister to keep him company." The bawd asked, "Where is he from?" Brother Six replied,

> "Now that man—it's all quite strange—
> Arrived here, he told me, from Beijing.
> He's all set on meeting your darling daughter.
>   He isn't wearing anything special,
> But surprisingly, he has lots of money at hand
> And acts like someone who spreads it widely.
>   He wants a whore to join him while drinking,
> And that's the reason I've come here today!"

The bawd asked, "How do you know that he spreads it widely?" "When he sent me on this errand," Brother Six replied, "he gave me ten coins." The bawd replied, "You're impressed by ten coins? Here in these lanes of misty flowers, I've seen ten ounces of silver and more."[3] But Brother Six said, "You've reached old age in vain. Have you never seen the other kind of coins?" The bawd asked, "What coins? Let me have a look!" Brother Six produced a gold coin and handed it to the bawd. As soon as she saw it, the bawd was flabbergasted and said, "Uncle Six, how many of these does he have?" Brother Six replied, "Who knows?"

> Little Brother Six told the old madam,
> "Make sure not to despise that soldier!
> He freely dispenses his wealth based on righteousness!"
>   When the bawd heard that the god of wealth had arrived,
> She felt in her heart an itch that she couldn't scratch,
> And from a branch, she plucked a nice polite phrase,
>   And said, "Let me go and look him over
> To see what kind of soldier he might be."

The bawd said, "I'll first go with you and have a look." "Rightly so," Brother Six said. "'What one sees with one's eyes is a fact; what one hears with one's ears may be fake.' Even if I were to talk till the dragons cried out, you still wouldn't believe me." The bawd said,

「你不知俺指著嗄來，不過指著這兩個孩子過日子。小
二姐性子又嬌，縱然不接皇帝，也要一個班配，我不去
看看，惹的他邊牆決臉的怎麼過？」那鴇兒跟著六哥，
同到了酒店，說道：「客在那里？」六哥道：「在樓上。」
鴇兒就待上樓，那六哥沒搬了佛動心來，不好上樓，遂
高聲叫道：「樓上的客招顧著，佛動心上樓去了。」那
萬歲在樓望的眼穿，聽的樓下吆喝，把那簷毡帽一推，
擡頭觀看。

睜龍眼仔細瞧，進來個老媽媽。鬢邊白髮光光乍，臉上的皺
紋無其數，口裏當門少兩牙，雖然風騷年紀大。萬歲爺心中
驚異，佛動心每哩是他？

皇爺說：「六哥兒，我著你去搬那佛動心，你怎麼叫了
一個『鬼見愁』來了？」說著，那老鴇子上的樓來，看
見萬歲穿的平常，就淡了半截心。走到近前，多揆了兩
多揆，叫聲姐夫，我這裏拜哩。那些護駕的大小鬼，見
他無禮，一個扯腿，一個按頭，那虔婆哎喲了一聲，撲
咚跪在地下，磕頭無數。

衆鬼使好促狹，打虔婆滿面花，撲咚跪在牀兒下。翻身磕頭
如搗蒜，頭上硼了些大疙瘩，鬆髻梳妝俱輪下。樓板兒響成
一塊，把六哥好不諕煞！

4   Guests in a courtesan house are called "brother-in-law."

"Don't you know whom I manage? I make my living managing these two kids. The younger, second sister, has been spoiled, and if it isn't the emperor she has to serve, at least it has to be a fitting partner. If I don't go over to have a look, she'll just stonewall me, and then what?"

The bawd followed Brother Six, and when they together arrived at the inn, she asked, "Where is this guest?" Brother Six replied, "In the upstairs room." The bawd immediately wanted to go upstairs. Since Brother Six had not been able to fetch Buddha's Lust, he felt uneasy about going upstairs, so he loudly called from below, "As requested by the upstairs guest, Buddha's Lust is coming up!" In his room, the emperor had been waiting impatiently, so when he heard his shouting and calling, he pushed his brimmed felt hat aside, and lifted his gaze to have a good look.

> His dragon eyes dilating, he intently watched
> And saw an old madam enter his room:
> The white hairs on her head shined brightly!
> The wrinkles spread across her cheeks,
> And two front teeth were missing.
> Despite her charms, she was advanced in years.
> The emperor was filled with fright and wonder:
> Buddha's Lust couldn't be her!

The emperor said, "Little Brother Six, I told you to fetch Buddha's Lust. How come you told this Devil's Grief to come?" While he spoke, the old bawd ascended the stairs. When she saw how commonly the emperor was dressed, her desire had already halfway paled. When she came closer, she curtsied twice and said, "Brother-in-law,[4] I present my bows." When the big and small ghosts that protected His Majesty saw that she showed no respect, one pulled at her legs and another pushed her head down, so that she gave a shout and, kerplunk, fell flat on her face, kowtowing without end.

> Those ghostly servants loved a practical joke.
> They so beat up the madam that she saw stars,
> And, kerplunk, knelt down before his couch.
> Rolling around, she kowtowed as if smashing garlic,
> And on her head quite a few bumps arose.
> Her fake bun came undone and swirled to the ground.
> The planks of the floor banged so loudly
> They caused Brother Six quite a scare!

那六哥聽的樓板響成一塊，說：「不好了！俺乾爺打老
鴇子哩，我去勸他。」六哥上的樓來，看見那虔婆磕頭，
遂說：「乾爺，一稱金雖是個賤人，有些體面，見了大
人，也只是拜拜，今日給你磕頭，是十分尊你，你只顧
著他磕起頭來無數。」萬歲說：「老鴇，你起來罷。大
熱天勞動你這一遭，沒甚麼給你，又叫你磕頭。」那老
鴇子扒起來，戴上鬆髻，自思想：好蹺蹊！又沒見他一
個錢的東西，怎麼磕了這一些頭？我平日見上人也不過
拜他兩拜。定了一定，方才問道：「長官，你是那裏？」
萬歲說：「我是北京。」媽兒道：「你當的是那一營的
軍？」萬歲說：「我當的是十三營裏的軍。」老鴇說：「只
有九標十二營，那有十三營呢？」萬歲說：「是新添的
一營。我在京就是十三營，我出了京，依然是九標十二
營了。」

萬歲爺笑嘻嘻，叫虔婆你聽知，從頭對你說詳細：十三營裏
我爲首，奉差由此到寧西。久聞令愛多標致，你着他陪我一
晚，窮軍家有分薄儀。

媽兒自思：這花子盡是寡嘴，薄厚在那裏？遂下樓就
走。萬歲道：「他沒相中我。他若去了，再請二姐就難
了。自古道：錢成錢成，無錢不成。老鴇子，你回來，
我給你幾兩銀子，你去買件衣服穿罷。」
十兩銀放在桌，金豆兒取一盒。鴇兒本是個愛財貨，

---

5   The surname of the old bawd is Jin 金 (gold).

When Brother Six heard the floor planks banging so loudly, he said
to himself, "Shit! My adoptive father is giving that old bawd a beating. I
have to talk to him!" When Brother Six came upstairs, he saw the madam
kowtowing, so he said, "Adoptive Father, this One Stone-Weight of Gold[5]
may be vile, but she still has her status. When seeing a noble, she only
performs some bows. Kowtowing to you here today, she's honoring you
in the extreme. You should take into consideration that she has kowtowed
to you without end!" The emperor said, "Old bawd, rise up! In this stifling
heat, I have bothered you to come, and while I have nothing to give you, I
also told you to kowtow." The old bawd crawled up, put her fake bun back
on, and thought to herself, "How weird! Even without seeing one of these
coins of his, why did I kowtow so much? Usually when I meet superior
persons, I only bow once or twice."

Once she had finally recovered herself, she asked, "Sir, where are you
from?" The emperor replied, "I'm from Beijing." The madam asked, "And
in which battalion do you serve?" The emperor answered, "I'm a soldier
in the thirteenth battalion." The old bawd said, "There are only nine regiments and twelve battalions. How can there be a thirteenth?" The emperor
replied, "This is a newly added battalion. When I was in Beijing, there
were thirteen battalions, and now that I've left Beijing, there are still nine
regiments and thirteen battalions."

> His Majesty the emperor said pleasantly,
> "Now dear madam, please listen to me.
> I will tell you all in detail from the start.
>   I am the head of the thirteenth battalion
> And was passing through on my way to Ningxi.
> But I have heard about your daughter's beauty.
>   If you'll let her accompany me for one night,
> I, a poor soldier, will provide a small gift."

The madam thought to herself, "This beggar is all talk. Where's that small
gift?" She set out to go downstairs to leave. The emperor concluded, "She
has the wrong impression of me, but if she leaves, it will be impossible to
invite second sister again. Since ancient times it has been said, 'Cash and
only cash accomplishes, and without cash nothing is accomplished.'" "Old
bawd, please come back. I will give you some ounces of silver so that you
can buy some new clothes."

> He placed ten ounces of silver on the table.
> He also took out a box of gold beans.
> The bawd was at heart a cash-loving type,

見了銀子花了眼，刮打著嘴兒笑呵呵，我不收下恐見錯。多挼著拜了又拜，叫姐夫口似蜜多。

　　鴇兒說：「乍會初逢，敢蒙姐夫照顧。」萬歲說：「照顧不大。這銀子是給你的，這豆子是給你那閨女的見面錢。」媽兒道：「我連這孩子的都捎了去罷。」萬歲說：「你放心。二姐若來，宿錢另奉。」

老虔婆心裏乖，不重客只重財，低袖多挼拜兩拜。我去失陪休心困，到家就著二姐來，千萬要你多擔待。小二姐年紀幼小，他自來沒見黑白。

　　皇爺說：「你放心。我雖帽破衣殘，却是個幫襯子弟。」鴇兒接了銀子，下樓去了。未知後事何如，且聽下回分解。

6　Is still inexperienced.

So on glimpsing the silver, her eyes saw stars!
She licked her lips and laughed loudly.
"It would be impolite not to take these."
   All atremble, she bowed once and bowed again.
As she spoke, her words were sweeter than honey.

The bawd said, "Having barely met during our first encounter, I wouldn't dare, dear brother-in-law, to accept this present." But the emperor said, "This is only a small present. This silver is for you. These beans are the assignation money for your dear daughter." The bawd said, "I will take all of it with me, along with the part for my daughter." The emperor said, "Don't worry. When second sister comes, the sleepover fee will be paid separately."

This old madam was quite shrewd.
She didn't value the patron; she only valued his wealth.
With lowered sleeves, all atremble, she bowed repeatedly.
   "I will go now and leave you, but don't be worried.
As soon as I get home, I'll order second sister to come.
On all accounts I have to ask you to be tolerant:
   Little second sister is still quite young in years
And never in her life has seen black and white."[6]

The emperor said, "Don't worry. My hat may be torn and my clothes may be worn, but I am an understanding playboy." After the bawd had accepted the money, she went down the stairs.

   If you don't know what happened next, please listen to the following chapter.

第十回 佛動心風塵自歎 老鴇兒打罵施威

話說那鴇兒下樓來見了六哥。六哥說：「你老人家這一遭可好麼？」婆子道：「先苦後甜。起初頭磕了頓頭。我合他敘些了家常，他說給我分薄禮，只當是給我幾個錢，可給了我一錠銀子，我掂量著有十來兩銀子；不足爲奇，還給了我一盒金豆。」六哥說：「你認的麼？」鴇兒道：「我自來沒見，黃登登的，待說是珍珠，又沒有眼，誰家有黃珍珠來？不是金豆是甚麼？」鴇兒照著六哥拜了兩拜，說：「您六叔，說不盡虧你看顧俺。」六哥說：「怎麼不看顧別人？一來是您娘們掙的，二來也是俺引進一場。」鴇兒說：「不著你，這東西是天上吊下來的，地下跑出來的，科枝上長的樹上結的？」六哥道：「閑話少說，你到家著二姐快來。」鴇兒辭了六哥，出了店房，自己尋思：我收了人家銀子，小二妮子那奴才他若不來時，我只得拿出利害來，給他個狠手，死活從他。按下虔婆發恨不題。且說佛動心本姓劉，原是揚州人，一個武官之女。八歲父母雙亡，落在姑娘手裏。他姑娘貪財，賣在他院中。長到十二三歲，出脫的如花似玉，才有了佛動心之名。一日夢見紅光罩體，請了遍退來算了一卦，說他有娘娘之分。他就一心要接皇帝，總不見客。那老虔婆又著實愛惜他，

10   Buddha's Lust bemoans her poor fate in the windy dust;
The old bawd shows her might by whipping and cursing.

Now let me tell you, the bawd came down the stairs and met with Brother Six, who asked, "Old lady, was your visit successful?" "'First bitter, then sweet,'" the old woman replied, "At the beginning I kowtowed to him, and told him some of our house rules, and he said he would give me a small gift. I thought he would give me a few coins, but he gave me one ingot of silver that felt on the hand like more than ten ounces. That silver wasn't even the strangest thing. He gave me a box of gold beans!" Brother Six asked, "How did you recognize them?" The bawd replied, "I've never seen them before, but they were bright yellow. You might think they were pearls, but they lacked pupils, and who has yellow pearls? What could they be but gold beans?" The bawd bowed twice to Brother Six, saying, "Uncle Six, I cannot fully express my gratitude for your patronage." Brother Six replied, "Why would I not patronize you? First of all, you women have earned it, and only secondly was it my recommendation." "If it hadn't been for you," the bawd said, "would this stuff have fallen from Heaven? Would it have leaked up from the earth? Would it have grown on a branch? Or grown as fruit on a tree?" Brother Six said, "No more talk! Go home and tell second sister to come." After the bawd had taken her leave of Brother Six and left the inn, she thought to herself, "I have accepted that man's silver, but if that slave, little second girl, refuses to come, I'll have to rely on my cruelty—and then it will be up to her whether she wants to live or die!"

Let's not talk about the madam getting angrier and angrier. Rather, let me tell you that Buddha's Lust was originally surnamed Liu and hailed from Yangzhou. She was the daughter of a military officer, but when she was eight, both of her parents died. She ended up in the hands of an aunt who loved money and sold her into the ward. By the time she was twelve or thirteen, she was as pretty as a flower and re-sembled jade, and only then did she acquire the name Buddha's Lust. Dreaming one day, she saw her body covered by a red glow, and when she asked a fortune-teller to predict her future, he said that she was des-tined to become an empress. So she only wanted to receive the emperor and never saw any other guests. The old madam truly cherished her

　　遂給他十個丫頭；伏侍他住在一座南樓上。這佛動心又
　　自己畫了一個皇帝影像，懸在帳中，朝夕禱告。等了二
　　年，見皇帝不來，自己又長成了，每日家思量這風塵下
　　賤，將來如何結果，不由的心酸落淚。
佛動心自思量，每日家待君王，那君王再不見影兒傍。身子
落在火坑裏，鴇於怎肯許從良？將來弄一個甚麼樣！悶來時
思思念念，不由人一陣恓惶。
　　這一日佛動心正然悲嘆，忽見那喜鵲兒來那簷前喳喳的
　　叫喚了幾聲。說：「喜鵲，你錯叫了！這煙花巷裏有甚
　　麼喜事？」猛擡頭看見皇爺的御影，說：「我從算卦以
　　後，我就傳下皇爺的影像，燒香念佛，供養了你三年，
　　不見萬歲在那裏，枉費了辛勤。」
燒上香拜主公，口兒裏自咕噥，燒香念佛的成何用？買命算
卦接皇帝，竹杆種火落場空，也是奴家前生命。佛動心滿心
好惱，胡瞞怨恨罵先生。
　　那二姐在南樓上痛哭不題。且說那老鴇兒進的院來，徑
　　到南樓

1　The only way for a registered courtesan to escape her vile status as a prostitute was to marry a commoner. For this to happen, her lover had to buy her freedom by paying a hefty sum to the bawd and apply to the authorities to change her status.
2　A chattering magpie was believed to announce the arrival of a loved one.
3　A set phrase to denote a lack of positive results.

and had provided her with more than ten serving girls to wait on her in her southern upstairs room. Buddha's Lust drew the emperor's portrait and hung it up inside her bed curtains, and each morning and night she prayed to him. She waited for two years, but no emperor made an appearance. As she grew up, she thought each day how vile her life was in the windy dust. Wondering what the future would bring, she was habitually overcome by bitter grief and sobbed.

> Buddha's Lust thought to herself,
>   "Every day I waited for my lord and king,
> But I haven't seen even his shadow.
>   My body has fallen into this pit of fire.
> How might the bawd allow me to marry out?[1]
> How will I end up in the future?"
>   Despondently, she thought and pondered,
> Involuntarily filled with frustration.

Just when Buddha's Lust was giving in to sad sighs that day, she suddenly saw a magpie appear before the eaves and chatter a few times.[2] She told it, "Happy bird, you chatter at the wrong place! What kind of happy affair can there be in this lane of misty flowers?" When she lifted her head, she saw the image of His Imperial Majesty and said, "Ever since I had my fortune told, I have preserved this image of the emperor. I have lit incense and recited the name of the Buddha. I have revered him for three years, but I haven't seen any emperor. All my efforts have been in vain!"

> Burning incense, she bowed to her lord
> While she softly mumbled her prayers.
> "What's the use of burning incense and reciting the name of the
>   Buddha?
>   When that fortune-teller predicted that I would receive the
>   emperor,
> He planted fire inside a bamboo tube, and it fell into an empty
>   space![3]
> But alas this must have been my karmic fate."
>   Buddha's Lust was overcome by a burning anger,
> Bearing a grudge, she cursed the fortune-teller.

Let me not mention that second sister was bitterly weeping in her southern upstairs room. Rather, let me just tell you that upon entering the ward, the old bawd went straight to the ground floor of the southern

底下一片混罵，罵了一回，便叫丫頭：「小二妮子那裏
去了？」二姐南樓聽見，說：「不好了！俺媽娘往常時
拿著我合掌上明珠哇是的，何等愛我；今日不知吃了誰
家的酒了，又不知吃了誰家的引子，連我也找算起來
了。我且下樓接他一接去。」

佛動心無奈何，下樓來接虔婆，接到樓上讓了坐。戰戰兢兢
旁邊站，花言巧語似蜜多，百樣奉承他不樂。老賤人眉頭不
展，謔殺了二八嬌娥。

二姐說：「媽娘，你不在後房自在，來南樓何事？」老
虔婆抹下臉來說：「我沒事就不來！人家那當姐兒的也
是當姐兒，春裏是春衣，夏裏是夏衣；你也是個姐兒，
我來問你要幾兩銀子使使。」二姐道：「媽娘，你胡突
了麼？我身邊又沒有客，可那裏的銀子？」鴇兒道：「好
奴才！你自己說了罷：俺老的老，小的小，每日掙給你
吃，幾時是個了手？」

一稱金把臉抹，叶麻上平聲叫賤人你忒也差，歪頭瞥腦的濟
著咋？吃穿二字你不管，逐日把我巴結煞。世間要你中做
嘎？今後晌若不接客，准備著打發你歸家！

老鴇子怒狠狠的罵下樓去，來到後房，

4　Yeast causes flour to rise, so the term suggests "rising anger."
5　Zhang Tai 2019 (687) prints the five characters making up this phrase in a smaller font,
suggesting that they are a prose interjection in the song, not to be sung but quickly
recited. The manuscript reproduced in Pu Songling 2009 (127) writes these five smaller
characters in a double column, suggesting rather that the phrase should be understood
as a direction to the performer to raise his voice. My translation is tentative.

building, cursing all the while. When she had cursed for some time, she called, "Serving girls, where has that little second girl gone off to?" When second sister upstairs heard this, she said, "Oh no! The madam has always treated me as a bright pearl in the palm of her hand, loving me dearly. But today I don't know where she's been drinking, and I don't know where she's eaten the yeast that makes her want to settle accounts with me![4] I had better go downstairs to welcome her."

> Buddha's Lust could do nothing
> But go downstairs and invite the madam
> Up into her room and let the madam sit down.
>   Trembling and shivering in fear, she stood at the madam's side;
> Her flowery and crafty words might be steeped in honey,
> But for all the flattery, she was as unhappy as before.
>   That old creature's brow remained locked in a frown,
> Scaring to death that pretty maiden of sixteen!

Second sister said, "Madam, why have you not gone to your back room downstairs to rest and instead come to this southern upstairs room?" The old madam said with a stern face, "I wouldn't come without reason. Those who serve as sisters in a house also have to act as sisters, so that in spring they can wear spring clothes and in summer can wear summer clothes. You are one of the sisters, so I've come to collect a few ounces of silver for expenses." Second sister replied, "Madam, have you lost your mind? I am not seeing any guests, so where would I get silver?" "You damned slave!" the bawd said. "Tell me something; young and old, we work hard each month to provide you with food. When will this come to an end?"

> This One Stone-Weight of Gold showed a stern face;
> *Shouting at the top of her voice,*[5]
> She shouted, "You no-good lowlife!
> With your tilting head and turtle brain, you're no help at all!
>   You don't worry at all about the words 'food' and 'clothes'!
> Day in and day out, you know only how to fawn on me.
> So what possible use are you?
>   If from now on you don't receive customers,
> I'll prepare to send you back home!"

The old bawd descended the stairs in a towering rage, cursing all the while, and when she came to the back room downstairs, she said,

叫丫頭把那鞭子給我泡上。丫頭們聽說，驚魂千里，說：「咱媽又不知待打誰哩！」少不得把那大盆擡來，打上擔水，泡著鞭子。鴇兒道：「你去叫小二妮子來的。」丫頭聽說，跑上南樓，叫道：「二姐姐，咱媽請你哩。」二姐道：「媽娘才來到樓上罵了我一場，幾乎鞭子落在身上。」丫頭道：「二姐姐呀，逐日守著的人，你不知道他那性麼？咱媽又好吃盅酒，吃不多，又好醉了。今日不知他那裏吃了盅酒，到了後房裏睡了一霎，醒了說道：『我才把小二妮子罵了一場，諕著那孩子了。快請他來，我給他陪個不是。』我才來請你。」那二姐明知是待打他，無計奈何，下了南樓，跟著丫頭來到後房，看見虔婆說：「兒才冲撞媽娘，只可憐孩兒流落在他鄉。」二姐雙膝跪下。老鴇子用手挽起說：「我的兒，你起來罷。我有句話合你說，只怕你不依從。」二姐道：「家有千口，主事一人，不依你，待依誰？」鴇兒道：「你聽那先生說等皇帝，那皇帝又不來，可不耽誤了你？我合你說：揀那使大錢的，先接一個，掙他幾兩銀子，咱娘們且救急。日後再不着你接客，你可等那皇帝罷。」二姐說：「別的罷了，這個叫我難以從命。」媽娘道：「你真果不從？我一頓打死了你，只當掉了這幾百兩銀子！人是苦蟲，不打不成！我憐到你幾時！」怒冲冲把二姐採住，可就打起來了。

老虔婆怒冲冲，採住了紅喜星，每日疼你成何用？一手摟住青絲髮，鞭子一舉不留情，

6　A water-soaked whip will be heavier.

"Maids, soak my whip!"⁶ When the serving girls heard this, they were
scared witless and asked, "Who's the madam going to beat?" But they
brought out the biggest tub and fetched a load of water to soak the whip.
The bawd said, "Go and fetch that little second girl!" The serving girls
ran upstairs to her room and said, "Second sister, our madam is asking
for you!" Second sister replied, "The madam came a moment ago to my
room to curse me out. It was almost like being whipped!" The serving
girls said, "Second sister, you live by yourself all the time. Don't you know
what she's like? Our madam likes to drink a beaker of wine, and if she
doesn't drink too much, she just gets drunk. But today she had a beaker
of wine somewhere, and after she slept if off in her room, she woke up
and said, 'Just now I cursed out that little second girl, scaring the hell
out of her. Quickly, call her over, so I can make amends.' That's why we
came to ask you down."

Second sister knew quite well that the madam wanted to give her a
beating, but as she saw no way out, she could only follow the maids to
the backroom downstairs. Seeing the madam, she said, "A moment ago I
offended you, madam. Please pity your child, lost far from home." When
second sister knelt down on both knees, the old bawd pulled her up and
said, "My child, please rise! I have something to say to you, but I fear you
will not obey me." Second sister replied, "'There might be a thousand
people in the house, but there is only one master.' Whom would I obey
if not you?" The bawd said, "Ever since you heard the words of that fortune-teller, you have waited for the emperor, but no emperor has ever
shown up. Isn't that ruining your life? So I tell you: pick some big spend-
ers and start by receiving one, so that you can earn some ounces of silver
and our problems will be solved. After that, I won't order you to receive
customers again and will let you wait for your emperor." Second sister
replied, "Anything else would be fine, but I cannot accept this order."
The madam said, "You really are going to disobey me? If I beat you to
death this time, it'll just be losing an investment of a few hundred ounces
of silver! People are pitiable insects that will not grow without beating.
How long can I go on loving you?" In a terrible rage, she grabbed second
sister and started to whip her.

> The old madam was in a terrible rage
> And tightly grabbed that red star of joy.
> "What's the use of cherishing you each day?"
> With one hand she held onto her shiny black hair.
> Once the whip was raised, it knew no compassion!

嫩嫩的皮兒難扎掙。小二姐冤聲不住，叫親娘饒我的殘生。

那虔婆打了二十多鞭子，就不打了，叫丫頭給我泡著乜鞭子，歇歇再打。說道：「你穿着衣服支架子麼？是你掙的麼？」叫丫頭給我剝了，只剝的赤條條的。二姐跪在那旁邊，見那水盆裏泡的那鞭子無數，自家說道：「老賤人實落落的要打，再打我就捱不的了。自古道：『猛風入井團團轉，為人何不順時行？』我將好言哄他哄他，若信了，我上南樓上吊尋死，抹頭服毒，都在於我。」

小二姐見識高，叫媽娘你聽著：我今接客休心躁。今晚若有客來到，就是叫化也留下嫖，無錢難說乾懂樂。老鴇子滿心歡喜，我的兒這就是了。

那老鴇子聽的說接客，走近前來，兩手抱住二姐說：「我的兒！我怎麼打你這些！」叫丫頭：「拿衣服來，給你二姐姐穿上，赤條條的甚麼道理。」二姐穿上衣服。媽兒又道：「拿坐來，站的這孩子慌了。」二姐坐下。媽兒又道：「拿酒來，給你二姐姐壓驚。」二姐道：「你就忘了麼？我從小酒肉不吃。」媽兒道：「我就忘了。」叫丫頭：「把盅子接下，壓的你姐姐手疼。」

老虔婆心裏懂，叫二姐你聽言：酒樓有個軍家漢，

7   To abstain from meat and alcohol as well as pungent spices is an act of piety in Buddhism.

Her tender skin was unable to withstand its blows.
   Little second sister cried for mercy without end,
Shouting, "Dear mother, spare my poor life!"

When the madam had administered her twenty lashes of the whip, she stopped and ordered the serving girls, "Soak me more whips. I'll take a rest and then whip her again." And she said to second sister, "Do those clothes that you wear look good on you? Did you earn them with hard work?" She ordered the serving girls, "Strip her!" So they stripped her stark naked. Second sister was kneeling to one side, and as she saw that no end of whips were being soaked in the tub, she thought to herself, "That old creature is determined to whip me, and when she does, I won't be able to bear it. Since ancient times it has been said, 'When a fierce wind enters the well, all the water turns around. So why should a human being not follow along?' I will mislead her with some kind words, and once she believes me, I will go upstairs to my room and hang myself or take poison, whichever I decide."

Little second sister, choosing the smartest way,
Said, "Dear mother, please listen to me.
From now on I'll take customers, don't worry!
   If a customer comes to visit tonight,
I will let him sleep with me even if he's a beggar,
But without money, there cannot be talk of providing pleasure."
   The old bawd was filled with joy at these words,
"My darling child, this is the way it should be!"

When the old bawd heard that she would see customers, she rushed forward and embraced her, saying, "My child, how could I give you such a lashing?" And she ordered the serving girls, "Get second sister her clothes. She can't stand there stark naked!" When second sister had put on her clothes, the madam said, "Get her a seat! This child has been standing long enough." When second sister had taken a seat, the madam said, "Get her some wine, so that second sister can get over her fright." But second sister said, "Have you forgotten? Since I was young, I haven't had any alcohol or meat."[7] So the madam said, "I had forgotten!" She ordered the serving girls, "Take that beaker! It's so heavy that it hurts your sister's hands."

The old madam was happy at heart
And said, "Listen, second sister.
A soldier is staying over at the inn,

仗義疎財手段大，十兩銀子見面錢，金豆一盒九個半。我的兒你陪他一晚，哄著他使些憨錢。

小二姐喜氣生；叫媽娘你是聽：富貴貧賤前生定，要接皇帝沒修下，且顧家中時下窮，掙他幾兩來費用。咱又無園林桑棗，全憑著和氣爲生。

　　鴇兒說：「我兒，正是這等。只爲咱這日子貧窮，若是那幾年，我還掙出錢來了，我也不肯。你快去南樓梳妝，出院去罷。」那二姐守著虔婆，不敢啼哭；離了他媽，就放聲大哭，上南樓去了。千想萬想，走又沒處走，待要尋死，又不得空。這樣苦楚，惟有心知。不知佛動心出院不出院，且聽下回分解。

8　*Heqi* 和氣 (union of ethers) may be rendered as "friendship," but here the term more likely refers to sexual intercourse (*heqi* 合氣).

And he disperses his wealth on the basis of righteousness, a big
   spender!
He gave ten ounces of silver to make your acquaintance,
And this box of gold beans weighs nine and a half!
    My child, when you keep him company tonight,
Sweet-talk that guy into foolishly spending more cash!"

Little second sister was filled with joy
And said, "Dear madam, please listen!
Wealth and nobility, poverty and vile status, are set by fate.
    I wanted to receive the emperor, but lack that karma.
So, considering the desperate poverty of our family,
I will earn some of his silver to meet our needs.
    As we don't have gardens or groves, mulberry trees or fruit
      trees,
We must rely on the union of ethers to make a living."[8]

"My child," the bawd said, "that is indeed the way it is. It is all because we
are so desperately poor these days. If I still had the years, I would be able
to make some money and wouldn't have agreed to whip you. Now quickly
go to your room and get dressed to leave the ward." In the presence of the
madam, second sister didn't dare cry, but when the madam had left her,
she fell to loud wailing. Once she had gone upstairs to her room, she pondered her situation from all angles: there was nowhere she could run too,
and she wouldn't have a chance to commit suicide. This bitter misery she
would have to suffer in silence. If you don't know whether Buddha's Lust
went outside the ward, please listen to the following chapter.

第十一回 二姐被逼怨老鴇 丫頭定計哄朝廷

話說二姐哭上南樓，望著揚州叫了聲爹娘：「你閃的我好苦也！」一發尋思一發恨，可就傷感起來了。

第一怨怨爹娘，只顧你早先亡，撇的孩兒沒頭向。七歲落在姑娘手，賣在煙花去爲娼，朝打暮罵無指望。你死在黃泉之下，怎知兒苦處難當！

第二怨怨姑娘，罵潑賤太不良，心如蛇蠍一般樣。爹娘死去託了你，圖財就把天理傷，老天只在頭直上。我合你那輩子冤恨，害的我進退恓惶！

第三怨怨賤人，罵虔婆忒狠心，我死在黃泉把你恨。好家人養的兒合女，打著合人家漢子親，良心天理順不順？眼望著家鄉遙遠，誰是我六眷的親人？

---

1   "The Yellow Springs" refers to the underworld, the world of the dead.

11　Second sister, put under pressure, resents the old bawd;
The serving girls devise a scheme to fool the emperor.

Let me tell you, second sister, weeping, ascended the stairs to her southern upstairs room. Facing the direction of Yangzhou, she repeatedly called to her parents, "You abandoned me to a life of suffering!" The more she pondered, the angrier she became, until finally she was overcome with grief.

"My first resentment is toward my parents:
You cared only for your early quick deaths,
Abandoning your child to a lack of recourse.
　At the age of seven, I fell into the hands of my aunt,
Who sold me to a brothel to become a prostitute—
Beaten at dawn, reviled at night, a life without hope.
　You died and now stay below the Yellow Springs.[1]
How can you understand my unbearable misery?

My second resentment is toward my aunt.
I curse her as a vile lowlife without any morals,
With a heart like that of an adder or scorpion!
　When my parents died, they entrusted me to you,
But coveting cash, you violated all rules of nature.
Yet Old Heaven hovers above your head!
　In which prior life did we form this vengeful feud?
You've harmed me so much I don't know what to do.

My third resentment is toward that scum.
I curse that old madam as too cruel by nature.
I'll hate you even when I'm dead at the Yellow Springs!
　As a child I was raised by a decent family,
But you force me to sleep with some unknown fellow.
Is that in keeping with your conscience and morals?
　I stare toward my home village so far, far away.
Who on earth are my family members and relatives?

第四怨怨青天，生下奴苦難言，俺又沒把天條犯。既在空中為神聖，這樣苦人在世間，也該睜眼看一看。若不是前生造孽，現放著劍樹刀山。

第五怨怨自家，想前身作事差，今生落在他人下。照照菱花看看影，叫聲薄命的小冤家，幾時捱彀打合罵？到不如懸梁高弔，一條繩命染黃沙！

　　話說那佛動心在南樓慟哭不題。他那丫頭裏有兩個聰明雅致的，二姐極喜他，因着自家待接皇帝，便一個叫金墩，一個叫玉座。二人上前說：「二姐姐，媽娘請你去說什麼來，回來只管哭？」二姐道：「說嘎到是小事，一頓鞭子幾乎打死！」丫頭說：「哎喲！爲什麼就打？」二姐道：「嗔我不接軍漢，就打呢。」丫頭道：「好異樣！你待不去接，着別人去不的麼？」二姐道：「那天殺的冤家，指名字單要我。」丫頭道：「咱就去罷，爲什麼受他那打？那漢子既單要你，還是愛你，他那裏有殺場哩麼？」二姐道：「你去的道容易！」丫頭說：「不去可怎麼著呢？」二姐道：「我情願吊殺死在樓上！」丫頭道：「姐姐，你好嘲！這點小事就上吊，若大似這個着呢，就該怎麼着呢？」

有金墩把頭搖，叫姐姐你好嘲，那裏犯著就上吊？轉了快活不算帳，還得他銀子一大包，

My fourth resentment is directed toward Blue Heaven:
You gave me life, but my sufferings are unspeakable,
Even though I never transgressed any heavenly injunction.
    Since you are a divine sage up in the sky above,
While people on earth are suffering in this manner,
You should open your eyes and take a good look!
    It must be because of a sin committed in a prior life,
That I now face trees of swords and hills of knives!

My fifth resentment is toward myself.
I must have acted wrongly in previous lives,
So in this life I've ended up lower than others.
    When I look in the mirror and see my reflection,
I call out, "My little friend, how poor is your fate!
How long can you bear the beating and cursing?
    It would be better to hang myself from the highest beam
And end my life with a single cord, dyeing the earth!"

Now let us leave Buddha's Lust weeping in her upstairs room. Two of
her serving maids were intelligent and beautiful, so second sister loved
them. Because she was waiting to receive the emperor, she called one of
them Golden Stool and the other Jade Seat. These two stepped forward
and said, "What did the madam say to you to make you weep like this on
your return?" Second sister replied, "What she said isn't the issue. She
almost whipped me to death!" The serving girls exclaimed, "Why did she
whip you?" Second sister said, "She was angry that I refused to receive
some soldier, that's why!" The serving girls said, "How strange! If you
didn't want to receive him, why didn't she tell someone else to go?" Second sister replied, "The damned fiend ordered me by name." The serving
maids said, "So let's go! Why should you suffer her beating? If he asked for
you specifically, he must love you and not want to kill you." Second sister
replied, "You think it's that easy to go?" The serving maids retorted, "But
what will you do if you don't go?" Second sister said, "I'm happy to hang
myself and die here in my room!" The serving girls replied, "Sister, you're
ridiculous! If you'd hang yourself over such a trifle, what would you do if
things were even worse?"

Golden Stool shook her head
And said, "Sister, you're ridiculous!
How could this be worth hanging yourself?
    To the contrary, there's pleasure beyond reckoning,
And in addition you'll get a large packet of silver.

世間嘎似這個妙？若是我三宵兩夜，管着他拿不住瓦刀。

　　金墩勸勾多時。二姐說：「誰像你那不值錢的貨！」二姐罵了金墩幾句，依舊柳眉雙蹙，杏眼含愁。到是玉座在旁說：「我有一計。」二姐忙問：「何計？快快說來。」好丫頭笑嬉嬉，勸姐姐休撇急，我有一條絕妙的計。咱觪同到玉火巷，你可藏的嚴實實，俺㑉上樓把你替。那軍家辨什麼眞假，咱只顧哄他的那東西。

　　二姐聽說，滿心歡喜，遂笑道：「你眞果肯替我？」丫頭道：「十八的大姐做媳婦，還等不到黑天哩。」

　　二姐又笑了笑道：「只怕你替不過。」丫頭道：「那漢子不過是聞名，他見了你幾遭？他就嫌模樣差些，也只說是有名無實，出上他不嫖就是了，咱媽娘知道哩麼？穿上衣裳咱去罷。」二姐聽說，進了繡房。

擦了眼去梳妝，穿幾套好衣裳，蛾眉淡掃嫦娥樣。朱唇一點櫻桃口，十指尖尖玉笋長，眞如一朵花初放。粧成了丫環也愛，上合下仔細的端相。

　　二姐打扮的齊齊整整，下樓去辭老鴇。

2　In other words, "I would exhaust him in bed until he had no strength left."

> What in the world could be as wonderful as this?
>   If it were me who stayed with him a few nights,
>   I'd make sure that he couldn't even hold a trowel!"[2]

When Golden Stool had tried to talk her around for quite a while, second sister said, "Why are you so vile?" Second sister cursed her, but then she contracted her willow-leaf eyebrows into a frown while her apricot eyes were filled with sorrow. Then Jade Seat said, "I have a plan!" Second sister promptly asked her, "What kind of plan? Please tell me, now!"

> The kind serving girl, all smiles,
> Urged her, "Second sister, don't panic!
> I've come up with a marvelous scheme!
>   The three of us will go together to Jade-Fire Lane,
> But you will have to hide yourself carefully.
> The two of us will go upstairs and take your place.
>   That soldier will be unable to tell true from false.
> We'll sweet-talk him out of his stuff."

When second sister heard this, she was filled with joy and said with a smile, "Are you really willing to substitute for me?" The servant girls replied, "'When a girl of eighteen has become a bride, she cannot wait for nightfall.'" Second sister laughed and laughed again, saying, "My only fear is that you won't be able to pull it off." The servant girls said, "That fellow has only heard your name. Has he seen your face? Even if he finds our features not to his liking, he can only say that the facts don't live up to the fame. All that can happen is that he doesn't sleep with us, and how would the madam find out about that? Put on your clothes and let's go." When second sister heard this, she entered her embroidery room.

> She rubbed her eyes and did her toilet,
> Putting on some of her finest clothes,
> Her curved eyebrows lightly drawn, like Chang'e's.
>   A little dot of red gave her a cherry mouth;
> Her ten tapering fingers were jade bamboo shoots.
> She truly resembled a flower about to bloom!
>   Her toilet finished, even the serving girls loved her,
> As they carefully inspected her from head to toe.

When second sister had dressed herself to perfection, she came downstairs and said goodbye to the old bawd.

佛動心把頭低，忍不住淚恓恓，哭哭啼啼下樓去。未曾進房擦了淚，見了虔婆笑嬉嬉，得罪媽娘休生氣。爲兒的待不接客，咱娘們要吃飯穿衣。

　　二姐說：「媽娘，我來給你磕頭，好去接客。」鴇子道：「好兒，磕什麼頭。像你大姐姐，我養活他恁麼大小，還沒給我磕個頭，不想你這孩子倒有禮數。好兒，我不怪你，你去罷。」那二姐出了後房門，仍是一陣心酸。佛動心低著頭，未出門淚交流，叫不應的龍天佑。萬丈火坑沒有底，今日方纔初上頭，幾時孽債填還勾？罵一聲狠心的老鴇，我合你那世裏冤仇！

佛動心出院門，小脚兒印香塵，更比月裏嫦娥俊。聲聲環佩叮噹噹，從容款步擺繡羅裙，未曾過去香一陣。笑一笑千金也難買，引掉了人的眞魂。

　　二姐出院，有［西江月］一首爲証：

　　　蓮步輕盈出戶，芳塵印去無蹤。行來楊柳弄春風，好似花枝擺動。

3　The last three characters of this line read *long tian you* 龍天佑. Zhang Tai 2019 (691) reads these as the name of a historical person, Long Tianyou (1644–1690), who was renowned for his virtue. This would result in the following translation of this line, "As she called on the unresponsive Long Tianyou." I do not find Zhang's interpretation convincing.

Buddha's Lust lowered her head
And could not stop herself from crying
As she walked down the stairs.
    Before she entered the room, she rubbed her eyes,
And when she saw the madam, she was all smiles,
"I offended you, mother, but please don't be angry.
    Your daughter did not want to receive any guests,
But we women need food to eat and clothes to wear."

Second sister said, "Madam, please allow me to kowtow to you before I leave to see my customer." The bawd replied, "Dear child, why would you want to kowtow? Even your elder sister, whom I raised for many years, has never kowtowed to me. I never thought that you would have such a sense of decorum. Dear child, I'm not blaming you for anything. Just go." Second sister left the room, still filled with bitter sadness.

Buddha's Lust lowered her head.
Before she left the house, her tears fell
As she called on an unresponsive Dragon Heaven for help.[3]
    "This fiery pit of ten thousand rods is bottomless!
Today is the very first time I take on a customer.
When will I ever pay off my debt of bad karma?"
    She cursed that unfeeling old bawd,
"In what life did you and I form this feud?"

When Buddha's Lust went out of the ward,
Her little feet impressed the fragrant dust.
She was even prettier than Chang'e in the moon!
    Note upon note, her girdle pendants tinkled and jingled.
Walking with measured steps, she stroked her gauze skirt.
Even before she passed, her fragrance engulfed one.
    A thousand ounces could not buy a single smile
That would entice the true soul of any man on earth.

There is a lyric to the tune of "West River Moon" that describes second sister leaving the ward:

With lotus steps she graciously goes out the door,
But their impressions in the dust leave no trace.
When walking, she is a weeping willow in spring winds
And resembles a flowering twig set swaying.

巫山神女出現，仙姬私下天庭。相思撇在路途中，拾
得歸家害病。

二姐出離宣武院，往玉火巷來。未知何如，且聽下回
分解。

---

4 Witch Mountain (Wushan 巫山) is a peak in Western Hubei overlooking the Yangzi.
Legend has it that the goddess of this mountain once appeared to a king of the ancient
state of Chu in his dream and shared his couch. On leaving, she told the king that she
appeared during the daytime as rain and clouds on the mountain.

The goddess of Witch Mountain[4] appears to men;
An immortal maiden secretly descends from Heaven.
Here on earth she scatters lovers' yearning on the road.
Pick it up and back home you'll suffer that illness!

Second sister left the Displaying Martiality Ward and went to Jade-Fire Lane. If you don't know what happened next, please listen to the following chapter.

第十二回 佛動心瞞怨小六哥 武宗爺假怒小佳人

話說那佛動心出的院門，不一時來到酒店。六哥道：
「辛苦了你！該著轎子接你去方是，就著你步行了來。」
遂請二姐到了房中，讓了坐，遂即斟上一盅茶，說道：
「請茶了。」

請二姐吃盅茶，定定神解解乏，我且問你一句話：無事不出
宣武院，你來小店做什麼？誰敢勞動你尊駕？面帶着無限憂
色，莫不是受人的戲答？

六哥道：「你沒事不出院來，是接客來麼？」二姐道：
「別人不知道，你也不知道麼？我從幾時接客來？」六
哥道：「正是呢，你接的是皇帝呀，待接什麼客？」二
姐道：「我今日出院，不知虧了誰來！」

佛動心怕婆娑，俺今日受折磨，不知虧了那一個？多虧那個
精扯淡，害殺人的小哥哥，想來待他不曾錯。這一番作成看
顧，准備着給他念佛。

六哥道：「你這意思說的是我麼？」二姐說：「你害的人
進退兩難，還打四

12　Buddha's Lust is filled with resentment against little Brother Six;

His Majesty the Martial Ancestor feigns rage at the little beauties.

Let me tell you, Buddha's Lust left the ward and soon arrived at the inn. Brother Six said, "We should have ordered a sedan chair to carry you here! Instead, we had you walk the whole way." He invited second sister to his downstairs room, where he offered her a seat and poured her a beaker of tea, saying, "Second sister, please have some tea."

> He invited second sister to have a beaker of tea
> To settle her mind and recover from fatigue,
> "Please allow me to ask you a question.
> 　You don't leave the ward without reason.
> So why on earth have you come to our inn?
> Who dared trouble you to make this journey?
> 　Your face is covered with unlimited sorrow.
> Could it be that you have been pressured?"

Brother Six said, "You don't leave the ward without reason. Have you come here to see a guest?" Second sister replied, "Other people may not know, but you don't know either? Since when do I see customers?" Brother Six said, "That's right! You will only receive the emperor! What customer are you seeing?" Second sister said, "I don't know whom I have to thank for leaving the ward today!

> I, Buddha's Lust, feared the old woman,
> And that's why I suffer this misery today.
> I wonder, whom do I have to thank for this?
> 　I'm afraid I have to thank that damned prattler,
> That little brother who deserves to be killed,
> Though as far as I know, I never treated him badly.
> 　This time he has arranged this great opportunity,
> So I am ready to recommend him in my prayers."

Brother Six said, "Are you talking about me?" Second sister replied, "You harm people and leave them nowhere to turn, and still you pretend

不知呢！」六哥道：「好奇事！你接客不接客，累着我那大腿根哩，上我的帳？」

佛動心氣囔囔，小六哥你好促狹，合俺娘說的是什麼話？自從你才出門，狠心媽娘就打殺，一霎幾乎作精下！那鞭子雨點相似，險些兒逼殺俺奴家！

六哥道：「逼什麼？你掙了錢來我待使哩，怨人喇喇的。你還回去不的麼？」二姐道：「我不接客，我也不回去。」六哥道：「俺家裏既沒有皇帝，你就不該來。你來要帳來呀，可是來探親來呢，可是看朋友來呢？要帳俺又不該你嘎；探親呢，俺合您娼家有什麼親？若是看朋友，你是個丫頭家，俺又沒合你拜交，只怕你來看相厚的來。你又不接俺，俺又不嫖你，沒要緊。既不接客又不去，待怎麼樣？」二姐笑道：「我不出院罷了，我既出院，就有點事。」

佛動心笑嘻嘻，叫六哥你聽知：我安排人兒將我替，哄了別人哄不的你。奴家還要好央及，萬萬休要給俺撒了氣。我若是陪你乾爺，你就該叫我親姨。

六哥道：「小捶辣骨！你央及我，你可就先罵我。我可仔不給你撒湯。」慌的二姐笑了笑說：「罷罷！咱從幾時不玩來？你休怪我，我還拜你拜。」六哥道：「你且說，人家給你了見面錢，搬的是你，你待著誰替你？」

not to know anything?" Brother Six replied, "This is strange! Whether or not you want to see customers doesn't concern me at all, but you hold it against me!"

> Buddha's Lust was now quite angry.
> "Brother Six, don't joke with me.
> What did you discuss with my madam?
>   As soon as you left through the gate,
> That cruel madam set about whipping me.
> One more lash and I would have become a ghost!
>   The whip came down on me like drops of rain.
> She had nearly killed me!"

Brother Six said, "So why blame me? Will I get some of the money you make? You're filled with resentment, but you can go back, can't you?" Second sister said, "I will not see any customers, and I won't go back either." Brother Six said, "There's no emperor here, so you shouldn't have come. But since you did come, you must have some purpose. Did you come here to visit a relative? Or did you come here to see a friend? You're wrong to fault me in this. No one here could be a relative of a prostitute, and since you're a wench, we're not true friends. I can only think that you've come to see someone you're close to. You're not here to see me, and I'm not your customer, but that isn't important. However, what are you doing here, if you're not seeing a customer and you're not leaving?" Second sister said with a smile, "I should not have left the ward, but since I have, there's just one small thing."

> Buddha's Lust, wrapped in smiles,
> Said, "Brother Six, now please listen.
> I have arranged for someone to take my place.
>   We can fool someone else, but we can't fool you,
> So I implore you from the bottom of my heart:
> Please don't, under any circumstances, spill the beans!
>   If I end up together with your adoptive father,
> You will, of course, have to call me dear Auntie."

Brother Six said, "You little slut! You ask for my help, and in the same breath you curse me. Of course I won't spill the beans!" A flustered second sister laughed and said with a smile, "Let's leave it at that! Since when can't we have some fun? If you don't blame me, I'll bow to you." Brother Six said, "Tell me, someone gave you money to make your acquaintance, and here you are, so who's substituting for you?"

二姐指著丫頭道：「他䞕。」六哥看了看道：「只怕替不過呀。」二姐道：「你休管俺，他認的是誰。」六哥道：「隨你的便。」二姐道：「金墩你先去。」金墩說：「六哥哥，你給俺報報。」六哥道：「只會賣酒，不會給你撈毛。」金墩扭了扭道：「不給俺報罷！小撕廝你三十里、五十里不知道路徑，走上叉道去了，身量大叫你背着我哩。」

好金墩急忙忙，辭二姐出了房，抖抖精神把樓上。一脚深來一脚淺，心裏盤算腿兒慌，上去樓臺走了樣。一脚兒跌在地上，好一似倒了堵高牆。

那金墩上去樓臺，把嘴兒拄了又拄，施展着上前說話。貪往前看，沒提防當路一個脚㴲子，絆了一脚，跌了三四尺近遠。萬歲諕了一驚：「是什麼人，怎麼不說話，樓著乜黑影裏？是怎麼說呢？」那金墩扒起來，抖搜了抖搜那衣裳，拿捏着拜了兩拜，說道：「是我。」皇爺說：「你是誰？」金墩說：「你搬的是誰？」皇爺說：「我搬的是佛動心。」金墩說：「我就是那佛動心呢。」有金墩走向前，叫姐夫咱有緣，媽娘着我來陪伴。幸遇姐夫待玩耍，村賣俏吃先講錢，稱了銀子好進院。萬歲爺嗤的聲笑了，這奴才不值個低錢。

金墩雖有些模樣，那裏看在萬歲眼裏，遂笑道：「你自己看不見你自己，

---

1   That is, her heart was beating as rapidly as the counters are moved on an abacus.

Second sister pointed to the serving girls and said, "These two!" Brother Six looked them over and said, "I'm afraid they won't be able to pull it off." But second sister said, "Don't worry about us. Does he know any of us?" So Brother Six said, "Have it your way."

Second sister said, "Golden Stool, you go first." Golden Stool asked, "Dear Brother Six, please announce me." But Brother Six said, "I only know how to sell wine, I can't be your pimp." Golden Stool pouted her lips and said, "So don't announce me. You little nobody, if we lose our way after thirty or fifty *li* and come to a fork in the road, I'll have you carry me on your back, since you're such a big guy!"

> Good Golden Stool was in quite a hurry;
> Having left second sister outside the room,
> She roused her spirits and ascended the stairs.
> One step was heavy, the next one was light;
> Her heart was an abacus,[1] her legs went weak.
> As she ascended the stairs, she lost courage.
> She stumbled and fell on the planks of the floor
> As if a high wall had come tumbling down.

When Golden Stool went up the stairs, she pouted her lips again and again, displaying how she would step forward and speak. Eagerly looking in front of her, she didn't notice the leg of a chair blocking her way. When it hit her leg, she stumbled three or four feet forward. The emperor was startled. "Who's there? How come you don't say a word, but lurk there in the shadows? What's going on?" Golden Stool scrambled up, straightened her clothes, and, bowing with airs, said, "It's me." When the emperor asked, "But who are you?" Golden Stool replied, "Whom did you send for?" When the emperor said, "I sent for Buddha's Lust," Golden Stool replied, "Then I am Buddha's Lust."

> Golden Stool, stepping forward,
> Said, "Brother-in-law, we have a karmic bond.
> The madam ordered me to keep you company.
> It's my good fortune you want to have fun,
> But selling snacks, first you set a price.
> Weigh out the silver, then I can return."
> His Majesty laughed with a snort,
> "This common slave isn't worth a cropped coin!"

Even though Golden Stool wasn't bad looking, she couldn't please the emperor, who said with a smile, "You have never seen yourself.

待我誇你誇。」金墩說：「你可誇的我好着些，我見了
人好支架子。」

佛動心你站下，聽着我把你誇：窄窄金蓮半尺大，鼻子孔好
似灶突樣，兩根黃毛一大抓，櫻桃小口瓢來大。莫不是東洋
大海潮，出來的巡海夜叉？

金墩道：「哎喲！我屬煎餅的，你誇攤了我了！」皇爺
說：「我再誇你一誇罷。」

拆破襖做背褡，大補丁白線巴，栗子布裙彭彭乍，汗巾破了
沒顏色，紫花布鞋扣上花。纂兒不勾棗核大，滿臉上搽些土
粉，好一似發了粉的東瓜。

金墩說：「俺就乜麼樣哩？」萬歲笑了一笑，說道：「等
我再給你數數那些孤老罷。」

耍和尚接扛夫，錢十個酒一壺，土炕上褪下半截褲。那腥臊
爛臭的邋遢兔，雞毛店裏那無賴徒，青天白日把蠶蛾婪。哝
殺人這般模樣，還想著要把人虜！

那金墩羞愧滿面，跑下樓來，叫聲姐姐：「替不的了！」
二姐問道：「怎麼着來？」

2   A yaksha is an ugly demon. One of the popular tales in Pu Songling's *Strange Stories of Make-do Studio* is called "The Yakshas and the Sea Market" (*Yecha haishi* 夜叉海市). In this tale, a handsome young man traveling at sea is blown by a typhoon to an island inhabited by yakshas, where his beauty is despised as ugly.
3   A common metaphor for breasts.
4   Rabbits are well-known for their sexual activity. The term also refers to male prostitutes.

Let me praise you." Golden Stool replied, "You'd better praise me well, so I can present myself to others."

> "Buddha's Lust, now stand there
> And listen while I praise you:
> Your tiny golden lotuses are more than half a foot.
>   Your nostrils look like the openings of chimneys,
> Your two tufts of brown hair are one big handful,
> And your small cherry mouth is as big as a gourd.
>   You must be a yaksha[2] patrolling the ocean
> And emerging from the eastern sea!"

Golden Stool said, "Oh, I'm a baked cake! You've praised me flat." The emperor said, "Let me praise you again!

> Your vest is made of a tattered coat,
> With a big added piece stitched with white thread;
> That chestnut linen skirt balloons out all over.
>   Your handkerchief is torn and faded;
> Flowers are tied to your nankeen shoes;
> Your buns[3] aren't even as big as the pits of dates.
>   You have cheap powder caked all over your face,
> So you look like a moldy old winter melon."

Gold Stool said, "Do I really look like that?" The emperor laughed and said, "Now let me enumerate your patrons!

> You invite monks and receive porters:
> For ten coins and one jug of wine,
> You'll pull down your pants on a *kang*!
>   Those malodorous stinking rabbits in rags[4]
> And lowlifes from chicken-feather inns[5]
> Will shag such a cheap tart in broad daylight.
>   Your appearance is totally disgusting,
> But still you hope to catch a man."

Overcome by shame, Golden Stool ran down the stairs, shouting, "Sister, I can't take your place!" When second sister asked her why,

---

5   "Chicken-feather inns" are places that provide the poor with a place to sleep. They provide not beds, but rooms filled with chicken feathers in which guests can sleep to ward off the cold.

金墩撅著嘴說道：「那漢子光貶扯人，又是瓢，又是桃哩，夜叉哩，東瓜哩！」玉座說：「你好出醜！你就是豬八戒家生的那孩子，弄出那些醜樣子來了。你看我去。」二姐說：「你可好生著。」玉座平日嘴尖舌巧，快語花言，便說：「不是我誇句海口，調嘴頭也招住他了。」二姐說：「千萬仔細着！這一遭替不下來，剃頭匠吆喝，可就沒了換頭了。」

叫姐姐不要忙，休拿我當尋常，人物還在金墩上。況且生來嘴頭巧，話是出馬一條槍，姐姐休愁把心放。憑着我去賣風俏，管着他叫我親娘。

玉座出了房門，賣弄他那輕狂，就忘了裝着那名妓的體統，典雅的行持，改不了那梅香的樣子，把兩根腿輪打開，懂懂的好似那馬耍蹄、驢打槽，兵天嗑地的走上樓來，說：「姐夫，我這裏拜哩。」皇爺說：「你是什麼人？」玉座道：「我可就是那佛動心了呢。」皇爺說：「你這宣武院裏佛動心有頭號、二號麼？」玉座說：「怎麼頭號、二號呢？」皇爺說：「方纔去了一個，又來了一個。」玉座說：「那是假的，我是真的。」萬歲聽說，看了一看，笑道：「你比那一個的模樣還略強點。」

武宗爺笑顏生，你強他一丁丁，坑合蓆差一迷迷縫。赤淌臉兒半欄腳，若在山溝頂蓆柵，你的生意比他興。看起你千般扭捏，這可就不值個操閧。

---

6   Zhu Bajie (Pigsy) is a character in the sixteenth-century novel *Journey to the West* (*Xiyou ji* 西遊記). As a pig spirit, he has the ugly features and sexual appetite of a pig.

7   There is no space between a *kang* and the mat placed on it.

Golden Stool pouted her lips and said, "That guy really drags you down. First I'm a gourd, then a peach, a yaksha, or a winter melon!" Jade Seat said, "You've exposed your ugly side. You must have been born in the family of Zhu Bajie⁶ to show so much ugliness. Just watch me go!" Second sister said, "Be careful!" Jade Seat had all her life been someone with a sharp tongue. "I'm not bragging about my rhetorical skills, but once I open my mouth, I'll subdue him!" Second sister said, "Be very cautious. If you can't pull it off, the barber who shaves heads will have to yell—there's no back-up head."

> She said, "Dear sister, don't be concerned
> And take me as somebody totally ordinary.
> My figure is better than that of Golden Stool.
>   Moreover, from birth I've been a shrewd talker.
> My tongue is my lance when I sally forth.
> Sister, don't be upset and set your worries aside.
>   Trust that I'll show off my charms.
> I'll make him call me 'Mommy' for sure!"

When Jade Seat left the room, she showed off her light-hearted bravado and forgot to adopt the demeanor of a famed courtesan with scrupulous behavior. Unable to shake off the manner of a servant, she walked with large steps, as happily as a horse trying out its hooves or a donkey kicking its trough. She stomped up the stairs and said, "Brother-in-law, let me bow to you." The emperor asked, "Who are you?" Jade Seat replied, "I am Buddha's Lust." The emperor asked, "Does the Displaying Martiality Ward have a number one Buddha's Lust and a number two Buddha's Lust?" Jade Seat said, "What do you mean by a number one and a number two?" The emperor said, "One just left, and here comes another!" Jade Seat said, "That one was a fake. I am the real one." Hearing this, the emperor had a good look, and said with a smile, "You do look somewhat better than the first one."

> His Majesty the Martial Ancestor smiled,
> "You indeed look a tiny bit better than she:
> The infinitesimal seam between the *kang* and the mat.⁷
>   With your sunburned red face and half-bound feet
> And working from a mat shed in a mountain gully,
> Your business would be busier than hers.
>   But if one looks at your thousands of postures,
> They don't earn a single round of applause."

玉座說：「少誚罷，俺相與的都是上人上官的。」萬歲嗤了一聲說：「我着你可暈着我了。」

嘴兒大胭脂塗，臉兒黑宮粉糊，怎麼上的那娘子數？死了老婆的窮光棍，十年沒人叫丈夫，纔叫你去縫縫褲。佛動心若是這等，那無名的就不是個人乎？

那玉座把頭扭了扭，說道：「褒貶是買主。待說我好罷，又恐怕要的宿錢太多了；說不好，糊突着玩玩罷了。」

叫姐夫休胡嘲，我看你無個操，故意才把皮來燥。車軸脖子油光臉，門樓頭來鼻子糟，心裏倒比那齊整的俏。那知道追懂賣笑，也跟著糊突聞騷。

萬歲爺氣昂昂，罵一聲他髒娘，我今說你休要嚷。自家裝着黃花女，胸前兩塊乍胖胖，行動又帶些奴才樣。好歪貨不流水快走，近前惡心的我慌！

玉座聽說，怒冲冲的當面就還上了．

有玉座怒冲冲，叫姐夫理不通，

Jade Seat said, "Don't chide me. I associate only with superior persons and high officials." The emperor said, "I say, you make me dizzy!

> With your big mouth and ample rouge,
> Your dark face and smeared powder,
> How can you be counted among the whores?
>   Only a poor bare stick whose wife has died
> And hasn't been called 'husband' for ten years
> Would have you mend the seam of his pants!
>   If Buddha's Lust is indeed of this high quality,
> Then those without fame must not be human!"

Jade Seat turned her head away and said, "It's up to the buyer to evaluate the wares. If you say that I'm fine, you're afraid that my fee for the night will be too much. But if you say I'm no good, we can just muddle through and have fun."

> She said, "Brother-in-law, don't mock me,
> In my opinion, you lack any integrity,
> And you scorch my skin on purpose.
>   You have a neck like an axle, your face shines with oil;
> You have a head like a gateway, and a nose that's rotten.
> But inside are you still more handsome than decent types?
>   What do you know of seeking pleasure and selling smiles?
> All you've heard of romance comes from bungling fools!"

> His Majesty was overcome with rage
> And he cursed her out as a dirty sleazebag.
> "I'm telling you to shut your trap!
>   You may pretend to be a virgin maiden,
> But those flaps on your chest are too fat.
> Your behavior reeks too much of a slave!
>   You're crooked goods, and if you don't leave as fast as you can,
> You'll get a taste of a man who's had it!"

When Jade Seat heard this, she was overcome by fury and flung it back in his face.

> Jade Seat was overcome by fury
> And said, "Brother-in-law, you're not making any sense!

好人不識好人敬。靸鞋說破還沒破，布衫說青又不青，氈帽說硬又不硬。你只像宣武院裏，俺支使的那個琴童。

萬歲大怒，罵了一聲賤人，拿起鞭子打將下去。

大丫頭說話擺，擺著尾搖着頭，皇帝氣惱龍眉皺。奴才大膽忒無禮，走的慢了把筋抽，若還回來打你個够！萬歲爺一聲吆喝，好玉座顛下了酒樓。

玉座激惱了萬歲，撞下了樓來。未知後事如何，且聽下回分解。

8 A "lute boy" is a gentleman's servant, so named because he carries his master's lute (or seven-stringed zither, as the case may be). The suggestion is that the boy also may share his master's bed, and that the "lute boy" employed in a courtesan's house is a catamite.

You don't appreciate respect when it's shown to you.
  I'd call your soft boots worn, but they're not yet worn;
I'd call your linen gown blue, but then it isn't blue;
I'd call your felt hat stiff, but then it isn't stiff.
  You look like that little lute boy[8]
We order about in the Displaying Martiality Ward.

 The emperor exploded with rage and shouted, "Vile creature!" Then he grabbed his whip to beat her.

When the serving girl was done speaking,
She wagged her tail and shook her head.
But the angered emperor frowned his dragon brow.
  "You brazen slave, you lack all decency!
If you run too slow, I'll pull out your tendons!
And if you dare come back, I'll whip you to a pulp."
  His Majesty the emperor gave one shout,
And kind Jade Seat tumbled down the stairs!

 When Jade Seat had angered the emperor, he pushed her down the stairs of the wine house. If you don't know what happened next, please listen to the following chapter.

第十三回 二姐初承御面歡 丫頭再定金蟬計

話說那玉座跑下樓來，諕的面如金紙，低頭無言。
大丫頭撅著嘴，半晌無言頭不回，諕的兩手無了脈。進門叫
聲二姐姐，吃不盡你無限虧，幾乎成了王邦貴。若是不連顛
帶跑，險些兒捱頓好捶！

丫頭下的樓來，叫聲姐姐：「替不的了！」二姐道：「怎
麼替不的？」丫頭道：「若光論嘴頭，我也照的住他；
只末了一句話，說的他就惱了。」二姐道：「你說什麼
來？」丫頭道：「我說他像咱家支使的那小琴童，他就
惱了，一頓鞭子就打下我樓來了。」二姐道：「奴才好
大膽，你就敢說他那個！虧了他性子好，若打你一頓
時，死不了也發過昏。」六哥道：「極好！叫您姊妹們
來接客來，叫您來罵客來麼？您媽娘若知道了，你有死
無活！」二姐道：「你弄的這等模樣，可叫誰替我？」
玉座道：「他原搬的是你，還得你去。」二姐聽說，滿
心好惱。

佛動心痛傷懷，想是我命裏該，

---

1   Wang Banggui is otherwise unknown.

13   Second sister is smiled upon by
His Imperial Countenance for the
first time;
A servant girl comes up with yet another
cunning scheme of substitution.

Let me tell you, Jade Seat ran down the stairs, with lowered head and not saying a word, so scared that her face looked like gilded paper.

> The big servant girl pouted her lips
> And remained silent a while, not turning around,
> So scared that no pulse was perceptible in either arm.
>   Entering the room, she cried, "Second sister,
> I cannot absorb your limitless misery!
> I nearly ended up like Wang Banggui!¹
>   And if I hadn't run off, head over heels,
> I might have received a sound trashing!"

When the servant girl came downstairs, she cried, "Second sister, I cannot substitute for you!" Second sister asked, "Why can't you substitute for me?" The servant replied, "If it were all just talk, I could give as good as I got. But I really pissed him off with what I said last." Second sister asked, "So what did you say?" The servant girl replied, "I told him that he was just like the little lute boy we employ, and he got so angry that he whipped me down the stairs." Second sister said, "Slave, how brazen to call him that! You're lucky he was so kind! If he'd given you a real whipping, you'd have fainted or else died." Brother Six remarked, "It serves you right! We told you to come and see a customer. Did we tell you to revile him? If your madam learns of this, you're dead!" Second sister said, "Now that you've messed things up, whom can I get to substitute for me?" Jade Seat replied, "He wanted you, so you'll have to go." When second sister heard this, she was terribly vexed.

> Buddha's Lust was deeply saddened inside:
> "I suppose that this must be my fate.

前生欠下風流債。欲待不上酒樓去，回去拷打怎麼挨？受不盡他無限害。想當是我錯了，就死了也不該出來。

我命苦對誰言，有煩惱積心間，我好將誰胡瞞怨？卻是奴家前生命，煙花相伴亂人眠，不管老少俺陪伴。到晚來無窮的夫主，天明了大不相干。

二姐滿眼落淚。丫頭道：「姐姐不要哭了，咱還有一計。」二姐姐道：「什麼計？」丫頭道：「咱今上樓去，見了姐夫，你只說樓上不是耍的去處，咱進院去玩的罷。哄他到院裏擺上酒來，姐姐你就先讓 /(左言右不)酒，只說是洗塵三杯，迎風三杯；俺這十個丫頭，每人也讓他三杯；他是鐵人，也就管醉了他。打發他睡了，你藏在旁裏，俺陪着他睡一宿。到了五更頭上，俺早些起來，你可去那牀頭上坐着。他若醒了找你，你可說我在這裏。他說你早起來爲何，你說院裏的規矩，從來這麼樣。不愁哄不了他。」二姐道：「奴才不要着那熟話來哄我。我欲不上樓，受不了老鴇子氣，少不了我自己去普白。六哥，你給我報報，我好上樓。」六哥道：「報什麼？俺家又沒有皇帝，你去罷。」二姐陪笑道：「大人不見小人過，你就合俺一般見識。不接客掙不了錢去，回家媽娘打我，你就看的上？」六哥道：「這話你早在那裏來？你等等，我給你報報。」

2   As a whore, she will sleep with any man without forming a lasting attachment.

In an earlier life I failed to repay a debt of romance.
　　If I don't go up to his room in this wine house,
How can I bear the beating on my return?
I couldn't take that endless torture.
　　I made a mistake right at the start:
Even facing death, I should never have left the ward!

"Whom can I tell the misery of my life?
This vexation is building up in my breast,
But against whom can I carry a grudge?
　　This must be my fate determined by a prior life.
Like smoke and fire, I will sleep with any man.[2]
Old or young, I have to accommodate them all.
　　Those innumerable husbands when evening falls
Will mean nothing to me by the break of dawn!"

As second sister wept uncontrollably, the servant girl said, "Sister, don't weep. I have still another scheme." Second sister asked, "What kind of scheme?" The servant girl replied, "We will go upstairs, and when you have greeted brother-in-law, you just tell him that his upstairs room is not a place to have fun, and that we should go to the ward to amuse ourselves. Once you've sweet-talked him into going to the ward, we set out wine and you invite him to drink. You say there are three cups to wash off the dust and three cups to welcome him. Each of us ten serving girls will also offer him three cups. Even if he's a man of steel, we'll get him drunk. When we take him to his bed, you hide yourself to one side, and I'll sleep with him for the night. If he wakes up and looks for you, you must say 'I'm here!' And when he asks why you got up so early, you just say that it's a set rule of the ward, and that it's always been that way. Don't worry. We'll be able to fool him." Second sister said, "Slave, don't fool me with your smooth talk. I don't want to go upstairs, but I cannot bear that old bawd's rage, so I have to go and take care of this matter. Brother Six, please announce my arrival so that I can go upstairs." Brother Six replied, "Why should I announce you? There's no emperor at our place either, so just go!" But second sister said with a smile, "'A great man doesn't notice a small man's faults.' Are you as stupid as I am? If I don't see the guest, I cannot make any money, and when I get home, the madam will beat me. Can you live with that?" Brother Six said, "Where did you learn to talk that way? Just wait and I will announce you."

上樓臺走一遭，叫乾爺你聽着：我說的那人兒親身到。萬歲
爺聽說擺擺手，若是假的快開交，休要再來瞎胡鬧。適剛纔
生些好氣，我這裏正自心頭焦。

六哥道：「乾爺說的是那裏的話！有第二個佛動心麼？」
萬歲說：「我兒，方纔你沒來嘎，滿樓上都是佛動心，
把我好不混煞！叫我一頓鞭子打下去了。別要叫他上來
了。」六哥道：「這是真的來了。」萬歲聽說大喜，說：
「叫他上樓來吧。」

上小樓拜軍家，恰合是一枝花，紅娘子一笑千金價。上穿一
身紅衲襖，綠羅裙上石榴花，紅繡鞋窄半礤大。迎仙容會他
一面，好姐姐閉月羞花。

二姐上樓，口稱姐夫道：「賤奴來遲，望乞恕罪！」萬
歲一見，心中大喜，走向前去，把二姐攙起說：「久仰
大名！窮軍無緣，今日纔得相會。六哥兒看坐來。」二
姐坐下，那萬歲上下觀看，果然不比尋常。

萬歲爺仔細觀，亞楊妃賽貂蟬，

---

3   The Chinese text has *hongniangzi* 紅娘子. The term may be used as the name of a spider, but more likely the author intends Hongniang, the spunky servant girl Yingying 鶯鶯, the heroine in the famous love comedy *The Western Wing* (*Xixiang ji* 西廂記, ca. 1300), by Wang Shifu 王實甫.

4   Concubine Yang 楊貴妃 was the favorite consort of emperor Xuanzong (r. 712–756) of the Tang dynasty. The elderly emperor showered her relatives with favors. When the Sogdian general in Chinese service An Lushan 安祿山 (d. 757) rebelled, she and her relatives were blamed for causing the rebellion. When An Lushan's troops approached the capital in the spring of 756, the emperor and Concubine Yang fled, but his guard insisted that he should allow her to commit suicide before they agreed to proceed. Since

He made the trip to the second floor
And said, "Adoptive father, please listen.
That girl I talked about has arrived in person."
    When the emperor heard this, he rubbed his hands,
"If it's another impostor, please send her away.
Don't let her come again to create a ruckus!
    A moment ago I flew into quite a rage,
And right now my heart is still fuming!"

Brother Six said, "Adoptive father, what are you saying? Is there a second Buddha's Lust?" The emperor replied, "A moment before you came, the whole building was filled with Buddha's Lusts, confusing me no end! I had to whip them downstairs, so don't let them come here again." Brother Six said, "It's the real one this time." On hearing this, the emperor was overjoyed and said, "Tell her to come upstairs."

When she came upstairs and bowed to the soldier,
She was quite a sprig of flowers.
One smile from this pretty maid[3] was worth a thousand ounces!
    She was dressed in a red jacket,
Pomegranate flowers decorated her green gauze skirt,
And her red embroidered shoes measured half a span.
    Welcoming her immortal charms on their first meeting, he said,
"This fine sister obscures the moon and shames the flowers!"

When second sister came upstairs, she said, "Brother-in-law, please forgive me for being so late." As soon as the emperor saw her, his heart was filled with joy, and helping second sister up from kneeling, he said, "I had long heard about your fame, but as I, a poor soldier, lacked the karma, we meet only today. Brother Six, go get a seat!" Second sister sat down, and the emperor observed her from head to toe. She was indeed extraordinary!

His Majesty observed her in all detail:
She equaled Concubine Yang, and surpassed Diaochan![4]

the ninth century, the tragic passion of emperor Xuanzong has remained a popular subject in Chinese classical and vernacular literature. Diaochan 貂蟬 is renowned as one of China's Four Beauties. She had been promised to the General Lü Bu 呂布 (d. 198). When he learned that she had been defiled by his master the dictator Dong Zhuo 董桌 (d. 192), he murdered Dong Zhuo, as intended by the man who had presented Diaochan to Dong Zhuo.

輕盈好似趙飛燕。一雙杏眼秋波動，兩道蛾眉新月彎，朱唇紅似胭脂瓣。若不是前生福分，那能勾話他一詀？

萬歲爺動龍心，觀不盡俏佳人，身材窈窕天生韻。三宮六院人多少，比他風流沒半分，也是寡人有緣分。就嫖上一年半載，能使我幾布政司金銀？

> 萬歲說：「有花無酒不成樂，有酒無花不成歡。如今兩般都有，不樂更待何時？」

高樓上擺酒席，一件件都整齊，六哥斟酒雙手遞。爺看二姐不轉眼，二姐害羞把頭低，人兒越看越標緻。萬歲爺愛的極了，使不的叫他聲御妻。

> 那六哥先給萬歲斟了個喜盃，就該二姐斟了。二姐斟酒未送過去，就滿臉通紅，羞愧難當。

小二姐面飛紅，沒奈何斟上盃，無精無彩把酒送。萬歲接酒龍心惱，這個奴才不志誠，陪我陪的沒有興。這妮子心高志大，他眼裏也沒有孤窮。

---

5   Flying Swallow Zhao (Zhao Feiyan 趙飛燕) was originally a professional dancer. When Emperor Cheng (r. 32–7 BCE) of the Han took a fancy to her, he moved her into the palace and eventually made her his empress.

6   The "happy cup" takes the place of a wedding cup during a regular wedding ceremony.

In grace and charm she was like Flying Swallow Zhao![5]
   Autumn waves rippled in her almond eyes,
And her moth eyebrows were curved like the new moon.
Her crimson lips were redder than a rouge petal.
   If it weren't for his good fortune from a past life,
He'd never have been able to touch her even once.

His Majesty the emperor's dragon heart was stirred.
He could not take his eyes from this fine beauty.
Her figure was lovely: a Heaven-shaped harmony!
   "Of all the women in my palaces and courtyards
None possesses even half as much sophistication.
This can only be because We have a karmic bond.
   If I philandered here for six months or a year,
How many provincial treasuries would that exhaust?"

The emperor said, "'A flower without wine gives no pleasure; wine without a flower does not bring joy.' But if both are present, then let's enjoy them!"

In the upstairs room a banquet was laid out,
With everything in its rightful place.
Brother Six poured the wine and offered it with both hands.
   His Majesty could not take his eyes off second sister,
While second sister bowed her head, filled with shame.
The more he watched her, the more beautiful she was.
   His Majesty was overcome by love,
But it was impossible to call her "my imperial wife."

Brother Six first poured a happy cup for the emperor,[6] and then it was second sister's turn to pour. But before second sister presented it, she blushed heavily, overcome by shame.

Second sister blushed even behind her ears.
With no way out, she had to pour a cup,
And quite dispirited, she presented the wine.
   Receiving the wine, the emperor felt annoyed:
"This slave truly lacks sincerity.
How can she not be delighted to serve me?
   This wench is too proud and ambitious.
In her eyes, even We count for nothing!"

萬歲說：「一盅酒也不用心斟的。他若再斟酒，我自有
道理。」那二姐把酒杯乾，又斟上遞於萬歲。萬歲接那
盅子撒了半盅，把二姐衣服沾了一塊。二姐心中不悅，
說：「姐夫這麼一條漢子，一個盅子也端不住，把人的
衣服都沾了！」萬歲說：「什麼好衣服哩！」二姐道：「不
是好衣服，你也拿幾件來麼？」萬歲說：「我家裏那梅
香做澱布的還嫌這行子哩。」二姐說：「你笑殺我了，
說那大話！你若有，不該穿件好的來支架子麼？」萬歲
說：「我穿着這衣服，你好合我坐的；我穿那好衣服來，
你就合我坐不的了。」二姐聽說這話，吃了一驚，方才
猛擡粉面，斜轉秋波，細細的打量萬歲。

耳垂肩貌堂堂，龍眉細鳳眼長，好似那泥搯的韋陀像。雖然
是個軍家漢，他的像貌不尋常，豈止遠在王龍上。待說是私
行的天子，怎沒有一騎從王？

　　二姐看罷，暗暗的笑了笑道：「長官，賤人不敢動問貴
姓大名？」萬歲道：「這丫頭上下打量了我一回，就開
口盤問，真是個怪孩子。待我混他一混。」便道：「你
問我怎的？你又不嫁我。我是個響馬，你盤問盤問拿起
我來罷！」二姐被萬歲批了幾句，就羞的低了頭說：「姐
夫好喬性兒！每哩既犯相與，就不問問麼？」萬歲說：
「從頭裏睄睄巴巴的，又問什麼？」二姐便不言語了。
略停了一停，便說：「咱院裏去玩的罷。」

小二姐便開言，酒樓上不好玩，

7　Earlobes hanging down to the shoulders are one of the physical characteristics of the
　　Buddha.
8　Skanda (Weituo 韋陀) is one of the protective deities of Buddhism.
9　In fiction and drama, a person who has fallen in love with someone may ask for that
　　person's name in order to gather the information needed to initiate wedding negotiations
　　between the two families.

The emperor said, "Even one beaker of wine she cannot pour out diligently. If she pours me another, I'll find a way to handle her." Second sister wiped his wine cup and poured another to hand to the emperor. When the emperor took the beaker, he spilled half of it, drenching some of second sister's clothes. Second sister was displeased and said, "Brother-in-law, what kind of man can't even hold a beaker? You've drenched my clothes!" The emperor said, "Are they good clothes?" Second sister replied, "If they're not, get me some that are!" The emperor said, "The serving girls at my place wouldn't use that stuff for their mops." Second sister responded, "You make me laugh with your bragging. If you had nice clothes, wouldn't you be wearing them and cut a better figure?" The emperor replied, "As long as I wear these clothes, you can sit beside me. Once I wear my good clothes, you cannot sit beside me." On hearing these words, second sister was startled. Only then did she raise her powdered face and cast the emperor a sideward glance to measure him up in detail.

> With his ears hanging down on his shoulders,[7] he was
>   impressive.
> His dragon eyebrows were fine, and his phoenix eyes long.
> He clearly resembled an image of Skanda[8] sculpted from clay.
>   Though he might be only a common soldier,
> His features were truly extraordinary.
> He far surpassed more than just Wang Long!
>   But if he were a Son of Heaven traveling incognito,
> How come there wasn't one mounted guard with this king?

Having scrutinized him, second sister darkly smiled and said, "Sir, could I make so bold as to ask your name?" The emperor thought, "This wench has taken the measure of me from head to toe, and as soon as she opens her mouth, she starts questioning me. She's truly an exceptional girl! I can't wait to fool around with her!" So he said, "Why do you ask such things? You're not going to marry me.[9] I'm a mounted bandit, so you must be questioning me to have me arrested." When second sister was chided by the emperor, she lowered her head in shame and said, "Brother-in-law, you're quite quaint. How can I not ask you any questions if we want to be good friends?" With that, second sister fell silent for a while. Then she said, "Let's go to the ward to amuse ourselves."

> Little second sister addressed him as follows,
> "This room in a wine house is no place for fun.

請爺就到宣武院。那邊樓上極清淨，琴棋書畫件件全，朝夕服侍也方便。說的爺一心要去，跳起來攜手相攙。

那萬歲臨行取出銀子一錠，叫六哥：「我的兒，我帶的銀子不多，暫且收下權當酒菜資，等我那小廝們來時，自有包補你處。」六哥道：「乾爺說的是那裏的話！休說吃這一頓飯，就是吃幾年兒也不要錢。」萬歲說：「我的兒！你到有孝心。不是你自家的買賣，伙計們多衆口難調。賺了錢就好；若折了本，就說是小六哥他乾爺吃去了，你怎麼擔待起？」六哥說：「小兒就無禮了。」遂把銀子收了。二姐叫丫環牽馬，即同萬歲往院中來了。

有丫環把馬牽，小二姐邁金蓮，領爺去向宣武院。六哥說乾爺進院去玩耍，忙裏偷閑我問安，一日一遭把你看。萬歲爺滿心歡喜，我的兒休負前言。

萬歲說：「我一起沒出門子，來到這裏，人生面不熟的，不認的一個人。你早晚的看看我，我好多玩幾天。」六哥便說：「二姐到了院裏，好生服侍俺乾爺。沒有銀子來我店裏取。你若慢待俺乾爺，就是給我沒體面了。」二姐道：「你放心罷，我身邊還有第二個人麼？我不敬他待敬誰？」六哥道：「正是。」他君妃二人進院。未知後事如何，且聽下回分解。

Sir, let's go to the Displaying Martiality Ward!
    Over there the upstairs room is quiet and clean,
With a lute and a go board, calligraphies and paintings.
There it's more convenient to serve you from morning till night."
    As soon as she said this, her patron was eager to go,
He jumped up and took her hand to help her rise.

Before leaving, the emperor took out an ingot of silver and called Brother
Six, "My son, I didn't bring much silver, but please take this for the moment
for the wine and food. Once my underlings have arrived, I will be able to
help you out more." Brother Six replied, "Adoptive father, what nonsense!
Forget about this one meal. Even if you had your meals here for a full year,
as your son I wouldn't want any money!" But the emperor said, "My son,
you show great filial piety, but this is not your business alone. You have
many partners, and they all have their opinions. Things are fine as long as
you make money, but when you lose capital, they'll say it's because of the
food and drinks for the adoptive father of little Brother Six. How could you
live with that?" Brother Six said, "Then I cannot but take it." After he had
accepted the silver, second sister told her serving girls to lead the horse
and set out for the ward with the emperor.

The serving girls led the horse
While second sister walked on her golden lotuses,
Leading her patron to the Displaying Martiality Ward.
    Brother Six said, "As you're going to the ward for fun,
I will visit you there in spare moments.
I'll come once a day to see how you are doing."
    His Majesty the emperor was filled with joy:
"My son, please make sure to keep your word!"

The emperor said, "From the moment I left home and arrived here,
everyone's been a stranger! If you come and see me regularly, I can enjoy
myself there for a few more days." Brother Six then said, "Second sister,
once you're in the ward, serve my adoptive father well. If you lack silver,
come to my shop to get some. If you treat my adoptive father without proper
respect, it will ruin my reputation!" Second sister replied, "Don't worry!
Do I have another patron? Who else is there to treat respectfully?" Brother
Six said, "That's right." The lord and his consort went to the ward, and if
you don't know what happened next, please listen to the following chapter.

第十四回 守名妓萬歲裝憨 罵憨達二姐含忿

那萬歲別了六哥，心中自思：這丫頭怪歹歹的，休著他看破行藏。我只得裝作癡顛，瞞他一瞞。不說萬歲定計，且說二人順着大街而行，有許多子弟聽的佛動心接了客人，人人來看，個個景仰，觀不盡小二姐萬種嬌嬈，百般風流。

誇不盡女裙釵，似仙姬下瑤臺，怎樣流落在煙花寨？可惜海底珊瑚樹，挪來人間賤處栽，口裏稱獎心裏愛。街前人攢攢簇簇，小二姐難把頭擡。

那二姐見眾人跟著亂看，急自害羞；又見萬歲左右不離，說道：「姐夫，你怎麼一條漢子，還害怕麼？有狼哩？有虎哩？你死活的跟着我，怕人家拉了我去了麼？你待在前頭就在前頭，你待在後頭就在後頭，不前不後的，你到有些嚴緊。虧了我沒嫁了你；若是嫁了你，到分不了外哩，你會數着我的腳步走。」萬歲道：「這奴才嫌我辱沒他，我只是不聽他說。」見了一座牌坊，故意說道：「妙呀！這個什麼東西？」

---

1   A "skirt and hairpins" refers to a beautifully dressed woman.

14 Accompanying a famed courtesan, the emperor pretends to be simple; Reviling his idiotic silliness, second sister is filled with indignation.

After the emperor had said goodbye to Brother Six, he thought to himself, "This wench is truly exceptional! I must not let her see through my disguise. I'd better pretend to be a stupid fool to deceive her." Let's forget about the emperor's scheme for now, and instead I'll tell you how the two of them walked down the main street. There were quite a lot of playboys who had learned that Buddha's Lust was receiving a guest, so they all came out to watch. They could not take their eyes off Buddha's Lust's myriad graces and hundred charms.

> No admiration was enough for this girl, this skirt and hairpins,[1]
> Who looked like an immortal descended from Jasper Pond.
> How had she ended up in this encampment of misty flowers?
>   How pitiable that this coral tree from the bottom of the sea
> Had been ripped out and transplanted to this vile location!
> They sung her praises, and they loved her in their hearts.
>   The people on the street formed a dense crowd,
> And little second sister could barely lift her head.

When second sister saw that all these people were following her and observing her without restraint, she immediately felt ashamed. Noting that the emperor followed closely at her heels, she said, "Brother-in-law, how can you be such a strapping fellow and still be afraid? Are there any wolves? Or any tigers? Or do you follow me so closely because you're afraid people may pull me away? If you want to walk ahead of me, then walk ahead of me, and if you want to walk behind me, then walk behind me. But one moment in front and one moment behind is a bit too close for comfort. It's a good thing I'm not married to you, because then I couldn't hold it against you if you wanted to count my steps." The emperor thought, "This slave blames me for shaming her. I will act like I didn't hear anything." When he saw a ceremonial archway, he deliberately said, "Wonderful! What's that?"

萬歲爺會裝傻，那前頭是什麼？這家人家多麼大，衣架擡在
街上曬，兩個巴狗上頭扒，軍家見了心害怕，叫二姐流水快
走，你看他下來咬咱！

那二姐雖然也認出萬歲是個貴人，只是眾人屬目之地，
見他光弄那獸像，未免沒好氣，不待答應他，遂把頭一
擺。萬歲道：「你這是個啞蟬麼？我說是個衣架；不是
個衣架，就是個秋千架，又無繩子合坐板。」那二姐沒
好氣的說道：「好！把那慫達！這是一座牌坊。」萬歲
說：「那上頭是什麼？」二姐道：「那是故事，叫做『獅
子滾繡球』。」萬歲說：「好呀！人說宣武院齊整，果
然是實。」二姐道：「謹言！看人家打腿！這不是院裏。」
萬歲道：「不是麼？我只當進來鐵裏門，都是院裏來。」

二姐道：「院在前邊。」萬歲說：「咱進院看景去來。」
萬歲爺進院來，睜龍眼把頭擡，白眼神廟中間蓋。南北兩院
分左右，穿紅著綠女裙釵，鐵石人見了也心愛。一邊是秋千
院落，一邊是歌管樓臺。

那萬歲進的院來，觀不盡的樓臺殿閣，無數的美女佳
人，萬歲爺心中大喜。

眾佳人貌如仙，簾兒下露脚尖，

---

2   The patron god of prostitutes and pimps. He is usually said to have a red face and long
    white eyebrows.

His Majesty the emperor knew how to play the idiot.
"What kind of thing is that there ahead of us?
How tall are the people in that family?
   They've carried a clothes rack into the street
And two barking dogs are clinging to the top.
This sight fills this simple soldier with fear!
   Please, second sister, run as fast as you can!
Look, they're coming down to bite me!"

Now, second sister might have recognized that the emperor was a noble person, but here she was surrounded by onlookers, so when she saw him acting like a simpleton, she was displeased. Not wanting to answer him, she only shook her head. But the emperor said, "Have you gone mute? I say it's a clothes rack. And if it isn't a clothes rack, it must be a swing stand, but how come there are no cords or plank?" Second sister was annoyed and said, "What a simpleton! This is an archway." The emperor asked, "And what's on top?" Second sister replied, "That's a decoration called 'two lions toying with an embroidered ball.'" The emperor exclaimed, "Great! People all say that the Displaying Martiality Ward is so beautiful, and indeed it is true." Second sister said, "Watch your words! People might beat you up. This isn't the ward!" The emperor said, "Isn't it? I thought that as soon we entered the iron-clad gate, we were inside the ward." "The ward is ahead of us," second sister replied. The emperor said, "Let's go in and see the sights!"

His Majesty the emperor entered the ward.
His dragon eyes dilated, he lifted his head:
A temple to the white-eyed god[2] had been built in the middle.
   The northern and southern courtyards were divided left and
      right.
There the girls, skirts and hairpins, were dressed in red and
      green.
Even a man made of steel would be filled with love at first sight.
   On one side was a courtyard with a swing;
On the other side a terrace for music and song.

When the emperor had entered the ward, he could not take his eyes off its towers and terraces, halls and chambers, with their limitless beauties and charmers. The emperor was overcome with joy!

These charming girls looked like immortals.
Below the curtains they showed their small feet,

時時勾引男兒漢。³ 麝蘭薰的人心醉，油頭粉面站門前，見
人一笑秋波轉。便就是神仙到此，也忘了洞府名山。⁴

　　不說萬歲看景散心。且說這院裏有許多姐兒，正在那裏
議論佛動心，說一回，笑一回。丫頭們來說：「衆位姐
姐，你看佛動心接了皇帝來了！」這姐兒們聽說，一個
家開門的，上樓的，扒牆頭的，紛紛嚷嚷，無其代數。
那一個道：「你看這漢子臉上黃幹幹的。」一個家拍手
笑道：「都是小二妮子起的心高了，每日等接皇帝，不
想接了恁麼個人！」齊聲說道：「好皇帝！這皇帝來
嫖這一遭，可沾了這宣武院了，後來人裏頭就玩不的
了！」都不想這賤人說的這話，是個先兆。日後萬歲回
京，火燒南北院，改爲困龍宮，人就玩不的了。

宣武院衆佳人，都亂誚佛動心，這奴才終朝每日發下恨，不
接尚書合閣老，開手接個大操軍，就有銀錢也不趁。還不如
嫖客王龍，使數的小廝和家人。

　　萬歲微微聽的，便道：「二姐，宣武院裏這姐兒們到都
有些眼色。」二姐道：「什麼眼色？」萬歲道：「他說我
是個皇帝。」二姐道：「他是誚我。我有願在前，不接
平人，等着接皇帝。原是我沒有造化，接皇帝接下你
了。」萬歲自思：「這賤人們誚你佛動心接的不

3　Bright eyes.
4　In Chinese mythology, the gods and immortals are expected to have transcended desire.

And time and again they enticed men.
    The wafting musk entranced the heart.
With oiled heads and powdered faces, they stood at the door
To smile and wink with autumn waves[3] at any man they saw.
    And even if you were a divine immortal,[4] on arriving here
You'd forget your grotto palace in famous mountains!

Let's forget about how the emperor enjoyed himself by taking in the sights, and let me tell you that in the ward, there were many sisters busily discussing Buddha's Lust when their servant girls came and told them, "Sisters, have a look at Buddha's Lust receiving the emperor!" At that, the sisters all opened their gates, went upstairs, or clambered on walls, making a huge racket. One said, "Look how sallow his face is!" Another clapped her hands and said laughingly, "This is all because that small second girl set her ambitions too high! Day in and day out, she waited for the emperor. Who would have thought she would receive such a man!" And they said as if with one voice, "After this emperor has been whoring here a while, he'll have stained the Displaying Martiality Ward, and no one else will be able to have fun here." Nobody could have thought that the words spoken by these vile people would be a premonition. Later, when the emperor returned to the capital, he burnt down the northern and southern courtyards, transforming them into the Endangered Dragon Palace, so people could no longer go there for amusement.

The many beauties in the Displaying Martiality Ward
Were all wildly criticizing Buddha's Lust:
"That slave was too determined all the time!
    She didn't receive a minister or excellency,
But takes this big common soldier for her first.
Even if he has the cash, he's not suitable.
    He doesn't even measure up to the boys and servants,
Or the lowest underling, of our prize guest Wang Long."

When the emperor heard some of this, he said, "Second sister, these sisters in the Displaying Martiality Ward are really discerning!" Second sister asked, "What kind of discerning?" The emperor replied, "They all call me the emperor!" Second sister said, "They're chiding me! In the beginning, I made a vow that I would not receive commoners and would wait for the emperor. But I never had such good luck, and now the emperor I take in is you!" The emperor said to himself, "So these vile women chide you, Buddha's Lust, for taking in a patron who doesn't

> 像皇帝，難道就不像個人？怎麼說王龍家小廝強起我？
> 雖是背裏話，也不該褻瀆至尊。這賤人們還有幾天草
> 壽，且看他快活幾日，等文武們來時，火燒南北兩院，
> 抄殺賤人，方雪我心頭之恨！」

萬歲爺牢記心，等北京衆群臣，來時發發這心頭恨。南北兩
院抄殺了，科子王八抽了筋！笑我不如王龍俊，常言道人是
衣裳，爲君的到不如庶民？

> 萬歲說：「這奴才們笑我，我頭信粗一粗村給他們看
> 看。」把那破布衫衫扯了一個偏袖，一步三搖搖將起來。
> 這萬歲穿的軨鞋是江彬做的，雖無穿着走路，但年歲久
> 了就爛了；那鞋掌子印著那溜道上邊嗤的一聲，抓下來
> 了半邊，走一步刮打一聲。姐兒們就笑小二姐這孤老雖
> 不是皇帝，像是個彎子的朋友。衆人道：「怎麼見的？」
> 姐兒道：「你不見他走着，脚底下還打着板麼？」丫頭
> 聽說，笑成一塊。那萬歲見人笑他，一發裝起嘲來了，
> 站在塘路上，可就講起他那鞋來了。

實指望出好差，掙兩錢好換鞋，誰想破的溜丟快。這鞋原是
報國寺，二百大錢買將來，穿了沒有五年外。聲聲說運氣不
濟，怎麼就這樣破財！

---

5   The Requiting the Nation Monastery (Baoguosi 報國寺) is a Buddhist monastery in
     Beijing. Originally established in the Liao dynasty, it was destroyed in the early Ming,
     but fully restored in 1466. The open courtyards of urban temples and monasteries often
     provided spaces for markets and fairs.

look at all like the emperor? But how can they say that I don't look like a man? How can they say that Wang Long's nobodies are better than me? These things may have been said behind my back, but they still should not calumniate the Most Supreme. The rotten lives of these vile women may last a few more days, but let's see how many are days of pleasure. When the civil officials and military officers arrive, I can cleanse this hatred in my heart only if I burn down the northern and southern courtyards and seize and kill all these vile people."

> His Majesty the emperor committed all this to memory.
> "I will wait for the arrival of my officials from Beijing,
> And when they arrive, I will vent this rage in my heart!
>   I will confiscate the northern and southern courtyards
> And pull out the tendons of all these harlots and pimps
> For deriding me as not as handsome as that Wang Long!
>   The proverb says that clothes make the man.
> How then can I as lord be less than the common herd?"

"If these slaves laugh at me," the emperor said, "I'll show them boorish behavior!" Holding onto one sleeve of his torn linen gown, he started to sway three times with every step. The loose boots the emperor was wearing had been made by Jiang Bin, and while he hadn't traveled in them before, they still had deteriorated with age. Walking on the rough road, one of the soles nearly ripped off with a sharp tearing sound, and it slapped on the ground with every step. The sisters had a good laugh: "Second sister's patron may not be the emperor, but he does look like a soothsayer." When people asked in what way, the sisters said, "Don't you see that even while walking, he's still beating his clappers?" When the servant girls heard this, they collapsed with laughter. The emperor noticed they were laughing at him, and he started to act even more foolishly by addressing those boots:

> "I had hoped that you would serve me well on my mission.
> Now I must scrape the money together to get new boots!
> Who'd have thought that you'd fall apart as quickly as this?
>   At the Requiting the Nation Monastery,[5] I acquired
> These boots for two hundred big copper coins,
> And I haven't even worn them for five years!
>   Every voice told me: you lack sufficient good fortune,
> But how could I so rapidly lose my investment?"

萬歲揚聲，二姐羞的極了，低低的叫聲：「姐夫，咱進
院罷。到裏頭叫丫頭們給你錐錐，幾丟刮打的叫人笑
話。」萬歲說：「我夜來使了幾個皮錢，稱了一兩好蔴，
待錐錐鞋來，爲着搬你就耽誤了，還在那酒樓上哩。去
給我取來，我吊着進去罷。」二姐擠了擠眼道：「你年
紀不大，這麼忘事？我纔見你使了五錢銀子買了兩付
火煙紅扣線帶子，你送了我一付，還有一付你弔不的
麼？」萬歲道：「支什麼架子！蔴線還沒有，那裏的扣
線帶子？你把那頭繩子解下來，我弔着罷。」二姐沒可
奈何，把那裙帶子解下一根來，遞於萬歲。萬歲接過
來，把腿擱在石凳上綁那脚。二姐囂極了，走向前去奪
過來，打了個死扣子，說道：「丫頭，架著您憨達進去
罷。」把萬歲推進院去。那萬歲猛然擡頭，見那樓前有
一白菓樹，樹上掛着一個鸚哥。萬歲一見，哈哈大笑。
萬歲爺笑哈哈，那樹上是什麼？綠毛雞白日裏上了架，通紅
一個彎彎嘴，他叫丫頭來看茶，花言巧語會說話。小二姐滿
心好惱，是誰家他這憨達。

萬歲道：「二姐，眞果是百里不同風，俺那裏雞架都靠
着屋簷底下，你這裏雞架掛在樹上，天還沒黑就上了
架。」二姐道：「那是鸚哥。」萬歲說：「俺那鸚哥白白
的，你這鸚哥怎麼綠綠的？」二姐道：「那白的朝廷家
纔有。」萬歲道：「瞎話！俺又不是朝廷家，俺家裏也
有白鸚哥。二姐，你把這鸚哥送給我吧，好合俺那一個
配對。」二姐道：

6   "Leather coins" are small, thin copper coins minted in the Ming dynasty.

As the emperor raised his voice, Buddha's Lust was filled with shame and she said softly, "Brother-in-law, let's go into the ward. Once inside, I will tell the serving girls to stitch it together for you. With all those slapping noises, people make jokes about you." The emperor replied, "Last night I spent quite a few leather coins[6] and bought an ounce of hemp because I wanted to stitch these boots. But because I had ordered you, I forgot about the hemp, and it is still at the inn. Go and get it for me, and I will wait here for you outside the ward." Second sister squinted her eyes and said, "You're not that old! How can you be so forgetful? A moment ago I saw you spend five *qian* of silver to buy two flaming red knotted-thread belts. If you give me one, you still have the other. Can you wait for that?" The emperor replied, "What do you mean? I don't even have any hemp thread, let alone a belt? Take off one of your girdles—I'll wait for you!" Second sister had no choice but to take off one of her skirt girdles and hand it to the emperor. The emperor took it, placed his foot on a stone bench, and tied the belt around it. Overcome by shame, second sister stepped forward, and yanked it in a solid knot. Then she said, "Girls, take this simpleton inside," and pushed the emperor into the ward.

The emperor lifted his head and saw a ginkgo tree in front of the high house and a parrot in a cage hanging from the tree. As soon as the emperor saw these, he laughed loudly.

His Majesty the emperor laughed loudly.
"What is that bird there up in that tree?
A green-feathered chicken roosting in daytime!
    With its red curved beak,
It's telling the servant girls to serve the tea.
It knows how to speak in flowery language."
    Little second sister was quite annoyed:
"Where on earth did this idiot come from?"

The emperor said, "Second sister, it's true that 'customs are different every hundred miles.' With us, the chickens go to roost below the eaves, but here with you, the chicken is hanging in the trees. It's not yet dark, but the bird has already gone to roost!" Second sister said, "This is a parrot." The emperor replied, "Our parrots are white, so how come this parrot is so green?" Second sister said, "White ones are found only in the palace." The emperor replied, "Nonsense! I am not the emperor, and I have white parrots at home. Second sister, please give this parrot to me, so I can mate it with mine." Second sister said,

「姐夫臨走時願送。」萬歲道：「這一溜三間寢房，那
一間是你的？」二姐道：「當中這一間就是賤人的。」
君妃二人攜手進了寢房。未知後事如何，且聽下回分
解。

"I will give it to you when you leave, brother-in-law." The emperor asked, "Which is your room in this suite of three rooms?" Second sister replied, "The room in the middle is mine." Holding hands, the lord and his consort entered the bedroom.

If you don't know what happened next, please listen to the following chapter.

第十五回 弄癡獃武宗作戲 嫌辱沒二姐含羞

　　話說那萬歲進的房來，觀不盡的琴棋書畫。

進房來四下觀，琴棋畫列兩邊，羅幃一帶香薰遍。牙牀錦被
鴛鴦枕，紅羅軟帳掛牀邊，磚場不響花氈墊。就是揀粧鏡
架，也典雅不像塵凡。

　　萬歲觀罷說：「二姐，你是本處人。可是遠方來的呢？」

　　二姐說：「不提起家鄉便罷，若是提起家鄉，無限傷
　　心。」

痛煞我女裙釵，一陣陣痛上心來，前生造下冤孽債。甘心寧
做莊家女，賤人原不戀章臺。誰肯救出我天羅外？到幾時把
火坑跳出，南無佛吃了長齋。

　　萬歲說：「這丫頭問了問他那家鄉，就無休無歇的哭起
　　來了。一來是他不願風塵；二來見我帽破衣殘，怕風月
　　行中姊妹們嗤笑他，他怎麼不惱？他既嫌我，我總裏裝
　　一個嘲獃，辱沒他辱沒。」

1　Mandarin ducks were believed to mate for life, so a long headrest for two people was
　called a "mandarin-duck cushion."
2　One of the names of the courtesan quarter in the Tang dynasty capital Chang'an.

15   Pretending to be a moron, the Martial
           Ancestor puts on a play;
           Resenting the humiliation, second sister
           is overcome by shame.

Let me tell you, when the emperor entered the room, he could not take his eyes off the lute and the go board, the calligraphies and the paintings.

> Entering the room, he looked around:
> Lute and go board, calligraphies and paintings, were arrayed on
>   both sides,
> And the gauze curtains were suffused with a fine fragrance.
>   An ivory couch, a quilt of brocade, a mandarin-duck
>   cushion.[1]
> Pliant bed-curtains of red gauze were hung around the couch,
> And the tiled floor didn't squeak under the felt mat.
>   Even the mirror-stand for a woman to make her toilet
> Was elegant, without a whiff of vulgarity.

When the emperor had seen all this, he said, "Second sister, are you from these parts or from some distant place?" Second sister replied, "If you hadn't mentioned my home village, things would be fine. But now that you've mentioned it, sadness pervades me.

> This pain is killing me, a girl, a skirt and hairpins,
> The pain, wave upon wave, overwhelms my heart
> In my former life, I created a debt of guilt and karma.
>   From the bottom of my heart, I'd rather be a peasant girl.
> I, this vile person, never felt any love for the Patterned Terrace.[2]
> Who will save me so that I may escape Heaven's net?
>   If I can ever jump out of this pit of fire,
> I'll praise the Buddha and keep to the fast all my life."

The emperor thought, "That wench! I ask her one question about her home village, and she starts weeping without pause or end! First of all, she detests a courtesan's life, and second, she fears that the sisters in the guild deride her because my hat is torn and my clothes are worn. But since she resents me, I'll keep acting the fool to humiliate her more."

那萬歲看見一張八步牀，便說：「這是什麼？」二姐道：「這是八步牀。」萬歲道：「我看看。」走到近前，把那紅羅帳一掀，看見上邊懸着御影，深深唱了一大喏，說：「阿彌陀佛！這明是座廟呢，你怎麼說是張牀？」二姐說：「是座娘娘廟，你怎麼不磕頭朝奶奶？」萬歲說：「是座爺爺廟。」二姐說：「也不是爺爺廟，也不是娘娘廟，那是北京皇爺的御影。」皇爺說：「這是正德麼？這行子好快腿，我昨日在京裏還見他，怎麼又跑了這裏來了，藏在你這屋裏？」二姐說：「是他那影像。」皇爺說：「他那影怎麼來在這裏？」二姐說：「我有晚做夢，神靈來警我，說道：『佛動心，你不要接客了，等着接皇爺罷。』天明請先生算卦圓夢，他說的與夢相同。我請丹青手來傳下御影，供養了三年了。」便叫丫頭：「把御影請起，多燒些金紙銀錢，打發他升天去罷。」萬歲道：「這丫頭到有誠敬哩。」遂又滿屋裏瞅，見那琵琶絃子挂在牆上，就說：「這一張琵琶合這一具絃子，好不齊整！」二姐嗤的聲笑了，說：「你放着我的罷！勾我受的了！」萬歲說：「這不是琵琶絃子麼？」二姐說：「這琵琶該說一面，絃子該說一旦，誰家說一張、一具呢？」萬歲說：「哦！是這麼說。」行說着，見一個小丫頭從房裏拿出一把琥珀如意來。萬歲看見，流水擺手說：「小奴才好不成人！好不邋遢！」

萬歲爺會撒顛，小二姐家不嚴，這把杓子是中看。滑滴溜的彎彎把，到給丫頭拿看玩，溓了怎麼去成飯？萬歲爺裝嘲胡混，小二姐心不耐煩。

3　A large couch that provides space not only for bedding, but also to sit.
4　Sacrificial money made of paper.

So when the emperor saw the eight-pace couch,[3] he asked, "What is this?"
Second sister replied, "This is an eight-pace couch." He said, "Let me have
a look!" He walked over, pulled the bed-curtains of red gauze aside, and
saw his imperial portrait hanging there. Loudly shouting his respect, he
said, "Amitābha Buddha! This is obviously a shrine. How can you call it
a couch?" Second sister replied, "This is a shrine to Her Majesty. How
come you don't kowtow to Her Majesty?" The emperor replied, "This is
a shrine to *His* Majesty!" Second sister explained, "This isn't a shrine to
Her Majesty, and it isn't a shrine to His Majesty. It's an imperial portrait
of the august ruler in Beijing!" The emperor said, "Is this Right Virtue
then? That guy must have fast legs! I still saw him when I was in Beijing
yesterday, so how can he have run here and hidden himself in this room?"
Second sister said, "This is his portrait!" The emperor asked, "And how did
his portrait end up here?" Second sister replied, "One night I had a dream
in which a god, coming to warn me, said, 'Buddha's Lust, don't receive
any customers. Wait for the emperor.' That morning I asked a soothsayer
to tell my fortune and explain my dream, and what he said corresponded
with my dream. I asked a painter to paint me a portrait of the emperor,
and I have venerated him now for three years." Then she said, "Girls, take
the imperial portrait down. Burn some gold paper and silver coins[4] and
send him off back to Heaven." The emperor thought, "She's quite sincere
in her respect!"

He glanced all around the room. When he saw a four-string lute and a
three-string banjo, he said, "This lute and banjo are neat." Second sister
laughed derisively and said, "Get lost, you make me cringe." The emperor
said, "But isn't this a lute and a banjo?" Second sister replied, "This lute
should be called a *pipa* and this banjo a *sanxian*. Who calls them a lute
and a banjo?" The emperor said, "Oh, so that's what they're called!" As
he spoke, he saw a serving girl take an amber *ruyi* scepter from the room.
He immediately clapped in his hands and said, "That little slave has no
manners! How dirty!"

> His Majesty the emperor was a fool:
> "Second sister, you're way too lax!
> This spoon is actually quite beautiful.
>   It gives off a glow and has a curved handle,
> Yet you allow a serving maid to play with it.
> If it gets soiled, how will you scoop up the rice?"
>   The emperor played a muddle-headed simpleton,
> Annoying little second sister beyond all measure.

小二姐氣狠狠，叫姐夫你好村，你在那鴇子窩裏困？頭圓耳大方方臉，看你皮毛也像個人，怎麼這樣不幫村？你說了這些俏語，幸虧了旁裏無人。

　　萬歲說：「我自來沒見光景。你嫌我辱沒你時，你教些乖給我，早晚給你支架子如何？」那二姐沒好氣，全不答應。萬歲自思：「好奴才！果然嫌我嘲。我找法作索他作索。」攛頭看見桌子上一把箏，說：「二姐，那是什麼東西呢？」那二姐嬌聲怪氣的說：「是箏！」萬歲說：「是什麼整置的？」那二姐嗤的一聲笑了，說：「姐夫，你兩個可班配：你也是木頭，他也是木頭。」皇爺說：「你也笑話我。我還會嫖哩，可不知他中做什麼？」二姐說：「你也嫖不出好嫖來；他還強起你，他中壓。」萬歲說：「壓著怎麼樣？」二姐說：「中聽。」皇爺說：「好呀！待我也壓壓。」

萬歲爺好嗑牙，這物兒甚可誇，我也上去壓一壓。湊到近前看了看，施轉着待往桌上扒。二姐忙向問你待囉？一聲休不曾說了，乓的聲成了些木查。

　　二姐忙道：「下來下來！了了了不的了！」皇爺說：「你說中壓。」二姐道：「不是這麼壓，支起馬來秫秸葶拉曲。就許你上去壓來麼？仔細顧你壓了，俺娘知道打我怎麼處？」皇爺說：「你休惱。等著我回了北京，把那天下的好木匠叫了他來，

---

5   "Pressing" (*ya* 壓) here also has the meaning of playing the zither (pressing the strings at the appropriate spots).

6   The words translated as "playing a song" (*laqu* 拉曲) may also be understood as "pulling them down." So we get "Rather than lifting a horse as high as the sorghum stalks, you had better pull the ears of sorghum down when feeding the animal."

Little second sister really got angry,
"Brother-in-law, you are so dumb!
What nest of quails did you sleep in?
   A round forehead, big ears, a square face—
By the looks of your skin, you must be human.
So how can you be as stupid as that?
   If you say such nonsensical things,
It's your good luck that there is no one else here!"

The emperor said, "I've never seen such a thing. When you resent me for bringing shame on you, you should teach me to become smarter, so I can make a better impression." But second sister was displeased, and didn't answer him at all.

   The emperor thought to himself, "That slave! She really resents my silliness! But I'll find a way to play a trick on her." Lifting his head he saw a zither on the table and asked, "Second sister, what kind of thing is that?" Filled with irritation, second sister said, "A zither!" The emperor asked, "What is it made of?" Second sister snorted as she laughed and said, "Brother-in-law, the two of you make a nice pair: you are made of wood, and so is the zither." The emperor said, "You're making a joke! I may be able to go whoring, but I don't know what the zither is good for." Second sister replied, "You're not even a good whoremonger, so that zither is better than you, since it's good for pressing."[5] The emperor asked, "When it's pressed, then what?" Second sister said, "Then it's good listening." The emperor replied, "Great, let me press it a while."

His Majesty the emperor chattered on:
"This thing indeed merits our praise.
Let me go and press it for a while."
   Stepping forward, he had a good look,
Then leaned forward to clamber on the table.
Second sister immediately asked, "What do you—"
   The words froze in her mouth, and she fell silent
As the zither was smashed into smithereens.

Second sister hastily called, "Come down! Come down! You can't do this!" The emperor said, "It is good for pressing!" Second sister said, "Not that kind of pressing! Lifting the horse to the highest ear of sorghum: playing a song![6] Who told you to go up there and sit on it? Never mind that you pressed it, but what will I do when my madam learns about this and I get a beating?" The emperor said, "Don't be upset! Wait until I return to Beijing. I'll order all the best craftsmen to come here and have

做些還你娘們。若就要，我出上銀子買。」二姐沒奈何，只得罷了。那萬歲又看見牀下有一把夜壺。

萬歲爺笑哈哈，佛動心你好邋遢，茶壺放在牀底下。沒有蓋子閉着口，暴上灰塵怎麼頓茶？早知道查髒嫖你囉？那萬歲故撒風顛，二姐說好個大獃瓜。

皇爺說：「二姐你好髒！俺那裏茶壺放在桌子上，使布蒙着還怕淉了；你這裏放着牀底下，那客來到家，怎敢刷淨了茶壺，那客待中去了。」二姐說：「這是夜壺。」

皇爺說：「這是夜壺麼？我知道了：您娘們酒量大，白日裏客來客去的吃不足興，到晚上無有宿客了，吃了好睡覺，故叫做夜壺。」二姐說：「這是溺壺呀。」

萬歲爺笑一聲，嘴兒短不相應，人兒怎麼照的正？放着外頭不大好，放着裏頭悶騰騰，不知你是怎麼用？佛動心無言可答，只羞的滿面通紅。

那二姐低頭半晌無言，遂丟了個眼色，那丫頭把好夜壺藏了。二姐自思道：「我看這人相貌出奇，必然不在人下，可怎麼這麼嘲獃？想是我看錯了人麼？」二姐反覆躊躕，心裏有些兩可的意思。未知後事如何，且聽下回分解。

---

7 A traditional Chinese chamber pot for use by men comes with wide spout, and so somewhat resembles a teapot.

8 On the art of physiognomy in traditional China, see Wang 2020.

them make a few for you all. And if you want one now, I'll come up with the best silver." Second sister had to let the matter rest.

The emperor also saw that there was a chamber pot under the bed.

> His Majesty the emperor laughed loudly,
> "Dear Buddha's Lust, you are quite dirty!
> You've placed the teapot[7] under the bed!
>   It doesn't have a cover and its spout is closed.
> How can you keep the tea exposed to dust?
> Had I known how dirty you are, I wouldn't have sought you out."
>   As the emperor pretended to be raving mad,
> Second sister thought, "What a moron!"

"Second sister, how dirty you are!" the emperor said, "At our place the teapot is placed on the table, and even if we cover it with a cloth, we still fear the tea may be dirtied. But here you put it under the bed. If a guest comes to your place and wants to wipe the teapot clean, he will leave right away!" Second sister said, "That is the chamber pot for the night." The emperor said, "This is a chamber pot for the night? I get it! You women sure can drink, and as guests come and go during the daytime, you drink without end. When evening falls and you have no guest staying for the night, you drink till you fall asleep, so that's why it is called a night pot!" Second sister said, "This is the piss pot!"

> His Majesty the emperor laughed loudly.
> At a loss for words, second sister could not answer.
> How could anyone give him a proper reply?
>   "If I place you outside, you will be of no use;
> If I place you inside, I'll feel sulky.
> I don't know how one best makes use of you!"
>   Buddha's Lust didn't know how to answer,
> And felt so ashamed that she blushed all over.

Her head lowered, second sister remained silent for quite a while. Then she gave a wink, and a serving girl hid that fine chamber pot.

Second sister thought to herself, "By his looks, this man has an exceptional physiognomy, and he definitely does not serve under others, but how can he be such an idiot? Could I have made a mistake in reading his face?"[8] Second sister kept on turning this over in her mind, torn between opposing thoughts.

If you don't know what happened next, please listen to the following chapter.

第十六回 武宗爺鬪兩般寶貝 佛動心驚一套琵琶

話說這老鴇子問道:「丫頭,你姐夫進了院了不曾?」
丫頭說:「來了多時了,在房中坐著哩。」媽兒聽說,
吩咐南樓擺下酒桌,「把您姐夫請來樓上。」丫頭聽說,
來到房裏說:「二姐姐,俺老媽南樓擺酒,特來有請。」
二姐頭裏走,皇爺後跟,來到南樓。萬歲自思:「我這
龍衣萬一被丫頭們看見不好,便道:「窮軍家只好住那
矮屋,見了高樓我就暈了。」二姐說;「聽的說有暈船的,
有暈轎的,可沒聽的說有暈樓的。你既是暈樓,叫丫頭
架着你罷。」萬歲說:「不好,我慢慢的走罷。」遂即
兩手扭過那後襟來,把兩個御腔垂兒兜的緊緊的,直
着兩根腿,一步一步捱上樓去。那樓下的丫頭們亂笑:
「你看這姐夫窮的一條褲子也沒有,還來鬪哩!」眾人
說:「你怎麼知道?」丫頭道:「你看他兩腿不敢離開。」
眾人道:「怎麼說?」丫頭道:「離開腿,他怕解官元寶
打開鞘,漏出整腚來了。」眾人笑罷,萬歲合二姐上的
樓來。老鴇子歡天喜地,口稱姐夫:「賤人有罪了!我
待合孩子去請來,家裏無人,我就說着孩子去罷。我家
裏擺酒給你洗塵。不知你幾時就來了,有失迎接。」

---

1   *Zhengding* 整腚 in speech can mean both "the complete silver ingots" and "buttocks."
The translation is an attempt to catch something of that wordplay. The escort here is
refers to an official who supervises the transport of large amounts of silver.

16   The Martial Emperor triumphs with two superior treasures;
Buddha's Lust is startled by one performance on the lute.

Let me tell you, the old bawd asked, "Girls, has your brother-in-law already entered the ward?" The serving girls answered, "He's been here already for quite some time. He's sitting in her room." On hearing this, the madam said, "Set out a table with wine in the southern wing and invite your brother-in-law to come upstairs." The serving girls went into the room and said, "Second sister, our madam has set out wine in the southern upstairs room, and we've come to invite you there." Second sister walked ahead, and the emperor followed her. When they arrived in the southern wing, the emperor thought, "I cannot allow these serving girls to see my dragon robe." So he said, "A poor soldier like me should stay only in a low room. As soon as I see such high stairs, I become dizzy." Second sister said, "I've heard about people becoming dizzy on a boat or in a sedan chair, but I've never heard about people becoming dizzy because of stairs. But if you feel dizzy, I'll have a servant girl support you." The emperor said, "That won't do. I'll walk very slowly." So he pulled the back of his gown with both hands tightly around his imperial buttocks and ascended the stairs step by step with stiff legs. The serving girls below the stairs collapsed with laughter, "Look at this brother-in-law! He is so poor that he doesn't even wear pants, and he still comes here to whore!" The others asked, "How do you know?" The serving girl said, "Just look at him! He doesn't dare spread his legs." And when they asked what that meant, the serving girl said, "When he spreads his legs, he is afraid the escort will open the package of his large silver ingots and his bare buttocks will show!"[1]

By the time they were done laughing, the emperor and second sister had ascended the stairs, and the old bawd, beaming with joy, addressed the brother-in-law: "Please accept my humble apologies! I had wanted to accompany my child in inviting you, but as there was no one else at home, I told my child to go so that I could set out the wine for you to wash down the dust of the road. Not knowing you'd arrived, I didn't welcome you properly."

正德爺上樓來，老鴇兒笑顏開，歡天喜地忙接待。茶才吃罷
斟上酒，十個丫頭排列開，席前跪下將爺拜。一個個吹彈歌
舞，門外頭唱將起來。

　　皇爺見丫頭們唱的中聽，聲音嘹亮，故意的顛憨，聽了
一聽，放下酒盅道：「那吱吱啞啞的是做什麼？」二姐
說：「是丫頭唱詞。」萬歲說：「俺家那唱詞都在臉前裏
唱，你這裏另一樣規矩麼？」二姐道：「俺這賤人家規
矩是這等，來房裏唱恐怕聽了清音去了，姐夫見他的
過。」皇爺說：「我不怪他，叫他們進來唱。」二姐說：
「叫你們進來唱哩。」十個丫頭進的房來，兩邊站下，
彈動絲絃唱起來了。

眾丫頭奉主公，蕭管笛共銀箏。一枝花帶着新水令，玉美人
相稱紅衲襖，江兒水上混江龍，步步嬌唱出情兒動，雁兒落
腔正字巧，沽美酒引吊了魂靈。

　　丫頭唱罷，過來討賞。皇爺說：「他那是做嗄，扒下起
來的？」二姐說：「他那是討賞。」皇爺說：「怎麼是討
賞？」二姐說：「他唱詞你聽了，問你討些賞賜，買胭
粉搽。」萬歲說：「給他什麼？」二姐說：「給他銀子，
或給他錢。」萬歲說：「有那個着不是窮漢了。我可給
他嗄？給他把

2   The tunes listed in this lyric belong to the dramatic repertoire.

When Right Virtue ascended the stairs,
The old bawd showed him a smiling face
And, beaming with joy, hastened to welcome him.
    As soon as he had drunk his tea, she poured him wine.
The ten serving girls all lined up in a row
And knelt before the table to bow to him.
    Each of them could play an instrument, sing, and dance,
And outside the gate they started to perform a song.

The emperor noticed that these girls were singing quite well and their voices were clear, but he deliberately acted the fool. Having listened for a while, he put down his wine beaker and asked, "What is that screeching and moaning for?" Second sister replied, "Those are the serving girls singing a song." The emperor said, "At our place anyone singing stands in front of you, but here you have a different rule?" Second sister said, "The rule in our humble house is this. If they come inside to sing, one fears that the brothers-in-law listening to their performance might find something to blame." The emperor said, "I will not blame them. Tell them to come inside to sing." Second sister said, "He tells you to come inside and sing." When the ten serving girls entered the room, they took up position on both sides and started to play their stringed instruments and sing.

These serving girls amused the main guest
With all kinds of flutes and a silver zither:
"A Sprig of Flowers" followed by "New Water Tune."
    "The Red Jacket" fitted with "The Jade Beauty."
"The River-Disturbing Dragon" on "The River's Stream."
"Each Step Lovely" was sung in a heart-stirring way.
    "The Goose Descends" was sung with the tune correct and the
        words adroit,
While "Buying Fine Wine" robbed one of one's soul![2]

When the serving girls had finished their songs, they came over [and kowtowed] to request a reward. The emperor said, "What are they doing, crouching down and getting up?" Second sister replied, "They are requesting a reward." The emperor asked, "What for?" Second sister replied, "They have sung a song, and you have listened, so now they're asking you for a token of appreciation so that they can buy makeup." "What should I give them?" the emperor asked. Second sister replied, "You can give them either silver or coins." The emperor said, "If I had that, I wouldn't be poor. So what should I give them? I'll give them

豆子罷。」丫頭道：「俺不要，俺有。」皇爺說：「你有
什麼豆子呢？」丫頭道：「俺有黃豆、黑豆、菉豆、豌
豆、還有茳豆。」皇爺說：「你那豆中吃；我這豆不中
吃，只中看。給你把，若是如意就拿了去，不如意在着
我的。」

萬歲爺笑嘻嘻，褡包裏取東西，一把金豆撒在地。丫頭一見
花了眼，搶的搶來拾的拾，這種豆兒眞有趣。佛動心見了也
睜眼，什麼人使這個東西？

那丫頭一個家碰頭磕腦的搶拾，崩了一個滾在二姐面
前，二姐蝦腰拾起。萬歲說：「你好眼皮子薄！賞了丫
頭的東西，要他何用？」二姐說：「一起沒見這般東西，
我待看看。」萬歲說：「你待看時，等小廝們來時抗兩
布袋來給你看。」二姐說：「你家裏有多少，你說這大
話？」皇爺說：「二姐，一處不到一處迷，你到咱家裏
看看，雜糧困一般。」二姐道：「我不聽你乜風話。」
皇爺說：「你拿乜琵琶來崩一個我聽聽。」二姐道：「你
好村！這琵琶是彈一曲，彈一套，或是彈四板，那裏有
彈一個的？」皇爺說：「憑你彈什麼罷。」那丫頭拿過
琵琶來，遞於二姐。二姐自思道：「這長官嘲頭嘲腦的
聽什麼琵琶，我有王三姐夫送我一條汗巾，我拿出來謅
謅，他貪看汗巾，就忘了彈琵琶了。」

佛動心取汗巾，拿出來派灰塵。從來沒見汗巾俊：

some beans!" The serving girls said, "We don't want any beans! We have plenty of beans." The emperor asked, "What kind of beans do you have?" The serving girls replied, "We have soybeans, black beans, green beans and round beans, and we also have cowpeas." The emperor said, "Your beans can be eaten, but my beans can't. They're only for show. I'll get them for you. If you like them, take them away, and if not, I'll keep them for myself."

> His Majesty the emperor was smiles all over
> As he took some gold beans from his satchel.
> He scattered a handful of them on the ground!
>   Once the serving girls glimpsed them, they saw only stars.
> Some grabbed them and others picked them up.
> The gold beans were fascinating!
>   Buddha's Lust also stared at them [and said],
> "What kind of man uses such things?"

The serving girls crashed together and bumped heads with one another as they gathered them up. One bean dropped and rolled in front of second sister, who bent to pick it up. The emperor said, "You must have seen little of the world. These things are to reward serving girls with, why would you want one?" Second sister replied, "I have never seen such a thing, so I wanted to have a look." The emperor said, "If you want to look at them, wait till my underlings arrive carrying two sacks of them for you." Second sister asked, "How many of them do you have at home, bragging like that?" The emperor said, "Second sister, 'If you haven't been to a place, you don't know about it.' When you come to our place and have a look, it's as common as corn stacks!" Second sister replied, "I'm not listening to your crazy talk!"

The emperor said, "Get a lute and play something for me." Second sister replied, "How boorish you are! On a lute one plays a song, or a suite, or perhaps four beats. How can one just play 'something'?" The emperor said, "Play whatever you like!" A servant girl took down the lute and handed it to second sister, but second sister thought to herself, "This guest is a moron and an idiot. How can he appreciate the lute? I have this handkerchief that brother-in-law Wang gave me. Let me take it out to distract him. If he becomes obsessed with inspecting it, he'll forget about me playing the lute."

> Buddha's Lust took out the handkerchief.
> She got it out and wiped away the dust.
> Never was a handkerchief so pretty!

中間織的鸞交鳳，兩頭童子拜觀音，雞素排草偏相襯。琵琶上一來一往，逗精神調他那汗巾。

　　萬歲道：「這奴才不彈琵琶，光調他的汗巾子，望我誇他。我打總的折折他的架子。」說道：「二姐放着琵琶不彈給我聽，弄那塊臭裹脚頭子怎的？不怕涴了手？」

二姐說：「你看看是裹脚頭麼？這是王姐夫從杭州來送我的汗巾，吃了飯好擦嘴。我看你一點手巾也沒有，吃了飯着便什麼擦嘴？」皇爺說：「只怕沒給我嘎吃；家吃的飽飽的，脫了這鞋合這襪子，逗樓下這裹脚來擦一擦便是。」二姐道：「好髒！」皇爺說：「髒麼？你乜汗巾子還跟不上我這裹脚也是有的。你且彈琵琶我聽罷。」二姐道：「你始終忘不了這琵琶。我還有一把好扇子哩，我再拿出來謅謅。」

小二姐逗精奇，取出扇甚整齊，扇面都是眞金砌。上邊畫着湘妃影，頂上寫着道子題，王右軍寫的行書字。這才是眞正古董，拿出去百兩也值。

　　萬歲道：「這奴才又謅他的扇子哩。我誇他一誇。」遂說：「二姐一把好扇，我也有一把好扇。你拿過來我看看，我也給你看看。」二姐道：「不看罷，熱手拿黃了。今日天黑了，明日你看兩遭罷。你就搧起這扇子了麼？你只搧那八根柴、小油紅，暑伏天使兩錢買的粗蒲扇，忽打忽打罷！」皇爺說：「我不看你

3　When the ancient sage king Shun died, his widows drowned themselves to become the goddesses of the Xiang River in Hunan. Wu Daozi (680–c. 760) was a famous painter of the Tang dynasty, known for his paintings of deities.

4　Wang Xizhi (303–361) is famous for his cursive calligraphy.

In the middle was woven a pair of phoenixes;
On both sides children paid homage to Guanyin.
The pattern and arrayed flowers perfectly suited each other.
    As it moved back and forth over the lute,
She did her best to distract him with the handkerchief.

The emperor thought, "This slave doesn't play the lute, but only tries to distract me with her handkerchief, wanting me to praise it. I will definitely pull down that façade." So he said, "Second sister, why do you set the lute down without playing, and instead wave about that piece of your stinking foot-binding cloth? Aren't you afraid of soiling your hands?" Second sister replied, "Do you take this for a piece of foot-binding cloth? This is a handkerchief that brother-in-law Wang brought with him from Hangzhou and gave me to wipe my mouth after eating. As far as I can see, you don't have a handkerchief at all, so how will you wipe your mouth after eating?" The emperor said, "My only fear is that you will give me nothing to eat. When I've eaten my fill, I'll take off these boots and socks and roll my foot-wraps together to wipe my mouth with." Second sister responded, "That's so dirty!" But the emperor said, "Your handkerchief can't measure up to my foot-wraps, and that's a fact. Just play that lute for me." Second sister thought, "So you haven't forgotten about the lute. I also have a fine fan. Let me take it out to distract him."

    Little second sister gave it her best
    And took out a fan that was very beautiful.
    The face of the fan was all gilded with gold.
        Above was an image of the Xiang River goddess
        That was claimed to have been painted by Wu Daozi.[3]
    The calligraphy was done by Wang Xizhi.[4]
        Now this was an authentic ancient curio
    That was worth a hundred ounces!

The emperor said to himself, "Now this slave wants to distract me with her fan. Let me praise it." So he said, "Second sister, that's a fine fan. I also have a fine fan. If you hand it to me to have a good look, I will also let you see mine." Second sister replied, "You'd better not take a look. If you hold it in your hot hands, it may turn yellowish. It's already getting dark, so look at it twice tomorrow. Do you want to fan yourself? You'd better use one of those thick reed fans sold for two coins during the hot days of summer, one reddened with a little oil and made of eight sticks that can stir up a storm!" The emperor said, "Then I won't look at your

那扇子了。且彈琵琶我聽罷。」二姐說：「你沒忘了這
琵琶，少不得要彈彈了。」

小二姐心裏焦，抱琵琶懶待調，少頭沒尾彈一套。不憂不喜
不誠敬，把這長官哄醉了，丫頭陪他去睡覺。好歹的留他一
晚，到明日打發他開交。

那二姐胡套了一彈。萬歲說：「這奴才像個會彈的，他
不待彈給我聽，我自有道理。」那萬歲穿的那綁腿靸鞋
沉重，那樓板聲音又響亮，故意撲咚撲咚的使那脚蹋。
二姐說：「放著琵琶不聽，你踩嘎哩？」萬歲說：「我給
你打着板哩。」二姐說：「你打的是什麼板？」萬歲說：
「我打的不是板，你彈的也沒有點。」

萬歲爺笑嘻嘻，你不該把人欺。人物雖醜心裏趣，琴棋六藝
誰不曉？花裏胡哨也記的，才來進院當子弟。你彈的少頭無
尾，拿着俺當了癡愚。

二姐自思：「這長官初進院時，有些憨樣；這一回我看
他像精細了。是的，我把琵琶彈一套好的，他聽過來，
就是俏裏裝村；若是聽不過來，就是村裏裝俏了。」

小二姐把絃調，這長官像不嘲，只怕還是村裏俏。懷抱琵琶
別改調，

fan. Just play the lute for me." Second sister said, "You haven't forgotten about the lute, so I'll have to play a little."

> Little second sister felt quite annoyed,
> Holding the lute, she lazily tuned it
> And played a suite without head or tail.
> Without sorrow or joy, it lacked all sincerity.
> "Once we have tricked this guest into getting drunk,
> One of the servant girls will go and sleep with him.
> For better or worse, we'll let him stay for one night;
> Tomorrow at dawn we'll then send him on his way."

Second sister lackadaisically performed a piece. The emperor said to himself, "This slave gives the impression of being someone who is able to play, but she doesn't want to play for me. I know how to handle this." Now the loose boots tied around his shins were quite heavy and the floor planks of the upstairs room resounded loudly, so he purposely stamped his feet with a boom. Second sister said, "Why are you stamping and not listening to the lute at all?" The emperor replied, "I am stamping out the measure." When second sister asked which measure, the emperor replied, "I'm not beating out any measure, because your playing has no rhythm."

> His Majesty the emperor was all wrapped in smiles.
> "It isn't befitting for you to bamboozle people.
> A man may look ugly, but can still be quite smart!
> Who doesn't understand the six arts, music, and games?
> Only after I mastered them, to some degree at least,
> Did I enter the ward to become your patron.
> Your playing was without heads or tails
> Because you considered me a stupid fool."

Second sister thought to herself, "When this guest first entered the ward, he was something of a simpleton, but now he seems to be so knowledgeable. Let me take the lute and play one suite well. If he can figure that out, he must be a smart guy pretending to be dumb. But if he can't, he's a boor pretending to be smart."

> Little second sister tuned the strings.
> "It seems as if this guest is not so dumb,
> But I fear he's only pretending to be smart."
> Holding the lute in her arms, she changed the tune,

滿江紅捎帶着月兒高，傾心吐膽彈一套。武宗爺微微冷笑，
這琵琶傳授不很高。

　　二姐聽說，把琵琶放下說：「我只當你怎樣知音來呢，
誰想你是胡猜。你說我傳授不高，這宣武院裏三千姐
兒，就沒有彈過我的。你說這大話，你會彈麼？」萬
歲說；「我只是沒開興哩。若是待彈，脚指頭也彈的中
聽。」二姐說：「見你那口來，還沒見你那手。好漢子
當面就彈。」二姐自思：「他會接就會彈，不會接就不
會彈。」二姐遞了個懷抱日月。萬歲說：「好賤人！真
果拿着我當憨瓜。」使了個順手牽羊，接過琵琶，且攔
住不彈說：「這賤人誇他的汗巾子，我也有條汗巾，拿
出來謅謅罷。」

龍袍裏取汗巾，拿出來愛煞人，乾坤少有汗巾俊：當中二龍
把珠戲，九曜星宮兩下分，二十八宿謹相遜。趁上帶香茶龍
盒，羊脂玉碾就的穿心。

　　萬歲將汗巾一展，照的樓上赤旭旭的，祥光出現。二
姐擡頭看見，打了一罕：這長官說話風張風勢的，他
的東西到有些古怪，花花鼇鼇的這是什麼？便問：「姐
夫，你拿的是什麼？」皇爺說：「是我擦嘴的點澆汗
巾。」二姐道：「是那裏來的，這樣齊整？」萬歲道；「遠
著哩！是日南交趾國進奉來的。」二姐道：「是給你的
麼？」皇爺說：「是給朝廷的。」二姐道：「給朝廷的你
怎麼拿著呢？」皇爺說：「我對你說罷。

5　More literally, this phrase might be rendered "Performing a 'walking off with a goat on
　　the sly'."
6　The Nine Dazzlers are the sun and the moon, the five planets, and two particularly bright
　　stars. The twenty-eight (lunar) lodges are a series of constellations that over the course
　　of the year mark due south at the moment of dawn.
7　Mutton-fat jade is a high-quality whitish jade.
8　The name of an ancient kingdom in the area of southern Vietnam.

> So "Full River Red" was followed by "The Moon So High."
> She put her heart and soul into the suite she played.
>   His Majesty the Martial Emperor coldly smiled,
>   "Your skill on the lute is not all that great!"

When second sister heard this, she put down the lute and said, "I thought that perhaps you understood music, but who'd have known you were only guessing? You say my skill isn't that great, but among the three thousand sisters in the Displaying Martiality Ward, no one plays better than I do. You make such big claims, but can you play?" The emperor replied, "I have no inclination to. But if I played, I could play well with my toes!" Second sister said, "We see your mouth, but we haven't seen your hands. A brave man would play right in front of us!" Second sister thought to herself, "If he accepts the lute, he'll be able to play it, but if he doesn't, he cannot play." Second sister pushed the lute into his arms, and the emperor said to himself, "That vile creature! She really considers me a simpleton." Quite at ease,[5] he accepted the lute, but then stopped himself from playing, saying to himself, "That vile creature prided herself on her handkerchief, but I have one as well, so let me take it out to distract her."

> He took a handkerchief from his dragon robe,
> And when he pulled it out, it was lovely in the extreme.
> Nowhere on Earth could one find such a pretty handkerchief!
>   In the middle were two dragons playing with a pearl,
> And the palaces of the Nine Dazzlers were arrayed on both
>   sides,
> While the Twenty-Eight Lodges followed each other.[6]
>   It was fit for carrying a dragon box of fragrant tea
> Or a ring sculpted from mutton-fat jade.[7]

As the emperor unfolded the handkerchief, it lit the upstairs room with a red glow, as an auspicious aura appeared. When second sister lifted her head to look, she was amazed: "This guest speaks and acts madly, but his things are exceptional. What do all these colors mean?" So she asked, "Brother-in-law, what did you take out?" The emperor replied, "It's a moistened handkerchief for wiping my mouth." Second sister asked, "Where is it from? It is so neat!" The emperor replied, "From far, far away! It is a tribute gift from the country of Jiaozhi in the far south."[8] Second sister said, "And they gave it to you?" The emperor replied, "It was given to the court." Second sister asked, "Then how did you get it?" The emperor answered, "Let me explain. Here in the provinces,

你看我在外邊沒體面，我在京裏也像個人。這朝廷的愛臣是江彬，我合他垂髮相交，俺兩個極厚。夜晚間俺兩個吃起酒來，他拿出來謅，我說：『江彬，你這汗巾是那裏的？』他說：『是外國進了來給萬歲的；萬歲使殘了，就賜了我一條。』我說：『江彬，皇家的東西，你拿着犯法，你送給我罷。』他就兩手奉獻。朝裏皇帝有這汗巾，朝外我也有這汗巾，除了俺兩，別人再沒有這汗巾了。」二姐聽聽，深深的拜了兩拜說：「賤人買命算卦，該接皇帝。也是我福分淺薄，接不着大駕；仗賴姐夫的洪福，給我那聖上的汗巾看看，死也甘心！」萬歲說：「你看不的。」二姐說：「我就奪！」跳了一跳，貪慌拘那汗巾，把桌子上酒壺拐倒。二姐只羞的面紅過耳，叫丫頭拿溅布來。皇爺說：「不用，隨便的使使罷。」萬歲把那汗巾窩攢起來，照桌面上一抹。二姐說：「姐夫好不成人！這樣東西就拿著溅了桌子！」皇爺說：「這行子不拂桌子，要他何用？」二姐說：「乾給我我也不要了。」那萬歲撛着那汗巾，迎風一抖搜，只聞的香風一陣，那上頭半點酒珠也無，異樣的新鮮。二姐見了，胸膛上長起草來，就慌了心，說道：「姐夫，你給我看看罷。」萬歲說：「我自是不給你看。」二姐把嘴一撅說：「你不給俺看罷，俺也不要了。你還彈你那琵琶罷。」萬歲說：「這奴才見了我這汗巾就慌的乜樣，我再拿出那扇子來謅謅。」萬歲從那扇囊裏取出扇子來了。

取扇兒在手中，滿樓上耀眼明，寶貝原是西番貢。仙人畫就錘金面，巧工雕成象牙櫃，

9   The word here translated as "flabbergasted" is *huang* 慌, which has the same pronunciation as *huang* 荒 (the same character but without the heart radical) meaning "overgrown."

you may think I have no status, but back in Beijing I cut quite a figure. The most favored minister at court is Jiang Bin, and he and I have been close friends since we were young. One night when the two of us were drinking, he took this out to distract me, and I said, 'Jiang Bin, where is this handkerchief from?' And he said, 'This was a tribute gift of a foreign country for the emperor, and when the emperor soiled it, he gave it to me.' I said, 'Jiang Bin, you're breaking the law taking the emperor's things. You'd better give it to me.'" So he presented it to me with both hands. At court the emperor has a handkerchief like this, and outside the court, I also have one. Apart from the two of us, no one else has one." When second sister heard this, she made two deep bows and said, "When I, this vile person, had my fortune told, I learned I was destined to receive the emperor. But my luck was too thin, so I never received His Majesty. But, brother-in-law, if you with your huge good fortune allow me to have a look at the handkerchief of our Sage Superior, I will be happy even in death!" The emperor said, "You cannot!" But second sister said, "Then I'll take it!"

She jumped up, and in her sudden desire to grab the handkerchief, she overturned the wine jug on the table. Blushing even behind her ears, second sister called for a serving girl to bring a rag, but the emperor said, "No need! Let's just use what we have at hand." The emperor rolled up the handkerchief and wiped the table. Second sister exclaimed, "Brother-in-law, you have no common sense! How can you clean the table with such a thing?" The emperor replied, "What's the use of this rag if we don't use it to clean tables?" Second sister replied, "Now I don't want it anymore, even if you gave it to me for free!" But when the emperor held the handkerchief in his hands and shook it out, there was a fragrant breeze and not half a drop of wine was to be seen on it anymore; it was miraculously fresh and clean! When second sister saw this, grass grew over her bosom; completely flabbergasted,[9] she said, "Brother-in-law, please let me have a good look." But the emperor said, "I still won't let you look." Second sister pouted and said, "If you don't let me have a look, it's fine. I don't want to anyway. Why don't you go and play the lute."

The emperor thought, "When this slave saw the handkerchief, she went out of her mind. Now I'll take out a fan to distract her." So the emperor took a fan out from its case.

> When he took the fan and held it in his hands,
> The whole room was dazzled by its bright light.
> This treasure was a tribute from a western nation.
> An immortal had painted the hammered-gold surface,
> And a clever craftsman had sculpted the ivory handle.

才然一舉香風動。拿出來霞光萬道，閃一閃瑞氣千層。

萬歲拿出那扇子一搖，滿樓上清香宜人。二姐看見諕了一驚：這長官的東西件件出奇。他拿的這把扇也看的過，但那個棋榴我可沒見。這萬歲爺扇子上是一科月明珠扇墜，二姐那裏曉的。二姐說：「好齊整扇呀！借過來我搧搧。」皇爺說：「手熱盪青了。今日天黑了，明日搧四遭罷。什麼好扇哩，不過是八根柴、小油紅，暑伏天使兩三錢買的蒲扇，怎麼好給你搧？」二姐說：「姐夫，你偏記的俺這裏合你出對字哩。俺說盪黃了，你就說盪青了；俺說搧兩遭，你就說搧四遭。你是八寶羅漢之體，你就合俺這賤人一般見識？有酒裝給你吃，當面就回席。俺也不看扇子了，還彈琵琶我聽罷。」皇爺說：「你是個什麼人，我就彈給你聽？」姐說：「孤老婊子玩耍罷，誰着你彈給我聽！」皇爺說：「這話有理。」萬歲爺龍心歡，抱琵琶定了絃，先彈一套昭君怨，鴻門設宴方丟下，然後緒上九里山。二姐聽罷心忙亂，看長官風風勢勢，誰想有這樣絲絃。

萬歲彈了一套，二姐吃了一驚：這長官何曾嘲來！遂不見的把椅子往前一拉，來親近萬歲。萬歲說：「這奴才眼裏有了我了，我也撒撒。」把椅子往一邊一拉。二姐嬌滴滴的說：「姐夫，俺眼裏有了你了，你就眼裏沒了俺！」皇爺說：「眼裏有俺，不過知道我這腰裏還有幾兩銀子。你娘們待算給我的。」二姐說；

10 The first-generation disciples who were taught by the Buddha in person and so received the full truth of his teaching. Their statues may be found in Buddhist monasteries.

11 In contrast to the tunes performed by second sister, which were common love songs, the pieces performed by the emperor are all inspired by great events in Chinese history. "Wang Zhaojun's Grief" expresses Wang's grief as she leaves the emperor who loves her to marry a barbarian chief in order to ensure peace. "The Swan Gate Banquet" was inspired by a famous meeting of Xiang Yu and Liu Bang, at which the latter only barely escapes a assassination plot. "Nine-Mile Mountain" evokes the final defeat of Xiang Yu at the hands of Liu Bang's general Han Xin 韓信 (d. 196 BCE).

> As soon as one waves it, it arouses a fragrant breeze.
> When he took it out, it gave off multicolored rays of light;
> In a flash, it emitted a thousandfold auspicious aura!

When His Majesty the emperor took out the fan and waved it once, the whole upstairs room was filled by a pleasing fragrance. Second sister was startled: "This guest's things are miraculous! I've seen fans like the one in his hand, but I've never seen such a pendant." The fan pendant was a full-moon pearl, but how could second sister know that? Second sister said, "That is a pretty fan! Lend it to me so I can use it to fan myself." But the emperor said, "With your hot hands, it would turn black. It's already dark. Tomorrow you can use it to fan yourself four times. What's so special about this fan? It's only a reed fan that I bought during the dog days of summer for three coins, reddened by a bit of oil and made of eight sticks." Second sister said, "Brother-in-law, you have a good memory! I set you the first line of a parallel couplet: I said it would turn yellowish, and you said it would turn black; I said two times, and you said four times. You may be an eight-treasure arhat,[10] but your knowledge is just the same as that of me, this vile person. I'll get some more wine for you to drink, and then we can return to our meal. I'm not going to inspect your fan, just play the lute for me." The emperor said, "Why should I play the lute for someone like you?" Second sister replied, "We're a patron and a whore amusing themselves. Who's ordering you to play for me?" The emperor replied, "That makes sense."

> His majesty the emperor was pleased at heart;
> Holding the lute, he tuned the strings
> And performed "Wang Zhaojun's Grief" first.
> As soon as he had finished "The Swan Gate Banquet,"
> He followed it up with "Nine-Mile Mountain."[11]
> Hearing him, second sister was perturbed:
> "By the looks of it, this guest is a raving madman,
> But who knew he could play the lute like this!"

After the emperor had played one suite, second sister felt shocked. "This guest isn't a fool at all!" She silently pulled her chair forward to be closer to the emperor, who said to himself, "Now this slave takes notice of me. Let me fool her once more." When he pulled his chair away from her, she said seductively, "Brother-in-law, now I that take notice of you, you don't take any notice of me." But the emperor replied, "If you take notice of me it is only because you know I still have some ounces of silver in my belt, and you women want to relieve me of those." Second sister said,

「俺不過是個女孩家，俺會放響馬，扯溜子，倒飽頭算
計你？不過是愛你那好絲絃。」皇爺說：「好什麼！不
過是胡亂撥幾點子，合狗跑門那是的。」二姐道：「又
來了。我且問你：你這絲絃教的教不的？」皇爺說：「教
不的，我怎麼學來呢？」

小二姐滿心歡，叫姐夫你聽言：你居家搬來宣武院，悶來咱
在一處玩，跟着姐夫學清彈，三千姊妹管你飯。你只是情吃
情穿，比當軍受用的自然。

萬歲道：「多蒙盛意。只是俺這家人家人口太多，吃穿
你就難管了。況且不是蘋婆，不是李子的，住在院裏甚
是不雅。」二姐道：「這可怎麼處？」二姐低頭尋思。
未知後生出個什麼計策，且聽下回分解。

12　Apple and plum here probably stand for cheap commodities.

"I'm only a girl. How can I spur on my horse, grab a fleeing man, and turn his bones upside down to relieve him of his money? It's only because I love the way you pluck the strings!" The emperor replied, "What was so good about it? I was just playing wildly, like a dog randomly scratching the door." Second sister said, "There you go again! But let me ask you, can you teach me to play like that?" The emperor replied, "How can I teach you what I never learned?"

> Little second sister was overcome with joy
> And said, "Brother-in-law, please listen!
> You should live here in the Displaying Martiality Ward.
>   When you feel lonely, we can amuse ourselves together;
> I can learn from you, brother-in-law, how to play the lute,
> And three thousand sisters will take care of your food.
>   You'll be able to eat what you want and wear what you want
> And have a much better life than that of a common soldier!"

The emperor replied, "Many thanks for your kind intentions! The only problem is that there are so many members of my household that you couldn't take care of their food and clothing. Moreover, I am not an apple or plum,[12] so it would be demeaning for me to live in the ward." Second sister said, "How can we solve that?" With lowered head she pondered the matter.

If you don't know what scheme she came up with, please listen to the following chapter.

第十七回 弄輕薄狂言戲主 觀相貌俊眼知君

話說二姐見萬歲不肯來院裏住，故意躊躕了一回，問道：「姐夫，你家有銅牀沒有？」萬歲笑了一笑，說道：「佛動心，你說的是那裏的話！朝廷家有龍牀，大人家有八步牀、頂子牀，小人家有脚牀，監裏有框牀，食店鋪有活落牀，棉花鋪有亞車牀，沒見人家有銅牀。」二姐說：「我問的是你家裏動了葷了沒？」萬歲道：「咱家是小人家麼？跳起來吃葱吃蒜的，殺豬宰羊的也斷不了。」二姐說：「我問的是大婚。」萬歲把眼一瞪說：「殺豬宰羊還不是大葷？仔等的殺個人吃麼？」二姐說：「我問你娶了妻小了沒。」皇爺說：「我是個夯人，不說是娶了老婆了沒，我知道什麼是小婚、大婚。你問的是老婆麼？有七八十個還多哩。」二姐道：「你又風上來了。從來道一妻二妾三奴婢，誰家就有七八十個呢？」皇爺說：「我是哄你。若有這麼些人口，我家裏籮升籮斗的給他什麼吃。」二姐說：「妙呀！你那起初雲你說金豆子就合雜糧困那是的，被我一句話詐出家當來了。你何不娶一個有生色的？」皇爺說：「我有那個念頭，只是搜尋不着好的。」

二姐說我的哥，你既說沒娶婆，我給你當家也當的過。今日既然接着你，我索性跟你去張羅，

1 *Tongchuang* 銅牀 (bronze couch) has the same pronunciation as *tongchuang* 同牀 (sharing a couch: a bed partner, a wife).
2 The word *hun* 葷 (meat, nonvegetarian food that is heavily flavored with such condiments as garlic and onions) has the same pronunciation as *hun* 婚 (a wedding, a marriage).
3 "A formal marriage" here translates *dahun* 大婚, which the emperor deliberately misunderstands as "big meat."

Displaying frivolity, foolish words offend the ruler;
Observing features, clever eyes recognize the lord.

Let me tell you, when second sister saw that the emperor was unwilling to move to the ward, she purposely hesitated for a while and then asked, "Brother-in-law, do you have a bronze couch?"[1] The emperor smiled and said, "Buddha's Lust, what are you talking about? The emperor has a dragon couch, major families have eight-pace couches and four-posters, common people have raised couches, in prisons they have restraining couches, in restaurants they have noodle couches, and in cotton workshops they have ginning couches. But I've never seen anyone with a bronze couch." Second sister replied, "I was asking you whether you use meat."[2] The emperor said, "Are we such a poor family? We jump up and eat onions and garlic, kill pigs, and slaughter sheep without interruption." Second sister replied, "I was asking about a formal marriage." The emperor, his eyes dilated, said, "Doesn't killing pigs and slaughtering sheep count as 'big meat'?[3] Or do you want me to kill a man and eat him?" Second sister replied, "I am asking whether you are married!" The emperor said, "I am a dense guy. You didn't say, 'Have you taken a wife?' What do I know about small meat and big meat? If you're asking me about my wives, I must have more than seventy or eighty." Second sister said, "There you go, raving mad again! The saying has always been 'one wife, two concubines, and three slave girls.' Who has seventy or eighty?" The emperor replied, "I'm joking. If there were that many people, we'd have to buy rice by the peck and bushel, and what could we give them to eat?" Second sister said, "Wonderful! In the beginning you said that you had gold beans piled up like corn stacks. But now one sentence is enough to make you confess your family situation. Why haven't you found a charming wife?" The emperor replied, "I intend to, but so far I haven't found a good one."

Second sister said, "Dear elder brother,
Since, as you have said, you don't have a wife,
Let me be your housekeeper—I'm up to the job!
    Because I am receiving you today,
I'll do my best to trap you in my net,

省的又接第二個。你休愁烟花拙懶，情管俺轉不下吆喝。

皇爺說：「你媽娘不知要多少銀子？」二姐說：「只要三千兩銀子。」皇爺說：「吃不盡沒有的虧。」二姐說：「待嫁我自有道理。我還有幾兩私房銀子，給俺媽娘罷。」皇爺說：「我就有銀子娶了你去，我家裏人口太多，給你什麼吃？」這二姐見萬歲百樣的推託，他就撒起嬌來了：「你放心過日子，我自有法治。」

佛動心發狂顛，拿着爺作戲玩。把我娶去宣武院，駝到北京順天府，房子賃上五七間，憑着模樣把錢轉。不要你糴升糶斗，管叫你情吃情穿。

皇爺冷笑了一聲說道：「別的生意還好做，這般賣買難做。」二姐不識進退，又嚶嚶的笑道：「好多道哩，做一遭就慣了麼？」萬歲聽說，龍顏大怒。

萬歲爺氣沖沖，罵奴才養漢精，放你娘的狗臭銃！捶的桌面乒乓響，身子跳起眼圓睜，倒把二姐諕了個掙。忙跪倒說咱兩戲耍，沒人處什麼正經。

So as not to have to receive another man.
　　Don't fear that as a misty flower I will be stupid and lazy,
　I would never demean myself by shouting and yelling."

The emperor said, "How much silver would your madam want?" Second
sister said, "Only three thousand ounces." The emperor said, "There's
never an end to the misery of lacking funds." But second sister said, "As
long as you want to marry me, there's a solution. I have a few ounces of
savings that I can give to the madam." The emperor replied, "Even if I had
the silver to marry you, there are too many people in my family. What
would I give you to eat?" When second sister saw that the emperor was
coming up with all kinds of excuses, she put on her charm and said, "You
can spend your time here without any worry. I'll find a way to solve this
problem."

　　Buddha's Lust was mad with rage
　　And made His Majesty the butt of her sarcasm.
　　"You marry me here in the Displaying Martiality Ward,
　　　Then carry me with you to Beijing in Shuntian Prefecture.
　　And once you have rented a house of five or six rooms,
　　I can rely on my beautiful figure to make some money.
　　　You won't have to buy any grain by the peck and bushel.
　　I'll make sure you can eat and wear whatever you want!"

The emperor smiled derisively and said, "All the other trades one can engage
in, but this kind of business is impossible." Second sister didn't know how
to proceed, so she said with an innocent smile, "It's such a good business!
Once you've done it, don't you get used to it?" When the emperor heard
this, his dragon face was suffused with rage.

　　His Majesty the emperor was overcome by rage
　　And reviled her as a slave and an adulterous slut.
　　"Just blow it out your stinking dog's ass!"
　　　He pounded on the table until it rattled.
　　And as he jumped up with wide-opened eyes,
　　He scared the wits out of second sister!
　　　She knelt down quickly, saying, "The two of us were just
　　　　joking!
　　Why do we have to be prim and proper with no one else
　　　around?"

二姐見皇爺惱了，只諕得骨軟筋麻，走到近前雙膝跪下，只稱姐夫：「賤人不識輕重，無心說出，追悔無及！」萬歲始終是愛他，見嬌滴滴的一聲哀憐，早把怒氣消入爪哇國去了。向前用手扯起來說：「你是妓女，我不濟是個嫖客，你不該罵我。」二人坐下，那二姐悶悶不足。萬歲說：「二姐，你照舊玩耍。你若待學絲絃，我願教你。」二姐聽說，才滿心歡喜，滿斟一盃遞於萬歲。萬歲說：「我不吃了。天色已晚，咱睡覺去罷。」二姐笑道：「你不吃就是怪我。」

佛動心弄嬌柔，若愛奴飲這甌，無心小失丟開後。萬歲本情不待吃，又怕心上人兒羞，伸開御手忙忙受。接過來不曾落案，一骨磈灌下咽喉。

萬歲飲乾，那佛動心還待讓他。萬歲便叫丫頭綽出殘席，安排寢帳，收拾睡覺。

衆丫頭急慌忙，鋪下了象牙牀，紅袖亂拂銷金帳。安下一個鴛鴦枕，熏籠裏面又添香，般般事兒皆停當。萬歲說二姐睡罷，到明朝再耍無妨。

佛動心也不言語，暗暗的思量：「今晚原是哄他，這個計策已是行不的了。」這二姐坐在燈下躊躇不定。

When second sister saw how upset the emperor was, she was so scared that her bones went weak and her tendons went numb, so she rushed forward and knelt down on both knees, exclaiming, "Brother-in-law, I, this vile person, didn't realize how hurtful that might be. I spoke without thinking, and now my regret comes too late." The emperor still loved her, and when he saw how she beseeched him with her seductive voice, he quickly dispatched his rage to the country of Java. Stepping forward, he pulled her up with his hand and said, "You are a courtesan, and I'm bad enough to be a whoremonger, so you shouldn't curse me." They sat down, but second sister was quite dispirited, so the emperor said, "Second sister, let's have fun like before. If you want to learn how to play the lute, I'm happy to teach you." On hearing that, second sister was filled with joy. She poured a full cup and handed it to the emperor, but he said, "I won't drink anymore. It's already dark. Let's go to sleep." Second sister said, "If you won't drink, it means that you still blame me."

> Buddha's Lust played the coquette:
> "If you love me, you will drink this cup.
> Forget about that inadvertent little slip!"
>   The emperor actually didn't want to drink,
> But fearing his beloved would feel ashamed,
> He hastily stretched out his hands to take it.
>   He never put it down on the table,
> But poured it down his throat in one gulp!

When the emperor finished the cup, Buddha's Lust still wanted to distract him, but the emperor called for the serving girls to take away the remainder of the meal, arrange the bed-curtains, and make things ready so that they could go to sleep.

> Quickly, the serving girls
> Spread out the bedding on the ivory couch,
> Their red sleeves brushing the gold-spangled curtains.
>   They laid down a mandarin-duck cushion,
> Added some incense to the incense burner,
> And prepared everything in a perfect manner!
>   The emperor said, "Second sister, get some sleep.
> Tomorrow morning we'll have fun again for sure."

Buddha's Lust didn't say a word, but secretly thought to herself, "The plan for tonight was to fool him, but the scheme didn't work." As second sister sat next to the lamp, she was beset by doubts and couldn't make

萬歲看了看那兩個丫頭，只管丟他那眼色，敦敦的看他姐姐。萬歲起的身來說道：「恁又不說長，又不道短，是待弄什麼鬼兒算計我麼？丫頭們快去罷，我待關門哩。」把丫頭們趕下樓去，烹的一聲關上樓門，便說：「二姐，咱睡了罷。」二姐羞答答的說：「請長官先睡，奴便來也。」這萬歲急自待脫衣服，怕漏了行藏，笑道：「二姐想是您害羞，我吹煞燈罷。」撲的一聲，把燈吹煞，然後解衣上牀。

萬歲爺解了衣，叫一聲我的妻，過來罷弄什麼勢。二姐無奈把羅裙解，說從來沒曾出門子，酸甜還不知是什麼味。萬歲爺點頭會意，佛動心咬定了牙根。

二人交歡已畢。二姐說：「我每日裏等皇帝，皇帝到沒等着，却等着你了，這也是前世注定的。我看你雖不是個皇帝，久後定然有大好處。」皇爺說：「二姐，你錯相了，窮軍家有什麼好處？」二姐說：「不然，人眼慢俗，我却有個小斤稱。你若是合不着我的意思，今晚上高低還費些事兒；如今還待說什麼哩，我這身子已是屬了你了。你若肯要我，就窮我也受的，身價你不要愁；若是不肯娶我呢，是我合該命盡，一死無大災，就是媽娘殺了我，我可也斷不肯迎新送舊了。」皇爺說：「二姐放心，我定然娶你就是了；萬一娶不成，我也定是教會你那琵琶。」二姐半晌無言，笑着說道：「真正是我這命盡了！」萬歲驚問：「這話怎麼說呢？」

up her mind. The emperor saw that the two serving girls kept winking at her and were watching her with concern. He got up and said, "You don't say this, you don't say that—do you want to take advantage of me with some mean trick? You girls should leave so that I can close the door." He chased them downstairs, slammed the door of the upstairs room, and said, "Second sister, let's go to bed." Overcome by shame, second sister replied, "Sir, you go to bed first. I will follow in a moment." The emperor wanted to take off his clothes right away, but afraid that his secret might be exposed, he said with a smile, "Second sister, you must be nervous. I'll blow out the lamp." With a puff he blew out the lamp, and then he took off his clothes and got on the couch.

> When His Majesty the emperor had taken off his clothes,
> He called to her, "My wife,
> Please come over here. What are you waiting for?
>> Second sister, having no choice but to take off her gauze
>> skirt,
> Said, "I have never gone outside the gate to be with a man,
> So I don't yet know how this will taste."
>> The emperor nodded his head in understanding,
> And Buddha's Lust clenched her teeth.

After the two of them had united in pleasure, second sister said, "Every day I waited for the emperor, but all my waiting was in vain, since all I got was you. This too must have been predetermined by our previous lives. But though you may not be the emperor, I think you will eventually achieve a major position." The emperor replied, "Second sister, the conclusion you draw from reading my face is wrong. What kind of major position can a poor soldier ever achieve?" But second sister said, "You're wrong. 'People's eyes despise the common,' but I have my own little scales. Even if you disagree with me, spend a little tonight. And there's something else I want to say. This body of mine already belongs to you. If you want me, I can suffer the worst poverty, and you won't have to worry about the price of my body. But if you don't want me, it will mean the end of my life. My death wouldn't be a disaster. Even if my madam kills me, I will never agree to prostitute myself." The emperor replied, "Second sister, don't worry. It's the right thing for me to marry you. And if by some chance I cannot marry you, I will still teach you to play the lute." Second sister remained silent for quite a while and then said with a smile, "So my life has truly come to an end!" The emperor was startled and asked, "Why do you say that?"

佛動心淚如麻，你有心愛奴家，奴家也願把你嫁。原是實心愛嫁你，嫁你原不用琵琶，既是從良要他囉？你分明不娶我的樣式，到如今還說什麼！

萬歲說：「這妮子到有這眼力。」疾忙抱過粉頸，摟定纖腰說：「二姐休惱，我方才是試試你的心。既然這等，我軍家自有制度。我雖窮可也不用你那私房。小廝們來時，或者還帶些錢來，三千兩銀子也還難不住我。」二姐說：「你休哄我呀。」萬歲說：「我從來是金口玉言，不會撒謊。」二人說的投機，各各歡喜，交股而眠。

纔睡下鼓二敲，紗窗外月正高，紅羅帳裏明明照。萬歲爺才把鼾睡打，一條花蛇甚蹊蹺，口鼻耳眼都鑽到。二姐見金龍出現，只諕的魂散魄消！

萬歲沉沉睡去，那金龍出現，把二姐諕的氣也不敢喘，搐在被窩裏暗想：「人都說真命天子定有龍蛇鑽竅，只怕這長官是個皇爺！」這二姐心下躊躕，忽然萬歲翻身醒來，問道：「你還沒睡着哩麼？」二姐說：「還沒哩。」遂將那櫻桃小口兒靠在萬歲耳邊說：「賤人不敢動問，你實說你是什麼人？」萬歲說：「好奇呀！叫長官叫了一日了，怎麼又問？」二姐說：「我看你不像個軍家。」萬歲笑道：「這又奇了！

4   To Buddha's Lust, the lute is a courtesan's means to lure customers.

> Buddha's Lust dissolved into tears,
> "If you have the desire to marry me,
> I will happily become your wife.
>   I would truly love to be your wife,
> But if I marry you, I'll have no use for a lute.
> What would I use it for once properly married?[4]
>   You've showed clearly that you won't marry me,
> So what is there left for me to say?"

The emperor said to himself, "This wench has such powers of discernment!" He hastened to embrace her powdered neck and said, holding her slender waist in his arms, "Second sister, don't be annoyed! I was only testing your determination. This soldier will find a solution to our situation. I may be poor, but there's no need to use your private savings. When my underlings arrive, they may bring some money with them. Even three thousand ounces of silver shouldn't be a problem." Second sister said, "Don't fool with me!" The emperor responded, "I've always believed that a man should stand by his word. I can't tell a lie!" When they had reached this happy conclusion, they were contented and fell asleep with legs intertwined.

> They had slept only till the second watch sounded
> When outside the silk window the moon rose high,
> Spreading its light inside the red gauze bed-curtains.
>   While His Majesty the emperor was snoring away,
> A colored snake—truly a miracle to watch—
> Bored through his mouth, his nostrils, his ears and eyes!
>   When second sister saw this gold dragon manifest itself,
> She was so scared her souls dissolved and her spirits fled!

With the emperor in a deep sleep, the gold dragon manifested itself, scaring second sister so much that she didn't even dare to catch her breath. Hiding herself under the coverlet, she thought, "People say that a true Son of Heaven is bound to have dragons and snakes bore through his body orifices, so this officer must actually be the emperor!" While second sister was beset by doubt, the emperor suddenly turned and woke up. "Haven't you fallen asleep yet?" he asked her. "No," she answered, "not yet!" Then she placed her little cherry mouth against the emperor's ear and whispered, "I don't dare ask you, but tell me who you truly are!" The emperor answered, "How strange! You called me 'officer' all day, so why are you asking again?" Second sister said, "In my opinion, you are no soldier." The emperor said with a smile, "This is even stranger!

你說像個什麼人呢？」二姐說：「賤人不敢說，你像個皇帝。」萬歲笑道：「可是你說我的話，你風了麼？我現問你：怎麼見的來？」

佛動心將爺誇，你裝歎又做什麼？看你不在人以下。常言貴命真天子，往往七竅現龍蛇，你就合着這句話。適剛才花蛇上面，險些兒將奴諕殺！

萬歲聽說有蛇，故意吃驚道：「好營生，好營生！諕殺我！想是這樓上有蛇，咱到明日搬了罷。」二姐道：「不是，這是貴人的真體，將來必然大貴。」萬歲道：「胡說！做個窮軍漢，貴從何來？」二姐道：「這到不在哩。」

叫軍爺你聽着：劉志遠也是窮家，景兒作的勾天那大。我癡心每日等皇帝，等了個人兒異樣殺，將來由了那先生的卦。奴便就打水挨磨，似三娘受苦不差。

二姐說了一會，各各睡去。萬歲忽然睜眼，天已大明。那二姐一宿不曾睡著，困乏極了，睡的好不甜美！萬歲恐怕露了馬腳，輕輕的起來，扎挂停當。那二姐方纔翻身，枕邊不見萬歲，慌忙扒起來。萬歲已將樓門開放，丫頭們紛紛鬧鬧，端洗臉水的，拿手巾的，替二姐梳粧的，不一時梳洗停當。

---

5   Liu Zhiyuan started out as a poor farmhand, but eventually became the founder of the Later Han dynasty (947–950).

Then tell me what I look like." Second sister said, "I don't dare say so, but you seem to be the emperor!" The emperor replied with a smile, "How can you say that? Have you gone mad? Let me ask you, Why do you think so?"

> Buddha's Lust praised His Majesty,
> "Why are you once again playing the simpleton?
> In my opinion, you're not one to stand below others.
>   People say that one fated to be a true Son of Heaven
> Will have dragons and snakes manifest themselves
> Through his bodily orifices, and that just happened here.
>   Just a moment ago a colored snake slid up your face,
> Scaring me half to death!"

When the emperor heard there was a snake, he pretended to be frightened and said, "What? You're scaring the hell out of me! There are snakes here? I'm leaving tomorrow!" Second sister reacted, "That's not true! It's a true sign of greatness! You're to achieve a high rank in the future." The emperor said, "Nonsense! I'm just a poor soldier. Where would such nobility come from?" But second sister said, "Don't worry about that."

> She said, "Officer, please listen to me!
> Liu Zhiyuan was only a poor soldier too,[5]
> But his situation became as great as Heaven.
>   Each day I foolishly waited for the emperor,
> Waiting for someone who was exceptional,
> So that the future would fit the soothsayer's prediction.
>   I'll be happy to haul water and push the mill
> And suffer the same misery as Li Sanniang."

After second sister had talked for a while, they both fell asleep. When the emperor opened his eyes, the sky was already bright. Because second sister hadn't slept during the night, she was now sleeping quite sweetly. Afraid that his secret might be exposed, the emperor sprang up and carefully dressed himself. Only when second sister turned to find the emperor gone from the cushion did she scramble up. The emperor had already opened the door of their upstairs room, so the serving girls crowded in, some carrying face-washing water, others bringing towels to help second sister make her toilet, and in a moment she was dressed to perfection.

紗窗外日兒高，纔剛剛梳洗了，扶頭熱酒忙拿到。酒兒最愛穿杯飲，琵琶喜從懷裏教，樓中一片絃聲鬧。這一番君妃歡樂，勾引出作死的沖霄。

這是佛動心初出茅廬第一功。未知後事如何，且聽下回分解。

6　A wedding couple actually drank cups of wine with intertwined arms.
7　When the warlord Liu Bei was in dire straits, he and his sworn brothers Zhang Fei and Guan Yu 關羽 (d. 219) sought to enlist the services of Zhuge Liang 諸葛亮 (181–234) as an adviser. On their first and second visit to his humble dwelling, Zhuge Liang refused to receive them, but when they had demonstrated their sincerity by visiting him a third time, he received them and outlined his grand strategy for them. Soon after leaving his "thatched cottage" he assisted Liu Bei in gaining a major victory.

Outside the silk window the sun had risen high,
But only then were her hairdo and toilet done,
And wine was brought in to congratulate the couple.
    She loved drinking the wine by exchanging cups.[6]
And he taught her the lute as she sat in his lap,
The whole room filled by the sounds of stirred strings.
    The shared joy of lord and spouse in this moment
Attracted that suicidal Wang Long!

This was Buddha's Lust first achievement upon leaving the thatched cottage.[7]

    If you don't know what happened next, please listen to the following chapter.

第十八回 婢送帖寶客欺心 鬼弄人二姐得意

話說這兵部王尚書，有個兒子名叫王龍，包着佛動心的姐姐賽觀音，住在北樓，隔着南樓不甚遠。這一日王龍在北樓正坐，忽然一陣南風，只聽的絲絃盈耳。

王沖霄在醉鄉，這聲音在那厢？一陣一陣聲響亮。院裏的絲絃我都聽過，高煞的腔調也只尋常，聽來那是這般樣。不知是那裏子弟，一句句唱出了京腔。

王龍說：「大姐，你聽聽南樓絲絃甚是出奇。」大姐說：「老王，你擡人擡在天上，滅人滅在地下。你可是隔壁聽音。你說是誰彈？乜是我二妹子跟我學了兩套，每日等皇帝，那皇帝也不來了，多管是悶極了，合丫頭們彈。」王龍說：「瞎話！這絲絃不同。南北二京好絲絃我也見過，我也能彈，這絲絃在我以上，不在我以下。」說的大姐心裏恍惚，巴着南樓聽了聽，果然美耳。遂根問丫環。

賽觀音問丫環，南樓上是誰玩？丫頭從頭說一遍：

1 When Zhu Yuanzhang founded the Ming dynasty, he established its capital at Nanjing, the Southern Capital. But when his son Zhu Di had successfully rebelled in Beijing, the Northern Capital, he did not move to Nanjing. His successors too remained in Beijing, which became the seat of the government. But the organs of central government at Nanjing, such as the Six Ministries, were never abolished.

18　A maid delivers a note: a prize guest has a devious mind;

Ghosts manipulate the man: second sister enjoys satisfaction.

Let me tell you, Minister Wang of the Ministry of War had a son named Wang Long. The patron of Buddha's Lust's elder sister Guanyin's Equal, he was staying in her upstairs room in the northern building, not too far from the southern building. One day Wang Long was sitting in the northern upstairs room when he heard the sound of stirred strings carried on a gust of southern wind.

> Wang Long had not yet recovered from his stupor.
> "Where might this music be coming from?
> With every gust, the sound becomes clearer.
> 　I have heard the playing of everyone in the ward,
> But the melodies of even the best performers are mediocre,
> So what am I hearing of such high quality?
> 　Where did this whoremonger come from,
> Singing each line to the proper capital tune?"

Wang Long said, "Big sister, just listen! The music from the southern building is quite exceptional." Big sister replied, "Old Wang, when you praise someone, you praise him to the sky, and when you destroy someone, you bury him in the ground. You're hearing music from the other side of the wall. Who do you think is playing? Those are the two suites that my younger sister learned from me. Every day she waits for her emperor, but no emperor has ever shown up. She must be bored out of her mind, so she is playing the lute with her servant girls." "Nonsense!" Wang Long said, "This music isn't the same. I've heard the best music of the Southern and Northern Capitals,[1] and I can play it too. But this playing is better, not worse, than mine." Hearing his words, big sister became unsure, and when she listened facing the southern building, the music did indeed sound great, so she asked the servant girls.

> Guanyin's Equal questioned the serving girls,
> "Who is playing in the southern upstairs room?"
> The servant girls informed her from the beginning:

二姐昨日接了客，帽子破來衣又殘，那人是個軍家漢。 那
王龍聽說不信，這事兒古怪刁鑽。

丫頭說了一遍。王龍說：「瞎話！他還不接我，怎麼肯
接那軍家？」大姐道：「依着我，這奴才接個叫花子，
我才自然；他若接個鄉宦人家的公子，我也不笑他。這
個京花子宥甚麼希罕哉！」王龍說：「咱把酒來頓的熱
熱的，另整菜屬，請那長官來唱着吃酒如何？ 」大姐
說：「叫他來吧，得請他！你呢，他就擔的個請字？」
王龍道：「我爲的不是那長官，我爲的是佛動心。我給
那個長官體面，佛動心也有體面。」大姐道：「這奴才
不宜擡舉。」王龍道：「怎麼就不宜擡舉？」遂叫家丁
王興拿個帖子來。王興拿過了一個十二折的全柬來。
王龍顚了兩顚說：「他擔不的使這全柬。」嗤的聲把那
十一折扯下，將一個單帖鋪在桌上，寫道：「通家侍教
生王龍拜。」

寫拜柬是王龍，舉霜筆胡弄窮，這遭送了殘生命！大限到了
合該死，太歲頭上去點燈，死在眼前如做夢。王冲霄欺心抖
膽，南樓上去請朝廷。

王龍把拜柬寫的停當，叫丫頭把這帖下在南樓上，給你
二姐夫。你說北樓王姐夫有請。丫頭道：「俺二姐夫不
來着你呢？ 」王龍說：「休說我給他請柬，我就叫他，
他也不敢不來。」丫頭道：「不是他不來，俺二姐夫穿
的衣服襤褸不堪。」王龍說：「是了，你二姐夫是個窮
漢麼？你着

---

2   The date of one's death.
3   The planet Jupiter, which needs twelve years to circle the sun. It is a star of disaster.

> "Yesterday second sister received a patron.
> His hat is torn, and his clothes are worn.
> By the looks of the guy, he's a common soldier."
>   But Wang Long refused to believe their tale:
> "This business sounds weird and fishy to me!"

When the serving girls had told their tale, Wang Long said, "Nonsense! She wouldn't even receive me, so how could she receive a common soldier?" Big sister said, "If I had my way, that slave would receive a beggar. But if she received the son of some local official family, I wouldn't ridicule her. What's so special about this beggar from the capital?" Wang Long replied, "How about us warming up the wine nicely, putting out another set of dishes, and inviting that officer over to sing and drink?" Big sister said, "Don't invite him, order him to come! Do you need to 'invite' a man who can't bear the weight of that word?" Wang Long replied, "I'm not doing it for the officer. I'm doing it for Buddha's Lust. If I increase the officer's status, I increase her status." Big sister said, "That slave doesn't deserve to be lifted up." But Wang Long said, "Why doesn't she deserve to be lifted up?"

He thereupon told his servant Wang Xing to get him an invitation card. Wang Xing got him a card complete with twelve folds. Wang Long nodded twice and said, "He's not worth a full card," and ripped off eleven folds. He spread the one-sheet card on the table and wrote, "Compliments of your friend and student Wang Long."

> The one who wrote the card was Wang Long.
> By lifting the brush he brought disaster down,
> And this time he caused his own death!
>   The great term[2] had come, so he was fated to die.
> On the head of the Great Year,[3] he lit a lamp.
> So his death was approaching, as in a dream!
>   That devious Wang Long had the courage
> To invite the emperor in the southern room!

When Wang Long had neatly written the card, he told a serving girl, "Deliver this card to second sister's man in the southern upstairs room and tell him, 'You are invited by brother-in-law Wang of the northern upstairs room.'" The serving girl asked, "And if second sister's man refuses to come?" Wang Long said, "Forget about the invitation card. If I ordered him, he wouldn't dare not come." The servant girl replied, "It might not be that he refuses, but that his clothes are all unpresentable rags." Wang Long said, "Indeed. Isn't second sister's man poor? Just tell

他來，我不嫌他衣破。人生十指尚有長短，富貴還有高低，也齊不的，天下有幾個跟上我的？丫頭，你對那長官說：「俺大姐夫請你哩。你若去時，陡然富貴就是陡然富貴，常常富貴就是常常富貴。」丫頭問道：「怎麼是陡然富貴？」王龍說：「他若來時，唱給我聽了，答應的我歡喜，賞他一桌酒，合你二姐姐吃哈，臨走再賞他二百錢，可不是陡然富貴麼？」丫頭又道：「常常富貴呢？」王龍說：「若中支使，留着他當個門下，做一個家丁，扎掛他給他絲綢穿着，強似他們當軍，可不是常常富貴麼？」丫頭道：「俺不說。俺到那裏說了，看你不給他，顯的是俺說瞎話。」王龍道：「我在你奴才們身上撒謊誆他麼？若是他答應的歡喜，豈止絲綢，人皮襖子我也做的起。」丫頭道：「俺到那裏就照樣說哩。」王龍說：「張口爲願，怎肯撒謊呢。」

有王龍差丫環，你快去把帖傳，那裏的子弟我看一看。丫頭聽說往下跑，上的南樓站一邊，王姐夫請去會一面。到那裏用心奉承，管給你換了衣衫。

丫頭上的樓來，把請帖給了二姐夫，說北樓王姐夫有請。二姐說：「多拜上罷，你二姐夫遠路困乏，不赴席罷。」萬歲聽的道，遂說：「二姐，他着人來請，咱不去怎麼說？恐怕咱回不起席麼？」二姐說：「這是北樓上王姐夫請你。」皇爺說：「有請柬麼？」丫頭說：「有。」皇爺說：「拿來我看。」丫頭把柬帖遞於萬歲，見是一個單紅帖，

him to come. I won't blame him for his worn clothes. The ten fingers are of unequal lengths: there's high and low wealth and status; they can't be equalized. How many people in this wide world are my equal? Girl, tell that officer, 'Big sister's man is inviting you. If you go, sudden wealth and status is sudden wealth and status, and continuous wealth and status is continuous wealth and status.'" The serving girl asked, "What is sudden wealth and status?" Wang Long said, "If he will sing for me when he comes and is pleasant company, I will reward him with a table of wine to enjoy with second sister, along with two hundred coins when he leaves. Isn't that sudden wealth and status?" The serving girl then asked, "And what is continuous wealth and status?" Wang Long said, "If he is fit for service, I will keep him in my household as a servant and will outfit him with silk clothes. That's far better than being a soldier. Isn't that continuous wealth and status?" The serving girl said, "I won't tell him that. If I tell him that and it turns out you won't give it to him, then I'd be the one who had lied." Wang Long said, "Would I use slaves to spread lies and deceive him? If he turns out to be pleasant company, it won't be only silk: I can make him a jacket of human skin!" The serving girl said, "Then I will tell him exactly that." Wang Long said, "Each word from me is a solemn vow. How could I lie?"

> Wang Long dispatched a serving girl:
> "Now hurry over there and deliver my card.
> I want to see that whoremonger over there."
>   Being told to go, the girl hurried downstairs,
> And in the southern room she stood to one side.
> "Brother-in-law Wang would like to meet you.
>   And if over there you diligently serve him,
> He will provide you with a new set of clothes."

When the serving girl had arrived in the upstairs room, she handed the invitation card to second sister's man and said, "You're invited by the brother-in-law of the northern upstairs room." Second sister replied, "Please report with all due compliments that second brother-in-law is still exhausted after his long journey, and won't join the meal." When the emperor heard this, he said, "Second sister, he has sent someone to invite me, so why shouldn't I go? Are you afraid that I cannot invite him for a meal in return?" Second sister said, "It's brother-in-law Wang of the northern upstairs room who is inviting you." The emperor said, "Is there an invitation card?" The serving girl replied, "Here it is!" The emperor said, "Let me have a look." The serving girl handed the invitation card to the emperor, who saw that it was a single sheet with

有核桃大字。萬歲一見，心中大有不忿：「好一個割頭
的奴才！我連一個全帖也擔不起了，給我這一個單帖
子！」丫頭見萬歲猶豫不定，恐怕不去，遂說道：「姐
夫，你去有好處。俺大姐夫許着給你做人皮襖子。」萬
歲說：「怎麼說做人皮襖子？」那丫頭把王龍的話從頭
學了一遍。皇爺說：「好呀！又賞我錢，又給我酒吃，
又給我做人皮襖子？找上門來的買賣，我還不去做，待
等甚麼？」萬歲翻過那帖子來記了一筆：某年某月某
日，王龍親許人皮一張。——那王龍未曾見皇爺，先
立了一張死文書給萬歲拿着，大夢不覺。皇爺說：「二
姐，咱赴席去罷。」

小二姐聽的說，拉住了萬歲爺，暗把手兒捏一捏。那王龍
行子眼目大，行動不動就稱他爺，逢人慣把架子扯。像是
你這個模樣，到那裏看他嘴撇。

萬歲說：「二姐你放心，到那裏見了王家那小撕廝，他
情管給我磕頭。」二姐說：「你又發風哩！他貴壓當朝，
財帛甚重，志大胸高，吃酒中間磕你頓拳頭！」皇爺
說：「你放心大膽，咱去罷。」

萬歲爺要下樓，佛動心不敢留，只得隨在身子後。手裏捏着
兩把汗，口雖不言心裏愁，這回醜兒可丟個勾！那萬歲洋洋
不睬，一步步花落水流。

characters as big as walnuts. On seeing this, the emperor's heart filled with rage: "Damn slave! I'm not good enough for a complete card? He sent me this one-sheet?"

When the serving girl saw that the emperor could not make up his mind, she was afraid that he might not go. She said, "Brother-in-law, it's in your interest to go. Big sister's man has promised to make you a jacket of human skin." When the emperor asked what she meant by a jacket of human skin, the serving girl repeated what Wang Long had said from the beginning. The emperor said, "Great! He'll reward me with money, he'll reward me with wine and food, and he'll also make me a jacket of human skin, even before I agree to do business with him. What am I waiting for?" The emperor turned the invitation card around and noted on the backside, "On this day, this month, this year, Wang Long promised one jacket of human skin." Before Wang Long has even seen the emperor, he has handed his own death warrant to the emperor. But he hasn't yet woken from his big dream! The emperor said, "Second sister, let's go and join the meal."

> When little second sister heard these words,
> She pulled His Majesty the emperor back
> And secretly pinched him with her nails.
>   "Wang Long thinks too much of himself.
> Whatever happens, he mentions the minister;
> When meeting people, he always puts on airs.
>   A man dressed like you
> Will there be met only with scorn."

The emperor said, "Don't worry, second sister. When we get there and I've greeted that nobody Wang, he will definitely knock his head to the ground." Second sister said, "You are raving mad again! His nobility surpasses that of the current emperor! His treasures are many, and his ambition unbridled. During the meal, he'll knock your head with his fists!" "Don't worry," the emperor said. "Be brave. Let's go."

> His Majesty the emperor wanted to go downstairs,
> And as Buddha's Lust did not dare stay behind,
> She had no option but to follow him.
>   She clenched her fists, which were drenched with sweat,
> And though she kept silent, she was filled with fear
> That many an unpleasant incident might occur.
>   The emperor was self-confident and unconcerned:
> Every step was "a falling petal, a flowing stream."

這萬歲下的樓來，早慌了那些大小鬼使，恐怕王龍禮貌不周，一陣神風先到了北樓，把王龍圍住。那王龍打了一個支使子，根根毛豎着。說道：「大姐，不好了！這長官有森人毛，未曾請他來，我這心裏戰兢兢的。」大姐說：「這兩日酒多食少，只怕是勞碌的。」王龍說：「不是，我今日做了一個夢極不好。睡到三更時分，只聽的耳邊風響，天地齊轉，我睡的那寢室倒了一間。」大姐說：「是也不算不好，這夢中何足爲憑？」大姐正然圓夢，丫頭來報：「那長官來了。」王龍說：「大姐，他來怎麼處？我下樓接的接他。」大姐說：「那就跌了你那尚書公子的架子。等他上的樓來，合你作揖着，你只還個半簽，就勾了他的了。」一言未了，萬歲爺可就上樓來了。

萬歲爺上樓來，王龍見伴不睬，長官失迎休見怪。久聞大名不曾會，作下揖去頭懶擡，鬼使按倒將爺拜。王冲霄昏迷了半晌，樓板上扒不起來。

萬歲上的樓來，王龍大辣辣的說：「久仰大名，作揖了！」萬歲裝了個不識事務的，把簷毡帽一按，上席坐下。王龍又說：「作揖。」鬼使走上去，按着頭的，擰着腿的，輪了個跟頭，如鷄啄碎米，點了個無其代數。王龍暈了一陣，自家也不知是什麼意思。二姐在旁喜的目瞪癡迷，自思這事出奇，就是老王暈風發了罷，怎樣朝着他仔管磕頭？這長官定然不是個尋常人。不表二姐暗暗稱奇。那大姐心高膽大，全不思量，

When the emperor descended the stairs, he created a panic among those ghosts great and small who feared that Wang Long would behave improperly, and in one gust of divine wind, they arrived in the northern upstairs room to surround Wang Long. Wang Long sneezed, and his hair stood on end. He said, "Big sister, something's wrong. This officer gives me goose bumps even before he's arrived. My heart is trembling and shaking!" But big sister replied, "These last two days you have drunk too much and eaten too little. I'm afraid you've tired yourself out." Wang Long said, "That's not it. Last night I had a dream that was extremely inauspicious. I slept till midnight, then suddenly heard a roaring storm. Heaven and Earth were spinning, and the bedroom collapsed." But big sister said, "That doesn't count as inauspicious. And how can you rely on dreams?" Just when big sister was interpreting his dream, a serving girl reported, "The officer has arrived." Wang Long said, "Big sister, what should I do now that he's here? Let me go downstairs to welcome him." But big sister said, "That would undercut your status as the son of a minister. Wait for him to ascend the stairs and greet you, and then you just nod. That should be enough for him." Before she had finished speaking, His Majesty the emperor came up the stairs.

> As His Majesty the emperor ascended the stairs,
> Wang Long saw him, but pretended to ignore him.
> "Officer, don't blame me for not welcoming you.
>   I've long heard about you, but we haven't yet met."
> When he nodded his head, he was unable to lift it.
> The ghosts were pushing him down and forcing him to bow!
>   Wang Long lost consciousness for quite a while
> And couldn't scramble up from the floorboards.

When the emperor arrived upstairs, Wang Long said with a swagger, "I have long heard about you. Be my guest!" The emperor acted as though he understood nothing, and pushing down his brimmed felt hat, he sat down in the seat of honor. Wang Long said once again, "Be my guest!" The ghosts had him walk forward, and as they pushed down his head and twisted his legs, they turned him around on his heels like a chicken picking up scattered rice, causing him to hit the floor again and again. Wang Long was dizzy and had no idea what he was doing. At the side, second sister was dumbfounded and delighted, thinking to herself, "How bizarre! Even if old Wang is so dizzy that he's lost his mind, why is he kowtowing to him? This officer definitely is not some common man!"

Let's not talk of how second sister secretly cheered the situation. Big sister was proud and courageous, and without any further thought

氣冲冲的就說：「老王，你發窩子風哩麼！」跑到近前，
拉着王龍那胳膊說：「你起來罷。 打折了他牛腿了麼？
你拜他做嗄？」也是那神鬼撥亂，那王龍起了一起，乒
的一聲，一頭碰在大姐的嘴上，只碰的牙齒凌落，滿口
流血。

小大姐害牙痛，心裏焦罵王龍，我到扯你你到掙。或是您親
達來是您祖，仔怕是您親祖宗，見了磕頭這麼盛。小大姐滿
心好惱，這一回胡哭了王龍。

王龍誤誤掙掙的扒了個甚時，纔扒起來，張着那口沒嗄
說。老鴇子說：「王姐夫，我說你家去罷，你再不聽，
你這暈風不發的利害了麼？」王龍道：「正是，前日發
的還好，今日發的我暈頭暈腦的，眼都花了。 我看長
官合那皇帝呀是的。」皇爺說：「這一陣風發的才是。」
二姐說：「王姐夫給你磕了這麼些頭，你只管支架子。」
二姐歡天喜地，大姐一陣好惱。

羞煞了小大姐，佛動心把嘴撇，姐夫前生造下的孽。常時見
人不唱喏，今日磕頭這麼些，喜的二姐沒休 歇。賽觀音惶
恐不盡，佛動心說了又說。

那佛動心極會戲弄王龍說：「王老爺是個大官。」王龍
說：「是北京兵部尚書，就待中入閣哩。」二姐說：「俺
大爺是進士。」王龍說：「是進士，江西提學。」二姐說：
「俺二爺

---

4   A presented scholar (*jinshi* 進士) is one who has passed the triennial metropolitan
     examinations.

she said in a rage, "Old Wang, have you become an idiot?" She rushed forward and pulled him up by his arm, saying, "Get on your feet! Have you broken your legs? Why are you bowing?" But because the divine ghosts were playing havoc, as soon as Wang Long got up, he bumped his head into big sister's face with such force that her teeth fell out and her mouth filled with blood.

> Big sister's mouth was hurting like hell.
> Greatly annoyed, she cursed Wang Long.
> "I was pulling you up, but you had to struggle!
>   Or do you think he's your grandfather?
> Are you afraid he is your ancestor,
> So you kowtow to him without end?"
>   Big sister was filled with exasperation
> While Wang Long was utterly befuddled.

Muddle-headed Wang Long struggled for a long time before he could scramble to his feet. Wide-mouthed, he knew not what to say. The old bawd remarked, "Brother-in-law Wang, I told you to go home, but again you didn't listen to me. Didn't you have a terrible attack of dizziness?" Wang Long replied, "Yes. That attack of a few days ago was manageable, but during this attack today, I felt so dizzy that my head was spinning and I saw stars. That officer looks like the emperor!" The emperor said, "That was only a moment of madness." Second sister said, "Brother-in-law Wang kowtowed so often to you, and you just sat there!" Second sister was overjoyed, but big sister was quite annoyed.

> Big sister was filled with shame,
> And Buddha's Lust pursed her lips:
> "This is bad karma created by brother-in-law in an earlier life!"
>   Ordinarily, when seeing people he wouldn't even greet them,
> But now he kowtowed so many times,
> Filling second sister with unlimited joy!
>   Guanyin's Equal was totally bewildered,
> While Buddha's Lust just kept talking.

Buddha's Lust took the opportunity to tease Wang Long, saying, "His Excellency Wang is a high official!" Wang Long replied, "He heads the Ministry of War in Beijing and will soon join the council of state." Second sister said, "And your eldest brother is a presented scholar?"[4] Wang Long replied, "Yes, he is a presented scholar and serves as intendant of education for Jiangxi." Second sister said, "And your second brother is

也是官。」王龍說：「是二甲進士，寧夏巡按。」二姐說：「你父子俱是大官，見了人不作揖麼？」王龍說：「怎麼不作揖？」二姐說：「你見了二姐夫，怎麼就磕頭呢？」王龍說：「多嘴多舌的小殺才！我怎麼給他磕頭？我這二日有暈風，今早晨又吃了兩盅酒，長官來他是個客，我不接他麼？那瓜子皮擦了我找一個跟頭，怎麼是磕頭？我不合你駁嘴，看椅子來我坐下。」

有王龍要坐下，大小鬼錐子扎，屁股害疼坐不下。起來欠去心不定，一把椅子左右拉。皇爺說王龍坐下罷。眞天子放了大赦，那小鬼才不扎他。

王龍拉過椅子來，才待坐下，那鬼使錐子往上一扎。王龍說：「不好了！有了毒蟲了！」大姐說：「你失張答怪，甚麼毒蟲？你起來我坐。」這大姐輕舉粉臀，尖伸妙腚，略坐了一坐，果然刺疼難忍。兩個就不敢坐的了。王龍只說是他痔瘡發了，又自思道：「我堂堂一個公子，今日這屁股也不助興，仔可站着，是他的小廝這裏伺候他麼？我走着合他說話，好折嚚！」王龍一行走着道：「長官，你是北京，你可在那一塊裏住？你貴姓甚麼名字？不是斗膽問你，你早晚惹下事時，叫家父好給你說個情。」萬歲也不入耳，說：「王官，你合遊營似的影支支的，你在桌頭上坐下罷。」王龍得了金口玉言，拉過椅子來，坐下試了試不疼，方才坐下。王龍見皇爺大大的，又叫他王官，心裏就大不自在，說：「長官，咱兩人叙叙好相與。」萬歲說：「咱萍水

also an official?" Wang Long replied, "He is a presented scholar of the second class and serves as regional inspector for Ningxia." Second sister said, "So father and sons are all high officials. When meeting people, don't they just nod to them?" Wang Long replied, "Of course they just nod." Second sister said, "Then why did you kowtow to my man as soon as you saw him?" Wang Long replied, "You glib-tongued little creature! I didn't kowtow to him! These last few days I've had dizzy spells, and early this morning I drank two beakers of wine. When the officer came, he was a guest, so I had to welcome him. I didn't kowtow to him, I slipped on a melon peel! But I'm not going to argue with you. Get me a chair so I can sit down."

> When Wang Long wanted to sit down,
> Ghosts big and small pricked him with an awl,
> So he couldn't sit down for the pain in his ass.
>   To stand or to sit, he couldn't make up his mind,
> And he pulled the chair to the left and the right,
> Until the emperor said, "Wang Long, sit down!"
>   When the true Son of Heaven issued a pardon,
> The little ghosts promptly stopped their pranks.

The moment that Wang Long pulled over a chair and wanted to sit down, the ghosts caused an awl to stick out and prick him. He cried out, "Ouch! I've been stuck by a scorpion!" But big sister said, "You're so skittish! What scorpion? Get up, and let me sit there." Big sister lightly lifted her powdered buttocks, pointedly stuck out her marvelous rear, and sat down for a while, but the pain of the stabbing was indeed intolerable! So neither of them dared sit down. Wang Long assumed that his hemorrhoids were acting up, and thought to himself, "I may be an impressive young man, but today my butt is acting up, so I have to keep standing. But am I this nobody's servant, waiting on him? Let me talk with him while I walk around. What a shame!" As Wang Long walked around, he said, "Officer, you're from Beijing, but where do you live? What is your surname? I'm not just brazenly asking questions. If you get into trouble at some point, I can have my father put in a word for you." The emperor did not answer, but said, "Sir Wang, you look like a ranger, fluttering this way and that! Just sit down on top of the table!" When Wang Long received this jade order from the golden mouth, he pulled a chair over and tried it out. Only when he felt no pain did he sit down.

When Wang Long saw that the emperor was quite tall and that he called him "Sir Wang," he felt uneasy and said, "Officer, the two of us should converse as friends." The emperor replied, "We have met by

相逢，有甚麼親戚？」大姐便說：「王姐夫，你就稱他長官，他就稱 你王三爺罷。」萬歲說：「我雖當着個窮軍，那江彬合我有點親戚，我也只叫他名字，生平不會叫人爺。你叫我長官，我叫你王官，都是一個官兒，有什麼不好？」王龍見說叫江彬的名字，也就不求全了。叫大姐快給我擺酒。萬歲說王龍待擺酒，我故事他故事，說：「王官，你待擺酒麼？說你的姓來，我過日好回席。」王龍不答。 皇爺說：「主官貴姓甚麼？怎麼不答應？」王龍說：「長官，你戲我哩，叫我王官，又問我貴姓，敢仔我姓王？」萬歲說：「混帳！我就沒見王官就是姓王。我道是長官，我就姓長 麼？」王龍道：「我實在姓王。」萬歲說：「果眞？」王龍說：「這姓有假的麼？」萬歲說：「只怕你爹爹多問不到，你休計較。」王龍說：「長官你謳了，你合我玩不起呀。你敢說你嫖的是妹妹，我嫖的是姐姐，咱是連姻，就該笑玩；這不是官親，玩不的呀！」萬歲說：「玩玩不差。」那賽觀音心中不悅，說：「好京花子！俺請你來吃酒來，說許你要俺來麼？我給王姐夫報報仇。」東西擺下兩桌，萬歲在左邊，王龍在右邊。大姐斟上一盅酒，分明待給王龍，他就故事萬歲說道：「二姐夫酒到了。」萬歲大喜，說道：「好姐兒！有眼色！」那萬歲起坐伸手去接，大姐說：「誰待給你哩！」二姐看不上，說道：「俺又沒曾來趕你的酒吃，你原是請俺來的，你不該眼底無人。你斟酒待給大姐夫，就給大姐夫；給二姐夫，就給二姐夫；你分明待給大姐夫，可怎麼故事二姐夫？」小大姐微微冷笑。

---

5   Wang Long addresses the emperor as *zhangguan* 長官 (officer). The emperor addresses Wang Long as *Wang-guan* 王官 (Sir Wang). Both terms share the element *guan* (official).

accident, and there is no blood relationship between us." Big sister said, "Brother-in-law Wang, you just call him 'officer,' and he can call you 'Third Master Wang.'" The emperor reacted, "Though I'm only a poor soldier, I have a certain relation to Jiang Bin, so I call him by name. Never in my life have I called anyone 'master.' If you call me 'officer,' I will call you 'Sir Wang.' In that way we are both 'sir.'[5] Wouldn't that be best?"

When Wang Long heard him say that he called Jiang Bin by his personal name, he didn't seek details, but rather ordered big sister to set out the wine. The emperor said to himself, "If Wang Long wants to set out the wine, I can play his joke back on him." "Sir Wang," he said, "are you going to set out the wine? Please tell me your surname, so I may invite you for a meal in return one day." When Wang Long did not reply, the emperor said, "Sir Wang, what's your surname? Why don't you answer?" Wang Long replied, "Officer, you're mocking me. You call me 'Sir Wang' and still ask me for my surname. My surname is Wang, of course." The emperor said, "Baloney! How is 'Sir Wang' surnamed Wang? I'm called officer. Does that mean I'm surnamed 'Off'?" Wang Long replied, "My surname truly is Wang." The emperor said, "Indeed?" Wang Long replied, "Could that be a fake name?" The emperor said, "I just worry that we can't consult your father on this. Please don't hold it against me." Wang Long replied, "Officer, you're talking trash. We can't make jokes about that. You claim you are patronizing younger sister, and I am patronizing elder sister, so we are related by marriage and should have some fun together. This is not some official relation than cannot be joked about." The emperor reacted, "Joke or not, it's all the same to me."

Guanyin's Equal was quite displeased and said, "What a beggar! We asked you to come over for some wine, but does that mean we gave you permission to make fun of us? I will get revenge for brother-in-law Wang." Everything had been set out on two tables, with the emperor seated to the left and Wang Long to the right. Big sister poured a beaker of wine that she clearly intended to present to Wang Long, but to make fun of the emperor, she said, "Here is your wine, second sister's man!" The emperor was quite happy and said, "Dear sister, you show discernment!" But when he rose from his seat and stretched out his hands to take the wine, big sister said, "Who's going to give you anything?" Second sister was offended and said, "I've never come to sponge off your wine and food. It was you who invited us. You shouldn't disdain people that way. If you want to pour wine for your man, just give it to your man, and if it's for my man, then give it to him. How can you make fun of my man when you clearly intended to give it to your man?" Big sister coldly smiled.

佛動心你瞎星星，接了個營裏兵，你就拿着當眞果的敬。一日的孤老甚麼帳？湯他一湯你就疼，從頭裏只管逞靈聖。叫二姐休要弄像，我還要使煞你乜咕噥。

　　大姐回頭合王龍說：「小二妮子旣然這等，咱索性氣煞他。」王龍道：「依你怎麼樣？」大姐叠着兩指道：「我說出一個法子來。」未知後事如何，且聽下回分解。

"Buddha's Lust, you're blind in both eyes
By taking some garrison soldier as a patron
And respecting him as if he were the real thing.
    How can he foot the bill of one day of whoring?
Touch him once, and you are racked by pain.
From the beginning he's been playing tricks.
    I tell you, second sister, don't give yourself airs,
Or I'll make sure you dare only to whisper!"

Big sister turned around and said to Wang Long, "If little second wench is going to act like that, we should drive her mad with rage!" Wang Long answered, "What do you think we should do?" Big sister put one finger on top of another and said, "I'll tell you the plan." If you don't know what happened next, please listen to the following chapter.

第十九回 天子愛妃齊奪翠 姐兒嫖客共含羞

話說王龍問大姐的法兒，大姐說：「他是個軍家，只會跑馬射箭，他知道甚麼。吃酒中間，你就說啞酒難吃，咱行個令。他若不會行，輸了酒，咱可取笑。」那王龍聽的說這話，就等不得，一盅酒乾了，叫賽觀音：「拿過令盅來，咱行一個令。」

有王龍叫長官，開懷飲玩一玩，從來啞酒吃不慣。輸家吃酒贏家唱，拆白道字要一般，打乖奪翠各人占。違令者罰酒三杯，飲酒處決不虛言。

二姐聽說行令，着忙說：「姐夫，他待行令，你會不會？你會就合他行；你若不會，丟一個眼色，我給你點着。」萬歲說；「你放心，休說是行令，就是諸樣事，我不在人以下。」行說着，王龍就拿個骰子盆來，說：「長官，咱行個令，誰可做官呢？也罷，咱點骰爲證，擲着誰，誰就是令官。」萬歲說：「贏什麼呢？」依着王龍是贏酒，大姐說；「老王休合他贏酒，輸了着他到肯吃。合他贏銀子。那長官不知帶了幾兩銀子來閬院，給他一個割根齊查，贏他個罄淨，叫他院也嫖不的，人也爲不的。」王龍說：「此計大妙！」說道：「長官，俺輸了的罰

1 *Jiuling* 酒令 is a general term for verbal drinking games. These often involve coming up with parallel lines that have to be constructed according to given specifications. Such specifications might be written on slips pulled out of a jar at random. The person who failed to come up with a fitting line lost the game and had to drink a cup of wine as punishment.

19   The Son of Heaven and his beloved
spouse equally take first place;
Elder sister and her whoring patron are
both filled with shame.

Let me tell you, Wang Long asked big sister for her plan, and she said, "He's a military man. He can only ride a horse and shoot a bow, what else does he know? While you're drinking, tell him, 'Dumb wine is hard to swallow: let's amuse ourselves with wine commands.'[1] If he cannot play the game and loses, he has to drink. Then we can make fun of him." When Wang Long had heard that, he couldn't wait, and when he'd finished only one beaker of wine, he ordered Guanyin's Equal, "Get the cup with the commands, so that I can come up with a command."

> Wang Long cried, "My officer,
> To drink to our hearts' content, we should play a game,
> Since from ancient times no one loves to down dumb wine.
>   The loser has to drink the wine, and the winner will sing.
> It's as fun as splitting characters to make up words.
> Anyone can win by being smart and taking the prize.
>   If you fail to satisfy a command, the fine is three cups of wine,
> And that you have to drink isn't just idle talk."

When second sister heard them talk about wine commands, she became anxious and said, "Brother-in-law, do you know these wine commands that they want to play? If you're good at them, then play with them, but if you are not good at them, I'll wink to give you hints." The emperor said, "Don't worry. Say nothing of wine commands, I'm second to none in everything." While they were speaking, Wang Long brought out the dice bowl. He said, "Officer, who will be the judge when we're playing wine commands? Fine, let the dice make the decision. Whoever throws the highest number will be the judge." The emperor said, "What are we playing for?" If it were up to Wang Long, they'd play for the wine, but big sister said, "Don't play for wine. If he loses, he will be only too happy to drink it all. Play for silver. The officer has brought who knows how many ounces of silver to come whoring in the ward. Clean him out completely, so he can't hang out here in the ward, and he's done for." Wang Long replied, "Great plan!" So he said, "Officer, our fine for losing

銀二十兩，吃酒三盅。」萬歲說：「賽觀音輸了呢？也
是二十兩？誰出？」王龍說：「我出。」萬歲說：「佛動
心輸了我出。」王龍拿過骰子來，擲了個九點，該是在
手。王龍說：「妙呀。」說：「長官，我待行個正經令麼，
怕你說不上來；行個俗俗的令罷，要兩頭一樣。」萬歲
說：「請先說。」王龍遂說道：「兩頭一樣是個磚，一去
不來灶突裏煙。煙煙，休煙，我打夥搬磚，壘竈窩添
柴煙。」皇爺接令就行道：「兩頭一樣是塊地，一去不
來是個屁。屁屁，夜夜出來看景致，一個景致沒看了，
惹的王龍龜聲噪氣。」王龍說：「京花子沒道理！行令
罷，許你罵我來麼？」大姐說：「我給你報一報仇罷。」
遂說道：「兩頭一樣是盤耙，一去不來是句話。畫道兒
長官帶着皮帽子。」二姐接令到行道：「兩頭一樣是張
弓，一去不來是陣風。風來了，雨來了，王龍背了鼓來
了。」皇爺秉手道：「王官恭喜了！」王龍道：「什麼
喜？」萬歲道：「封了你一個忘八頭，還不喜麼？」

萬歲爺笑一聲，王冲霄面通紅，長官掃了俺的興。砌裏答撒
的精光棍，油嘴滑舌會嫖風，不想這花子能行令。王冲霄心
中火起，只一口乾了一令盅，。

萬歲說：「還行不行？」王龍說：「怎麼不行！」拿起骰
子來，擲了萬歲的一個令官。大姐說：「這樓上極邪，
慣好輸令官。咱今遭贏回來了。長官快行令來。」

2   "Turtle" also commonly designates a pimp.
3   Implying baldness. Bald people were the object of ridicule.
4   Pimps often acted as the musicians when courtesans performed. The small orchestras
     that accompanied dramatic performances were led by the drummer.

will be twenty ounces of silver, and you have to drink three beakers of wine." The emperor asked, "And if Guanyin's Equal loses, will it also be twenty ounces? Who will pay?" Wang Long said, "I will pay!" The emperor replied, "If Buddha's Lust loses, I will pay."

Wang Long took the dice and threw a nine, which meant that he would be the judge. Wang Long said, "Wonderful! Officer, I had wanted to use a phrase from the Classics, but I'm afraid you wouldn't come up with anything. So let's use a very common phrase. I want something the same on both sides." The emperor said, "Please go first." Wang Long said, "Two sides the same make for a brick. / What goes and doesn't return is chimney smoke. / What smoke, what smoke! / Don't cause such smoke! / We'll get together and bring the bricks. / Build a proper stove, / And add firewood smoke." It was the emperor's turn to come up with a matching phrase, so he said, "Two sides the same make for a piece of land. / What goes and doesn't return is a fart. / When he blows a fart, / He comes out each night to look for the sights, / But not a single sight does he see. / So Wang Long croaks in rage like a turtle!"[2] Wang Long said, "This capital beggar has no decency! We're playing a game. Does that allow you to revile me?" Big sister said, "I will get revenge for you!" Then she said: "Two sides the same make for a platter with ears. / What goes and doesn't return is a spoken word. / Set the rules. / This officer's hat is made of skin."[3] Second sister was the next, and she said, "Two sides the same makes for a bow. / What goes and doesn't return is a gust of wind. / The wind has come; / The rain has come. / Wang Long is carrying a drum on his back."[4] The emperor grasped his hands and said, "Sir Wang, congratulations!" When Wang Long asked what for, the emperor replied, "You have been appointed head of pimps, isn't that reason enough?"

> His Majesty the emperor laughed out loud,
> While Wang Long's face flushed red:
> "This officer is ruining all my pleasure!
>   Dressed in rags he is a bare stick, pure and simple.
> Oily-mouthed and glib-tongued, he knows his way.
> Who would have thought this beggar was good at games?"
>   A fire started raging inside Wang Long's heart,
> As he downed his punishment in one gulp.

The emperor said, "Are we continuing or not?" Wang Long replied, "Of course we are!" He took the dice, and according to the roll, the emperor was the judge. Big sister said, "This upstairs room is jinxed: it's usually the judge who loses. This time around, we'll recoup our losses. Officer, let us have a command!"

萬歲說：「我要一個天上飛禽是什麼，地下走獸是什麼，路旁古人是誰，那古人拿的是什麼，三什麼兩什麼，打死那什麼，我來的慌些，沒看是公甚麼，母什麼。」王龍道：「你是令官，你先說來。」萬歲說道：「天上飛禽是隻鵯，地下走獸是隻虎，路旁古人是漢高祖。漢高祖使着開山斧，三斧兩斧劈死那隻虎。那一時我走的慌些，沒看是公虎是母虎。」王龍接令行道：「天上飛禽是老鴉，地下走獸是匹馬。」萬歲道：「輸了！上字不合下字的音。」王龍說：「怎麼算輸了？」萬歲說：「就不算。路旁古人呢？」王龍說：「罷了，我沒了古人了。強龍不壓地頭蛇，我合這狗頭賴罷。」遂說道：「路旁古人是俺達，」萬歲說：「可輸了！您達怎麼就是古人？」王龍說：「俺達七八十了，做到尚書，眼前就入閣了，還算不是古人麼？」鵯兒道：「王姐夫，你從幾時這麼賴來？王老爺百年之後，改朝換代，纔稱的是古人。」王龍道：「用你來管閑事麼！」遂又說道：「是俺達。俺達達拿着三股叉，三叉兩叉叉死那匹馬。那一時我來的慌些，沒看是公馬是母馬。」二姐遂說道：「天上飛禽是鳳凰，地下走獸是綿羊，路旁古人是楚霸王。拿着混鐵槍，三鎗兩鎗刺死那綿羊。那一時我走的慌些，沒看是公羊是母羊。」萬歲說：「大姐說罷。」大姐道：「天上飛禽是隻牛，」萬歲說：「且住了。這牛有翅麼？他會飛麼？」王龍說：「長官不要賴罷。你沒見那山水牛麼？他也是會飛的。」萬歲道：「就算山水牛。地下走獸呢？」大姐道：「可沒了走獸了。」

5　Gaozu (Lofty Ancestor) of the Han is Liu Bang (d. 195 BCE), the founder of the Han dynasty.

6　The final word of the first line is *ya* 鴉 (crow), while the final word of the second line is *ma* 馬 (horse). These words may rhyme in popular song, but do not rhyme according to the rules for classical poetry as they belong to different tonal groups (*ya* has a level tone, and *ma* a deflected tone).

7　Xiang Yu (232–202 BCE).

8　A small insect.

the emperor said, "I want the names of a bird that flies in the sky, of an animal that runs on the ground, of an ancient person by the side of the road, of the thing that he is holding in his hands, of what he kills with it, and of what, in my haste, I failed to distinguish as to whether it is male or female." Wang Long said, "You're the judge: you should start." The emperor said, "The bird flying in the sky is a bustard. / The animal running on the ground is a tiger. / The ancient person by the side of the road is Gaozu of the Han,[5] / and Gaozu of the Han uses a mountain-clearing ax. / With three or two strokes of his ax, he kills a tiger, / But at that moment I fled in such a panic / That I failed to see if it was a male or female tiger." Wang Long followed on his lines and said, "The bird flying in the sky is the crow, / The animal running on the ground is a horse." The emperor interrupted him, "You've lost! The last word of the first line doesn't rhyme with the last word of the second line."[6] Wang Long said, "How can that count as losing?" The emperor said, "All right, I won't count it. What about the ancient person by the side of the road?" Wang Long said to himself, "Damn it! I don't have an ancient person by the side of the road. A strong dragon doesn't put down a snake in the grass. How am I going to bluff my way out against this shithead." So he said, "The ancient person by the side of the road is my dad." The emperor said, "Now you've truly lost. How can your dad be an ancient person?" Wang Long replied, "My dad is almost eighty. He's become a minister and will soon join the state council. He doesn't count as an ancient person?" The bawd intervened, "Brother-in-law Wang, since when can you bluff like that? His Excellency Wang can only be counted as an ancient person after another century, when there will be another dynasty!" Wang Long said, "Who asked you?" So he said, "It's my dad. / My dad is holding a trident, / And with three or two stabs of that trident, he stabs the horse to death. / But at that moment I fled in such a panic / That I failed to see whether it was a male or female horse." Second sister thereupon said, "The bird flying in the sky is the phoenix, / The animal running on the ground is the sheep. / The ancient person by the side of the road is the Hegemon King of Chu.[7] / The Hegemon King of Chu is holding an iron lance. / With three or two stabs of that iron lance, he stabbed the sheep to death. / But at that moment I fled in such a panic / That I failed to see whether it was a male or a female sheep." The emperor said, "Big sister, your turn." Big sister said, "The bird flying in the sky is an ox." The emperor said, "Now hold it! Does this ox have wings? Can it fly?" But Wang Long said, "Officer, don't bluff. Have you never seen a mountain-flood ox?[8] Those can fly." The emperor said, "So let's count it as a mountain-flood ox. But what about the animal that runs on the ground?" Big sister said, "I don't have any running animal!"

王龍把大姐瞪了一眼。大姐道:「可悶煞我了!只怕我是走獸,我又只兩根腿。也罷,合他賴罷。」遂說:「地下走獸是個粉頭,路旁古人劉武周。劉武周拿着個大杵頭,三杵頭兩杵頭,杵死那個粉頭。那一時我來的慌些,沒看是公粉頭,是母粉頭。」老鴇子說:「小大妮子,你待死麼?怎麼越大越糟囤了!這粉頭還有公母麼?大姐夫稱上銀子罷。」王龍無計奈何,稱上了四十兩銀子。

萬歲爺笑哈哈,叫鴇子斟大杯,二姐喜的如酒醉。粉頭也有公合母,耕地的牛兒都會飛,堪合王龍是一對。萬歲說:這長臍粉頭,王冲霄扎他大虧。

萬歲合二姐拍手大笑。大姐羞的滿面通紅,無言可答,遂乾了令盅。心中不服,便說:「糟糟!是別人行令着,俺輸了。我也行個令,各人要有翅無毛,後待四句詩,上下不叶音的輸。」萬歲說:「請。」大姐先說:「我占一個蚊子。」二姐說:「我占一個蜂子。」王龍待說我占一個蒼蠅,還沒說出來,交別了口說:「我占一個蜻蜓。」萬歲說:「我占一個蒼蠅。」王龍說:「我待占個蒼蠅來,未曾開口就錯了,倒被長官占了去了。我這蜻蜓也不弱的。」萬歲說:「大姐請先罷。」大姐說道:「我做蚊子實是強,貴賤皮肉我先嘗。吃的肚兒大大的,花枝底下去乘涼。」

9   The word translated as "trollop" is *fentou* 粉頭 (powdered head), a common term for prostitutes.
10 Liu Wuzhou 劉武周 (582–622) was one of the warlords following the collapse of the Sui dynasty.

Wang Long stared at big sister with eyes wide open, so big sister said, "I'm screwed! I'll have to be the running animal, even though I have only two legs. Fine, I'll bluff my way out!" So she said, "The animal running on the ground is a trollop.[9] / The ancient person by the side of the road is Liu Wuzhou.[10] / Liu Wuzhou is holding a big stamper in his hands, / And with three stamps of his stamper, two stamps of his stamper, / He stamps that trollop to death. / But in that moment I came in such a panic / That I failed to see whether it was a male or female trollop." The old bawd said, "You big wench, do you want to die? The older you get, the more muddle-headed you are! Do you have male and female trollops? Big sister's man, you will have to weigh out the silver." Wang Long was forced to weigh out the silver.

> His majesty the emperor laughed out loud
> And ordered the bawd to pour a large cup.
> Second sister was so pleased she seemed drunk:
>   "Among trollops you have males and females,
> And the oxen that plow the fields can fly.
> They form a fitting parallel to Wang Long!"
>   The emperor said, "This long-dick trollop!"
> Wang Long suffered a major loss.

The emperor and second sister clapped their hands and laughed heartily. Big sister felt so ashamed that she blushed all over her face, but she couldn't find a retort, and so emptied the beaker that she had to drink as punishment. Then she said, "My bad luck! I lost because other people set the theme. But let me give the command! Everyone has to come up with creature with wings but no hair, to be followed by a four-line poem. If the lines don't rhyme, you lose." The emperor said, "You first!" Big sister went first and said, "I choose the mosquito." "I choose the bee," second sister said. Wang Long wanted to say, "I choose the fly," but before he could say so, his mouth got twisted and out came "I choose the dung beetle." "I choose the fly," the emperor said. Wang Long said, "I had wanted to choose the fly, but even before I opened my mouth, I mixed things up, and now the officer has taken the fly. But my dung beetle will prove just as strong!" "Big sister, please go first," the emperor said. Big sister said,

> As the mosquito, I am strongest:
> I am first to taste the flesh of high and low.
> And when I have eaten my fill and my belly is bloated,
> I enjoy the cool shade below blooming branches.

二姐接令即行道：「我做蜂子實是強，百般花蕊我先嘗。吃的肚兒飽飽的，蜂窩裏頭去乘涼。」萬歲接令說道：「我做蒼蠅實是強，朝廷御筵我先嘗。珍羞百味吃個飽，天華板上去乘涼。」王龍說：「這京化子他占的不奇，說的到好。我這蜣螂怎好出口？」萬歲說：「王官怎不行令？」王龍說：「我另占何如？」萬歲說：「酒令大如軍令，使不的另占。」王龍前思後想，沒計奈何，遂說道：「我做蜣螂實是強，」王龍自思：不好，蜣螂就該吃屎了。代不說可又怕輸了。遂又說道：「……諸般屎尖我先嘗。吃的肚兒大大的，拱著個彈兒做乾糧。」鴇子大笑道：「王大姐夫你好髒！一盅酒甚麼大要緊，就吃起屎來了？拿過銀子來吃酒罷。」

老鴇子這一聲，羞犯了王老冲，二姐笑的眼沒縫。萬般東西都不吃，單單揀着吃大恭，

Second sister followed this with

> As the bee, I am strongest:
> I am first to taste the nectar of the hundred flowers,
> And when I have taken so much that I'm truly satisfied,
> I enjoy the cool shade in the hive.

In his turn the emperor followed this with

> As the fly, I am strongest:
> I am first to taste the imperial banquet at court.
> I eat my fill of the hundred dishes and exquisite delicacies
> And then enjoy the cool shade on the ceiling boards.

Wang Long said to himself, "This capital beggar! His topic isn't exceptional, but he phrased it well. How can I come up with a good poem on the dung beetle?" The emperor said, "Sir Wang, why don't you take your turn?" Wang Long replied, "Can I choose another topic?" But the emperor said, "The discipline in wine commands is as strict as in the military: changing topics is not allowed!" Wang Long racked his brains but saw no way out and eventually said,

> As the dung beetle I am strongest:

But then he thought to himself, "Damned! A dung beetle has to eat shit!" He wanted to keep silent, but he was also afraid to lose, so eventually he said,

> I am first to taste all kinds of shit.
> And when I have eaten my fill and my belly is bloated,
> I push the ball that serves as my rations.

The bawd laughed heartily and said, "Brother-in-law Wang, you are too dirty! Is a beaker of wine so important that you start eating shit? Get the money and drink the wine!"

> These few words of the old bawd
> Filled Wang Long with utter shame.
> Second sister laughed till her eyes nearly shut,
>   "He doesn't want to eat anything else,
> But chooses to dine exclusively on turds—

從來沒見這蹺蹊性。叫丫環斟水與他，漱漱口好掇令盅。

王龍着二姐笑的羞愧難當，把眼瞪了幾瞪，幾番待要發作，又尋思是自己說的，又怕人說他，憊頭搭腦的，不言不語的。萬歲道：「王官休惱，我行一個令給你散散心罷。」王龍道：「甚麼令？」萬歲說：「名爲急口令，天下一百單八府，各府一個字，說爺是什麼，娘是什麼，後生下什麼，伸什麼手，取什麼壺，斟什麼酒，張什麼口，吃什麼酒，什麼酒乾。上字不合下音，算輸。」王龍說：「長官請占。」萬歲說：「我占龍慶府。」王龍乖覺，便揀一個好名色的說：「我占一座歸德府。」大姐說：「我占一座廬州府。」二姐說：「我占一座鳳陽府。」萬歲說：「我是令官，我就先行罷。」「我占的是龍慶府。俺爺是公龍，俺娘是母龍，后來生下我這小龍。伸龍手，取龍壺，斟龍酒，張龍口，吃龍酒，龍酒乾。」王龍說道：「是這麼說麼？我另占一府何如？」萬歲道：「違令者罰！」王龍低頭自思，難于開口，只管不說。萬歲說：「我替你說了罷。」「你占的是歸德府。你爺是公龜，你娘是母龜，後來生下你這小龜。伸龜手，取龜壺，斟龜酒，張龜口，吃龜酒，龜酒乾。」二姐接令說道

11　The first character used in writing the place name Gui'de 歸德 (return to virtue) has the same pronunciation as the character *gui* 龜, which means turtle. "Turtle" is a common term for a pimp. I here write "Gui'de" with an apostrophe separating the two syllables to avoid confusion with the English word "guide."

12　The first character used in writing the place name Longqing 龍慶 means "dragon."

All my life I've never seen such a weird character!"
    Wang Long ordered a serving girl to fetch some water
So he could rinse his mouth before taking the cup.

At second sister's laughter, Wang Long felt unbearable shame. He glared at her and was about to blow his top repeatedly, but then he considered that he himself had said those words, and was afraid that the others would criticize him. He remained silent and despondent until the emperor said, "Sir Wang, let me issue a command that will lighten your heart." Wang Long asked, "What command?" The emperor replied, "This is a tongue twister. Take a word from the name of one of the one hundred and eight prefectures of the empire, and tell us who your father is, who your mother is, what your children will be, what kind of hand you stretch out, what kind of jug you take, what kind of wine you pour out, what kind of mouth you open, what kind of wine you drink, and what kind of wine is finished. If the lines don't rhyme, you lose." Wang Long said, "Officer, please make your choice." The emperor replied, "I choose Longqing." An alert Wang Long picked a beautiful place and said, "I choose Gui'de."[11] Big sister said, "I choose Luzhou," and second sister said, "I choose Fengyang." The emperor said, "I am the judge, so let me go first. I chose Longqing. My father is a male dragon,[12] my mother is a female dragon, and I will father dragon children. I stretch out my dragon hand, take the dragon jug, pour the dragon wine, open my dragon mouth, and drink the dragon wine until the dragon wine is finished." Wang Long said, "Is that how it's done? Can I choose another prefecture?" The emperor said, "Whoever breaks the rules will be fined." Wang Long pondered the matter with lowered head, and as he found it impossible to say his lines, he kept his mouth shut. But the emperor said, "Let me say it in your place. You chose Gui'de, so your father is a male turtle your mother is a female turtle, and what you father will be little turtles. When you stretch out your turtle hand, take the turtle jug, and pour out the turtle wine, you will open your turtle mouth, and drink the turtle wine till the turtle wine is finished." Second sister continued the game by saying,

：「我占的是鳳陽府。俺爺是公鳳，俺娘是母鳳，後來生下我這小鳳。伸鳳手，取鳳壺，斟鳳酒，張鳳口，吃鳳酒，鳳酒乾。」大姐又像王龍，面紅過耳，不則一聲。二姐笑道：「大姐姐，我替你說了罷。」「你占的是盧州府。你爺是公驢，你娘是母驢，後來生下你這小驢。伸驢手，

取驢壺，斟驢酒，張驢口，吃驢酒，驢酒乾。」

萬歲大笑。那王龍氣的氣充兩肋，無法可施，酒也不待吃，話也不待說。萬歲立起身來說：「王官，今日盛擾；我已是醉了，咱不吃罷。」王龍說：「聽見你的絲絃甚妙，還不曾領教，怎麼就說去呢？」萬歲說：「改日再玩罷。」遂同二姐下了北樓。未知後事如何，且聽下回分解。

---

13   The first character in Fengyang 鳳陽 means a male "phoenix."

14   The first character in Luzhou 盧州 is close in pronunciation to *lü* 驢, which means "donkey."

"I chose Fengyang. My father is a male phoenix,[13] my mother is a female phoenix, and I will bear little phoenixes. When I stretch out my phoenix arm, I take the phoenix jug and pour the phoenix wine. When I open my phoenix mouth, I drink the phoenix wine until the phoenix wine is finished." Big sister blushed just like Wang Long, not making a sound, so second sister said with a smile, "Big sister, let me say it for you. You chose Luzhou. Your father is male donkey,[14] your mother is a female donkey, and the children you will bear will be little donkeys. When you stretch out your donkey hand, you take the donkey jug and pour out donkey wine. And when you open your donkey mouth, you drink donkey wine till the donkey wine is finished."

The emperor laughed heartily, but Wang Long was so filled with rage that his sides hurt. Yet there was nothing he could do about it, so he didn't want to drink any wine or say anything. The emperor stood up and said, "Sir Wang, we have bothered you too much today. I'm already drunk, so let's not drink anymore." Wang Long replied, "I heard your wonderful performance on the lute, but haven't yet received your instruction. Why do you want to leave?" The emperor said, "Let's meet again another day." Thereupon he and second sister descended the stairs.

If you don't know what happened next, please listen to the following chapter.

第二十回 二姐含羞吹玉笛 武宗假意賣龍駒

　　話說二姐見萬歲口頭伶俐，全無一點鄙瑣處，心中大
喜。當下回到南樓，丫頭來點上銀燈，各人散去。二姐
把樓門關了，說：「長官，你先睡，我待吹燈哩。」二
姐一口把燈吹煞。萬歲將龍衣脫下，用青布衫浮皮一
裹，裹的合一個包袱相似，緊放在身子裏頭，方才睡
下。二姐一來熟了，二來心裏喜歡，也就解衣上牀來
了。

佛動心今夜中，有八分愛武宗。瘡口不敢說沒連縫，雖然路
兒還生澀，也是瘍裏帶着疼，不似昨日難扎掙。他二人玩要
了半夜，一覺兒睡到天明。

　　一宿晚景提過。二姐看見天明，早起梳粧。萬歲說：
「我還要睡，休着人來混我。」萬歲又睡了片時，見二
姐獨坐窗前，照那鏡兒。萬歲說：「你下樓去看看我那
馬，不知今夜餧他來沒？」萬歲把二姐調下樓去，方纔
起來，扎掛停當，梳洗完備。又彈了一回琵琶，下了一
回棋子，吃了早飯。萬歲說：「咱兩個悶騰騰的，不如
還合王龍混去。」二姐說：

20 Second sister conquers her shame and plays the jade flute;
The Martial Emperor deceptively sells off his dragon colt.

Let me tell you, second sister was very pleased when she saw how gifted the emperor was in repartee, and that he showed no sign of ignorance. Straightaway they returned to the southern upstairs room. Serving girls lit the silver lamp and then retired. After second sister had locked the door, she said, "Officer, you go to bed first. I will blow out the lamp." With one puff, she blew out the lamp. The emperor took off his dragon gown and wrapped it in the cover of his blue linen gown like a pack, which he placed close to his person. Only then did he go to bed. Second sister had become experienced, and she also had come to like him, so she took off her clothes and ascended the couch.

> This night Buddha's Lust
> Loved the Martial Ancestor eighty percent.
> Her wound could not yet be said to have fully healed.
> But even though the road was still raw and constricted
> And there was still some pain with an itch,
> It was not as hard a struggle as the first time.
> The two of them had their fun for half the night,
> Then fell asleep, sleeping till the sky turned bright.

So much for that night. When second sister saw that the sky was bright, she quickly got up and made her toilet. But the emperor said, "I still need some sleep, so don't let anyone bother me." After the emperor had slept for a while, he saw second sister sitting before the window looking into a mirror. "Please go downstairs and have a look at my horse," the emperor said, "to see whether it was fed last night." Only after the emperor had tricked second sister into going downstairs did he get up, dress himself properly, comb his hair, and wash his face.

After playing the lute, engaging in a game of go, and eating their breakfast together, the emperor said, "It's boring with just the two of us. We should get together with Wang Long again." Second sister replied,

「昨日是他請咱，咱去就罷了；方纔擾了他，怎好自己
又去？」萬歲說：「有個指頭。」二姐說：「什麼指頭？」
萬歲說：「我正愁着那馬沒人餧養，不如賣給他罷。」
二姐說：「你來到院裏就賣了馬，也不好看像。」萬歲
說：「這不過暫且令他替我餧着，何妨呢。」二姐說：
「賣給人還待要的哩。」萬歲說：「你不要愁，我用着了，
他自然兩手奉獻。」商議已定，下的南樓，這話不表。

再說王龍在北樓，與大姐定計，要贏萬歲。

王冲霄在樓中，尋方兒把氣爭。大姐便說有法令，軍家錢財
看的見，賭場裏合他顯顯能，務要贏的他掉了腚。腚溝裏夾
上稱桿，管叫他一溜崩星！

二人正自商議，萬歲合二姐到了。王龍拱了一拱說：
「我就待着丫頭去請，你來的正好。」萬歲說：「夜來
取擾。今日無事可也不來，有一件事要來求玉成。」王
龍說：「什麼事？」萬歲說：「若說出來，休要笑恥。」

叫王龍休笑話，無銀子使什麼？一匹好馬賣了罷。兩頭見日
走千里，不用鞭子腿不夾，三百兩銀減半價。宣武院把馬賣
了，當子弟玩耍玩耍。

"Yesterday he invited us, and we went there. We just bothered him, so how can we go there on our own initiative?" The emperor said, "I have a reason." When second sister asked what kind of reason, the emperor replied, "I'm worried that no one will feed my horse, so I had better sell it to him." Second sister said, "It would give the wrong impression if you sold your horse as soon as you arrived in the ward." But the emperor said, "I only want him to feed the horse for the time being. What's the problem?" Second sister said, "Will you still want it once you've sold it?" The emperor replied, "Don't you worry about it. As soon as I need it, he will freely present it to me with both hands." With that, they went downstairs.

Let's leave them now and return to the northern upstairs room and Wang Long, who was plotting with big sister about how to triumph over the emperor.

> In the upstairs room Wang Long
> Was seeking a way to vent his rage
> When big sister said, "I know a way!
>   That soldier must have limited money,
> So display your skill in gambling with him,
> And make sure you beat the pants off him.
>   With a scale-rod in his ass,
> We'll have him running like a shooting star."

While they were deliberating, the emperor and second sister arrived. Wang Long greeted them with folded hands and said, "You arrive at the right moment. I was just about to send a serving girl over to invite you." The emperor replied, "Yesterday we bothered you, so today we would not come without a reason. I have an issue that I hope you can solve for me." When Wang Long asked what kind of issue, the emperor said, "Don't laugh when I tell you."

> He said, "Wang Long, don't laugh at me:
> If I have no cash, how can I spend it?
> So I want to sell that fine horse of mine.
>   In only two days' time it ran a thousand miles,
> Without me using the whip or pressing its sides.
> Three hundred ounces of silver, at half the price!
>   After selling my horse in Displaying Martiality,
> I'll play the patron and enjoy myself in the ward."

大姐說道：「老王，你常說那騾子不是你的，是老爺的看騾，你待買匹馬。你買了他這馬罷。」王龍說：「我就忘了呢。長官，你只管吃酒，你那馬我管招顧你的。」便吩咐人北院取馬。不一時，把龍駒牽到。王龍走下樓看了一看，眞正好馬。說道：「我去試試。」

王冲霄造化低，一心裏把馬騎，金鞍玉轡牢拴系。院內跑了兩三趟，喜煞王龍作死賊，稱上三百冰花細。幾盤棋把他贏了，管叫他彈打雀飛。

王龍只誇好馬，就像一條龍，只聽的耳邊風響，平地駕雲。「這馬就值一千兩銀子，買了他的罷。遂稱給他銀子。再贏了他的，馬也是我的，銀子也是我的，銀馬都到我手。」王龍計算定了，上樓來叫道：「長官，我才試了試的那馬，說走一千是謊着了，極七八日也走不上一千。好歹買了來，給小廝們騎罷。休說有這馬，就是沒有這馬，給你三百兩銀子，結個朋友也不差。」大姐拉在一邊說：「老王，大牲口要個文約纔是。京花子什麼正經！賣幾兩銀子花費了，回了北京，見了他的主子，問道：『你那馬呢？』他昧了良心說：『到了山西遇着王龍，倚強欺弱，白問我要了去了。』他那主子若是個性好的人，寫一個火票來問你要了去；若是傲上的人，駕前一奉，就說尚書的公子短了差官的馬去了，可不連老爺的官傷着了麼？拿着銀子買不自在哩麼？不如問他要張

1　A mule that is used only for riding.

Big sister said, "Old Wang, you always say that that mule isn't yours, but rather that it is the show mule[1] of His Excellency, and that you want to buy a horse. Why don't you buy his horse?" Wang Long said, "I had almost forgotten. Officer, have some wine. I will definitely buy your horse." Thereupon they ordered someone to fetch the horse to the northern ward. Soon the dragon colt was brought over, and Wang Long went downstairs to have a good look. It was truly a fine horse, so he said, "Let me try it."

> Wang Long's fortunes took a dive.
> He was determined to ride the horse.
> Golden saddle and jade bit were securely fastened.
>   It ran a few rounds inside the ward,
> Greatly pleasing Wang Long, that suicidal thief,
> Who weighed out three hundred ounces of ice.[2]
>   In a few games of go, he would all win it back
> And have that guy fleeing like a hunted sparrow.

Wang Long could only praise the fine horse. It was like a dragon: he heard the wind roar in his ears as if he were suddenly riding the clouds! "This horse is worth a thousand ounces of silver, so let me buy it from him. Once I have weighed out the silver for him, I'll win it back. The horse will be mine and the silver too; silver and horse both will end up in my hands."

Once Wang Long had settled on this scheme, he went upstairs and said, "Officer, I have tried it out. You lied when you said that it could run a thousand miles. Even at its best, it could not do a thousand miles in seven or eight days. For better or worse, I'll buy it from you and have my servants ride it. Let's forget about the horse. Even without it, I will still give you three hundred ounces of silver. It's well spent to become your friend." Big sister pulled him to the side and said, "For such a big animal you need a contract. How can we trust that capital beggar? He'll sell his horse for a few ounces of silver and spend it all, but when he gets back to the capital and sees his superior, that man will ask, 'What about your horse?' and without any conscience he will say, 'When I arrived in Shanxi, I ran into Wang Long, that tyrant, and he took it from me for nothing.' If that superior is kind, he will write a warrant to claim it back from you, but if he's a proud person, he will report it to the Throne, saying that the son of a minister stole the horse of an emissary. Wouldn't even His Excellency become involved and be damaged? Even if you pay with silver, you can't be casual about it. The best thing is to ask him for a

文約，那怕他告御狀上本章，咱放着證見。」

賽觀音把心欺，弄巧語害正德。王龍耳軟無主意，隨邪聽了
賤人話，王龍吃了大姐虧，後來剝皮無人替。王冲霄被他調
轉，一心裏查考眞主。

王龍聽了大姐這話，回席坐下，說：「長官，咱吃了這
半日酒了，我就沒問你貴姓？」萬歲自思：「這廝問我
貴姓，我又不好說我姓朱。也罷，我混他一混。」這
萬歲拿起一雙箸來，向桌子上一指。王龍道：「長官慣
好弄鬼，問他貴姓不說，光指那桌子，你這個虎我就打
不開。乜桌子上只兩把壺，長官，你姓胡麼？」萬歲不
答，只點頭。王龍說：「妙呀！我就是個老神猜，我就
猜著你姓胡了。尊諱呢？」萬歲把簷氈帽一拉搭，伏桌
子上打盹。王龍說：「你這又是一個虎。尋尋思思的，
沒裏他是『胡尋思』，這又不像個人名，只怕是『胡想』。
我莽莽他罷。長官，尊諱是想？」萬歲又點頭。王龍
說：「又打破這個虎了。你的字呢？」萬歲說：「字是君
思。」王龍說：「你的號呢？」萬歲說：「你問的這麼親
切，待告着我不成？待我再混他一混。」拿起箸來往南
指了一指，往北指了一指。王龍說：「又是一個虎。三
個虎打破了兩個了。

2　High-quality silver.
3　The word for jug (*hu* 壺) has the same pronunciation as the surname Hu 胡.
4　The phrase translated as "deep in thought" is *xunxun sisi* 尋尋思思. The word *xiang* 想 means to think.
5　The two characters *junsi* 君思 may be rendered as "you think."

written contract. Even if he accuses you at court and submits a report, we would have proof."

> Guanyin's Equal, quite deceptive herself,
> Calumniated Right Virtue with clever words;
> Wang Long, with no ideas of his own, was easily taken in.
>   Following evil, he listened to that vile person's words
> And suffered misfortune because of big sister:
> When later his skin was flayed, no one took his place.
>   Wang Long was talked around by big sister
> Who convinced him to distrust the True Ruler.

After Wang Long had listened to big sister, he returned to the banquet, sat down, and said, "Officer, we've been drinking all this while, but I still haven't asked you for your surname." The emperor thought to himself, "He's asking me for my surname, but I can't very well tell him that my surname is Zhu. Fine, let me fool him." The emperor picked up a pair of chopsticks and pointed them to the table. Wang Long said to himself, "This officer is always playing tricks. When I ask for his surname, he points at the table instead of telling me." "I cannot solve this riddle of yours! On that table there are only two jugs. Officer, are you surnamed Hu?"[3] The emperor only nodded his head. Wang Long said, "Wonderful! I must be a divine riddle master, having guessed that you're surnamed Hu. And what is your personal name?" The emperor pulled his brimmed felt hat to one side and dozed off, leaning forward on the table. Wang Long said to himself, "Yet another riddle. Deep in thought. Could it be that he is Hu Xunsi? But that doesn't look like a personal name. I think it must be Hu Xiang.[4] Let me surprise him." "Officer, is your personal name Xiang?" The emperor again nodded his head. Wang Long said, "Another riddle solved! And your social name?" The emperor said, "My social name is Junsi."[5] Wang Long said, "And your alias?" The emperor said to himself, "He's asking all these personal details, does he want to lodge an accusation against me? Let me trick him again." He picked up the chopsticks and pointed once toward the south and once toward the north. Wang Long said to himself, "That's yet another riddle. I've solved two of the three riddles.

這花子多是樓上起號，只怕是『胡南樓』；他又往北指，只怕是『胡北樓』。是了，長官大號想是胡雙樓麼？」萬歲說：「然。」王龍說：「胡雙樓，你賣這馬給我，是個大牲口，要一個文約才是。」萬歲說：「不然拿筆硯來

我寫。」王龍笑道：「長官，你也識字麼？」萬歲道：「剛寫出我的名字來。」王龍說：「寫出來就是了。」

立文約胡君思，北京城一小旗，我是一個吃糧的。因爲無錢賣了馬，寶客王龍買了騎，三百兩銀子上了契。上寫着外無欠少，下隨着一並交支。

那萬歲立了文約，王龍拍手大笑。

有王龍喜重重，叫大姐你是聽：三百兩銀子幫他個淨。叫他窮的沒處去，收他門下做家丁，早晚帶着好聽用。若着他寫帖上帳，那小廝也倒聰明。

王龍說：「大姐，咱把他那銀子幫他個馨淨，着他有家難奔，有國難投。你可圓成着，你就說俺王姐夫雖是鄉宦家公子，他可極良善，長官你又沒了銀子了，怎麼回家？你給他做個管家不好麼？哄的他上了套着，那時在我。我叫他給我牽馬墜鐙，奉客唱詞；又寫了一筆好字，早晚給我上帳寫寫名帖不好麼？話是這樣說罷，咱可有甚麼方法贏他那銀子？」

6　Nanlou 南樓 means "southern upstairs room" while Beilou 北樓 means "northern upstairs room." Shuanglou 雙樓 means "paired rooms."

This beggar must have taken his alias from the upstairs room, so it must be Hu Nanlou, but he also pointed toward the north, so I think it must be Hu Beilou. I get it!" "Officer, your alias must be Hu Shuanglou?"[6] The emperor replied, "Indeed!" Wang Long said, "Hu Shuanglou, you are selling this horse to me. As it is a big animal, we need a contract." The emperor replied, "If so, get an inkstone and I will write one." Wang Long said with a smile, "Officer, do you know your characters?" The emperor replied, "I can just about write my own name." Wang Long said, "That will do."

> "The one establishing this contract is Hu Junsi,
> A common soldier from the city of Beijing.
> I am one who draws a ration of grain.
>   I am selling my horse because I am short of money.
> The precious guest Wang Long is the buyer.
> Three hundred ounces of silver seals the deal."
>   At the top he wrote, "Amount paid in full,"
> At the bottom he wrote, "Goods exchanged."

When the emperor established this contract, Wang Long clapped his hands and laughed loudly.

> Wang Long was extremely pleased
> And said, "Big sister, now listen to me.
> I'll help him get rid of those three hundred ounces.
>   I'll reduce him to such poverty he has nowhere to go.
> I'll take him into my household as another servant,
> Taking him with me at all times and using him.
>   If I let him write notes and do accounts,
> that little nobody may prove pretty smart."

Wang Long said, "Big sister, I'll help him get rid of all that silver and make sure he has no house he can run to and no country he can flee to. But you have to bring the matter to the perfect conclusion. You will say to him, 'Even though our brother-in-law Wang is the son of a local official, he is a good man. Officer, you have no money left, so how can you go back home? Wouldn't it be great if you became his major-domo?' Once you've sweet-talked him into falling into the trap, it will all depend on me. I will tell him to lead the horse and hold the stirrup, serve guests and sing lyrics. And as he can also write well, wouldn't it be great if he could do the accounts from early till late, and write notes and invitations? It sounds great, but how will I win all his money?"

大姐道：「這倒是小事。這花柳巷裏總是填不滿的坑，我待着他今日淨，就今日淨；待着他明日淨，就明日淨，有甚麼難處？雖是這麼說，姐夫，

你可留戀着才好。」王龍道：「怎麼留戀他呢？」大姐道：「你或是合他打雙陸，或是抹骨牌，或是下象棋，諸般的都合他試試。你再贏他的，我再騙他的，霎時間就着他淨了，值甚麼呢！」王龍遂即收了買馬的文契，兌了馬價銀子，二人鋪謀定計，要贏萬歲。未知後事如何，且聽下回分解。

7　The prostitution quarters.

Big sister said, "That is the easiest part. These flower and willow lanes[7] are a pit that can never be filled, so if we want him to be cleaned out today, he will be cleaned out today, and if we want him to be cleaned out tomorrow, he will be cleaned out tomorrow. What's the problem? Even so, brother-in-law, it would be best if you stay close to him." Wang Long asked, "How should I stay close to him?" Big sister said, "Play backgammon with him, or dominoes, or chess. Try him out in all of them. The more often you win, the more persuasive I will sound, and soon we'll have cleaned him out. How hard could it be?" So Wang Long accepted the contract for the sale of the horse and paid out its price in silver. Then the two set out on a scheme to triumph over the emperor.

If you don't know what happened next, please listen to the following chapter.

第二十一回 王冲霄賭博輸錢 武宗爺脫衣洗澡

話說大姐合王龍定計要贏萬歲，遂丟了個眼色，那丫頭將氣球拿過來。萬歲說：「我裝憨給他瞧瞧。」說；「乜個東西，丫頭你拿了去罷，我纔吃了飯。」丫頭抿着嘴笑，放在桌上。萬歲說：「二姐，他既有誠敬之心，咱就饒他，拿刀來切開我嘗嘗。」

萬歲爺會裝憨，叫王龍你聽言：南北二京我曾串，諸般光景見多少，這個棋榴甚稀罕。什麼東西下的蛋？叫丫頭拿刀切開，我嘗嘗是酸是甜。

那王龍鼓掌大笑道：「莊家不識木梨，好一個香瓜！」萬歲自思：「作死的王龍，眞果拿着我當個憨瓜。」說：「王官，這東西我曾玩過，一名叫行頭，也叫氣球。我也略會幾脚。」大姐說：「老王，你看這長官分明是拾查子說話，一行不知道，一雯就知道了。」王龍說：「正是呢。」說道：「長官，給你麼，可不許你切開吃了。」萬歲說：「不肯切開，咱可怎麼踢呢？」王龍說：「要踢故事，一脚踢不着，罰銀十兩。」萬歲說：「不妨，我還有二百銀子哩；那馬又賣了三百兩，我還踢幾脚。你過來，我合你踢踢罷。」

萬歲爺笑哈哈，叫王龍你聽着：

1　"Wood-pear" (*muli* 木梨) is one of the names of the quince. "Musk melon" (*xianggua* 香瓜) has the same pronunciation as "country hick" (*xianggua* 鄉瓜).

Wang Long loses his money by trusting
in gambling;
His Majesty the Martial Ancestor
undresses to take a bath.

Let me tell you, big sister and Wang Long settled on a scheme to triumph
over the emperor. They winked at a serving girl, who brought in an air-
filled ball. The emperor thought, "I'll pretend to be a simpleton," so he
said, "Girl, please take that thing away, I've just eaten." The serving girl
had to suppress a smile as she placed it on the table. The emperor said,
"Second sister, since she's so sincere, let her get a knife and cut it so I can
have a taste."

> His Majesty the emperor loved to play the simpleton.
> He called to Wang Long, "Now please listen to me.
> I've visited both the Northern and Southern Capitals,
>   So I've seen quite a lot of special sights.
> But this ball-shaped thing is extremely strange.
> What kind of creature could lay such an egg?
>   Have a girl bring a knife and cut it open,
> So I can taste whether it's sour or sweet."

Wang Long clapped in his hands and laughed loudly: "A farmer doesn't
know a wood-pear. What a musk melon!"[1] The emperor thought to himself,
"That suicidal Wang Long really takes me for an idiot." He said, "Sir Wang,
I've played with such things. It's called a toy or an air-filled ball. I sort of
know how to kick it." Big sister said, "Old Wang, look, this officer clearly
just repeats what others say, he doesn't understand anything, and then
suddenly he gets it." "Indeed," Wang Long said. Then, "Officer, it's yours.
But you can't cut it up." The emperor said, "Of course I don't want to cut
it up. How could we play kickball then?" Wang Long said, "If you want to
play kickball, the fine for failing to kick it once is ten ounces of silver." "No
problem," the emperor said. "I still have two hundred ounces, and then
I sold my horse for three hundred ounces, so I can still play for a while.
Come here, and you and I will play."

> His Majesty the emperor laughed loudly
> And said, "Wang Long, now listen to me:

休笑軍家不識貨。王龍踢在半空裏，皇爺使母雞倒端窩，脚脚踢的似天花落。王冲霄暗暗喝彩，打一罕好他賊哥。

　　王龍見踢不過萬歲，說：「長官，這氣球不是擡舉人的東西，跳跳答答的不好看相。我合你下棋罷。」丫頭擡下桌子，端上棋盤。萬歲說：「一盤多少？」王龍說：「一盤一百兩罷。」皇爺說：「不多不多。」擺下了一盤棋，王冲霄仔細思，萬歲只當閒游戲。寶客王龍朝不住，常往手裏去奪車，一盤回了勾二十遞。皇爺說你眞是受罪，你原來不是下棋。

　　萬歲贏了一盤。大姐說：「咱贏了一盤麼？」王龍說：「今日運氣不濟，把銀子贏給了別人了。」大姐說：「還合他下麼？」王龍說：「輸一盤就怕了他麼？」兩個又下不多時，那王龍被萬歲殺的如風捲殘雪，霜打敗葉，又輸了一盤。

有王龍自思量：這長官手段強，棋子又在我一上。連輸兩盤沒的說，只怨運氣好平常。走來走去沒頭向，便說道下棋不勝，打雙陸鬧上一場。

　　那王龍連兩盤輸了，說道：「長官，不合你下了。」萬歲說：「不下，

2　The "chariots" in Chinese chess can be compared to rooks.

Don't ridicule this officer as utterly ignorant."
　　Wang Long kicked the ball up halfway into the sky.
　　The emperor did "a hen scratching its nest upside down."
　　With each of his kicks, heavenly flowers rained down.
　　Wang Long could not but secretly express his praise,
　　"That scoundrel gives one the shivers. He's so good!"

When Wang Long saw that he could not beat the emperor at kickball, he said, "Kickball doesn't show people at their best since running and jumping don't make for a pretty sight. Let's play a game of chess." A serving girl cleared the table and set down a chess board. The emperor asked, "How much per game?" Wang Long replied, "Let's play for one hundred ounces." The emperor said, "That's not too bad."

　　The pieces were placed on the board,
　　And Wang Long really racked his brains,
　　As the emperor played completely at ease.
　　The precious guest Wang Long failed in his defense
　　And chariots[2] were repeatedly stolen from his hands.
　　The whole game was over in just twenty moves.
　　The emperor said, "You were really whipped!
　　It's clear that you never play chess."

The emperor had won the game, but big sister asked, "Did we win?" Wang Long replied, "Today I had back luck. I lost the money to the other guy." Big sister asked, "Will we play him again?" Wang Long replied, "Do you think I'm afraid of him after one loss? The two of them played again, but soon Wang Long was being destroyed by the emperor as if a storm was gathering scattered clouds and frost was killing yellowed leaves. He lost another game.

　　Wang Long thought to himself,
　　"This officer is an excellent player,
　　A much better hand at chess than me.
　　Forget about those two games that I lost,
　　I only resent my luck for running out."
　　Walking up and down without any hope,
　　He thereupon thought, "If I can't win at chess,
　　Let's play backgammon and have some fun."

When Wang Long had lost two games of chess, he said, "Officer, I won't play anymore with you." The emperor said, "If you won't play,

拿銀子來罷。」王龍道:「這二日食少事煩,棋神不附
體,合你打雙陸罷。你再贏了我,我總裏稱給你;我若
贏了你,咱就準了。」萬歲說:「一帖多少?」王龍道:
「一帖六十兩罷。」萬歲說:「不多。」王龍道:「錯了。
早知他這等仗義,就該合他一帖一千兩銀子,不勾連他
那青布衫剝給我。」叫丫頭:「拿雙陸來。」
雙陸盤端過來,將馬兒擺列開。有句賤言休見怪:一帖白銀
六十兩,輸了當時兌過來,或輸或贏不許賴。那萬歲贏了數
帖,極的那王龍眼裏插柴!

王龍說:「不合你賭了,我又輸了勾三四帖了。」萬歲
說:「多着哩。」王龍說:「這一雾我就輸了多少。」老
鴇子說:「王姐夫往日像個君子,今日像個小人。賭錢
是丈夫,賭乖不賭賴。我算着你整輸了十二帖。」王龍
說:「要這賤婆兒來管閒事!任我輸幾帖,我仔不合你
賭着呢。」萬歲說:「不賭了,拿銀子來。」王龍說:「給
你。」萬歲說:「拿算盤子來打打。」萬歲架着算盤,
王龍喝着,共該一千五百五十兩。萬歲說:「兌了罷。」
王龍說:「就兌。」二姐笑着說:「姐夫贏了,該我架天
秤。」那大姐還給王龍支架子,叫丫頭:「你休動姐夫
那箱子裏的銀子,零碎的就勾了。」那丫頭拿出來了一
布袋子,統了一大堆。二姐將天秤架起,瞧了一瞧說:
「早哩,早哩。」王龍說:「蹺蹊!我這銀子蟲子打了
麼?怎麼有堆堆沒分兩?」

bring out the silver." Wang Long replied, "These last two days I haven't eaten much and have been quite busy, so the god of chess didn't possess me. But let's play backgammon. If you triumph again over me, I will weigh out the total sum to you. But if I triumph over you, we are equal again." The emperor asked, "How much for each round?" Wang Long replied, "Let's say sixty ounces for one round." The emperor said, "That's not too bad." Wang Long reacted, "Damn it! If I had known earlier he's so easy with his money, I'd have suggested one thousand ounces per round. If he didn't have enough, I'd strip that blue linen gown off his back." And he ordered a serving girl to fetch the backgammon board.

> When the backgammon board had been brought,
> He arrayed the pieces in a row and said,
> "Don't blame me for making this humble statement:
>   We play for sixty ounces of fine silver a round.
> Whoever loses has to hand it over on the spot.
> Whether winning or losing, no lying allowed!"
>   When the emperor had won a number of rounds,
> Wang Long was so anxious that his eyes were on fire.

Wang Long said, "I shouldn't have gambled with you. I've lost again, some three or four rounds." The emperor said, "A few more, I'd think." Wang Long asked, "So how many rounds have I lost in this short period of time?" The old bawd remarked, "Brother-in-law Wang, in the past you seemed like a gentleman, but today you've acted small. When gambling for money, one has to be a real man. Gambling depends on wits, not on bluffing and cheating. By my reckoning you have lost a full twelve rounds." Wang Long said, "Who asked you, a vile madam, to meddle? I may have lost a few rounds, but I haven't been gambling with you!" The emperor said, "Get the silver if we're not gambling anymore." Wang Long replied, "I will." The emperor said, "Bring me an abacus so I can add it up." As the emperor calculated on the abacus, Wang Long shouted in surprise. In all, he owed one thousand five hundred and fifty ounces. The emperor said, "Now pay up, please." Wang Long replied, "I will." Second sister said with a smile, "Brother-in-law has won. I should get out the scales."

Big sister, still wanting to maintain Wang Long's status, shouted, "Don't touch the silver in brother-in-law's boxes. The loose silver should be sufficient." The serving girls brought out a linen sack and poured out a big pile. Second sister set up the scales and, after casting a glance at it, said, "Hurry up!" Wang Long said, "Strange! Have insects been at my silver? How come in that whole pile there isn't a single piece worth an

丫頭再拿那成錠的大元寶來，又大小搬出來了十數多個。王龍說：「勾了麼？」二姐敲了敲還差點。萬歲說：「差那點子待怎麼？饒了他罷。」那砝碼丟的緊了，只一跳，忽的一聲，把銀子撒在那樓板上，白花花的一大堆。

將銀子倒面前，叫二姐你聽言：幾兩銀子看的見，些須微禮休嫌少，權且當做胭粉錢，零碎墊手也方便。等着我那小廝們來到，自然還另送你宿錢。

大姐道：「老王，你眼瞎麼？看不見着你聽聽罷。我陪了你這一二年了，你給了我幾遭胭粉錢？頭一遭給了我二錢，第二遭給了我三錢。我說姐夫沒吃肉麼，倒腥了嘴哩，你就記在心裏，到了第三遭給了我五錢。你三遭共給了我一兩錢銀子。你看人家恁麼大一堆銀子，就盡做了胭粉錢。你枉是尚書家的公子，玷辱了子弟！」那王龍輸了這些銀子，心裏疼着，又被大姐誚了幾句，怎麼不惱！滿心裏火起。

有王龍心裏焦，這長官我猜不着。銀錢只當糞堆撩，千兩銀子買胭粉，牛皮上邊拔根毛，聲聲還說小廝到。頭一遭賞銀千兩，送宿錢不知多少。

大姐說：「老王，你到明日早起來，休出前門走，打後門裏走罷。」王龍道：「怎麼說呢？」大姐說：「看人家裂破你那嘴了！敢說道那王三爺，每日價妝人，請了那長官來唱給他聽來，

---

3   "A point" here would appear to mean a decimal fraction.

ounce! Serving girls, get those big ingots of fifty ounces!" So they also brought out more than ten bigger ingots, large and small, and Wang Long asked, "Is this enough?" When second sister checked, it was still one point off,[3] but the emperor said, "What do we care if he's one point off? Let him keep it." He swept the weights away and as the scale jumped, the silver scattered onto the floorboards into a brilliant white pile.

> He threw the silver down in front of her
> And said, "Second sister, listen to me:
> These few ounces of silver aren't much.
>   Please don't mind such a small gift.
> Use it for now as make-up money.
> These bits and pieces are handy to carry.
>   And when my underlings will have arrived,
> I will separately pay the sleepover fees."

Big sister said, "Old Wang, are you blind? If you can't see, just listen. I have kept you company for a few years, but how often have you given me any make-up money? The first time you gave me two *qian*, and the second time you gave me three *qian*. I said, 'Brother-in-law, you may not have eaten any meat, but it has made your mouth stink.' You remembered that, and the third time you gave me five *qian*. So altogether, you gave me one ounce of silver on three occasions. Look at this guy! He's giving that huge pile of silver as make-up money. You may be the son of a minister, but you have defiled all whoremongers!" Wang Long had lost all that money, which was smarting him, and now he was also vilified at length by big sister, so of course he was vexed. A fire was raging in his heart.

> Wang Long felt scorched inside.
> "This officer—I can't figure him out:
> He treats silver as if it were a pile of shit.
>   One thousand ounces of silver to buy cosmetics—
> Like one hair pulled from the hide of an ox!
> And again he says, 'When my underlings arrive.'
>   If he's giving her one thousand ounces to start with,
> Who knows how much he'll pay as sleepover fees."

Big sister said, "Old Wang, when you get up tomorrow morning, don't go out through the main gate in front, take the back door." When Wang Long asked, "Why?" Big sister said, "If you meet people, they'll grin at you, and I bet they'll say, 'That third master Wang thinks he's quite a man, but when he invited that officer over to sing him a song,

倒給他磕了頓頭，還贏了他一大堆銀子去了，可不囂煞了麼？」說的王龍默默無言。大姐又道：「你抖抖精神，咱再合他玩耍玩耍，不死不活的是做嗄呀？」王龍道：「不玩了，輸壞了銀子了！」便向萬歲說道；「長官，我原來是請你來領教來，你倒贏了我這些銀子，把彩都着奪了去了。我吃着酒，你唱一個曲我聽聽罷。」萬歲說：「我從來不唱給人聽。」王龍道：「你不唱，彈彈罷。我自不乾了，我給你做身綢子衣服。」萬歲道：「可是呀，你許下給我件人皮襖子，只怕這件衣服你做着難。」王龍道：「豈有此理！」萬歲果然彈了一套。王龍連聲喝彩說：「好絲絃！好絲絃！」萬歲道：「只怕你刮拾不的那衣服。」王龍道：「大丈夫一言既出，駟馬難追，我就不好反悔。」萬歲說：「多謝了。」王龍又灌了幾盅酒，千思萬想，沒處出氣；又見佛動心在旁洋洋得意，便道；「我別的弄不過他，或者我這身上穿的這衣服，他拿不出來。待我小小的形容形容他，也着他囂。」便說道：「酒後發熱了。丫頭拿個浴盆來，我合二姐夫待洗澡哩。」萬歲說：「這廝可惡！又待合我比衣服。」行說着，丫頭擡了水來。王龍賞了五錢銀子。遂即脫了衣服，大姐拿了來，抖搜了抖搜，「您看王姐夫好齊整衣服！」王龍說：「咱是窮的麼？昨日新打開了一箱，一疋尺頭做的。」二姐說：「王姐夫，你這一頂網子還是金圈哩。」大姐說：「妹妹，你那孤老有王姐夫這一頂網子麼？」

4　In Ming-dynasty times, Chinese upper-class men had long hair that they gathered in a hairnet under their cap.

he kowtowed to him and lost a huge amount of silver to him in gambling.' Wouldn't that be terribly shameful?" At that diatribe, Wang Long sank into silence. Big sister said, "Rouse your spirits! Let's play him again. What are you doing, sitting here more dead than alive?" Wang Long said, "I won't play. I've lost too much silver already!"

Then he turned to the emperor and said, "Officer, I invited you here to learn from you, but instead you won all that silver from me, and I let you get me down. Please sing for me while I drink my wine." The emperor replied, "I have never performed for people." Wang Long said, "If you won't sing, then play the lute. You don't have to do it for nothing. I will have a silk gown made for you." The emperor replied, "Indeed, you promised me a jacket made of human skin, but I worry that you'll have trouble making such a piece of clothing." Wang Long said, "Nonsense!" Then the emperor played a suite on the lute, for which Wang Long praised him repeatedly, saying, "A fine performance, a great performance!" But the emperor said, "I'm still afraid you won't be able to let go of that piece of clothing." Wang Long replied, "'Once a real man has given his word, not even a team of four horses can catch up with it.' I don't regret my promise." "Many thanks!" the emperor replied.

Wang Long poured some more beakers of wine and pondered the matter from all possible sides, but couldn't find a way to vent his anger. When he saw how deeply satisfied Buddha's Lust looked, he said to himself, "In all other matters I couldn't outperform him, but perhaps he can't match my clothes. Let me shame him with the comparison." So he said, "After all this wine, I'm feeling too hot. Girls, bring in a bathing tub so second sister's man and I can take a bath." The emperor said to himself, "This scoundrel is detestable! Now he wants to compete with me in clothing." While he was thinking this, the serving girls brought in the water. Wang Long rewarded them with five *qian* of silver and then took off his clothes.

When big sister had taken his clothes from him, she shook them out, "Just look how perfect these clothes of brother-in-law Wang are!" Wang Long said, "Do you take me for a pauper? A few days ago I had a box of new clothes made for me, using a whole bale of silk." Second sister said, "Brother-in-law Wang, this hairnet[4] of yours has a gold band?" Big sister said, "Little sister, does your patron have a hairnet like brother-in-law Wang's?"

那二姐心中不悅，說道：「甚麼網子！是混帳網子！雜毛網子！」大姐見他這等，一發將王龍的衣服，脫一件，說一件。說還未了，便叫丫頭：「怎麼不擡二姐夫的水來？他待脫下那青布衫子來支支架子哩。」一言未盡，兩個丫頭把水擡來。萬歲本不待洗，怕走漏了消息，被他突的心頭火起，便說：「我要洗洗。」

萬歲爺要脫衣，佛動心着了急。你的衣服不出奇，蠻子渾身是紬緞，你只一身粗布衣，休着他打了咱的趣。道姐夫等上一等，回南樓洗澡不遲。

皇爺說：「我也就着洗洗罷。」

衆丫頭擡水至，萬歲爺方脫衣。齊來跪下討賞賜，分明是把王龍壓，金豆子撒下各人拾。二姐歡喜大姐氣，衆丫頭兢兢戰戰，除皇家誰有這樣的東西？

丫頭得了金豆，百樣的奉承，將一個托盤，承着四箇肥皂，上頭頂着來獻給。萬歲待脫下來，恐怕人見了就知道他是皇帝，就連青布衫一齊脫下，窩鑽了窩鑽，遞於二姐。二姐看見了個龍爪，就待展開。萬歲流水擠眼，二姐方纔會意，包了辮在懷中。

Second sister was annoyed, and said, "What kind of hairnet? It's a messy hairnet, a bastard hairnet!" When big sister saw her reaction, she discussed Wang Long's garments as he took them off at even greater length. At the same time, she told the serving girls, "Why haven't you brought the water for second sister's man? He's going to take off that linen gown to give us a show." Before she had finished speaking, two serving girls had brought the water. The emperor didn't want to take a bath for fear that his secret might be revealed, but he was so offended by big sister that a fire raged in his heart, and he said, "I'll take a bath."

> When the emperor decided to take off his clothes,
> Buddha's Lust was overcome with panic.
> "Your clothes are so ordinary!
>   That rascal is dressed from head to toe in silks,
> Whereas you're dressed in rough linen.
> Don't let that fellow destroy our good cheer!"
>   She then said, "Brother-in-law, please wait a while.
> It won't be too late for a bath back in our room."

But the emperor replied, "I will take a bath right here."

> The serving girls brought in the water
> And the emperor began to take off his clothes.
> They knelt down, asking for a reward.
>   Clearly to show up Wang Long,
> He scattered gold beans among them,
> To second sister's pleasure and big sister's rage.
>   The serving girls were shaking and trembling.
> Who besides an emperor would have such things?

After the serving girls received these golden beans, they exerted themselves in a hundred ways to serve him. They brought out a plate with four pieces of soap and presented it to him, raising it as high as their heads. The emperor was about to take off his clothes, but afraid that people would know on seeing them that he was the emperor, he took everything off with his linen gown and rolled it all up, handing the bundle to second sister. When second sister saw a dragon claw, she wanted to unroll it, but the emperor quickly gave her a wink. Second sister grasped his intentions, and held the bundle tightly in her arms.

青布衫先脫了，藏起那袞龍袍。裏邊襯衣有兩套，不是紬來不是緞，件件都是極蹊蹺。汗衫全用珍珠造，穿著他夏天涼快，還打上冬裏熱燥。

　　萬歲脫下衣服，王龍合大姐也暗暗的打罕，只估不出是個什麼人來。

好衣裳件件精，賽觀音諕一驚。王龍也把腦兒掙，心裏猜他是響馬，猜來猜去不分明。惟有二姐明似鏡，自思量陪他兩宿，不知他就是朝廷。

　　二姐辫起萬歲那網子來說：「大姐姐，你看這網子上是二龍戲珠。」大姐說：「乜是二鱉瞅蛋罷了！」

萬歲爺怒上心，罵奴才賊賤人怎麼當面罵了朕？說我操軍我不惱，二鱉瞅蛋好難禁！幾時解了心頭恨，王龍剝皮的時節，碎刀子割這賤人！

　　那萬歲氣在心頭，滿面通紅。二姐將身子影着萬歲，說道：「姐夫穿上衣服，咱回南樓去罷。」萬歲聽說，出了浴盆，遂同二姐起行。王龍合大姐送下北樓來。未知後事如何，且聽下回分解。

He first took off his blue linen gown
And in it hid his twisting-dragon robe.
Beneath it he wore two sets of underwear.
　　They were made not of silk or satin,
And each was extremely exceptional.
His undershirt was all made of pearls.
　　It was cool when wearing it in summer,
And warm when putting it on in winter.

As the emperor was taking off his clothes, Wang Long and big sister were inwardly shaking, as they could not guess what kind of man would appear.

Each item of his fine clothes was superb,
So Guanyin's Equal suffered a fright,
And Wang Long wracked his brains.
　　They secretly guessed that he was a bandit,
But they couldn't figure out the truth.
Only second sister was as clear as a mirror
　　As she thought, "I've slept with him two nights in a row
Without realizing that he is the emperor!"

Second sister picked up the emperor's hairnet and said, "Big sister, look, this hairnet has two dragons playing with a pearl!" But big sister said, "That's two turtles eyeing an egg!"

His Majesty the emperor was filled with rage,
And [silently] cursed her, "You slave, you rotten slut,
How dare you curse Us out to Our face?
　　Say I'm a common soldier, I don't care,
But 'two turtles eyeing an egg' is hard to endure.
How can I vent this rage in my heart?
　　When that Wang Long will be stripped of his skin,
The hacking knife will chop up this common slut!"

The emperor was filled with rage and his face flushed. Shielding the emperor with her body, second sister said, "Brother-in-law, put on your clothes so we can return to the southern upstairs room." On hearing this, the emperor stepped out of the tub and departed with second sister. Wang Long and big sister saw them off as they descended the stairs.

If you don't know what happened next, please listen to the following chapter.

第二十二回 佛動心拜主求歡 王冲霄輸錢遷怒

話說萬歲離了北樓，南樓去了。王龍說：「大姐，不想那軍家的衣服，件件出奇，再估不出他是個什麼人來。」大姐說：「必然是個響馬，在那裏短了皇杠。不如拿起他來，送到當官，比這狗頭！」王龍道：「他那口裏常說合江彬有處，若是真果，可不壞了？」按下二人議論不提。且說二姐合萬歲回到南樓，滿心歡喜。

佛動心閉了樓，焚上香把主酬，三年志願今朝就。翻身便把皇爺拜，有點小失休記仇。萬歲拉住羅衫袖，說二姐行此大禮，我問你是什麼緣由？

萬歲說：「二姐，你嘲殺了！我在京裏串戲班，臨來時無甚可穿，我就開開戲箱，暗拿出來了幾件。才不過是哄那王龍。那件蟒衣是那戲子們穿的着裝皇帝的，百姓們穿了犯法。我怕他茄着我，我才着你藏了，怎麼你也信了麼？」

佛動心笑顏開，我每日也疑猜，誰想你把俺當嘲巴待。今日若還再信了，

22   Buddha's Lust, seeking pleasure, bows
to the emperor;
Having lost his money, Wang Long
redirects his rage.

Let me tell you, when the emperor had left the northern upstairs room and gone to the southern upstairs room, Wang Long said, "Big sister, I hadn't thought that every item of that soldier's clothing would be so exceptional. I have even less of an idea of who he is." Big sister replied, "He must be a mounted bandit who robbed an imperial transport somewhere. It would be best to arrest that shithead and send him to the responsible officials for an inquiry." But Wang Long replied, "He keeps saying he's a friend of Jiang Bin. If that's true, wouldn't we be in real trouble?" But let's forget the discussions of these two and tell what happened after second sister and the emperor returned to the southern upstairs room, their hearts filled with joy.

> When Buddha's Lust had locked the room,
> She lit incense in gratitude to her lord.
> "My vow of three years has come true today."
>   Falling on her knees, she bowed to His Majesty.
> "If I did anything wrong, please don't hold it against me!"
> The emperor held the sleeve of her gauze gown
>   And said, "Second sister, may I ask why
> You perform such a solemn ritual?"

The emperor said, "Second sister, you mock me! In the capital I joined a theatrical troupe, and because I had nothing to wear coming here, I opened the costume chest and secretly took some items. They'd only fool that Wang Long. The dragon robe is worn by the actors when they perform as an emperor. It's forbidden for a common citizen to wear it! I was afraid he would make fun of me, that's why I had you hide it. But how could you too buy into it?"

> Buddha's Lust broke into a smile.
> "I've been suspicious every day,
> But who would think you'd treat me as a joke?
>   If I still believed what you say,

可就眞眞是老獸，眼裏也沒珠兒在。就向爺禱頭千萬，也不要這樣蠢才。

　　萬歲說：「你這妮子，就合一個鬼靈精那是的！我只爲一時賭氣，就着你參透機關。我今日也不必背你了。」正說着，丫頭叫道：「姐姐開門，拿了酒飯來了。」二姐聽說，把門開放，秉起燭來，擺下酒飯，叫丫頭：「你們困乏了，各人休息去罷。」丫頭聽說，各歸房去。二姐把門閉了，雙膝跪下，口稱：「萬歲用膳。」萬歲道：「你說吃飯罷，休說用膳，看走漏了消息，被王龍知道了。」二姐說：「曉的了。」二人用過酒飯，二姐收拾牀鋪，與萬歲寐寢。

佛動心喜盈盈，比昨日大不同，千式百樣把朝廷奉。二姐忘了該呼萬歲，萬歲也迭不的叫梓童。天子庶民無品從，也不是金卯玉笋，要了耍萬古傳名。

　　一宿晚景提過。君妃早起梳洗已畢，萬歲穿上衣服，正待吃早飯，北樓已着丫頭來請。萬歲說：「備着酒飯，咱上北樓去吃罷。」二人同丫頭下了南樓，竟到北樓。王龍歡天喜地的接出來。萬歲說：「連日取擾，我今自也備了一盅水酒，攜來同樂。」王龍道：「通家何必費事？」二人上樓，拉開桌椅，擺下酒席，吃過三巡。王龍說：「咱不是這麼悶吃，還該找個法兒玩玩。」萬歲說：「子弟風流都使盡了，

1　This otherwise unattested phrase would seem to be based on the expression "golden branches and jade leaves" 金枝玉葉, which designates persons of imperial descent.

I'd truly be an idiot,
Like as if I lacked sight.
    I wish Your Majesty millions of years,
Since I don't want to be so stupid!"

The emperor said, "Little wench, you're as clever as a ghost. I let myself go for just a moment, and you saw through my secret. As of today I won't have to hide it from you." As he was speaking, the serving girls called, "Sister, please open the door! We're bringing the wine and food." Second sister opened the door. Holding a candle, she set out the wine and food, and said to the serving girls, "You must be tired. Go and have some rest." Being so told, the serving girls went to their downstairs room. Second sister locked the door, knelt down on both knees, and declaimed, "May Your Majesty enjoy this repast!" But the emperor said, "Just say 'Let's eat,' not 'Enjoy this repast.' Otherwise, word may spread, and Wang Long may hear." Second sister replied, "Understood!" When they had enjoyed their meal, second sister made the bed and went to sleep with the emperor.

Buddha's Lust was overcome by joy.
This night was different from before,
As she served the emperor in all possible ways.
    Second sister forgot that she should call him His Majesty,
And His Majesty didn't have time to call her Her Majesty.
The Son of Heaven and a commoner forgot all rank.
    Was this match not "a golden slit and a jade shoot."[1]
They had their fun, renowned for all eternity!

So much for the scenes of that night. The lord and his spouse got up and made their toilet. By the time the emperor had put on his clothes and was about to have breakfast, the northern upstairs room had already sent a serving girl to invite him over. The emperor said, "As the meal has already been set out, let's go to the northern upstairs room and enjoy a meal there. They went downstairs with the serving girl, and when they arrived at the northern building, Wang Long came out to welcome them, as happy as could be. The emperor said, "We have bothered you for a few days in a row, so today I brought a beaker of wine along to enjoy together." Wang Long said, "We're friends. Why go to such trouble?"

They went upstairs, and the tables and chairs were pulled out and the meal arranged. When they had drunk three rounds, Wang Long said, "We shouldn't be bored while we eat. We should find some other way to have fun." The emperor replied, "We tried out all the amusements of

可玩甚麼？」大姐道：「您倆投投壺罷。」王龍說：「正
是，我就忘了。我就合你投壺。」萬歲道：「隨意隨意。」
王龍說：「我着你贏怕了，我燒上香禱告禱告，贏你一
遭，我也遮遮囂。」萬歲說：「你就許點什麼何妨呢？」
丫頭擡過香案來，王龍焚香禱告。

王冲霄跪案前，衆神靈保佑咱，待合長官投回壺。諸般景兒
都弄過，遭遭罰酒又輸錢。這回仗托神靈面，保佑着王龍贏
了，殺幾個豬羊祭天。

　　大姐說：「我看你粧殺我了！怎麼禱告天地，許豬許羊
的？」萬歲說：「我也禱告禱告。」他也不磕頭，把手
望空一舉，說道：

上告玉皇老友前，下祝閻羅崔府官，城隍土地在兩邊站。要
着王龍贏了我，我就貶你上雲南，休要拿着當尋常看。你着
我君家贏了，殺幾隻癲象祭天。

　　大姐說：「花子又上來了風了！你是嘎人家，殺起象來
了？」萬歲說：「我有好親戚借出來了。」王龍說：「不
合你弄那寡嘴。你過來，咱投壺罷。」這王龍自幼在
學，不好讀書，慣好投壺。拿起那箭來顛了一顛，使了
個「蘇秦背劍」故事，扢噔一聲，投在壺裏。王龍喜的
抓耳撓腮。萬歲道：「乜個投箭法稀鬆平常，拿起隻箭
來撩到裏頭，人人都會，

2　Prince Cui is one of the underworld gods.
3　The ancient sage king Shun used an elephant to plow his fields while still a farmer. Elephants still live in the wild in the extreme south of China, but in Ming and Qing China, the overwhelming majority of the population would only have known the elephants that were kept by the imperial court in Beijing and that took part in some processions (or might be led out to take part in a pageant).
4　Su Qin 蘇秦 lived in the third century BCE. He is believed to have led a coalition of six states against Qin.

playboys. What other game is there?" Second sister said, "Why don't you play a game of pitch pot?" Wang Long said, "Right! I'd forgotten about that. I'll play pitch pot with you." The emperor replied, "As you wish." Wang Long said, "I've been beaten by you so often that I've grown scared. Let me burn some incense and pray to the gods. If I can win just once, I can cover my shame." The emperor said, "What could be wrong in your making a little offering? The serving girls brought the incense table over, and Wang Long lit incense and pronounced his prayer.

> Wang Long knelt down in front of the altar.
> "Divine gods, please protect and assist me.
> I will play a game of pitch pot with this officer.
>   We have already played all kinds of games.
> Time and again I was fined wine or lost money,
> So this time I rely on the help of you gods.
>   If you protect me, Wang Long, and help me win,
> I will slaughter some sheep and pigs to thank Heaven!"

Big sister said, "Why are you giving yourself such grand airs! Why pray to Heaven and Earth, promising them sheep and pigs?" The emperor said, "Let me also say a prayer." He did not kowtow, but just raised his hands toward the sky as he spoke.

> "I pray to my old buddy the Jade Emperor above,
> To King Yama and also to Prince Cui[2] below,
> And to the city gods and earth gods on both sides.
>   If you let Wang Long win this game against me,
> I'll banish the whole lot of you to distant Yunnan.
> Don't take this as something of no importance!
>   But if you make sure that this officer wins,
> I'll kill some mangy elephants to thank Heaven."

Big sister said, "Our beggar has gone mad again! What kind of person can slaughter elephants?"[3] The emperor replied, "I have relatives from whom I can borrow them." Wang Long said, "You shouldn't be all talk. Come here, and let's play." Wang Long from his earliest days in school never liked to study, but he always loved to play pitch pot. Picking up a dart, he turned it around and executed a "Su Qin swings the sword on his back,"[4] tossing it into the pot with a kerplunk. Wang Long was so pleased with himself that he scratched his ears and rubbed his cheeks.

The emperor said, "That way of throwing the dart is exceedingly mediocre. Everybody knows how to pick up a dart and throw it into the pot.

有什麼奇處？你看我投個故事。」那萬歲拿過箭來，照東牆上一摔，舞了幾個花，一投，插在壺裏。王龍大驚說：「是什麼故事？」萬歲說：「這是『珍珠倒捲簾』。」王龍說：「從來沒見。你再投一個故事我看看。」萬歲取過箭來，捻的滴滴溜的轉，往上一撩落下來，又插在那壺裏。王龍道：「這是什麼故事？」萬歲道：「這是『野鵓鴿尋窩』。」王龍說：「做這個你有個手法，我又不合你弄這個了。咱抹骨牌罷了。」

有王龍惱心懷，一心裏抹骨牌。空中像有鬼神在，天地人和偏向主，青黃雜牌推過來，王龍輸了沒的賴。王蠻子抹了又抹，邪骨牌有些怪哉！

抹了一回骨牌，王龍又輸了，只低這頭，長吁短嘆的。大姐道：「還有一件極不出奇的營生，你道弄的好，你合長官耍耍何如？」王龍說：「我這兩日輸掙了，也想不起是什麼來了。你說是嗄？」大姐說：「是跌六氣。」王龍說：「妙呀！就是這等。」這萬歲雖是個光棍皇帝，這一件他却沒學。便說：「這個不會。」王龍聽說不會，就越發纏起了，說：「這個不過是拿着六個錢撩下去，以慢多的爲贏，有什麼難處？」萬歲也極好勝的，看看不會就是一件短處。便說：「咱試試。可賭嗄呢？」王龍說：「一柱一百兩，就來不許試。」眞正聰明不過帝王，拿起錢來極樣仔。

萬歲爺架錢挴，像有鬼等着翻，

What's so special about that? Just watch the way I throw." The emperor took a dart and smashed it against the eastern wall, and it ricocheted straight into the pot. Wang Long was startled and asked, "What's that called?" The emperor said, "This is 'a pearl tumbling down the curtain.'" Wang Long said, "I've never seen that style. Show me yet another way to throw." The emperor selected a dart, twisted it around a few times, and threw it straight up. It too fell straight into the pot. When Wang Long said, "And what's that called?" the emperor replied, "This is 'a wild pigeon seeks its nest.'" Wang Long said, "If you can do that, it means you have the technique. I won't play this game with you anymore. Let's play dominoes."

> Wang Long was quite annoyed.
> Fully concentrating, he moved the stones,
> But it seemed as if the gods were present.
>   Heaven and Earth and Harmony sided with the ruler.
> Green, yellow, and mixed stones were pushed his way,
> And Wang Long lost, with no way to bluff his way out.
>   That rascal Wang shuffled them again and yet again,
> But those evil stones acted in a miraculous way.

After they had played dominoes for a while and Wang Long had lost again, he could only lower his head and heave sigh upon sigh. Big sister said, "There is still an exceedingly simple game, which you play very well. Why don't you play that with the officer?" Wang Long replied, "These two days I have only lost, and I cannot think of anything else. What did you have in mind?" Big sister replied, "Dropping the Six Ethers." Wang Long said, "Wonderful. Let's do that." Even though the emperor was a barestick emperor, he had never tried this game, so he said, "I don't know that game." When Wang Long heard that he didn't know it, he became even more insistent, and said, "In this game you take six coins and throw them on the ground. The one who throws the most backsides up wins. It's quite easy." Now the emperor was someone who very much liked to win, but it was a drawback that he had never played before, so he said, "Let me try. What are we playing for?" Wang Long replied, "Each time for one hundred ounces, and you can't try it out first." In truth, even the smartest guy cannot outdo an emperor. As soon as the emperor picked up the coins, he played quite well.

> His Majesty the emperor shook the coins in his hands,
> And it seemed as if there were ghosts awaiting his throw.

一跌就是六個慢。王龍輸的沒陽氣，拿起錢來就戰戰，用上心來只跌個斷。圪搭的把頭錢摔了，一聲裏罵地罵天。

王龍輸極了，一行稱着銀子，一行罵那頭錢。二姐在旁裏笑道：「你着俺大姐姐再給你尋個方法，那銀子今遭還輸不犯哩。」王龍正煩躁，又聽的二姐誚他，心頭火起，便說：「小科子！你領了您那孤老來，都把我銀子贏了去，我也不肯干休！」二姐羞的滿面通紅，半晌不語。萬歲跳起身來大罵：「好賊！你輸極了麼？誰給你出氣哩麼？」老鴇子吵起來，萬歲使性子走下北樓去了。未知後事如何，且聽下回分解。

As soon as he dropped the coins, he scored a full six!
   When Wang Long lost, the blood drained from his body.
He took up the coins, shivering with fear,
And for all his concentration, he scored only a zero!
   He smashed the six coins to the ground,
All the while cursing Heaven and Earth!

Wang Long was distressed by his loss, and while he weighed out the silver, he cursed the coins they had played with. On the side, second sister said with a smile, "You should have big sister find you yet another game. This time there's no end to the silver you've lost." Wang Long was already quite irritated, and when he also heard second sister sneering at him, a fire exploded in his heart, and he said, "Trollop! Even if the patron you brought here had won all my money, I wouldn't give up so easily." Second sister felt so ashamed that she blushed even behind her ears and didn't say a word for a long time. The emperor jumped up and loudly cursed him out, "You scoundrel! Have we cleaned you out? Who's going to get revenge for you?" When the old bawd started to shout, the emperor lost his temper and ran down the stairs.

   If you don't know what happened next, please listen to the following chapter.

第二十三回 賺嬌娥大姐定計 比根基萬歲生嗔

話說萬歲自從合王龍惱了，待了好幾日不曾上門。忽然一日，王龍又着丫頭來請。萬歲不去。鴇兒自己又來，說道：「二姐夫，你眞果怪他哩麼？他輸極了；什麼正經！宰相肚裏撐開船，你休合他一般見識。不過是那公子脾氣，疼他那銀子，就弄出那醜態了。這二日懊愧的合什麼呀似的。」

賭博的不害羞，爲乜錢就打破頭，銀子輸了一千六。賭場裏根基沒憑準，行說着好說把臉丟，轉一轉兒還依舊。就有些面紅面赤，又不是宿世冤仇。

鴇兒道：「適纔見姐夫不去，他訕的了不得，着小大姐央我來替他謝罪。他旣這等，二姐夫，你還是去呀，有仇哩麼？況且昨日是二姐不看頭勢，惹的他罵了一句，他又沒傷着姐夫。」萬歲的性兒也是好動不好靜的，極好合人打混，又被鴇兒百般相勸，也就沒了氣了。兩個又跟着媽兒往北樓來。王龍出來迎着，先給萬歲謝罪，說；「我昨日實着你贏極了，我就心焦了幾句，休要放在心裏。」又向二姐笑了笑：「二姐，

---

1   A description of the capacity for forgiveness of a great man.

23   Cheating a charming beauty, big sister
hatches a scheme;
Comparing backgrounds, the emperor
displays his fury.

Let me tell you, after the emperor had been annoyed by Wang Long, he
did not visit him for quite a few days. But suddenly one day Wang Long
once again sent a serving girl to invite him. When the emperor did not
go, the old bawd came in person and asked, "Dear guest, do you really
blame him? He was upset by his losses, so how could he restrain himself?
'Inside the stomach of the prime minister, one can punt a pole boat.'[1]
You shouldn't show the same attitude as he did. In his case, it's only the
peevishness of a young master who clings to his silver and so displayed
such ugly behavior. These last two days he's been regretting it more than
he can say.

> Because of his gambling, he lost all shame;
> Because of the money, he blew his top.
> He lost sixteen hundred ounces of silver.
>   His experience with gambling dens didn't help him.
> Speaking fine words, he showed a mean face,
> But he turned himself around into his old self again.
>   So even though his face turned red, even crimson,
> This was no karmic feud from your former lives."

The bawd said, "When he saw a moment ago that you refused to go, he
was utterly embarrassed and ordered big sister to implore me to offer his
apologies on his behalf. Since he feels that way, second sister's man, you
should go there. You're not archenemies, are you? Moreover, it was second
sister who misjudged the situation a few days ago, which led him to curse
her out. He didn't hurt you, brother-in-law."

Now the emperor's character was such that he loved action and not
quiet. He really loved to hang around with people, and he was also
urged on by the bawd in a hundred ways, so his rage disappeared. He
followed her to the northern upstairs room, where Wang Long came out
to welcome them. He first apologized to the emperor, saying, "You won
so much a few days ago that I got angry, but please forget about what I
said." He also gave second sister a smile and said, "Second sister, don't

你休怪我，我着你誚極了，就胡突心眼子，這二日好不懊悔煞！」

有王龍笑呵呵，叫二姐休怪我，昨日實是我的錯。就該脫下那小鞋底，照着嘴兒只管搯，打煞怨的那一個？但得你心中不惱，我就念一聲南無彌陀。

那大姐也來，二姐長，二姐短，花甜蜜語的，說那好話兒。二姐也就笑了。王龍說：「快擺酒來。」略不停時，將酒席擺的齊齊整整。

斟上酒彎彎腰，謝了罪又告饒，弄了多少虛旋套。長官既來我心喜，或是使碗又使瓢，咱把酒量鏢一鏢。萬歲爺連飲了十碗，不濟事王家那冲霄。

萬歲爺吃了十數碗，王龍不能招架，說：「咱還找個法兒。」大姐說：「罷呀！昨日不是找法來！」王龍說：「長官，咱今日可玩的安相相的，也休要賭錢了，咱下棋贏酒罷。」丫頭將棋盤端過，安下棋子，二人便下。

棋盤兒在面前，萬歲爺信手安，著著下的天花亂。王龍恐怕還輸了，手兒好似打巡欄，

2　Amitābha is the Buddha of the Western Paradise who will receive there the souls of all who sincerely call on his name.

blame me! You made such a sneering remark that I was utterly confused.
These two days I have been filled with regret!"

> Wang Long laughed loudly,
> Saying, "Second sister, don't blame me,
> A few days ago, things were truly my mistake.
>   I should strip off the soles of your little shoes
> And beat myself in the face with them.
> Whom can I blame if I hit myself hard?
>   If only you'd no longer be annoyed with me,
> I'd gratefully recite 'Hail Amitābha'!"[2]

Big sister also arrived, and she, with a 'second sister' here and a 'second sister' there, also spoke many friendly words as sweet as flowers and phrased like honey, so second sister also smiled. Wang Long said, "Set out the wine!" and in a short while a banquet with wine had been neatly laid out.

> He poured out the wine, deeply bending at the waist,
> Offering his apologies and asking for forgiveness,
> Engaging in no end of empty gestures and words.
>   "Officer, I am filled with joy now you've come!
> Let's use a bowl or perhaps a gourd,
> And see which of us can hold the most liquor!"
>   The emperor drank ten bowls without pause,
> While Wang Long was of no use at all.

When the emperor had drunk more than ten bowls, Wang Long could not continue the competition, and he said, "Let's find some other game!" Big sister said, "Forget about it! Didn't you find another game some days ago?" Wang Long said, "Today the two of us should amuse ourselves sedately. We shouldn't gamble for money; we should play a game of go for wine." After the serving girls brought in the go board and set out the pieces, the two started to play.

> With the go board in front of him,
> The emperor placed his pieces at will,
> And every move was dazzling.
>   Wang Long was afraid he might lose again.
> With each move his hand hovered in the air,

條條路兒躊躕遍。萬歲說狗屎棋子，一着兒下了半年。

下棋中間，大姐說：「二妹妹，他兩個下棋還早哩，我
有個琵琶譜兒，煩你給我改正改正。」大姐約着二姐下
樓來了。

賽觀音笑盈腮，請妹子下樓臺，那知他把心兒壞。合他到了
香房裏，琵琶譜兒丟在懷，殷勤就把二姐拜。相煩你耐心坐
坐，我到樓上看看再來。

這王龍輸了一盤，方纔安下棋子，大姐便回來了。王龍
道：「大姐，你合長官下着，我告一告便。」原來是這
王龍合賽觀音定下的一局。一來王龍每日愛想二姐，不
能到手；二來見萬歲戮乖奪翠，沒法治他，也要撮弄點
先頭；三來見佛動心得意的受不的，要觸注這個口。遂
合大姐計議定，誆在他沒人處，就幹起那「張飛掏鵪鶉」
的那事情來了。料想那當婊子的，他也沒有不依的。當
下王龍下的樓來，到了房裏，見二姐獨抱琵琶，在那裏
對那譜兒。王龍一步驀進，二姐放下琵琶，起身就走。
王龍當門截住，說道：「我來敬陪不是，你怎麼就待走
呢？」

王沖霄驀進門，叫一聲佛動心，你三爺實實愛你俊。若還遂
了我心意，一遭就許你十兩銀。搬過頭來把嘴兒印。佛動心
鶯聲怪叫，咭叮噹扯斷了羅裙。

3   This phrase is otherwise unknown but would appear to be a description of rape.

As he hesitated at length about each course of play.
　　The emperor exclaimed, "These dog-shit stones!
Each move takes you more than half a day."

While they were playing, big sister said, "Second sister, they've just started their game. I have a lute score that I would like to trouble you to correct for me." So big sister agreed to go downstairs with second sister.

With a smile all over her face, Guanyin's Equal
Invited second sister to go downstairs with her.
How could second sister know she had ill intentions?
　　When they had arrived in her room,
She pushed the lute score into second sister's hands
And solicitously bowed to second sister.
　　"Please wait here for me for a while.
I'll have a look upstairs and be back!"

Wang Long had lost a game and the two had just finished putting the stones in order when big sister arrived. Wang Long said, "Big sister, you play a game with the officer, so that I can go and wash my hands." In fact, this was a scheme Wang Long and Guanyin's Equal had agreed on. First of all, Wang Long had always loved second sister, but had never been able to lay his hands on her. Second, he saw that the emperor was too smart for him and stole the prize; he had no way to beat him, but still wanted to gain the upper hand. Third, he saw that Buddha's Lust was unbearably smug, and he wanted to stuff her mouth. So he had agreed on a plan with big sister to deceive her into going somewhere with no one around, so that he could do a "Zhang Fei stealing eggs from the pigeon."[3] He went to the room downstairs and saw second sister all alone with the lute in her arms following the score. When Wang Long suddenly entered, second sister put down the lute and got up to leave. But Wang Long blocked the door and said, "I came here to offer my apologies. Why do you want to run off?"

Wang Long hastily entered the door
And he called out, "Dear Buddha's Lust,
Your Third Master really loves your beauty!
　　If I can fulfill my desires, I promise you
Ten ounces of silver for just this one time."
He dipped his head and pressed his lips against hers.
　　Buddha's Lust screamed with her oriole voice
As he ripped off her gauze skirt!

那佛動心被王龍抱住，只急的柳眉倒豎，粉面通紅，一
聲怪叫。王龍死活不放。按下不提。且說萬歲正合賽觀
音下棋，一個丫環跑上樓來說：「大姐夫合俺二姐姐打
仗哩。」萬歲聽說，龍顏陡變，虎步如梭，轉下樓來。

萬歲爺下樓來，只聽的鬧垓垓，見王龍正在那裏行無賴。看
見萬歲纔撒了手，二姐頭鬆懷也開，丫頭扶出門兒外。萬歲
爺重重大怒，罵王龍作死的奴才！

萬歲大罵。王龍上前陪笑說：「不過是個婊子，是你的
自家老婆麼，就這樣生氣？」媽兒道：「你哄着我給你
請了客來，你可弄下這個繭，怨的二姐夫惱了麼？你休
做聲罷。」

萬歲爺怒如雷，罵王龍作死賊！因何不合你尊堂睡？天生就
剝皮貨，死在眼前尚不知，只顧弄你那花花勢！我看你裝模
裝樣，湯一湯沾了我那人兒！

王龍那公子性，素常降人是慣了的，誰敢說一個失字。
被萬歲罵了幾句，只氣得三尸神暴跳，兩眼圓睜，便
道：「氣煞我也！你不過馬前小卒，合我在一堆坐着，
就是擡舉你了，還說我玷辱了你的婊子！你自家估量估
量，我那點不如你？我就合你比比根基。」

In Wang Long's clutches, Buddha's Lust panicked, her curved eyebrows standing straight up and her powdered face gone red as she screamed at the top of her voice. No matter what, Wang Long wouldn't let her go, but for the moment no more about that. Let me tell you instead that while the emperor was playing a game with big sister, a serving girl came running up the stairs, shouting, "Big sister's man and our second sister are having a fight!" On hearing this, the emperor's face changed color, and with tiger steps fast as a shuttle, he ran downstairs.

> When His Majesty arrived downstairs,
> He heard only a terrible noise and saw Wang Long
> About to commit a scandalous deed.
>   Only when Wang Long saw the emperor did he release his grip.
> Second sister's hair was disheveled, and her collar undone.
> A serving girl had to support her as she went outside.
>   His Majesty the emperor was overcome by rage
> And cursed Wang Long out as a suicidal slave!

The emperor cursed him out at length, but Wang Long stepped forward with an unctuous smile and said, "She's only a whore! Is she your wife, that you're so angry?" The madam said, "You shut your trap! You sweet-talked me into inviting him as your guest, and then you play a trick like that on him! And you blame second sister's man for being upset? Shut up!"

> His Majesty the emperor raged like thunder
> And reviled Wang Long as a suicidal criminal.
> "Why don't you go and sleep with your mother?
>   You're a creature fit to be flayed.
> Your death is waiting for you, but you have no idea
> And just want to act the philanderer-in-chief!
>   Seeing how you act and behave,
> Your touch defiles that woman of mine!"

As a high-born young man, Wang Long was used to denigrating others, but who dared mention a single failing of his? Cursed out by the emperor, he became so enraged that the spirits of his body jumped up and down and his eyes bulged open. He said, "This drives me mad with rage! You're only a horse groom. If I let you sit with me, I'm already enhancing your status. And you say I defiled your whore! Think it over. Is there any way I'm lesser than you? Let's compare our backgrounds!"

萬歲說：「我那根基可不濟。」王龍道：「不消說，你
那祖宗關了銀來使了，掙了你這一名臭軍，你甚麼根
基！」

我父親在北京，生三子有大名：大哥曾把皇榜中，二哥寧夏
做巡按，只我王龍沒得成。看我讀書不中用，纔着我江湖奔
走，習會了買賣經營。

王龍說：「這就是我的根基。你可說來，撒謊支架子的
不是丈夫。」萬歲自思：「砍頭的貨，我也表表你聽罷。」
萬歲爺怒冲冲，罵王龍小畜生，我還比你有根莖。祖父雖然
賣豆腐，積下無限大陰功，山東泗水人人敬。後搬在北京城
裏，第一家天下聞名。

王龍說：「我就不說罷，你自己已是供出你的贓根基來
了。賣豆腐的後代，就勾了人的了，還說人沾了他哩。
近來不是在江湖上把性子忖了，先打你一個扁包，送到
官府，統上兩布袋銀子，還着你有死無活！」萬歲說：
「你有多少銀子，說着人死呢？」

王冲霄發大言，你聽我說銀錢。我那財貯你沒見，堆金積玉
敵國富，江湖河海有常船，

---

4 Zhu Yuanzhang, the founder of the Ming dynasty, was born in a very poor family. His
grandfather Zhu Chuyi 朱初一 lived for a while in Sishui (Sizhou) in Shandong Province.
One of the family trades was peddling tofu.

"My background is no good," the emperor replied. Wang Long said, "That goes without saying! Your ancestors scrounged some silver together and used it to buy you this stinking soldier position. What background could you have?

> My father resides in Beijing.
> He sired three sons, who all are quite famous:
> My eldest brother was listed on the imperial plaque,
>   My second brother is regional inspector for Ningxia,
> And only I, Wang Long, have no accomplishments.
> On seeing that I made no progress at all in my studies,
>   They told me to travel widely on rivers and lakes
> To learn the business of buying and selling."

Wang Long said, "That's my background. Now you tell yours. If you tell any lies or give yourself airs, you are no real man." The emperor thought to himself, "You damned creature! Let me describe my background for you."

> His Majesty the emperor was in a raging fury
> And cursed out Wang Long, "You little beast!
> My background is far better than yours.
>   Even though my ancestor was a tofu peddler,
> He amassed an unlimited store of hidden merit
> And was respected by all in Shandong's Sishui.[4]
>   Later he moved home to the city of Beijing
> As the first family renowned throughout the world!"

Wang Long said, "I don't have to say it, as you confess your dirty background yourself. As the descendant of a tofu peddler, you may qualify as human, but can you say that others defile you? If I hadn't dissipated much of my temper recently on rivers and lakes, I would have beaten you flat and then delivered you to the magistrate. Even if you were wrapped in two sacks of silver, I'd still have you killed without mercy!" The emperor said, "How much silver do you have that you can order a man's death?"

> Wang Long started to brag:
> "Listen to me tell you about our money:
> You've never seen so much stored treasure!
>   Our piles of gold and jade equal the dynasty's riches;
> We have freighters on the rivers and lakes, streams and seas.

銀錢不知有幾百萬。不是我誇句海口，我跟你萬個長官。

　　萬歲說：「你就是這麼大財主麼？」王龍說：「不濟麼？天下數一數二的！」萬歲說：「可唓嚇煞我了！我也不消把我那家當合你比，我說說我那小廝們的家當你聽聽罷。」

萬歲爺氣昂昂，叫王龍休逞強，你有多大小家當？空是兵部尚書子，銀錢能有幾百房？不如一個小廝管的賬。把你銀錢盡數拿來，河內常船，南京鋪子，地土宅子，老婆孩子，盡情算了，敵不過我一個莊子上的雜糧。

　　王龍說：「儘着你乜花花嘴，滿口胡叨，誰信呀？我且問你：你這麼些糧食，你有多少莊子呢？」

萬歲爺鼻子裏嗤，叫王龍你聽知：我的莊子十三處。管莊的小廝都威武，個個門口豎大旗，炮響三聲誰不懼？吹鼓手掌罷大號，小小廝給大小廝作揖。

　　王龍說：「你那小廝是個官麼？」萬歲說；「不是官麼？像你這樣東西也生出來了。」王龍大叫道：「好囚軍！氣死我也！」老鴇子見他兩個鬬起口來，說道：「二位姐夫消消氣罷。大姐夫，他年少的人，已是做出來了，還待治的哩麼？二姐夫請回南樓去罷。」萬歲氣忿忿的離了北樓，

I don't know how many millions of cash we have.
     I'm not exaggerating or boasting,
But I equal ten thousand officers like you!"

The emperor said, "Are you really such a moneybags?" Wang Long replied,
"Is that so wrong? We count as the very top of the world!" The emperor said,
"That amazes me! There's no need to compare the finances of my family
with yours, let me just tell you the finances of my underlings."

     His Majesty the emperor was filled with pride
     And said, "Wang Long, don't claim to be champion!
     How many possessions do you have in all?
        You are only the son of a minister of the Ministry of War,
     How many hundreds of rooms of silver and cash do you have?
     It must be less than an account managed by one of my servants!
        All your silver and cash, the river cargo boats, the pawn shops
           in Nanjing, the fields and the houses, your wives and your
           children.
        Added all up, it doesn't equal the grain stores of just one of my
           estates!"

   Wang Long said, "Whatever nonsense you spew from that grandstand-
ing mouth of yours, who would believe you? Let me ask you, With all that
grain, how many estates do you have?"

     His Majesty the emperor snorted
     And said, "Wang Long, listen and learn:
     The estates that I own are thirteen in number.
        The underlings in charge of those estates are mighty men.
     A great banner is erected in front of the gate of each one.
     Who doesn't feel fear when the cannon resounds three times?
        When pipers and drummers have given the great command,
     The small underlings all bow to the great underlings."

Wang Long said, "Are your underlings officials?" The emperor replied,
"What else could they be? They can also produce all those things of
yours." Wang Long loudly cried, "You criminal soldier, you're driving
me mad with rage!" When the old bawd saw them start to argue, she
said, "Gentlemen, please calm down! Big sister's man may be still quite
young, but he has already made his mark. What more should he want
to achieve? Second sister's man, please go back to the southern upstairs
room." Still steaming with rage, the emperor left the northern building,

一行走着，一行罵道：「我不剝他的皮，我不算手段！」萬歲合王龍惱了。到了次日，老鴇子備了一席酒菜，給他兩個合勸，自己來請。萬歲堅執不去。鴇子道：「二姐夫，你性子這麼喬。年小的人們，每日價可答頭在一堆子，什麼正經！」萬歲道：「你對王龍說，着他剝下他那皮來給我，我才去哩。」鴇子見請他不動，也就去了。待了二三日，萬歲正合佛動心在南樓上下棋，忽然王龍着個丫頭送了一封書來。萬歲拆開一看，上寫着：

多拜上老長官：俺不過玩了玩，你就拿着當象馬蛋。摟了摟腰兒做了個嘴，不曾湯着那故事尖，縱不然也少不了邊沿。你忒也認真，可笑我只當狗皮緣邊。

萬歲爺看罷說：「好欺心的狗賊！待我回他個帖兒。」寫就了書一封，回覆那小畜生，待中死矣還掙什麼命！我說不要你那皮襖罷，誰知你嬌性再不聽，定要脫下將我送。若還是真正好漢，剝皮時休要害疼。

萬歲自從寫了回書，兩樓上不犯往來。萬歲這裏彈，他那裏就唱；萬歲這裏睡了，他那裏鑼鼓喧鬧起來。萬歲好生痛恨！未知後事如何，且聽下回分解。

5　Something out of the ordinary.

and as he was walking, he cursed Wang Long out, "If I don't flay him, I'm useless."

The emperor and Wang Long were annoyed with each other. The next day, the old bawd set out a banquet with wine to persuade them to become friends again. She herself went to invite the emperor, but he stubbornly refused to go. The bawd said, "Second sister's man, you're too stubborn. Young people should nod to each other every day and spend time together. Why stand on principle?" The emperor replied, "Tell Wang Long to strip off his skin and give it to me. Only then will I go." When the bawd saw that she could not get him to go, she left.

A few days later, when the emperor and Buddha's Lust were playing a game of chess in the southern upstairs room, Wang Long suddenly sent a serving girl to deliver a letter. The emperor opened it and read,

> "To the old officer, with all due compliments:
> I was only having some fun with your girl,
> But you considered it an elephant's egg![5]
>   I took her in my arms, and I gave her a kiss,
> But I never even touched her triangular part.
> And even if I did, it was only the edge.
>   You're so serious that you're ridiculous.
> I take the issue to be just a piece of dog's skin."

When the emperor had read this, he said, "Lying crook! Let me write him a note back."

> When he had written his letter,
> He sent it back to that little scum.
> "On the brink of death, you still struggle to survive!
>   I thought that I should not insist on your jacket of skin,
> But who knew that in your arrogance, you wouldn't listen.
> Now I really want you to take it off and give it to me.
>   And if you really want to be a hero,
> Don't complain about the pain when you're flayed!"

Once the emperor had written this letter in reply, the two upstairs rooms interacted no more. When the emperor played the lute on his side, the man on the other side would sing, and when the emperor went to sleep on his side, the other man would create a ruckus with gongs and drums, so the emperor hated him deeply!

If you don't know what happened next, please listen to the following chapter.

第二十四回 窮秀才南樓謁見 都籤片御筆親封

　　話說這大同城有一個飽學秀才，姓胡，極會相面。家裏窮的壠地沒有，他自家說將來有百萬之富。人都笑他，就給他起了個混名叫胡百萬。又看着自家命裏該當沒有官星，因此上丟了那書本子，光弄那雜八戲，吹彈歌舞，件件都會。朋友們因他在行，常請他去吃酒幫嫖，承歡取樂。

胡秀才會幫閑，又會吹又會彈，況且又相極好的面。這手裏抓來那手裏撩，家無片瓦合根椽，沒個板查稱百萬。人都說這秀才薄命，他手裏拿不住個低錢。

　　這胡百萬別的還只尋常，只有吹笛彈箏，大同地裏就數他第一。那宣武院裏常請他去教吹教打，院裏的婊子沒有一個不合他熟的。那佛動心每日等皇帝，人人都笑；他獨不然，見一遭就誇獎一遭。這胡秀才，着幾位朋友請去吃酒鬧玩，數日不曾歸家。回家第二日，到了院裏，聽的說佛動心接了個軍家，心裏就老大驚疑，便到一稱金家去打聽。媽兒讓他坐下吃茶。

An impoverished student pays a visit to
the southern upstairs room;
A sycophant-in-chief is appointed by
the imperial brush in person.

Now let me tell you, in the city of Datong there was a learned student surnamed Hu. He was an excellent physiognomist. He was so poor that he didn't have even a single ridge of land, but he claimed that in the future he would be a millionaire. People all laughed at him and gave him the nickname Millionaire Hu. Since he also saw that the star of officialdom would never shine on him, he had thrown away all his books and only practiced various idle skills, becoming an expert in playing the flute and strumming the lute, as well as singing and dancing. Because he was so knowledgeable, his friends constantly invited him along when they went drinking and whoring.

> Student Hu was excellent company:
> He could play the flute and also strum the lute,
> And on top of that, could read faces quite well.
>   What he took in with one hand, the other hand doled out.
> His house had not a single roof tile, nor a single beam;
> He owned not a single bench, yet was called a millionaire.
>   People all said, "This student has such a poor fate
> That he cannot hold on to one cropped copper!"

In all other aspects this Millionaire Hu was quite mediocre, but he was counted number one in Datong City when it came to the flute and the zither. People in the Displaying Martiality Ward constantly invited him to teach these instruments, and there was no whore in the ward who was not acquainted with him. Back when Buddha's Lust was waiting for the emperor, other people all ridiculed her, but he alone did not, and whenever he saw her, he would praise her highly. Because some friends had invited him to accompany them drinking and cavorting, Millionaire Hu had not returned home for several days. The next day after his return home, he came to the ward and heard that Buddha's Lust had received a soldier. He was secretly greatly surprised, so he went to the Jin family to hear more about it. The madam asked him to sit down and have a cup of tea.

胡百萬便開言：在城外貪着玩，幾日沒到宣武院。聽的二姐接了客，煩你給我傳一傳，我和長官見一面。老鴇兒忙叫丫頭，快與他通報一番。

　　且說那萬歲正合佛動心悶坐，丫頭上樓說道：「下邊有胡百萬待來拜姐夫哩。」萬歲說：「他是個甚麼人？」二姐說：「他是個秀才，極會吹彈，我也曾跟着他學箏來。」萬歲自合王龍惱了，就是小六哥三兩日來看看，又不能住下，兀自沒人散悶。聽說胡秀才在行，心中大喜，便說：「叫他進來。」丫頭即忙下樓，說：「姐夫有請。」秀才聞請，就上樓來了。

胡百萬進樓房，將萬歲細端詳，翻身倒拜南樓上。萬歲纔待拱一拱，見他跪倒費思量，只說還是那幫閑的樣。萬歲爺連聲請起，胡百萬悚懼而恐惶。

　　胡百萬爬將起來，站在一邊。萬歲說：「請坐。」胡百萬說：「不敢。」讓了兩三回，方才坐下。萬歲說：「我合你一個朋友家初見面，怎麼這樣謙恭？這到着我心裏不安。」那丫頭見他磕頭，也都笑他。胡百萬也不肯當面說破。

胡百萬坐在旁，丫頭們笑他臟，給人磕頭是那裏的賬？百萬明知是天子，卻又不肯撒了湯。

Millionaire Hu thereupon asked her:
"I sought some fun outside the city,
And haven't come to the ward for a few days.
    I've heard second sister has received a guest,
So I have to trouble you to introduce me to him.
I'd like to have a meeting with that officer."
    The old bawd promptly ordered a serving girl
To hurry upstairs and announce his arrival.

Let me tell you, the emperor and Buddha's Lust were sitting there, bored.
The serving girl came upstairs and said, "Millionaire Hu is waiting downstairs to pay his respects to brother-in-law." The emperor asked, "What
kind of person is he?" Second sister replied, "He's a student, but very good
at the flute and the zither. I've studied the zither with him." Since the
emperor had fallen out with Wang Long, Brother Six had paid him a visit
every other day, but as he could not stay there, the emperor had no one to
cheer him up. So when he heard that student Hu was knowledgeable, he
was very pleased and promptly said, "Let him come in!" The serving girls
hurried downstairs and said, "Brother-in-law is waiting for you." At this
invitation, the student promptly went upstairs.

When Millionaire Hu entered the room,
He observed the emperor closely
And dropped down to bow to him in the upstairs room.
    The emperor was about to greet him with a nod,
But saw to his surprise that he was kneeling down,
And thought that this might be a sponger's way.
    Though the emperor repeatedly asked him to get up,
Millionaire Hu was still filled with fear and trepidation.

Millionaire Hu clambered to his feet and stood to one side. The emperor
said, "Please take a seat." Millionaire Hu replied, "I wouldn't dare." He
sat down only after he had been invited several times. The emperor said,
"You and I are friends. Why are you so deferential on our first meeting? It
makes me uneasy." When the serving girls had seen him kowtowing, they
all laughed at him, but Millionaire Hu wouldn't disclose the truth.

As Millionaire Hu sat down to one side,
The serving girls laughed at him for being a lackey,
"What's his deal, kowtowing like this to him?"
    The millionaire clearly knew that he was a Son of Heaven,
But he was unwilling to spill the beans, and so he said,

說爺是個王侯相，望後日風雲得志，看一眼莫要相忘。

　　萬歲說：「我果然封了王侯，你的終身都在於我；只怕你那學業無準，可也罷了。」

萬歲爺笑顏生，叫秀才你是聽：只怕你那咀兒不靈應。若還過日封王侯，凡事都與你盡情，些小富貴也保的定。但只是封侯何日，你給我說個分明。

　　胡百萬說：「學生學問淺薄，這個日子可就定不出來。」

　　萬歲說：「也罷，我聽的說你吹彈的極好，有琵琶在此，你彈一套我聽聽罷。」

胡百萬抱琵琶，切四象按九牙，彈了一套客窗話。萬歲聽罷微微笑，便叫二姐你聽咱，這彈和你相上下。一半點像內府傳授，但只是節奏還差。

　　胡百萬說：「軍爺真正知音。小生這琵琶從一個御樂的親戚學來，原沒有真傳，怎麼入的爺的尊耳！」萬歲說：「你的武藝那一件精呢？」胡百萬說：「都不精。」

　　二姐說：「他的箏好。」萬歲便說：「拿箏來。」

胡百萬接銀箏，一回重一回輕，兩手不住忙忙弄。起初好似簷前雨，

1　The ledges on the neck of lute and the frets on its body may both be made of ivory. The Chinese original distinguishes them by two different terms for ivory (*xiang* 象 [elephant, ivory] vs. *ya* 牙 [tooth, tusk, ivory]).

"Sir, you have the features of a prince or minister!
　　Once you have achieved your ambition,
Please don't forget me if you happen to see me."

The emperor said, "If indeed I will be ennobled as a prince or marquis, you can depend on me for the rest of your life. But I'm afraid your learning is off the mark. Too bad!"

His Majesty the emperor displayed a smile
And said, "Dear student, now please listen to me.
I'm afraid that your prediction will not come true.
　　But if I am ennobled as a prince or marquis,
Everything will be arranged as you wish.
I'll make you a promise of a modest wealth and status.
　　But first you have to tell me clearly:
On which day I will be ennobled?"

Millionaire Hu replied, "The scholarship of this humble student is too shallow to determine the exact day." The emperor said, "Forget about it. I've heard that you are an excellent musician. There's a lute here. Please play a suite for me."

Millionaire Hu took the lute in his arms,
Touched the four ledges, pressed the nine frets,[1]
And played the suite "Conversations of Travelers."
　　When the emperor had heard it, he smiled
And said, "Second sister, please listen to me.
His playing is about as good as yours.
　　It somewhat resembles the Inner Court teaching,
But has some mistakes in rhythm and beat."

Millionaire Hu said, "Officer, you truly understand music. I learned to play the lute from a relative of an imperial musician, so I never received the true transmission. How could it be fit for your appreciation?" The emperor said, "What do you excel at?" Millionaire Hu replied, "Nothing!" Second sister said, "He plays the zither very well!" The emperor said, "Then bring the zither."

Millionaire Hu took the zither,
Playing it loud and then soft,
His two hands busily moving about without rest.
　　First, the music resembled rain in front of the eaves.

次後還如百鳥鳴。皇爺聽罷龍顏動，說二姐你學嘎來，十停只得了三停。

　　胡百萬抓罷，萬歲大喜說：「這箏就是御院裏也沒有。」胡百萬慣幫嫖，幫襯語極會叨，奉承的萬歲心歡樂。回頭便把二姐叫，沒有別人你休囂，把那新學的琵琶領領教。佛動心一回彈罷，百萬說我也會了。

　　二姐跟着萬歲學了一套，彈出來委是中聽。胡百萬不住的喝彩。彈完了，胡百萬說：「我也會了。」萬歲不信，就叫他再彈。

胡百萬真蹺蹊，聽一遍不曾學，就照着樣兒彈一套。旁人聽着齊喝彩，真正不差半分毫。萬歲聽畢微微笑，這琵琶還差點死手，從今後休對彈了。

　　胡百萬遂磕了一個頭，起來說：「甚麼死手，軍爺說了罷。」萬歲鼓掌大笑道：「不對你說。」胡百萬說：「我再吹吹那笛給軍爺聽聽，咱交易了罷。」萬歲說：「你先吹吹我看，換過了換不過呢？」

胡百萬真會玩，將笛兒吹一番，悲切好似離羣雁。

Then it sounded like the chirping of birds.
Hearing it, the dragon face was moved.
    The emperor said, "Second sister, what did you learn?
You've barely achieved a third of his mastery!"

When Millionaire Hu was finished plucking, the emperor was very pleased and said, "This mastery on the zither is found not even in the Imperial Conservatory."

Millionaire Hu was an old hand at sponging,
And he knew how to please the patrons of whores.
His flattering words gave the emperor pleasure.
    Turning around, the emperor called, "Second sister,
With no one else present, there's no need for shame.
Let's hear the piece on the lute you just learned."
    As soon as Buddha's Lust finished playing,
The millionaire said, "I can play that too."

Second sister played beautifully the piece that she had learned from the emperor, and Millionaire Hu voiced his admiration. When she had finished playing, Millionaire Hu said, "I can play that too!" The emperor did not believe him and ordered him to play it.

Millionaire Hu was uncanny.
Upon hearing a suite he had never studied,
He could play it exactly as he'd heard it.
    His audience voiced their admiration,
Because there wasn't even the slightest difference.
But the emperor listened and said with a smile:
    "This performance still lacks some masterstrokes,
From now on don't play this piece for me again!"

Millionaire Hu kowtowed, then rose up and said, "What masterstrokes? Sir officer, please tell me." The emperor clapped his hands, laughed loudly, and said, "I won't tell you!" Millionaire Hu said, "I'll play something on the flute for you, and perhaps we can make an exchange." The emperor said, "First play, and then I'll see whether I'll make an exchange."

Millionaire Hu really knew how to amuse.
He took his flute and played for a while
So sadly that it resembled a lonely goose.

二姐沒嗄可當板，頭上拔下鳳頭簪。萬歲敲着連聲讚，說這笛委是大妙，得二姐唱一個崑山。

萬歲說：「這笛眞妙。二姐，你唱一個和他一和。」佛動心唱起來，可人意開人懷，教人魂散九霄外。百萬玉笛忙和起，聽不出是兩聲來。萬歲聽罷龍心愛，將酒杯一口飲盡，說一聲妙哉妙哉！

萬歲說：「佛動心唱的第一，胡百萬吹的第一。勞苦了您倆了，咱吃酒罷。我行一個令兒，要破一個謎，猜不方的罰。」胡百萬說：「請爺先說，好做個樣子。」萬歲說：「地上沒有天上有，人人沒有一人有。」二姐說：「是龍。」萬歲說：「二姐猜方了。」胡百萬罰一盅。二姐又說：「地下也有，天上也有，人也有。裏頭不見外頭的見。」萬歲說：「這是雲。」胡百萬說：「人那裏的雲？」萬歲說：「雲布、雲錦、雲履，穿着裏頭便不見，穿着外頭便見了。」胡百萬說：「是呀。我却說甚麼？」有金墩在旁裏斟酒，胡百萬說：「你替我尋思尋思。」萬歲說：「不許替。」金墩嘻嘻的只顧笑。萬歲說：「你若是有麼，你就說，算你的。」金墩說：「人不知他知，他不覺我覺。」萬歲說：「這是甚麼東西？」胡百萬說：「這個我可猜方了，這是他那肚子裏那私孩子。」萬歲大笑說：「我輸了。」罰了一盅。「你可說麼？」胡百萬說：「我也有了。人不知他知，他不覺我覺。」

2 A way of singing southern songs that had become popular in Suzhou in the sixteenth century. It remained the most fashionable style of performance in the seventeenth and eighteenth centuries. The most important instrument in Kunqu music was the flute.

3 Cloud shoes are cloth shoes decorated with a cloud pattern and curled-up tips. In the sixteenth century, they were outlawed as too luxurious for commoners. Cloud brocade (or Nanjing brocade) refers to the highest-quality multicolor brocade as produced in the imperial workshops in Nanjing. Cloud cloth refers to cloth decorated with a cloud pattern.

Second sister had nothing at hand to beat out the measure,
So she pulled a phoenix-head hairpin from her hair,
And as she beat the measure, the emperor kept praising him.
    He said, "Your mastery of the flute is truly wonderful,
So good that second sister should sing a Kunqu song!"[2]

The emperor said, "Your mastery of the flute is truly wonderful. Second sister, you should sing a song to accompany him."

When Buddha's Lust started singing,
It was pleasing and dispelled all sorrow,
Lifting one's souls beyond the Ninth Heaven!
    The Millionaire's jade flute hastily started following,
So one's ears could not distinguish the two voices.
Upon hearing this, the emperor's dragon heart loved it!
    He emptied a cup of wine in one gulp,
Saying only, "Wonderful, wonderful!"

The emperor said, "Buddha's Lust is the best in singing, and Millionaire Hu is the best on the flute. I have worn you two out, so let's drink some wine. Let's issue wine commands. Try solving a riddle, and the one who can't will be fined." Millionaire Hu said, "Sir, go first and tell us yours, so we'll have an example." The emperor said, "On earth you don't have it, but in Heaven you do. Other people don't have it, but one person does." Second sister replied, "A dragon!" The emperor said, "Second sister solved the riddle!" So Millionaire Hu is fined one drink. Second sister said, "On earth you have it and in Heaven you have it, and people also have it. Inside it you don't see it, but outside it you do." The emperor said, "A cloud." Millionaire Hu said, "What are people's clouds?" The emperor replied, "Cloud cloth, cloud brocade, and cloud shoes.[3] When you go through it, you don't see it, but when you get outside it, you see it." Millionaire Hu said, "Indeed. What can I say?" Golden Stool was pouring wine at the side, so Millionaire Hu said, "Come up with something for me!" But the emperor said, "No substitutions allowed!" But as Golden Stool kept smiling to herself, the emperor said, "If you have something, just say it. We will count it as yours." Golden Stool said, "Others don't know, but he knows. Yet he doesn't feel what I feel." The emperor said, "What could that be?" But Millionaire Hu said, "I can solve that riddle. It's the bastard child in her belly."

The emperor laughed loudly and said, "I lose!" He fined himself one beaker of wine and said "Your turn!" Millionaire Hu said, "I have one. Others don't know, but she knows. Yet she doesn't feel what I feel." The

萬歲說：「該罰！人說了的你怎麼又說？」胡百萬說：「我這個不合他一樣。」萬歲說：「是嘎？」胡百萬說：「是我這褲子裏的破爛流丟的，惟止家下給我胡做時他纔知道。」萬歲大笑道：「胡百萬，你有百萬之名，可怎麼還沒有條囫圇褲子？」胡百萬說：「這是人誚我，起了一個綽號。」萬歲說：「我管給你成就了這個名子。」

萬歲爺笑呵呵，胡百萬你聽着：放心有我也不錯。果然由了那封侯的話，百十萬銀子值甚麼，情管着你自在過。胡百萬慌忙跪下，磕的頭比那碎米還多。

胡百萬磕頭謝恩。萬歲說：「你休要忒認眞了，我的王侯萬一封不成，可不搭了你那些頭麼？」胡百萬說：「搭不了。」

武宗爺心裏歡，不由的開笑言，叫了一聲胡百萬。我若得了王侯位，給你本兒去轉錢，鹽商茶客從你的便。你若是做上幾載，運來時百萬何難？

胡百萬說：「小生命薄，本兒大了擔不的，給我一個別的頭向罷。」萬歲說：「有一個頭向你極會做的。」胡百萬說：「甚麼頭？」萬歲說：「給你一個都篦片頭，你可願做麼？」

萬歲爺開玉言，叫秀才且耐煩，將來封你個都篦片。幫閒嫖客屬你管，

emperor said, "You're fined! How can you say what someone else said?" However, Millionaire Hu said, "But mine is different from hers." The emperor said, "Indeed?" Millionaire Hu said, "It's a pair of pants that I've reduced to rags. When my wife fixes them somehow, she knows." The emperor laughed loudly and said, "Millionaire Hu, you may be called a Millionaire, but how come you don't even have a decent pair of pants?" Millionaire Hu replied, "It's a nickname people gave me to ridicule me." The emperor said, "I definitely will make the name come true for you."

> His Majesty the emperor laughed loudly:
> "Millionaire Hu, listen to me.
> Don't worry, you haven't done so bad by me.
>   If indeed I become ennobled as you predicted,
> What do we care about millions of silver?
> I'll make sure that you can live in ease."
>   Millionaire Hu hastily knelt down, kowtowing on and on,
> More times than the number of scattered grains of rice.

Millionaire Hu kowtowed to express his gratitude. The emperor said, "Don't take this too seriously! If by chance I don't become ennobled as a prince or marquis, all those times you knocked your head on the ground will have been in vain." But Millionaire Hu said, "It isn't in vain."

> The Martial Ancestor being pleased at heart,
> His face involuntarily broke into a smile,
> And he called out, "Dear Millionaire Hu,
>   If I obtain the rank of a prince or marquis,
> I'll give you the capital to generate money:
> Salt merchants and tea traders will follow your whim.
>   If you work in such a job for a few years,
> With some luck, the millions will come easy."

Millionaire Hu said, "I am destined to be poor, so I cannot bear the burden of so much capital. Please give me some other job." The emperor replied, "I know a job that you can do perfectly well." Millionaire Hu asked, "What kind of job?" The emperor said, "I'll make you the sycophant-in-chief. Is that a job you're willing to take?"

> His Majesty the emperor spoke his jade words,
> Saying, "Dear student, please don't be upset.
> In the future, I'll appoint you as sycophant-in-chief.
>   Spongers and whoremongers will be under your sway,

打那姐兒忘八的課稅錢，這個營生你幹不幹？丫頭們嗤嗤的怪笑，胡百萬喜地歡天。

　　胡百萬說：「這個頭向就強的別的。但只是口說無憑，求爺給一個帖兒做個憑信。」便拿了一幅柬帖來，遞在萬歲面前。萬歲此時有些醉意，乘着酒興大寫道：「欽差巡視兩京各院等處地方，都理嫖務，兼管天下幫閒都簽片。」胡百萬拿在手裏，磕頭謝恩。萬歲自從進院，不曾開興吃酒，今日不覺大醉。胡百萬見爺醉了，便說：「小生告辭，軍爺睡了罷。」萬歲說：「夜已深了，你合那丫頭們在樓下睡了，明日再玩。」

萬歲爺醉沉沉，叫秀才夜已深，你且合那丫頭們困。明日起來再玩耍，省的差人把你尋，休要去的無音信。胡百萬連聲答應，爺自睡不要擔心。

　　胡百萬答應一聲，下樓去了。未知後事如何，且聽下回分解。

And you'll collect all taxes on sisters and pimps.
Is this perhaps a responsibility you can manage?"
    The serving girls were giggling and laughing,
But Millionaire Hu was as pleased as could be.

Millionaire Hu said, "That's a better job than any other. But an oral promise provides no proof, so please, Sir, give me a note that may serve as
confirmation." He thereupon fetched a sheet of paper, which he placed
before the emperor. The emperor at that moment was slightly drunk and,
while under the influence, wrote in large characters, "Sycophant-in-Chief
dispatched to inspect the wards of the two capitals and comparable places
and regions, in charge of all matters concerning whoring, as well as all
spongers of the whole wide world." With this in his hands, Millionaire Hu
kowtowed in gratitude.

    Since he had entered the ward, the emperor had never drunk with such
abandon, but that day he became totally drunk. When Millionaire Hu saw
that the emperor was drunk, he said, "I had better leave. Sir officer, please
go to bed." The emperor replied, "It's already late. You go and sleep with
the serving girls downstairs, so we can amuse ourselves again tomorrow."

    His Majesty the emperor was utterly drunk,
    And said, "Dear student, it's already late!
    You go and sleep with the serving girls
        So that tomorrow when we get up and want to have fun,
    I won't have to send someone to find you.
    Don't go without leaving any information."
        Millionaire Hu repeatedly promised to do so:
    "Dear Sir, go to bed, and don't worry!"

Millionaire Hu made his promise and went downstairs.
    If you don't know what happened next, please listen to the following
chapter.

第二十五回 游妓院萬歲觀花 吹玉笛美人獻技

話說那萬歲醉了，睡到天明，便說：「二姐，夜來那胡百萬進來就磕頭，只怕他認出我來了。」二姐說：「也是有的。他相極好的面。人都笑我等皇帝，他不笑我。」萬歲說：「着人去叫他來罷。咱再合他玩耍，我可盤問他盤問。」二姐便叫丫頭去請他。丫頭說：「今夜裏任憑怎麼留他，他不住下，自己打着個燈籠，飛跑的去了。」

萬歲爺笑一聲，叫丫頭你是聽：想是他嫌你不乾淨。他家住在甚麼巷，隔着這裏幾里程？若是不遠你蹭一蹭。果然他宿在家裏，拉他來休要放鬆。

丫頭說：「我去找他去。」略不停時，丫頭回來說：「他夜來不曾歸家。」二姐說：「有了。」

佛動心想一週，半夜裏何處收留？有個去處他去的溜。東院裏有我好姐姐，名子叫做百花羞，秀才惟只合他厚。情管是在他那裏，不消去別處搜求。

丫頭說：「我就忘了呢，就是就是。」慌忙去了。

25   Visiting the courtesan quarter, the
emperor observes the flowers;
Playing her jade flute, a beauty presents
her skill.

Now let me tell you, the emperor was so drunk that he slept till the next
morning, when he said, "Second sister, last night Millionaire Hu kowtowed
to me as soon as he entered. I'm afraid he recognized me." Second sister
replied, "That's quite possible. He is an expert in reading faces. Everyone
else ridiculed me for waiting for an emperor, but he didn't." The emperor
said, "Have someone call him. While the two of us are enjoying ourselves,
I should question him." Second sister ordered a serving girl to invite him,
but the serving girl said, "Last night we could not keep him here by any
means. He flew off carrying a lantern!"

> His Majesty the emperor laughed out loud
> And said, "Serving girl, now listen to me!
> He must have disliked you for being unclean.
>   Which lane in the city does he live on?
> And how far is it from here?
> If it isn't too far, you must go there.
>   If he spent the night at his own place,
> Drag him here and don't loosen your grip!"

The serving girl said, "I will look for him." After a while she returned and
said, "He didn't return home last night." Second sister said, "I have an idea."

> Buddha's Lust pondered this for a while,
> "What place would take him in at midnight?
> I know the place where he usually goes.
>   In the eastern courtyard lives my elder sister,
> Whose name is Puts All Flowers to Shame.
> The student and she are extremely close.
>   He definitely must be staying with her,
> So there's no need to seek him elsewhere."

The serving girl said, "I'd forgotten. That must be it." And she hurried off.

有丫頭到東廂，胡百萬才下牀，臉兒洗得沒停當。罵了一聲天殺的，着俺像找白侍郎，你可弄那自在像。穿搭上流水去罷，這早晚還只顧麼倉。

胡百萬穿衣裳，罵一聲小淫娼，上頭撲面的甚麼樣？我這問您二姐姐，文書着他給一張，我可合你算算賬。那丫頭連推帶打，一陣風拉上樓房。

萬歲說：「你幹的好事！我着你休去，你怎麼就逃了？」胡百萬說：「他們又不留我，怎麼可強插白賴的死塞呢？」丫頭說：「好嚼舌根子的！我沒說你休去罷？」萬歲說：「這自然是你的不是。你竟揚長去了，又不怕人擔囂；我封了你一個大大的官兒，你又不早來謝恩。罰你給丫頭作個揖罷。」胡百萬說：「我寧只給佛動心磕頭，這揖可難作。」萬歲說：「你爲什麼半夜裏逃走了呢？你作揖還揀主麼？」胡百萬說：「不是揀主，他們都擔不的，看折煞他了。」

丫頭們笑哈哈，胡百萬你忒也誇，自家估着自家大。你說作揖就擔不的，你跪上試試看怎麼？秀才說話就恁麼乍。百萬說你留情意，再留我定是住下。

---

1   Vice-minister Bai refers to the famous Tang-dynasty poet Bai Juyi 白居易 (772–846), but it is unclear what incident is referred to as "seeking vice-minister Bai." Perhaps this is a reference to the story of the deliverance of Bai Juyi by Chan master Bird's Nest. Anonymous 1990, for instance, tells us that when the two arhats Luojia 羅迦 and Tina 提那 are seduced by the splendors of the human realm, they are banished to earth, and they promise that they will deliver each other. While Tina is reborn as Bai Juyi, Luojia becomes a holy monk, but when he dies without delivering Bai, the Buddha takes him to task on his return and sends him back to earth to save Bai Juyi, which he eventually does. Other versions of this legend may provide the Chan master and Bai Juyi with different celestial backgrounds.

When the serving girl arrived in the eastern section,
Millionaire Hu had just descended from the couch
And washed his face, but was not yet dressed.
    She cursed him under her breath, "You damn . . .
He makes me act like 'seeking vice-minister Bai,'[1]
But you are the very picture of leisure!"
    Get dressed so that we can leave as fast as the wind.
You're making me wear down my heels!"

Millionaire Hu put on his clothes
And reviled her, "You little whore.
What's with your slapdash makeup?
    I'll ask your second sister
To write out a statement
So that I can settle accounts with you!"
    The serving girl pushed him and beat him,
And like a gust of wind pulled him upstairs.

The emperor said, "You played quite a trick on me. I told you not to leave, so why did you flee?" Millionaire Hu replied, "They never tried to make me stay, so how can you so forcefully and groundlessly charge me with that?" The serving girl said, "Bite your tongue! Didn't we tell you not to leave?" The emperor said, "Of course this is your fault. You brazenly left, not fearing that others might have to bear the blame. And though I appointed you to very high office, you didn't arrive early to express your gratitude. As punishment, I order you to humbly greet the serving girl." Millionaire Hu said, "I will be happy to kowtow to Buddha's Lust, but I cannot humbly greet her!" The emperor said, "Why did you run off in the middle of the night? And why are you so choosy in whom you greet?" Millionaire Hu replied, "It's not that I'm so choosy. The problem is that they all wouldn't be able to bear it. The burden would break them!"

The serving girls laughed loudly:
"Millionaire Hu, you boast too much!
'Each considers himself the greatest.'
    You say that we cannot bear your greeting.
What would happen if you kowtowed?
Student, what you say is nothing but boasting!"
    The millionaire said, "Show me some mercy!
The next time you want me to stay, I will stay."

萬歲說：「着了極了，饒了你罷。我且問你：你會相面，你相着我現如今是甚麼人？若說着，賞銀二百兩。」

胡百萬笑吟吟，俺有眼也有心，你說俺就恁麼夯。頭上戴着簷氈帽，腰束皮鞓帶一條根，自然長官何消問。這兩日運氣極好，又插上這二百兩的白銀。

萬歲說；「你可相差了，就沒有裝做軍家的？」胡百萬說：「拿銀子來罷。」萬歲說：「相不着怎麼還敢要銀子？」胡百萬說：「軍爺請自家說是個甚麼人，我就不要了。」萬歲說：「我現是個京官。」胡百萬說：「若是個京官，我情願挖下眼來搓了。」萬歲說：「我實對你說罷，我是個皇帝。」胡百萬問二姐姐道：「眞果麼？我不信，我不信！誰家皇帝出來嫖院來？還肯自家說是皇帝？拿銀子來罷。」

萬歲爺笑哈哈，我本是盤問他，誰想倒着他盤問下。就給你銀子二百兩，休要拿着當土合沙，做條褲子好支架。你領我院中看看，那有名的都是誰家。

萬歲說：「二百銀子這是小事，我可不是爲你相的那胡突面。聽說院中三千姊妹，你就認的兩千七八。那名妓多少，你都領我去看看。」胡百萬說：「這自然是都籤片的職掌，怎敢推辭。」萬歲大喜，

The emperor said, "You're asking for trouble, but I forgive you. But let me ask you. You know how to read people's faces. Read my face, and tell me what kind of man I am. If you give the right answer, I will reward you with two hundred ounces of silver."

> Millionaire Hu displayed a grin,
> "I have the eyes; I have the mind.
> Do you think that I'm that dense?
>   On your head you wear a brimmed felt hat;
> A leather belt is wrapped around your waist.
> Of course you're an officer. Why even ask?
>   These two days my luck has been quite good,
> And now I get two hundred more ounces!"

The emperor said, "But you're wrong. Does no one dress up as a soldier?" Millionaire Hu said, "Get the silver!" The emperor said, "How dare you demand the silver when you've read my face wrong?" Millionaire Hu said, "Sir officer, please tell me who you are, and I won't demand it." The emperor said, "At this moment, I am a capital official." Millionaire Hu replied, "If you're a capital official, I'll gouge out my eyes." The emperor said, "Then let me tell you the truth: I am the emperor!" Millionaire Hu asked second sister, "Is it true? I can't believe it! What emperor ever left the capital to come whoring in the ward? How can you claim that you're the emperor! Get me the silver!"

> His Majesty the emperor laughed loudly.
> "I wanted to question him,
> But who thought that he would question me?
>   I will give you your two hundred ounces of silver,
> But please don't treat it like mud or dust.
> Have a pair of pants made so you can show off!
>   Now take me on a tour and show me the ward
> And tell me who the most famous courtesans are!"

The emperor said, "The two hundred ounces of silver is only a minor thing, but you don't get it for misreading my face. I've heard that of the three thousand sisters in the ward, you know around twenty-eight hundred of them. Now take me on a tour to see all the famous courtesans." Millionaire Hu said, "This is, of course, a responsibility of the Sycophant-in-Chief. How could I dare refuse?" The emperor was greatly pleased.

即時吃了酒飯，一同下樓。胡百萬說：「二姐沒本是走
不去罷？」萬歲說：「也罷，你在家叫人擺下酒席，回
來咱好玩耍。」

轉街巷曲彎彎，皇帝後秀才前，領着萬歲沿門串。出色名妓
八十個，武藝精通件件全，揀着門兒從頭看。看了勾五十餘
家，爺纔信自古才難。

二人走了五十餘家，有住下吃一盅茶的，有略坐坐就走
了的，有合胡百萬罵幾句的；都知道是二姐接的那軍
家，也都不甚尊敬，却都爲胡百萬的面子上，沒有不讓
坐坐的。萬歲肚中饑了，却又困乏，見那一般名妓都不
上眼，興致也就沒上來了。轉過牆角，又到了一家，見
那房舍甚是清雅，有一個姐兒迎將出來。

萬歲爺細端詳，打扮的淡素裝，年紀只在二十上；雖然不似
二姐美，風流却也不尋常，行持沒有那儣賴樣。見了爺拜了
兩拜，將二人請進香房。

到了房裏，胡百萬說：「這就是南樓上那位爺。」那姐
兒慌忙跪倒，磕了幾個頭兒，便說：「不知爺來，有失
迎接，賤人萬死！」

2   Because of her bound feet.

After they had first taken their meal, they went downstairs together, and Millionaire Hu said, "Second sister, you don't have what it takes to walk,[2] so you'd better not go." The emperor said, "Fine. You stay at home and have the serving girls lay out a banquet so that we can amuse ourselves on our return."

> They wound their way down streets and lanes.
> The emperor followed behind with the student in front
> Leading the way as they went from door to door.
>   There were eighty of the most beautiful courtesans.
> They excelled in all skills, perfect in each way.
> Selecting the gates, they visited all of these girls.
>   When they had visited over fifty households,
> The emperor realized, "Talent is always rare."

The two of them visited more than fifty houses. At some of them, they stayed to have a beaker of wine, but at others they only sat for a while before walking on. At some, Millionaire Hu was cursed out. They all knew that the soldier had been received by second sister, but they did not show him any respect. Yet out of consideration for Millionaire Hu, they all let the two of them sit down for a moment. The emperor began to feel hungry, and he also had become tired. When he saw that the common run of famous courtesans didn't take notice of him, his interest also declined. They turned a corner and came to yet another house, he saw that that building was extremely proper. A sister came out to welcome them.

> The emperor observed her closely:
> She was dressed in a delicate outfit,
> And her age was just over twenty.
>   Though not as pretty as second sister,
> Her charms were exceptional
> And she showed no signs of sloth.
>   On seeing His Lordship, she bowed twice,
> And invited them into her room.

Inside her room, the millionaire said, "This is His Lordship from the southern upstairs room." The sister hastily knelt down, kowtowing repeatedly, and then said, "Not knowing that Your Lordship had arrived, I failed to go outside to welcome you. This vile person deserves ten thousand deaths!"

萬歲爺暗疑猜，這個人好怪哉，怎麼聽說就將我拜？人人拿着不當事，忽然跑出個敬的來，萬歲便有幾分愛。要賞他白銀百兩，口不言心裏鋪排。

　　二人茶罷，美人便吩咐丫頭速備酒席。萬歲說：「窮軍家又沒有賞銀，那裏就有取擾的理。胡百萬，咱走罷。」美人那裏肯依。

那美人笑開言，叫聲爺休棄嫌，好容易見的爺金面。雖然沒嘎給爺吃，略把腿兒少蹺蹺，遽然去了不好看。胡百萬你若領了客去，我合你斷了咱往還！

　　胡百萬說；「這是他一點誠意，咱就擾他罷。」萬歲便忻然坐下。略不停時，酒肴甚是齊整。

武宗爺悶氣消，問一聲女多嬌，初逢不知是甚麼號？今日閑玩來到此，沒曾帶着銀子包，回時送個薄儀到。美人說增光萬幸，若說這賞賜何消。

　　胡百萬說：「他名子叫百花羞。」萬歲說：「哦！那百花羞就是你麼？」百花羞說：「就是賤人。」胡百萬說：「聽的誰說來？」萬歲說：「今早晨找不着你，佛動心說，有一個百花羞合他甚厚，必然是在那裏，因此知道這個名子。」又點點頭說道：

His Majesty the emperor was wondering to himself,
"This person behaves in a very remarkable manner!
Why does she promptly bow to me upon hearing him?
    All the others considered me unimportant,
But suddenly someone comes running to greet me!"
The emperor promptly felt a certain love for her
    And wanted to give her a hundred ounces of silver.
He said not a word, but promised himself that he would do so.

When the two had finished their tea, the beauty ordered her serving girl to quickly prepare a meal. The emperor said, "As only a poor soldier I don't have the money to reward you. How could I bother you? Millionaire Hu, let's go." But the beauty did not agree.

That beauty said with a smile,
"Sir, please don't disdain me,
It hasn't been easy to see your golden face.
    Even though I have nothing good to serve you,
Please sit here for a little longer.
It will look awkward if you leave so quickly.
    Millionaire Hu, if you take this guest away,
I'll have nothing more to do with you!"

Millionaire Hu said, "As this is her sincere wish, we should avail ourselves of her hospitality." The emperor happily sat back down. After a short while, a perfect meal was served.

The Martial Ancestor, his gloom dispersed,
Asked her, "Lovely lady,
As this is our first meeting, what is your name?
    Idly amusing ourselves today, I came here
And forgot to bring my purse of silver with me.
But on my return I will send you a small gift."
    The beauty replied, "Your presence is bliss.
Why do you have to talk about presents?"

Millionaire Hu said, "Her name is Puts All Flowers to Shame." The emperor said, "So you're Puts All Flowers to Shame!" She replied, "That's me!" Millionaire Hu asked, "From whom did you hear about her?" The emperor replied, "When we couldn't find you this morning, Buddha's Lust said that you are very close with Puts All Flowers to Shame, so you must be with her. That's how I know the name." Nodding his head, he

「是你眼色不差，果是個妙人兒，雅致溫柔，不同尋常。」百花羞說：「蒙爺的過獎，折煞賤人了！」萬歲說：「胡百萬可人沒有不會吹彈的。」那百花羞見爺問他，便去房裏拿出一隻玉笛，一攢牙笙，雕刻的異樣精美。笑了笑，將那笙遞於胡百萬。

一吹笛一吹笙，合起來好中聽，哀哀吹了兩三弄。知音天子上邊座，好好連誇四五聲，想那教笛時特把心來用。細聽他一字一句，合百萬一氣相同。

萬歲大喜說：「您二人這樣相厚，又是極好的一對兒。依我說，百花羞，你嫁了他罷。」二人聽說，一齊下來，兩手撲地，給爺叩了頓頭。

武宗爺笑哈哈，你磕頭為什麼？我不過是句閑常說話。幾十兩銀子還容易，出百兩以外就難咱，媽兒不知要多少價。點點頭說也罷也罷，且從容濟着我刷刮。

百花羞說：「軍爺這片好心，賤人離了火炕，給爺念佛。」萬歲說：「你嫁與不嫁，今後且不必提他。您二人且合我去南樓上玩耍玩耍，過日的事在我。」百花羞帶了丫頭，一同出門往南樓去了。

---

3 The mouth organ (*sheng* 笙) features a number of pipes of different lengths attached to one mouthpiece.

added, "Your choice is not bad. She is indeed a marvel, extraordinarily elegant and friendly!" Puts All Flowers to Shame said with a blush, "Sir, you praise me too much, I don't deserve such words!" The emperor asked, "Does Millionaire Hu have any friends who can't play the flute or lute?" When Puts All Flowers to Shame heard this question from the emperor, she went to fetch a jade flute from her room and an ivory mouth organ[3] carved in an exceptionally beautiful way. With a smile, she handed the mouth organ to Millionaire Hu.

> One played the flute, the other the mouth organ.
> As they harmonized together, the music was great.
> They played two or three pieces in the most moving way.
> The Son of Heaven, a true connoisseur, was seated at the
> head
> And repeatedly praised their playing: "Excellent, excellent!"
> He imagined how the flute teacher must have exerted himself.
> He listened carefully to her every word and phrase,
> As she harmonized with the millionaire and synchronized every
> breath.

The emperor was greatly pleased and said, "The two of you are so close and make such a fine duo! Puts All Flowers to Shame, I think you should marry him!" When they heard this, they knelt down and kowtowed to His Lordship with their hands on the floor.

> The Martial Ancestor laughed loudly.
> "Why are you kowtowing to me?
> It's just a conventional phrase!
> A few dozen ounces of silver are easy enough,
> But more than a hundred ounces becomes difficult.
> I don't know how much your madam asks for you."
> Nodding his head, he said, "So be it; so be it.
> Let me take my time to scrape it together!"

Puts All Flowers to Shame said, "Sir officer, when thanks to your kindness I can leave this pit of fire, I will recite the name of the Buddha for your benefit." The emperor said, "There's no need to bring up the matter of your marriage again. The two of you will have fun with me in the southern upstairs room. All expenses on me." Puts All Flowers to Shame took a serving girl along, and together they left for the southern upstairs room.

百花羞到樓門，看見了佛動心，跪下才把二姐問。你若到了安身處，也念念火坑受罪人，休忘了從小一處混。佛動心大驚失色，忙回禮跪倒埃塵。

二姐忙把百花羞請起來，說：「姐姐忽然行此大禮，這是爲何？」百花羞說：「是應當的。」
想妹妹掛心懷，怕爺嗔不敢來，誰想倒將奴錯愛。忽然到了俺家裏，沒點甚麼清處來，又許提出火坑外。這都是妹妹的體面，磕萬頭也是應該。

二姐說：「他的話俱聽不的。姐姐既有從良的心腸，也是易事。我還有幾兩私房銀子，那媽媽娘任拘要多少銀子，我管助成。」
萬歲爺笑一聲，佛動心你瞎支稜，開口就誵你那銀錢重。我問親戚借一借，定然拔他出火坑，臨時還有小陪送。我送他黃金萬兩，兩口兒快活一生。

胡百萬合百花羞又磕頭謝了恩。佛動心說：「你光叨大話，我看你合不煞口來着待說甚麼！」萬歲說：「你休管我。快拿酒來，咱四人痛快玩玩。」四人方才坐定，有一個丫頭拿上一個帖子來。萬歲問：

4	The sins of a former existence that created the karma causing her to become a courtesan.

Puts All Flowers to Shame arrived there
And greeted Buddha's Lust.
She knelt down and asked second sister,
   "If you found a spot to live in peace,
Think of me, suffering for my sins[4] in this pit of fire.
Don't forget that we've lived together since childhood!"
   Buddha's Lust blanched, greatly surprised,
And in return she too quickly knelt down in the dust.

Second sister hastily invited Puts All Flowers to Shame to get up again
and said, "Sister, why did you suddenly perform this solemn ceremony?"
Puts All Flowers to Shame replied, "It was fitting.

   "You, younger sister, have always showed concern,
But fearing the officer's wrath, I didn't dare come here.
Who knew he would actually show me his love?
   All of a sudden he appeared at my place,
Where I didn't have any pure place for him.
He has promised to free me from this pit of fire.
   This he did out of consideration for you,
This is why I should kowtow to you."

Second sister said, "You cannot listen to what he says. But as you
desire to marry a commoner, it's an easy matter. I still have some ounces
of private savings. I will help with however much silver your madam
may want."

   His Majesty the emperor laughed loudly,
"Buddha's Lust, you must be stone-blind!
You only open your mouth to lie about savings!
   I will borrow some silver from my relatives
And definitely pull her out of this pit of fire,
And when the time comes, I'll add a small wedding gift.
   I will give them ten thousand ounces of yellow gold
So the two of them can live in comfort all of their lives."

Millionaire Hu and Puts All Flowers to Shame once again kowtowed
to express their gratitude. Buddha's Lust said, "You're just making grand
claims. As I see it, you can't keep your mouth shut to think before you
speak." The emperor said, "Don't try to control me. Bring out the wine,
so the four of us can have a good time." The four of them had barely sat
down when a serving girl brought in a note. When the emperor asked

「是做甚麼的？」丫頭說：「是北樓上王姐夫請胡相公的。」胡百萬說；「你對他說罷，我不能去。」

萬歲說胡秀才，那王龍有錢財，你若不去看他怪。百萬笑道不妨事，他死的頭向待中來，他就惱些也沒害。他來時曾會他一面，看不上那嘴臉歪腮。

胡百萬說：「他也活不的幾日了，得罪他些也不差。」

萬歲說；「你那裏見的？只像你給我相的那面，那王侯在那裏哩？」胡百萬說：「若合我相那面似的，他就壞了。」萬歲說：「閒話休題，咱且吃酒罷。」

兩對兒並坐了，飲數巡興致高，各人顯出各人的妙。一個琵琶一個笛，一個打板一個簫，滿樓不住喧天鬧。四個人歡歡喜喜，只吃的譙鼓三敲。

萬歲聽見打三更，說道：「咱不耍罷。您二人明晨早來。」胡百萬合百花羞連忙答應，下樓去了。未知後事如何，且聽下回分解。

what it was, she said, "Brother-in-law Wang at the northern upstairs room invites Mr. Hu." Millionaire Hu then said, "Please tell him I cannot come."

The emperor said, "Student Hu,
Wang Long is quite rich.
If you don't go there he might blame you!"
    The millionaire said with a smile, "That's not an issue.
His death is only a few days away,
So who cares if he gets annoyed?
    I met him once in the past,
But I can't stand his crooked face!"

Millionaire Hu said, "He has only a few more days to live, so it doesn't matter if I offend him." The emperor asked, "How do you know? It must be like when you read my face. And where is my title of prince or marquis?" Millionaire Hu replied, "If it's as good as that prediction of mine, he's done for." The emperor, "Don't talk nonsense. Let's have some wine."

The two couples sat side by side,
And after some rounds the mood was joyous
As each displayed his or her marvelous skill.
    One plucked the lute, and one played the flute;
One beat the clappers, and one blew the pipes.
The whole building resounded with their music!
    The four of them had a wonderful time together
And kept on drinking till the midnight watch.

When the emperor heard the third watch being sounded, he said, "That's enough. You two come back tomorrow morning." Millionaire Hu and Puts All Flowers to Shame hastily promised to do so and went downstairs.

    If you don't know what happened next, please listen to the following chapter.

第二十六回 胡百萬幫嫖惹禍 張天師保主留丹

　　話說萬歲吃酒吃了半夜，到了天明起的身來，便問：
「胡百萬兩口子來了不曾？」丫頭說：「還沒哩。」「快
去叫他來的。」丫頭去不多時，回來說道：「來不的了。」
萬歲說；「怎麼來不的了呢？」

丫頭說胡秀才，他今早已是來，剛剛到了門兒外。王宅家人
把他請，說了聲不去就上來，揣衣服裂的條條壞。萬歲爺未
曾聽罷，罵一聲欺心的小奴才！

　　丫頭說：「百花羞着人給他買衣裳去了。買了來時，就
過來哩。」萬歲說：「快給他送三十兩銀子去，着他揀
着那上好的紬緞，多叫幾個裁縫，流水快做出來，扎掛
的一攙新，可來見我。」

慌的那佛動心，拿出了一包銀，差人去把秀才問。裁縫叫了
好幾個，一宿做了一攙新，走來更比常時俊。兩口兒早到樓
上，齊聲說謝爺天恩。

Millionaire Hu, a companion in
whoring, incites disaster;
Heavenly Master Zhang leaves a pill to
protect the Ruler.

Now let me tell you, the emperor kept drinking until midnight. As soon
as he rose the next morning, he asked, "Have Millionaire Hu and his
friend arrived?" "Not yet," a serving girl replied. "Then go tell them
to come!" The serving girl had not been gone for very long when she
returned and said, "They can't come." The emperor asked, "Why can't
they?"

> The serving girl said, "The student Hu
> Was already here this morning,
> But the moment they arrived outside the gate,
>   Wang Long's servants invited them over,
> And when he refused, they attacked him,
> Tearing the clothes he was wearing to rags."
>   Even before the emperor had heard it all,
> He reviled Wang Long as a "mean slave."

The serving girl said, "Puts All Flowers to Shame sent someone to buy
new clothes for him. After that, they will come over." The emperor said,
"Hurry and send her thirty ounces of silver so that she can choose the
best silk, and engage a few more tailors to make the clothes as quickly as
possible. When he is dressed in a completely new outfit, he should come
and see me."

> In a great hurry, Buddha's Lust
> Took out a package of silver
> And had someone take it to the student.
>   He engaged numerous tailors,
> And overnight they finished his outfit.
> Walking around, he was more handsome than ever!
>   He and his girlfriend quickly hurried upstairs
> And in unison thanked His Lordship for his grace.

萬歲說：「你相與着沒體面的軍家，又給你做不下主來；你不如去奉承奉承他，就不怪你了。」胡百萬說：「我不去，也不是怕爺嗔。」

窮雖窮志氣剛，任拘他怎麼降，臉兒難合心兩樣。叫我幾回我不去，無非就是嫌他髒，嘴臉叫人看不上？我只將冷眼觀蟹，看橫行能有幾場。

萬歲說：「快拿酒來，我給胡百萬壓驚。」

萬歲爺斟一盅，我給你壓壓驚，休爲煩惱就沒了興。百味珍饈忙拿過，四人依然鬧樓中，今朝更比昨朝勝。不說他君臣取樂，惱犯了寶客王龍。

且說那王龍辱了胡百萬一場，方纔心下少可；又聽的待了一日一宿，就上下一攛新了，依舊南樓作樂。暗暗的鼓那肚子，要害南樓一黨。

王冲霄悶騰騰，聽南樓彈唱聲，氣的整宿睡不定。難道尚書大公子，不如一個腌臢兵？我定然合他弄一弄。晝夜的越思越惱，找法兒要害朝廷。

---

1   "Walk sideways" (*hengxing* 橫行) also means engage in violence.

The emperor said, "You're hanging out with a soldier who has no status and who cannot act as your champion. You'd better go and suck up to him, so he won't blame you." But Millionaire Hu said, "I won't go. I don't fear his wrath.

> I may be poor, but I have my pride.
> Let him catch me; I won't give in.
> My face cannot be different from my heart!
>   However often he calls me, I will not go,
> All because I despise him. He is so mean
> That one cannot take a fancy to his face.
>   I will 'with a cold eye observe the crab'
> And see how often it can 'walk sideways.'"[1]

The emperor said, "Bring the wine, so I can quell the indignity Millionaire Hu had to suffer."

> His Majesty the emperor poured out a cup:
> "With this let me quell the indignity for you.
> Don't let this annoyance dampen your mood."
>   A hundred delicacies were fetched,
> And upstairs the four partied as usual.
> That day surpassed even the day before.
>   Say nothing about the joy of lord and vassal.
> It annoyed prize guest Wang Long!

Now let me tell you, Wang Long's feelings had improved only slightly after having roughed up Millionaire Hu. But after that day and night when the new outfit was being made, he heard them having a great time in the southern upstairs room as before. Inwardly, his belly ballooned with rage, and he wanted to do in the whole southern-upstairs-room gang.

> Wang Long was overcome by gloom.
> Hearing the music and song from the southern room,
> He was so mad that he couldn't sleep all night.
>   "It is not possible that the main son of a minister
> Cannot measure up to a scumbag soldier!
> I'll surely have it out with him for good!"
>   Day and night he kept thinking and pondering,
> Seeking how to do away with the emperor.

且說張天師正然誦皇經，偶然一陣狂風，大同的城隍參見。天師道：「有何事情？」城隍道：「萬歲隻身私行大同宣武院取樂，有王龍要害萬歲，一個文武不曾代來。今日玉皇聖誕，大小諸神都去慶賀，無人保駕，如何是好？」天師說：「也罷，我就下山保主一遭。」吩咐城隍去了，遂即出的門來。這天師古時有一陣祥雲，只爲他誤入斗牛宮，偷看了仙女，遂摘了他的祥雲，只給了他一陣黑風。遂畫了一個十字，兩脚踏住，念動咒語，吹口法氣，一陣黑風從地旋起，不多時來到大同。天師收了神術，兩脚踏立塵埃。遂自思道：「萬歲我曾去朝過幾次，他認的我，我也不好見他。現如今胡秀才是招財童子臨凡，他日近君王，不免托了他罷。」

張天師上大街，要訪那胡秀才。到了胡家大門外，打起卦板裝算卦，百萬忽然走出來。天師一見說聲怪，這一位天顏日近，怕目下有些奇災。

胡百萬大驚失色說：「先生，你也會相面麼？」天師說：「也略通。」百萬說：「我相着我往前交了好運，你怎麼就說我有災難呢？」天師說：「你的學業還淺。是你聽我講來。」

2　Celestial palaces.
3　The character ten (*shi* 十) has the shape of a cross.
4　One of the many gods of wealth, often depicted as a baby.

Now let me tell you, just when Heavenly Master Zhang was reciting the holy scriptures, he was suddenly visited by the city god of Datong, who came in a whirlwind. The Heavenly Master spoke, "What is your business?" The city god replied, "The emperor is visiting Datong incognito and is enjoying himself in the Displaying Martiality Ward. Now a certain Wang Long wants to kill the emperor, who did not bring a single civil official or military officer with him. Today is the birthday of the Jade Emperor, so all the big and small gods have gone there to offer their congratulations and there is no one to protect His Majesty. What should be done?" The Heavenly Master said, "Understood. I will descend the mountain to protect the ruler." Having given his instructions to the city god, he immediately went out through the gate.

The Heavenly Master in ancient times had an auspicious cloud for traveling, but it had been taken away because he had mistakenly entered the Dipper and Ox palaces[2] and spied on its immortal maidens. Now he had only a black whirlwind. So he drew the character for character "ten,"[3] stepped on it with both his feet, recited a spell, and blew out a breath of magic air, whereupon the black wind rose from the earth and shortly arrived in Datong. The Heavenly Master stored his magic away and stood with his feet in the dust. He thought to himself, "I have gone to court a few times to pay my respects to the emperor, and he knows me, so I had better not meet with him. But student Hu is an incarnation of the Lad Who Attracts Riches[4] and will become close to the emperor, so I had best entrust this to him."

> Heavenly Master Zhang walked down the street,
> Wishing to pay a visit to student Hu.
> Upon arriving outside the gate of his house,
>   He beat on his trigram board, pretending to tell the future,
> So the millionaire immediately came running out.
> As soon as he saw him, the Heavenly Master said, "Weird!
>   I'm afraid that this heavenly face so close to the sun
> Will soon suffer a strange misfortune!"

Millionaire Hu was greatly surprised and losing all color said, "Teacher, can you also read faces?" The Heavenly Master replied, "To a certain extent." The millionaire said, "I read my own face and learned that I would encounter good fortune, so why do you say that I will meet with disaster?" The Heavenly Master said, "Your learning is yet shallow. Listen to my explanation.

雖相法你也通，但未必如我精，不測的禍福你不能定。縱有
人間危難事，我袖占一課果分明，立時斷就生前命。胡百萬
聽說大喜，把天師讓到了家中。

胡百萬合天師到了一座密室中，作了個揖，讓了上堂，
遂求斷吉凶。天師起了一課，斷曰：

這個卦實是強，現如今侍君王，眼前就要遭磨障。文武不曾
帶一個，惟你朝夕常在旁，若有差池上誰的帳？那時節合家
大小，少不的一命無常！

天師說罷，胡百萬只諕的面如土色，慌忙跪下，只說：
「仙長救命！」

天師笑這無妨，只小心要提防，禍福只在頭直上。就是珍饈
合百味，拿來但要你先嘗，縱有失錯不妨帳。我送你一丸丹
藥，也是個起死良方。

天師便囊中取出一丸丹藥，遞於胡百萬，說道：「你近
中有一道鬼門關，却也無妨。把這藥丸交與你那得托的
拿着，你若有甚麼差池，這藥丸就能救你。」天師吩咐
已畢，出門去了。

5　Secretly, on his fingers.
6　The entrance to the underworld.

Even though you too understand physiognomy,
You're not yet as skilled as I:
You cannot determine an unfathomable fortune.
    Though you will encounter a crisis on earth,
Up my sleeves[5] I've clearly computed this case:
Soon you'll be freed from your karmic fate."
    On hearing this, Millionaire Hu was very pleased
And invited the Heavenly Master into his home.

Millionaire Hu took the Heavenly Master inside a secret chamber, and after he greeted him with a light bow and ceded the seat of honor to him, he asked him to determine his future fate. The Heavenly Master computed his case and concluded,

    "This hexagram is truly strong:
Right now you serve an emperor,
But soon you will meet with disaster.
    He did not bring a single official or officer,
So it is only you at his side, day and night.
If anything happens, who will be to blame?
    Then your whole family, both old and young,
Will lose their lives without exception!"

When the Heavenly Master had said this, Millionaire Hu was so terrified that his face looked like mud. Hastily he knelt down, crying, "Immortal Master, please save my life!"

The Heavenly Master smiled, "That's not a problem.
You just have to be careful and take precautions,
For disaster and blessing are hovering over your head.
    When it comes to his rare delicacies and hundred dishes,
You must make sure to take and taste them first.
If something goes wrong, it's not a problem.
    I will leave you this one round cinnabar pill:
The perfect recipe for resurrecting from death."

The Heavenly Master thereupon took a cinnabar pill from his bag, and as he handed it to Millionaire Hu, he said, "Very soon you will pass through Ghost Gate Pass,[6] but that won't be a problem. Entrust this pill to someone you can rely on to preserve it, and if something untoward happens to you, this pill will save you." After the Heavenly Master had given these instructions, he was gone.

胡百萬暗低頭，一邊想一邊愁，機關心裏安排就。忙忙走到
宣武院，藥丸交與百花羞，從頭說了前合後。他二人商議已
定，一雙雙來到南樓。

　　萬歲說：「您兩個去做甚麼的來？」胡百萬說：「爺睡着
了，俺各人家去料理料理，誰知得了一件奇事。」萬歲
說；「甚麼奇事？」胡百萬說：「遇見了一個算命的先
生，他給我算了一個卦。」萬歲說：「算的何如？」
見一個算卦人，他算我近至尊，至尊現交着潑雜運。着我頓
頓先嘗飯，朝夕休要放寬心，大小事兒加謹慎。若還是一腳
錯了，準備着滅了滿門。

　　二姐聽罷大驚。萬歲冷笑道：「這先生光叨瞎話。你每
日就是合我在一堆兒，我又不是皇帝，你怕怎的！」二
姐說：「是皇帝不是皇帝的，出上就依着他說。以後飲
食都着胡百萬過了目，方許進用；如是胡百萬不在這
裏，我自檢點。」萬歲點頭應允。
胡百萬已封官，從今後又加銜，兼管御廚的都簽片。二姐不
教他別處去，着他兩口住樓前，事事都打他眼中看。只爲着
給朝廷管膳，險些兒去給閻王幫閑。

　　這一日，萬歲待吃酒，丫頭樓下拿了一瓶酒來，放在胡
百萬面前。胡百萬說：「代我斟上一盅嘗嘗。」
胡百萬把酒嘗，吃一口噴鼻香，引的喉嚨裏饞蟲上。仰仰頭
兒只一灌，十二重樓一陣涼。

Millionaire Hu secretly lowered his head,
And as he pondered, he worried.
When he had come up with a plan in his mind,
    He hurried to the Displaying Martiality Ward,
Gave the pill to Puts All Flowers to Shame,
And told her the story from beginning to end.
    After they had discussed it in detail,
They went as a pair to the southern room.

The emperor said, "What have you two been doing?" Millionaire Hu said, "Sir, after you fell asleep, we each went home to take care of things. Who knew that something strange would happen?" "What strange thing?" the emperor asked. Millionaire Hu said, "I met a soothsayer, and he calculated a hexagram for me." The emperor asked, "And what was his conclusion?"

    "I met a soothsayer,
    And he calculated that I would serve the Most High,
    But that the Most High would meet with misfortune.
        He ordered me to first taste each dish you fancy.
    Day and night I should not slacken in my attention.
    I have to be meticulous in all matters, large and small.
        And if I make only a single mistake,
    My whole family will be wiped out."

When second sister heard this, she was greatly frightened, but the emperor said with a sneer, "This soothsayer is blabbering nonsense. You've been hanging out with me every day, and I'm not the emperor, so what are you worried about?" Second sister said, "Whether you are the emperor or not, it would be best to do as he says. From now on, you will only be allowed to eat or drink after it's been inspected by Millionaire Hu. And if Millionaire Hu isn't here, I will inspect it myself." The emperor nodded in agreement. So that day, when the emperor wanted to drink some wine and had a serving girl fetch a jug from downstairs, she placed it before Millionaire Hu, who said, "Let me pour out a beaker to taste it."

    To taste the wine Millionaire Hu
    Drank a mouthful. What a strong aroma!
    It brought out the gluttonous grub in his throat.
        Bending backward, he poured out the wine.
    So refreshingly cool, it gushed down his gullet.

霎時大害從天降，滿肚裏疼如刀割，叫一聲氣絕而亡。

萬歲和佛動心見胡百萬死了，大驚失色，雙雙落淚。百花羞說：「不妨不妨，前天那算命的早知有今日之難，給了一粒丹藥，想必靈驗。」即時叫丫頭把口拗開，把藥丸放在口內，灌上了一口清水。只聽的咕碌咕碌響了幾聲，藥已下去了。

拗開口灌下丸，頓飯時手動彈，忽然略把眼睛轉。哎喲一聲翻過來，一口鮮血吐牀前，萬歲諕的渾身戰。這酒是從那裏拿來？快與我問個根源。

丫頭諕的戰戰兢兢，跪在地下說道：「這是自家的酒，兩樓吃的都是，並無兩樣。」萬歲心下明白，說：「你起來。去罷，不干你事。從今以後，兩樓上人役不許往來。」

萬歲爺早得知，罵王龍作死賊，暗中定下絕戶計。若不虧了胡百萬，一樓大小死無疑。一回思量一回氣，戲犯妃子還容小可，這樁事值的剝皮！

萬歲叫人用心服侍胡百萬。胡百萬待了一宿就好了，君臣夫妻依舊南樓作樂。未知萬歲何日回京，且聽下回分解。

That very moment disaster descended from Heaven!
   He suddenly felt a stabbing pain in his stomach.
He cried out, breathed his last breath, passed away!

When the emperor and Buddha's Lust saw that Millionaire Hu had died, they blanched in fright, and both of them cried. But Puts All Flowers to Shame said, "It's okay; it's okay! That soothsayer yesterday knew of today's disaster and gave me a cinnabar pill that should work." She told a serving girl to wrench his mouth open, placed the pill in his mouth, and flushed it down with some clear water. With a gurgling sound, the pill had been swallowed.

They opened his mouth and flushed down the pill.
In the time it would take to eat a meal, his hands began to stir,
And abruptly his eyes moved a little bit too.
   With a cry of pain, he turned himself over,
And spat out a mouthful of red blood on the floor,
Scaring the emperor so that he shivered all over.
   "Where did you get this wine?
Make haste, get to the bottom of this!"

The serving girl was so scared that she was shaking all over. Kneeling down on the floor, she said, "This is our own wine. The two upstairs rooms drink the same, there is no difference!" The emperor already understood and said, "Get on your feet, this has nothing to do with you. From now on, the personnel of the two upstairs rooms are not allowed to mingle."

His Majesty the emperor already understood
And shouted, "Wang Long, you suicidal thief,
You secretly came up with this murderous scheme!
   If it had not been for Millionaire Hu's assistance,
Everyone in this upstairs room would have died!
The more I think about it, the more enraged I am.
   That you violated my spouse, I forgave as a small matter,
But for this, you really deserve to be flayed!"

The emperor ordered all to carefully attend to Millionaire Hu. After a night, he had fully recovered, so lord and vassal, husband and wife, continued to amuse themselves in the southern upstairs room.

If you don't know what happened next, please listen to the following chapter.

第二十七回 定國公衙內嚇奸 張太監井邊認馬

話說那在朝文武見萬歲久不登殿，個個疑惑；又聽小人的亂傳，皇帝出京私行。文武們與定國公議論，常常上本。國母着忙，叫那太監張永：「你這兩日間的江彬口詞何如？」張永叩頭說道：「那賊全無口詞。」國母大怒說：「領我密旨，同文華殿毛紀，三日追不出他的口詞，你各人頂上一刀！」張太監着忙。

張太監着了忙，領密旨離朝綱，戰戰兢兢魂飄蕩。見了萊州毛閣老，訴了一遍說的慌，毛紀愁鎖眉頭上。刑部監把江彬提出，他不招就立下法場。

　　毛紀、張永同到法司裏，即差人向刑部監提出江彬。毛閣老一見大罵道：「賣國的奸賊！今日不招，我是不合你干休了！」

毛閣老氣昂昂，罵奸賊太不良，好似三國曹丞相。王莽、蘇憲今何在？

1　Mao Ji 毛紀 (1463–1545) had been a tutor to the emperor when he was still the crown prince. During the Zhengde reign, he rose to ever higher positions. After the death of the Zhengde emperor, he was one of the officials who oversaw the succession. During the Jiajing reign, he would continue to hold high office for many years.

2　Cao Cao 曹操 (155–220), who in the final decades of the Han dynasty arrogated all power at court, reducing the emperor to a figurehead.

3　Wang Mang 王莽 (45 BCE–23 CE), the all-powerful minister of the final years of the Western Han, deposed the last emperor of the Western Han to found his own Xin dynasty. He ruled as its first and only emperor from 9 to 23 CE, when he was overthrown. Su Xian 蘇憲 was one of Wang Mang's henchmen, according to popular tradition.

The State-Stabilizing Duke scares a
        traitor at the Judicial Office;
        Grand Eunuch Zhang recognizes the
        horse by the side of a well.

Now let me tell you, the civil officials and military officers at court had
not seen the emperor hold audience for a long time, so they were all filled
with doubt. Moreover, they had heard rumors among the commoners that
the emperor had left the capital to travel incognito. The civil and military officials and the State-Stabilizing Duke discussed this and repeatedly
sent in memorials. The mother of the nation became impatient and said
to Grand Eunuch Zhang Yong, "What kind of confession did you extract
from Jiang Bin after those few days of interrogation?" Zhang Yong kowtowed and replied, "The thief refuses to confess to anything." The mother
of the nation was greatly enraged and said, "This is my secret edict: If you
and Mao Ji[1] of the Patterned Flower Hall cannot extract a confession from
him in three days, both of you will be beheaded!" Grand Eunuch Zhang
had little time left.

> Grand Eunuch Zhang had little time left.
> Having received a secret edict, he left the court,
> Shaking and trembling, with his souls all in turmoil.
>   Upon seeing His Excellency Mao from Laizhou,
> He told him everything, speaking in haste,
> And sorrow locked Mao Ji's forehead in a frown.
>   They had Jiang Bin fetched from prison.
> If he did not confess, he would be put to death!

Mao Ji and Zhang Yong arrived together at the Judicial Office and had
Jiang Bin fetched from the prison of the Ministry of Justice. On seeing him,
His Excellency Mao loudly reviled him, "You traitorous bandit, if you don't
confess today, we'll never let up on you!"

> His Excellency Mao was filled with rage,
> And shouted, "Villain, you are too evil!
> You're like Prime Minister Cao of the Three Kingdoms![2]
>   Wang Mang and Su Xian, where are they now?[3]

力比董卓、石敬瑭，心似趙高無兩樣。專想着篡朝奪位，我着你目下遭殃！

　　張太監大怒道：「人是苦蟲，不打不成！善便怎麼肯招？給我夾起來！」

張公公惱心懷，把江彬夾起來，攏了一攏無計奈。江彬每日爲官宦，知道這樣刑法怎麼捱。忽然尋法胡廝賴，在堂下聲聲叫苦，張太監你其實就不該。

　　江彬道：「張永，我保的是皇帝，你保的不是皇帝麼？當初萬歲出朝之時，你我同送出城去，怎麼只光夾我？」張永大叫道：「好奸黨！仇口咬着我麼？」

張太監咬碎牙，氣忿忿怒轉加，謀害主公犯罪大。老天不遂奸臣意，仇口咬我爲甚麼？我說合你對了罷。危難處一聲來報，千歲爺進了宮衙。

　　江彬不招，張永正在危難之際，從人來報：「千歲到了。」毛紀、張永接出門來。定國公問道：「追的口詞何如呢？」張永從頭至尾，說了一遍。定國公勃然大怒。

定國公怒冲冲，把銅錘舉在空，

4　Dong Zhuo 董桌 (d. 192) grabbed power in 189 and relocated the capital from Luoyang to Chang'an, but his reign of terror ended when he was murdered by his underling Lü Bu. Shi Jingtang 石敬瑭 (892–942) became the founding emperor of the Later Jin dynasty (936–946) after he had bought the support of the Liao dynasty by ceding sixteen prefectures in northeast China.

5　Zhao Gao 趙高 (258–207 BCE) was a eunuch who became all-powerful at the Qin court following the death of the First Emperor in 210 BCE.

6　Finger presses and shin presses are instruments of torture. They consist of two pieces of wood tied together with ropes.

Your power may compare to Dong Zhuo and Shi Jingtang,[4]
But your heart is exactly like that of Zhao Gao:[5]
　　You only desire to steal the state and grab the throne.
However, I'll bring disaster upon you right now!"

Grand Eunuch Zhang, greatly enraged, said, "Man is a miserable creature: without a beating nothing gets done. How is he going to be willing to confess if we treat him softly? Put on the presses!"[6]

Uncle Zhang was exasperated
And subjected Jiang Bin to the presses,
But tightened them to no avail.
　　Jiang Bin had been a palace official all his days,
So how could he stand this kind of torture?
But suddenly he found a way to weasel out.
　　In front of the hall he bitterly complained,
"Grand Eunuch Zhang, you shouldn't do this!"

Jiang Bin said, "I protect the emperor. Don't you protect him too? When the emperor left the court, you and I accompanied him through the city gate together, so why are you putting the presses on me?" Zhang Yong loudly shouted, "You nasty fiend! Are you trying to implicate me with your lies?"

Grand Eunuch Zhang gnashed his teeth.
His towering rage had only increased.
"Murdering one's lord is the greatest crime!
　　Old Heaven will not fulfill a traitor's desire.
Why do you implicate me with false words?
I say you and I should face each other in court!"
　　In this moment of crisis it was announced
That a prince had entered the compound.

Jiang Bin refused to confess. Just when Zhang Yong found himself in a tight spot, a servant announced that a prince had arrived, the State-Stabilizing Duke. The duke asked, "What kind of confession have you been able to extract?" Zhang Yong presented him with a complete account, at which the State-Stabilizing Duke exploded with rage.

The State-Stabilizing Duke, overcome by rage,
Lifted his bronze mallet high in the air,

頂梁穴上蹭一蹭。不說萬歲在那裏，一錘把你喪殘生，渾家大小殺個淨！有江彬哭聲不絕，叫千歲待我招承。

　　江彬說：「千歲息怒，臣願招來。」定國公怒道：「快忙說來，萬歲在那裏？」江彬說：「萬歲說私行看景，臨行曾對臣說，休要洩漏天機，非是小臣之過。倘若說出，朝中若有奸臣，萬歲路途有失，臣怎麼擔的起？千歲同合朝文武押着微臣找主。我主回來，饒臣不死；找不回來，情願伏罪。」定國公說：「暫且饒你不死。」毛閣老便傳衆文武俱齊集蘆溝橋下。張永說：「先往那一省去？」江彬說：「山西大同府。」衆文武聽說，大家急奔紅塵。

衆文武離順天，前過了居庸關，一路無辭忙似箭。饑餐渴飲來的快，過了一山又一山，那日來到宣府店。江彬說休要前走，密松林且把身安。

　　那江彬常串邊塞，走的極熟，向張公公道；「倘若黎民得罪主公，他若知信，萬歲有失，那時怎了！前邊有個密松林，不如暫且住下，你我進城訪主一遭。」張永說：「這話有理。」衆文武

7　Also known as Marco Polo Bridge, a long bridge across the Yongding River, completed in 1192. It is located ten miles southwest of Beijing.

And lightly grazed the top of Jiang Bin's skull.
  "If you don't tell where the emperor may be,
One blow of this mallet will destroy your life,
And your family, old and young, will be killed!"
  Jiang Bin kept weeping and weeping
And said, "Dear prince, let me confess!"

Jiang Bin said, "Dear Prince, calm yourself. I'm willing to confess." The State-Stabilizing Duke said, "Speak quickly, where is the emperor?" Jiang Bin replied, "The emperor said he wanted to travel incognito to take in the sights, and when he left, he told me that I should not expose his secret. So I am not to blame. If word got out and there was a traitorous minister at court and something untoward happened to the emperor while on the road, how could I take responsibility for that? Dear Prince, you and the officials and officers of the whole court should go and look for the emperor, with me as your prisoner. When our ruler has returned, please spare my life. But if he cannot be found, I accept my punishment." The State-Stabilizing Duke said, "We will spare you, for now."

His Excellency Mao informed the civil officials and military officers to assemble at Lugou Bridge.[7] Zhang Yong asked, "Which province should we look in first?" Jiang Bin replied, "Datong Prefecture of Shanxi Province." When the officials and officers heard this, they all rushed forward through the red dust.

The officials and officers left Shuntian
And advanced through Juyong Pass,
Eagerly speeding on, like an arrow, along the road.
  Eating when hungry and drinking when thirsty, they hurried
    on.
Having crossed one mountain, they crossed yet another,
And arrived at Xuanfu Inn that day.
  Jiang Bin said, "You should not go any further.
Rather, rest here in this dense pine forest."

Jiang Bin was well acquainted with the border regions and had traveled there extensively. So he said to Uncle Zhang, "What if the common people have offended the emperor, and they know we're coming and something untoward happens to him. What will we do then? Ahead of us is a dense pine forest, so it would be best to stay here for the time being. Then you can enter the city to search for the ruler." Zhang Yong replied, "What you say makes sense." The civil officials and military

在林中隱藏，張永、江彬二人進城來了。

他二人進大同，心裏想叫主公，你在那裏貪歡慶？串街過巷找一遍，不見萬歲影合蹤，怎不叫人心酸痛！他二人走頭無路，驚動監察神靈。

那萬歲該當回京，諸神撥亂着。王龍叫丫頭：「我買的那馬，今日飲了麼？」丫頭道：「還沒飲哩。」王龍說：「渴着我那馬，把你打一千！快給我去飲飲的。」丫頭聽說，不敢怠慢，淚恓恓的牽馬出院來了。

二梅香淚盈盈，那世裏少陰功，今生折磨咱的性。不是打來就是罵，奴才只當叫奶名，滿心冤屈合誰控？不如咱尋個無常，早死了另去脫生！

丫頭牽馬哭出院來。張永、江彬轉過頭看見龍駒。江彬說：「有了我的命了，那不是萬歲的坐馬？」張永聽說，猛然擡頭，急走了幾步，扯住那馬。那馬常和張永作伴，見了張永，唔唔的大叫，點頭磕腦，只是不會說話。張永道：「丫頭，這馬是誰的？」丫頭道：「是王三爺的。」張永道：「是你王三爺自家的呀，是他買的呢？」丫頭道：「是買的長官的。」張永道：「那長官現在那裏？」丫頭道：「在院裏。」張永道：「這馬是我的，被人拐出來了。那長官是個拐馬的，我正是來找他哩。」物見主必定取，張永牽着馬

officers hid themselves in the forest, while Zhang Yong and Jiang Bin
went into the city.

> The two of them entered Datong,
> Thinking in their hearts, "Lord,
> Where did you go for your fun?"
>   Following streets and crossing lanes, they searched,
> But they didn't see a shadow or trace of the emperor,
> And, of course, were filled with aches and pains.
>   The two of them had no idea where to go,
> Which moved the gods of inspection.

The emperor was destined to return to the capital. The gods confused
Wang Long so he told the serving girls, "Did the horse that I bought get
anything to drink today?" The serving girls said, "Not yet." Wang Long said,
"I'll give you a thousand lashes for letting my horse suffer from thirst. Hurry
up and give it something to drink." The serving girls dared not disobey this
order, and in tears they led the horse out of the ward.

> The two serving girls were awash in tears.
> "In our former lives we did few good deeds,
> So in this life we are made to suffer.
>   If we're not beaten, we're cursed.
> We slaves can call out only our mothers' names.
> To whom can we complain about injustice?
>   The best option by far is to seek death,
> To die quickly and seek rebirth elsewhere!"

Leading the horse, the servants girls wept as they left the courtyard. Turning a corner, Zhang Yong and Jiang Bin saw the dragon colt.
Jiang Bin said, "I'm saved! Isn't that the emperor's riding horse?" When
Zhang Yong heard that, he snapped his head up and ran a few steps
to grab the horse. The horse was used to Zhang Yong, so when it saw
him, it whinnied loudly and bobbed its head, since it didn't know how
to speak. Zhang Yong asked, "Girls, whose horse is this?" The serving
girls replied, "This belongs to Third Master Wang." Zhang Yong asked,
"Has this always been Third Master's property, or did he buy it?" The
serving girls said, "He bought it from an officer." Zhang Yong asked,
"And where is that officer?" The serving girls replied, "He is staying in
the ward." Zhang Yong said, "This horse is mine, and it was stolen. That
officer is a horse rustler, and I've been looking for him. When a beast
greets its master, it's bound to be taken." And Zhang Yong led the horse

往外走。那丫頭只急的抓耳撓腮，捶胸跺足。

二梅香淚滿腮，想是咱命裏該，從天降下災合害。今日井邊失了馬，到家拷打怎麼捱！尋思一回沒計奈。只爲那王龍該死，帶累了兩個裙釵。

二梅香投井而死。張永、江彬牽着馬來到林中，見了衆人，訴說了一遍。此時王尚書也在行營，衆人秉手說道：「王老先生恭喜！你家三公子與萬歲作伴，又買了萬歲的龍駒。」王尚書聽說，只諕的魂飛天外，魄散九霄了！

王尚書諕一驚，罵王龍小畜生，養活着他成何用！人家養兒防備老，不想他是個闖禍精，可把他達達送了命！實指望我主有賞，到不想不得回京。

便叫左右拿繩鎖來，將王尚書綁了。毛閣老遂暗傳號令，進了大同城。未知後事如何，且聽下回分解。

away. The serving girls were so upset that they scratched their heads, beat their breasts, and stamped their feet!

> The two serving girls dissolved in tears,
> "This has to have been predestined!
> From Heaven descend disaster and harm!
> Today we have lost the horse by the side of the well,
> And the beating we'll get on our return will be unbearable!"
> They thought and thought, but there was no way out.
> Only because Wang Long was destined to die
> Were these two "hairpins and skirts" involved.

The two serving girls threw themselves into the well and died. When Zhang Yong and Jiang Bin arrived in the forest leading the horse, they greeted the others and told the whole story. At that moment Minister Wang was also in the traveling camp, and his fellow officials clasped their hands and said, "Congratulations, Sir Wang! The third young master is not only accompanying the emperor; he has also bought the emperor's dragon colt!" When Minister Wang heard this, he was so scared that his souls fled beyond Heaven, and his spirits dispersed through the Ninth Heaven!

> Minister Wang was petrified
> And shouted, "Wang Long, you little beast,
> What was the use of raising you?
> When other people raise sons, it's to provide for one in old age,
> But who knew he'd only cause me disaster?
> He is bound to cost his old father his life!
> I had really hoped that our ruler would reward me,
> I never expected to be unable to return to the capital."

His fellow officials then ordered their underlings to fetch ropes and chains and tie up Minister Wang. His Excellency Mao secretly gave orders, and they entered the city of Datong.

If you don't know what happened next, please listen to the following chapter.

第二十八回 大姐繩縛王冲霄 萬歲火燒宣武院

話說衆文武進了大同，封了四門，扯起黃旗爲號。各官知道，齊來參見。這外官兒見了幾遭皇帝？來到黃旗下跪着張永，口稱萬歲。張永大笑道：「你是什麼人？」各官叩頭道：「俺是大同道、府、州、縣、總兵等官。」張永道：「萬歲來宣武院三個月了，你們還不曉得。快去點兵，把守城池，不要走了王龍。回朝上本，保你等沒事。」衆官領命去了。毛閣老傳令，快換朝服，手執牙笏，各按品從，各人俱要十分小心。衆文武齊聲答應。不一時，總兵點起的人馬，把宣武院團團圍住。

張公公把令傳，刀出鞘弓上弦，霎時圍了宣武院。南樓權當金鑾殿，文武百官把主參，禮拜已畢兩邊站。萬歲爺樓上正耍，衆文武誰敢高言。

衆文武行罷大禮，分班站立。萬歲正合胡百萬下棋，丫頭急忙傳報說：「不好了！有許多兵馬，將院圍了！

28 Big sister ties up Wang Long with a rope; The emperor burns down the Displaying Martiality Ward.

Now let me tell you, when the civil officials and military officers had entered Datong and sealed off the four gates, they raised a yellow banner as a signal. When the local officials learned of this, they all came to present themselves. How often have officials in the provinces seen the emperor? When they arrived below the yellow banner, they knelt before Zhang Yong, wishing him a long life of a myriad years. Zhang Yong had a good laugh and said, "Who are you all?" The officials kowtowed, identifying themselves as such officials as Datong's circuit inspector, prefect, administrator, magistrate, and general. Zhang Yong said, "The emperor has spent three months in the Displaying Martiality Ward, but you had no idea! Quickly assign soldiers to guard the city walls and its moats so that Wang Long cannot escape. When I report to court upon our return, I promise that you all will be safe." The officials accepted their orders.

His Excellency Mao conveyed an order that everyone should change into court dress and hold their ivory tablets of office, that each should take his place in the ranks and be extra cautious. The civil officials and military officers answered as with one voice. Very soon the infantry and cavalry assigned by the general had tightly surrounded the Displaying Martiality Ward.

> Uncle Zhang gave his orders:
> With drawn swords and strung bows
> Soon they encircled the ward.
> The southern upstairs room was now the Golden Bells Hall.
> The hundred civil and military officials paid their respects,
> And having bowed, they arranged themselves on both sides.
> Upstairs His Majesty the emperor was having his fun,
> But who among the officials dared raise his voice?

After the civil officials and military officers had kowtowed, they stood tall, arranged by rank. Just as the emperor was playing a game of go with Millionaire Hu, a serving girl rushed in to report, "Disaster! Lots of infantry and cavalry have surrounded the ward. And in front of the

大些穿紅的漢子，都在下邊哩。」老鴇子慌成一塊，話
都說不出來了。萬歲說：「休害怕，這是我那小廝們來
了。」不一時，江彬上樓，雙膝跪下，口稱萬歲：「臣
接駕來遲，赦臣不死！」萬歲大喜，說道：「愛卿，我
還待玩二日，你就來了。」江彬道：「合朝文武俱在樓
下伺候大駕。」萬歲即出樓門。文武見主，拜倒在地。
萬歲說：「卿家遠勞，免禮罷。」文武聽說，分班站立。
那王龍正在北樓，合賽觀音追歡取樂，忽聽的一片喧
嚷，忙叫丫頭去看。不一時，丫頭回來，跑的只吁吁的
喘，都面無人色，說：「了不的了！南樓上那個長官是
個皇帝！」丫頭還沒曾說完，那王龍從牀上就張將下來
了。

跌了個仰不踏，起不來就地爬，王龍此時才不乍。叫聲大姐
怎麼處？我不如裝個小忘八，跳了牆頭走了罷。賽觀音玉容
陡變，全不念枕上冤家。

大姐自思：「平日我得罪的皇帝也不少，不如拴住王
龍，送於萬歲，將功折罪。」便叫丫頭們快上來拿住王
龍，「咱去請賞。」十餘個人一齊下手，不一時將王龍
綁起來了。

賽觀音叫呱呱，我自家爲自家，姐夫你就怪點罷。王龍大罵
狠心婦，每日把我當親達，

---

1   During the Ming dynasty, officials of the imperial bureaucracy's highest ranks (one to
four) wore red.

house there are a lot of guys all dressed in red!"[1] The old bawd was so flabbergasted she could not say a word, but the emperor said, "Don't be afraid, my underlings have arrived."

Soon Jiang Bin came upstairs, knelt down on both knees, and wished him a long life of a myriad years. "Your servant has been dilatory in welcoming Your Majesty. Please spare your servant from the death penalty!" The emperor was very pleased and said, "Beloved minister, I'd wanted to stay here for a few more days, but here you are already!" Jiang Bin said, "The civil officials and military officers of the whole court are waiting for Your Majesty outside." The emperor thereupon went outside, and on seeing him the civil officials and military officers threw themselves down to make their bows. The emperor said, "You all have come a long way, so let's dispense with the ritual."

At that very moment, Wang Long was pursuing his pleasure with Guanyin's Equal in the northern upstairs room. When he suddenly heard the great clamor, he hastily ordered a serving girl to have a look. She soon returned, running so hard that she was panting. All color had drained from her face as she said, "It can't be! That officer in the southern upstairs room is the emperor!" Before the serving girl had even finished her words, Wang Long had already tumbled down from the couch!

> He tumbled down and lay flat on his back.
> He could not get up and crawled on the floor.
> Finally, Wang Long had lost all pretense.
> He yelled, "Big sister, what should I do?
> The best thing is to pretend to be a little pimp,
> Jump over the wall and run for my life!"
> Guanyin's Equal's jade face abruptly changed
> As she gave no thought to their shared passion.

Big sister thought to herself, "These days I have offended the emperor quite often, so the best thing I can do is to tie up Wang Long and present him to the emperor to lessen my punishment by my merit." So she said, "Girls, come quickly and grab Wang Long so I can ask for a reward." More than a dozen people laid their hands on Wang Long and very soon they had him trussed up.

> Guanyin's Equal said, "You silly fool,
> I myself have to look after myself.
> Lover, you should have been smarter!"
> Wang Long reviled her as a cruel bitch,
> "Each day you treated me like a daddy,

一朝失勢變了卦。賽觀音不言不語，把王龍獻於皇家。

　　大姐將王龍拴至南樓，見了萬歲跪下道：「王龍待跑，被賤人拴來見駕。望祈萬歲將功折罪。」王龍見了萬歲，只是磕頭：「臣有眼無珠，萬死萬死！」萬歲笑道：「王官，我不怪你。你許的我那白表紅裏的那人皮褂子，可給了我罷。」王龍只諕的癱倒在地。江彬說：「是你得罪着萬歲了，待要你匕皮哩。」萬歲傳令，叫錦衣武士，帶刀指揮上來，將王龍拿去剝皮草揎，消朕之大恨。

有王龍顫巍巍，罵大姐吃你的虧，千萬刀剮賊賤的輩！得罪朝廷都是你，臨危了還要獻諂媚，臨死咬的牙根碎。可憐是三聲礮響，將皮褂一並全追。

　　把王龍剝皮草揎，擡到樓前，立站不倒，面不改色。萬歲說：「王官，你死了也稱財神。」忽的聲面前陰風一陣，左轉三遭，右轉三遭，謝恩已罷，歸天不提。大姐跪下，口稱萬歲赦賤人不死。萬歲說：「你是妙人兒，又虧你幫襯，今日又來獻功。」叫江彬：「有北京捎來的那驢兒，牽來給大姐騎了去罷。」大姐說：「萬歲饒了賤人，賤人走了去罷。」江彬喝道：

But once I lose my footing, you change your tune!"
　　Guanyin's Equal said not a word in reply,
　　But presented Wang Long to the emperor.

Big sister took the trussed-up Wang Long to the southern upstairs room. She knelt before the emperor and said, "Wang Long wanted to run, but I had him tied up to appear before Your Majesty. I hope that your Majesty will limit my punishment on account of my merit." When Wang Long saw the emperor, he could only kowtow. "Your servant had eyes but lacked sight. I deserve to die a myriad deaths." The emperor said with a smile, "Sir Wang, I don't blame you. But you promised me a jacket made of human skin, red on the inside and white on the outside, so give it to me now." Wang Long was so scared that he fell down on the ground, paralyzed. Jiang Bin said, "As you've offended the emperor, he wants your skin!" The emperor gave his order, "Have the soldiers of the Brocaded Guard and their sword-carrying commanders come forward so they may strip Wang Long of his skin and fill it with straw to dissipate Our great hatred."

　　That Wang Long was shaking all over
　　As he reviled big sister, "You betrayed me!
　　You're a criminal slut who deserves to be cut to pieces!
　　　The one who offended the emperor was you,
　　But faced with danger, you hope to flatter and seduce him!"
　　About to die, he gnashed his teeth to smithereens.
　　　How pitiable! When the cannon had been fired three times,
　　His skin and his clothes were all requisitioned.

After Wang Long had been stripped of his skin and it was filled with straw, he was carried to the front of the building. There he stood erect without falling down, and his face did not change expression. The emperor said, "Now that you're dead, I appoint you the god of wealth." With a roar, a whirlwind arose before his face. It turned three times to the left and three times to the right. Having expressed his gratitude in this way, Wang Long went off to Heaven. But enough about that.

Big sister knelt down and exclaimed, "Your Majesty, please spare this vile person from death!" The emperor said, "You're a smart girl. We have not only benefited from your assistance, but today you have also presented merit." He ordered Jiang Bin, "You brought a donkey from Beijing. Lead it out, and let big sister ride it." Big sister said, "Allow me to leave now that you have pardoned me." But Jiang Bin shouted, "You

「好賊潑賤人！你得罪着萬歲了，給你木驢騎着哩！」剝去了大姐衣，碎鑼響破鼓槌，人人要看狼心肺。百樣裝的假面目，千人靠的臭囊皮，登時剮了個粉粉碎。一霎時油頭粉面，只剩了白骨一堆。

話說王龍剝了皮，封了財神，木驢剮了賽觀音，萬歲方息了心頭之火。那大同大小官員，都來朝參，說：「臣不知萬歲駕臨，有慢君之罪，俱該萬死！」皇上說；「你們都是有功的，每人加三級回衙理事。只把那張、王二舍拿來重責四十，發往雲南充軍，滿門家眷逐出爲丐。」衆官叩頭謝恩，領旨去了，各回衙門不提。萬歲說：「張永何在？」張永跪下說：「奴婢伺候。」萬歲說：「你領旨意向玉火巷李小泉家店裏，把我那乾兒宣來，不要驚諕着他。」張永領旨去了。話說那王尚書身帶繩鎖，自來投見，眼淚汪汪，伏在地下請罪。萬歲說：「王愛卿，你是好官，赤心爲國，並無私曲。王龍罪犯天條，本當處死，與你無干。」叫錦衣衛把繩鎖去了。王尚書去了繩鎖，換上官衣，同衆文武前來謝罪方畢。張永將六哥宣至南樓下邊，見了萬歲，雙膝跪下，口稱萬歲：

2　The wooden donkey was a wheeled contraption shaped like a donkey on which condemned prisoners were paraded through town before execution to allow people to vent their rage on the criminal.

criminal slut! You have offended His Majesty, and he will have you ride the wooden donkey!"[2]

> Big sister was stripped of her clothes.
> Cracked gongs resounded, and broken drums boomed.
> Everybody wanted to see her wolfish heart and lungs.
> Her fake cheeks and eyes made up in a hundred ways,
> That stinking leather bag on which a thousand men relied
> Were in one moment cut up and scattered like dust.
> In one instant her oiled hairdo and powdered face
> Were reduced to a pile of white bones.

Let me tell you, the emperor stilled the fire in his heart only after Wang Long had been stripped of his skin and been appointed as the god of wealth and after Guanyin's Equal had been cut to pieces on the wooden donkey. The high and low officials of Datong came to pay their respects and said, "Your servants were unaware of Your Majesty's visit. As we committed the crime of lèse-majesté we deserve to die ten thousand times!" But the emperor said, "You all have great merit, and each of you will be promoted three grades. Return to our offices to take care of business. Arrest the two young masters Zhang and Wang, administer them forty heavy strokes, and banish them to Yunnan to serve in the army. All their relatives should be driven out to beg on the street." The officials kowtowed to express their gratitude and received their orders. Then they returned to their offices. But no more about this.

The emperor said, "Zhang Yong, where are you?" Zhang Yong knelt down and said, "Your slave is waiting." The emperor said, "This is my order to you. Go summon my adoptive son from the inn of Li Xiaoquan in Jade-Fire Lane, but don't scare him!" Upon receiving this order, Zhang Yong left.

Now let me tell you, Minister Wang, tied up with ropes and chains, was brought to appeal to the emperor. His eyes awash in tears, he stretched himself out on the floor, asking to be punished. But the emperor said, "Beloved Minister Wang, you have always been a good official with loyal heart who loves the state and never gives in to partiality. Wang Long's crime offended the rules of Heaven, so he had to be condemned to death, but you were not involved at all." He ordered the brocade-uniform guards, "Remove his ropes and chains!" Minister Wang was freed of his ropes and chains and changed into his court robe, and all the civil officials and military officers came forward to express their gratitude.

Afterward, Zhang Yong brought Brother Six to the southern building. When he saw the emperor, he knelt down on both knees and called out,

「臣不識聖駕，言語不周，本當處死！」萬歲說：「我兒
休要害怕。我賜你金牌一面，掌管天下酒稅。八個花帽
錦衣、兩個撩衣太監侍奉你。」六哥叩頭謝恩。

小六哥是東斗星，他修的福不輕，是他老爺有積幸。萬歲一
見龍心喜，我兒靠前聽我封，天下酒稅屬你用。滿了官回朝
繳旨，加你個上寶司卿。

小六哥時道中，帶着花披着紅，鼓樂齊響往外送。花帽錦衣
有八個，撩衣太監跟二名，一時聲勢掀天動。往常時提壺賣
酒，平地裏春雷一聲。

　　萬歲說：「胡百萬保朕有功，更比不的別人。你待做個
甚麼官呢？」胡百萬說：「臣已受過封了。但臣命薄，
一個州縣也稱不的；又玩耍慣了，不願做官。」萬歲說：
「也罷，即賜你黃金三萬兩，一則酬你的功勞，一則給
百花羞作賠送。」二人叩頭謝恩。

都簽片是胡生，有御筆親標名，欽差嫖院人人敬。子弟幫客
齊上稅，天下忘八納進奉，

"Your servant did not recognize Your Majesty, so I was often amiss in my language and deserve to be condemned to death." But the emperor said, "My son, don't be afraid. I gift you with a golden plaque that puts you in charge of all taxes on wine throughout the empire. You will be waited on by eight soldiers of the brocaded guard with flowered hats and by two grand eunuchs with tucked-up gowns." Brother Six kowtowed to express his gratitude.

> Little Brother Six was an Eastern Dipper star,
> By his deeds he acquired considerable blessings,
> And because of his father, he enjoyed great favors.
>   As soon as the emperor saw him, he felt joy.
> "My son, come closer and listen to my words:
> Taxes on wine throughout the realm are yours.
>   When you come to court at the end of your term,
> I will promote you to director of palace seals."

> The right moment had come for little Brother Six:
> Carrying flowers on his head and dressed in red,
> He was escorted outside to the music of drums.
>   He had eight soldiers of the brocaded guard
> And two grand eunuchs with tucked-up gowns.
> His fame and power at that moment shook Heaven!
>   In the past he used to carry a jug and sell wine;
> Now out of the blue, spring thunder roared.

The emperor said, "Millionaire Hu, in protecting Us you showed even greater merit than others. What kind of office do you want?" Millionaire Hu replied, "Your servant has already received an appointment. My fate is poor, and I would not be up to a single district. Also, I'm used to loafing around. I don't want to become an official." The emperor said, "Fine, then. I will gift you thirty thousand ounces of yellow gold, first as a reward for your services, and second as a present for your wedding with Puts All Flowers to Shame." The two kowtowed to express their gratitude.

> Student Hu was the Sycophant-in-Chief.
> His name had been listed by the imperial brush
> As inspector of whoring quarters, respected by all!
>   Patrons and spongers all paid him taxes,
> Pimps throughout the realm sent him tribute,

十三省婊子把錢掙。眼看着青堂瓦舍，胡百萬天下聞名。

　　胡百萬自此以後，拿着萬歲御筆誥命，着天下的州縣給他拿稅，一年就有十餘萬兩，這是後話不表。萬歲說：「朕初進院時，有許多賤人貶斥朕身，羞辱不堪。朕有願在前，等文武們來時，火燒南北兩院，抄殺賤人，方削朕之大恨！」傳旨：「先開刀殺盡賤人，然後發火。」佛動心轉過來，哭盈盈淚滿腮，倒身便把皇帝拜。賤奴幼在媽娘手，撓頭赤足不成材，多虧媽媽好心待。看賤奴一宵恩義，饒了他血染長街。

　　萬歲說：「可沒有撒謊的皇帝。」說：「也罷，叫這兩院生靈快忙逃命，閃下一所空房子燒了罷。」張永吆喝道：「萬歲放了大赦了，叫這南北兩院科子忘八快忙逃命，待舉火哩。」

萬歲爺爲了情，忘八們得了生，鴇兒娘子齊逃命。忙忙好似喪家犬，雨打蜻蜓亂烘烘，漏網魚繁心不定。萬歲說快給我舉火，霎時間烈焰騰空。

　　怎見的那火勢呢？

And whores of the thirteen provinces made money.
In no time he had a tiled-roof brick mansion.
Millionaire Hu was renowned all over the world!

From that moment on, Millionaire Hu had the districts throughout the empire collect taxes for him by dint of this appointment by the imperial brush of His Majesty. In one year, he received more than a hundred thousand ounces. But this is a story for another day.

The emperor said, "When I first entered the ward, there were many vile persons who despised Us—an unbearable shame! So I made a vow that I would wait until the civil officials and military officers had arrived and then burn the southern and northern courtyard to the ground and kill these vile people. Only then will We have dissipated this great hatred!" He issued an edict, "First kill these vile people, and afterward set fire to it all!"

Buddha's Lust turned around,
Weeping piteously as tears streamed down her cheeks.
Throwing herself down, she bowed to the emperor,
  "This vile slave was raised by my madam from youth—
A good-for-nothing with bare feet and messy hair!
But fortunately, the madam always treated me kindly.
  Out of consideration for one night of affection,
Please spare her; don't let her blood dye the streets!"

The emperor thought, "But there cannot be a lying emperor!" So he said, "Fine then! Tell anything alive in the two courtyards to run for their lives and leave all their empty houses behind to be burned." Zhang Yong loudly proclaimed, "His Majesty has issued a general pardon and orders the trollops and pimps of the northern and southern courtyards with all speed to flee for their lives, as we are about to set it on fire!"

The emperor acted out of love
So that the pimps could survive
And the bawds and whores could flee for their lives.
  They scurried on like dogs without a home,
An unruly crowd of rain-drenched dung beetles,
Or fishes that slipped through the net, still afraid.
  The emperor said, "Now set fire to the place!"
In an instant, fierce flames ascended the sky.

What did that fire look like?

風攬火火攬風，起愁雲鎖碧空，刮刮砸砸火星迸。眞君獨占南方位，怒惱來時霹靂鳴。灰片片火烘烘，黑烟直射斗牛宮。磚合瓦乒乓亂響，宣武院一片通紅。

宣武院起了火，前後房一齊灼，狂風颼颼旋天刮。只爲着皇爺心歡喜，誰想臨行大揭鍋。二姐亂把金蓮跺，只因着萬歲玩要，宣武院成了荒坡！

二姐跪下，尊道：「萬歲，這院子燒的這麼馨淨，媽娘何處安身？」萬歲說：「你到是個好人，知恩不記仇。」叫江彬：「你曉諭那大同知縣知道，等朕回京，這虔婆給他一所宅子，按月關糧，叫他受用罷。」二姐、鴇子一齊謝恩。萬歲吩咐張永，侍奉劉妃後行，「文武保朕回京」。文武聽說，各分班列隊，排開御駕，礮響三聲，魚角齊鳴，大同合屬官員親送大駕回京。後來張永跟隨劉妃進京，到了宮裏，先去參見張娘娘，磕頭禮拜。娘娘道：「好一個俊俏人兒！」即忙一把拉起，說道：「我賜你鐵布裙，以後免你行禮，」列位們聽着：你說這裙子有鐵打的麼？不是這等講說，只是見娘娘不跪，不磕頭，就合穿着鐵裙子一般。你看佛動心一個婊子，一朝時來運至，享的何等榮華？有一首

The wind stirred the fire, the fire stirred a storm,
Raising gloomy clouds that were chained to the blue void,
As crackling and sputtering sparks exploded.
　　The True Ruler alone occupied the southern position,
When enraged the thunder resounded.
　　Ashes scattered, as the fire raged on and on,
And black smoke rose up to the palaces of Heaven.
　　As bricks and tiles blew up with a boom,
The Displaying Martiality Ward was all wrapped in red.

The Displaying Martiality Ward was on fire.
The houses in front and in back were all burning,
And a roaring tornado whirled up to Heaven.
　　All because the emperor had taken his pleasure there!
Who knew that upon departing he would overturn the pot?
Second sister wildly stamped her golden lotuses.
　　Only because the emperor had sought his pleasure there,
The Displaying Martiality Ward became a graveyard.

　　Second sister knelt down and said respectfully, "Your Majesty, where can my madam live, now that these courtyards have been burned down?" The emperor replied, "You're a good person who remembers favors and forgets feuds." And he ordered Jiang Bin, "Inform the magistrate of Datong district that after Our return to the capital, he should provide this bawd with a dwelling and a monthly allowance of grain for her use." Second sister and the bawd expressed their gratitude together.
　　The emperor ordered, "Zhang Yong, you will escort Concubine Liu to the capital. The civil officials and military officers will protect Us as We return to the capital." The civil officials and military officers formed groups according to rank and arranged an imperial procession. The cannon resounded three times, the painted horns blared, and all officials of Datong personally saw His Majesty off as he departed.
　　Later Zhang Yong followed Concubine Liu into the capital. When they arrived in the palace, she first paid her respects to Her Majesty Zhang. After she kowtowed and performed her bows, Her Majesty said, "What a charming person!" She hastily pulled her up and said, "I gift you an iron skirt so that you will not have to kneel." Dear audience, now listen: Do you think that this skirt was made of iron? That's not it. The term only meant that when visiting Her Majesty, she did not have to kneel and did not have to kowtow, just as if she were wearing a skirt made of iron. Consider what kind of glory the whore Buddha's Lust enjoyed as soon as her time had come and her fortune peaked! There is a lyric to

「清江引」贊張皇后的賢德，感嘆那劉妃的造化：
張后賢良天下少，看見二姐到，一把忙拉起，稱獎人兒妙，賜鐵裙伴君王直到老。
〔西江月〕正德一回嫖院，布衣穿起綾羅。王龍橫死是如何？只爲裝腔取樂。雖然紅顏薄命，鐵裙原是傳訛。聊齋愛惜女嬌娥，留在房中取樂。

3 Pu Songling.

the tune of "Clear River Prelude" that praises the wise virtue of empress
Zhang and admires the good fortune of Concubine Liu.

Empress Zhang's virtue is rare in this world:
When she saw second sister arrive,
She personally helped her to rise.
She praised her as a lovely person
And gave her an iron skirt to accompany the emperor as long as he lived.

    To the tune of "West River Moon"

Because Right Virtue went whoring,
Commoners came to wear fine silk.
Why did Wang Long have to die a cruel death?
Because in seeking joy, he behaved like a rogue.

Even though "fine face, poor fate"
And "an iron skirt" are all fables,
Liaozhai,[3] out of love for this charming woman,
Stayed inside his room to have his fun.

Bibliography

Editions

Pu Liuquan 蒲柳泉. 1970. *Liaozhai quanji* 聊齋全集 [Collected Works of Liaozhai]. [Compiled by Lu Dahuang 路大荒 and Zhao Tiaokuang 趙苕狂.] Guting shuwu. Reprint of Shijie shuju, 1936.

Pu Songling 蒲松齡. Lu Dahuang 路大荒, ed. 1986. *Pu Songling ji* 蒲松齡集 [The Works of Pu Songling]. 2 vols. Shanghai guji chubanshe. Reprint of Zhonghua shuju, 1962.

Pu Songling 蒲松齡. Sheng Wei 盛伟, ed. 1998. *Pu Songling quanji* 蒲松齡全集 [The Complete Works of Pu Songling]. 3 vols. Xuelin chubanshe.

Pu Songling 蒲松齡. Pu Xianming 蒲先明, ed. Zou Zongliang 邹宗良, ann. 1999. *Liaozhai liqu ji* 聊斋俚曲集 [The Rustic Songs of Pu Songling]. Guoji wenhua chubanshe.

[Pu Songling 蒲松齡.] 2009. *Xingyun qu* 幸雲曲. In *Shandong wenxian jicheng* 山東文獻集成, edited by Han Yuqun 韓寓群, vol. 48, 1–288. Shandong daxue chubanshe.

Pu Songling 蒲松齡. 2018. *Liaozhai liqu ji* 聊斋俚曲集 [The Rustic Songs of Pu Songling]. Qi Lu shushe.

[Pu Songling 蒲松齡.] 2020. *Liaozhai bubian Xingyun qu Zhengde biaoyuan* 聊斋补编幸云曲正德婊院 [A Compilation of Additional Texts by Pu Songling—Songs of the Imperial Visit to Datong: Right Virtue Goes Whoring]. In *Ershi shiji wushi niandai Shandong daxue minjian wenxue caifeng ziliao huibian* 20世纪50年代山东大学民间文学采风资料汇编 [A Compilation of the Collected Materials on Popular Literature Collected by Shandong University in the 1950s], collected by Guan Dedong 关德东 et al., edited by Guan Jiazheng 关家铮 and Che Zhenhua 车振华, vol. 2, 614–726. Shanghai guji chubanshe.

Zhang Tai 张泰, ann. 2019. *Liaozhai liqu ji jiaozhu* 聊斋俚曲集校注 [Collated and Annotated Edition of the Rustic Songs of Pu Songling]. 2 vols. Jiuzhou chubanshe.

Specialized Reference Works

Dong Zunzhang 董遵章. 1985. *Yuan Ming Qing baihua zhuzuo zhong Shandong fangyan lishi* 元明清白话著作中山东方言例释 [Explanations of the Shandong Dialect Expressions in Vernacular Works of the Yuan, Ming, and Qing Dynasties]. Shandong jiaoyu chubanshe.

Feng Chuntian 冯春田. 2003. *Liaozhai liqu yufa yanjiu* 聊斋俚曲语法研究 [A Study of the Grammar of the Rustic Songs of Pu Songling]. Henan daxue chubanshe.

Xu Fuling 徐复岭, comp. 2018. *Jinpingmei cihua, Xingshi yinyuan zhuan, Liaozhai liqu ji yuyan cidian* 金瓶梅词话醒世姻缘传聊斋俚曲集语言词典 [A Dictionary of the Vocabulary of *Plum in a Golden Vase, A Marriage to Awaken the World*, and *Rustic Songs of Pu Songling*]. Shanghai cishu chubanshe.

Zhang Shuzheng 张树铮. 2018. *Pu Songling baihua zuopin yuyan yanjiu* 蒲松龄白话作品语言研究 [A Study of the Language of the Vernacular Works of Pu Songling]. 2 vols. Shandong daxue chubanshe.

General

Abe Yasuki 阿部泰记. 2020. "*Zengbu Xingyun qu* de minjian wenxue tese" 增补幸云曲的民间文学特色 [Characteristics of *Zengbu Xingyun qu* as Folk Literature]. *Pu Songling yanjiu* 蒲松龄研究 2020 (3): 248–256.

Anonymous. 1990. *Niaowo chanshi du Bai shilang xingjiao* 鳥窩禪師杜白侍郎行腳 [The Trajectory of Chan Master Birds' Nest Conversion of Vice Minister Bai]. In *Baojuan chuji* 寶卷初集 [First collection of precious scrolls], 40 vols., edited and annotated by Zhang Xishun 張希舜, vol. 28, 1–45. Shanxi renmin chubanshe.

Barr, Alan. 1986. "Pu Songling and the Qing Examination System." *Late Imperial China* 7 (1): 87–111.

Cai Zaomin 蔡造珉. 2003. *Xiegui xie yao, citan cinüe: Liaozhai liqu xinlun* 寫鬼寫妖刺貪刺虐——聊齋俚曲新論 [Describing Ghosts and Monsters, Exposing Greed and Cruelty: A New Study of the Rustic Songs of Pu Songling]. Wanjuanlou.

Chang, Chunshu and Shelley Hsueh-lun Chang. 1998. *Redefining History: Ghosts, Spirits, and Human Society in P'u Sung-ling's World, 1640–1715.* University of Michigan Press.

Che Zhenhua 车振华. 2015. *Qingdai shuochang wenxue chuangzuo yanjiu* 清代说唱文学创作研究 [A Study of the Creation of the Chantefable Literature of the Qing Period]. Qi Lu shushe.

Chen Yuchen 陈玉琛. 1997. "Liaozhai liqu tonglun" 聊斋俚曲通论 [A Comprehensive Discussion of the Rustic Songs of Pu Songling]. *Pu Songling yanjiu* 蒲松龄研究 1997 (4): 121–136.

Chen Yuchen 陈玉琛. 2004. *Liaozhai liqu* 聊斋俚曲 [The Rustic Songs of Pu Songling]. Shandong wenyi chubanshe.

Chen Yuchen 陈玉琛. 2019. *Liaozhai liqu qupai changqiang yibaishou* 聊斋俚曲曲牌唱腔100首 [A Hundred Melodies for the Tunes in the Rustic Songs of Pu Songling]. Jinan chubanshe.

Chen Zhiyong 陈志勇. 2017. *Minjian yanju yu xishen xinyang yanjiu* 民间演剧与戏神信仰研究 [A Study of Popular Theater and Belief in the God of Theater]. Zhongshan daxue chubanshe.

Doleželová-Velingerová, Milena and J. I. Crump, trans. 1971. *Ballad of the Hidden Dragon: Liu Chih-yüan chu-kung-tiao*. Clarendon Press.

Feng Menglong, comp. Shuhui Yang and Yunqin Yang, trans. 2009. *Stories to Awaken the World: A Ming Dynasty Collection*, vol. 3. University of Washington Press.

Fujita Yūken 藤田祐賢. 1984. "Ryōsai zokkyoku kō" 聊斋俗曲考 [An Inquiry into the Rustic Songs of Pu Songling]. *Geibun kenkyū* 18 (1964): 29–43. Chinese translation: Itō Naoya 伊藤植哉, "Liaozhai liqu kao" 聊斋俚曲考 [An Inquiry into the Rustic Songs of Pu Songling]. *Pu Songling yanjiu jikan* 4: 157–168.

Fujita Yūken 藤田祐賢. 1988. "Keiō gijuku shozō Ryōsai kankei shiryō mokuroku" 慶應義塾所藏聊齋關係資料目錄 [A Catalog of Materials Related to Pu Songling at Keio University]. *Geibun kenkyū* 53: 117–157.

Geiss, James. 1987. "The Leopard Quarter during the Cheng-te Reign." *Ming Studies* 24: 1–38.

Geiss, James. 1988. "The Cheng-te Reign, 1506–1521." In *The Cambridge History of China*, vol. 7: *The Ming Dynasty*, pt. I, edited by Frederick W. Mote and Denis Twitchett, 403–439. Cambridge University Press.

Gong Bin 龚斌. 2001. *Qing you qianqianjie: qinglou wenhua yu Zhongguo wenxue yanjiu* 情有千千结——青楼文化与中国文化研究 [Thousands upon Thousands of Knots of Passion: Studies on Bordello Culture and Chinese Literature]. Hanyu dacidian chubanshe.

Goodrich, L. Carrington, and Chao-ying Fang, eds. 1976. *Dictionary of Ming Biography, 1368–1644*. 2 vols. Columbia University Press.

Goossaert, Vincent. 2022. *Heavenly Masters: Two Thousand Years of the Daoist State*. University of Hawai'i Press.

Guan Dedong 关德栋, ann. 1980. *Liaozhai liqu xuan* 聊斋俚曲选 [A Selection of Rustic Songs by Pu Songling]. Qi Lu shushe.

Guan Dedong 关德栋. 1997. "Du *Liaozhai liqu* zhaji" 读聊斋俚曲札记 [Desultory Notes on the Rustic Songs of Pu Songling]. *Pu Songling yanjiu* 蒲松龄研究 1997 (4): 1–9.

Hanan, Patrick. 1988. *The Invention of Li Yu*. Harvard University Press.

[He Mengmei.] Tkin Shen and James Legge, trans. 1843. *The Rambles of the Emperor Ching Tĭh in Këang Nan: A Chinese Tale*. 2 vols. Longman, Brown, Green, and Longmans.

Hu Shi 胡適. 1953. "*Xingshi yinyuan zhuan* kaozheng" 醒世姻緣傳考證 [Research on *A Marriage to Awaken the World*]. In *Hu Shi wencun* 胡適文存, vol. 4, 329–395. Yuandong tushu gongsi.

Hua Wei 華瑋. 2019. *Qingdai xiqu zhong de Mingshi zaixian* 清代戲曲中的明史再現 [The Representation of Ming History in Qing Drama]. Zhonghua shuju.

Idema, Wilt L. 2010. "Prosimetric and Verse Narrative." In *The Cambridge History of Chinese Literature*, edited by Kang-I Sun Chang and Stephen Owen, vol. 2, 343–412. Cambridge University Press.

Idema, Wilt L. 2014. *The Resurrected Skeleton: From Zhuangzi to Lu Xun*. Columbia University Press.

Idema, Wilt L. 2021. "Shan Ameng, *Shaanxi Songs of a Boudoir Beauty* (Also Known as *Zither Songs of a Boudoir Beauty* or *Marital Harmony*, and Credited to Pu Songling)." *Chinoperl: Journal of Chinese Oral and Performing Literature* 40 (1): 35–64.

Jin Xia 靳霞. 2019. "Zhengde weixing zhong 'Zhou Yuan zhaoqin gushi' yanjiu" 正德微行中周元招亲故事研究 [A Study of the Story "Zhou Yuan Marries a Wife" in the Incognito Travels of the Zhengde Emperor]. *Hanzi wenhua* 汉字文化 244: 64–65.

Ladstätter, Otto. 1960. *P'u Sung-ling: Sein Leben und seine Werke in Umgangssprache* [Pu Songling: His Life and His Vernacular Works]. Diss., Ludwig-Maximilians-Universität München.

Li Dengqiao 李登桥. 2012. "Liaozhai liqu zhong de gupai boxi tanxi" 聊斋俚曲中的骨牌博戏探析 [An Analysis of the Gambling on Dominoes in the Rustic Songs of Pu Songling]. *Pu Songling yanjiu* 蒲松龄研究 2012 (1): 85–91.

Li Dengqiao 李登桥. 2015. "Liaozhai boxi yu Ming Qing zhi ji Shandong boxi xisu tanxi" 聊斋博戏与明清之际山东博戏习俗探析 [An Analysis of Gambling as Described by Pu Songling and the Gambling Habits in Shandong in the Seventeenth Century]. *Pu Songling yanjiu* 蒲松龄研究 2015 (3): 161–169.

Li Wanying 李万营. 2016. "Ming Wuzong youxing lieyan gushi de wenben yanbian ji qi wenhua yiyun" 明武宗游幸猎艳故事的文本演变及其文化意蕴 [The Transformations in the Texts on the Tale of the Ming Dynasty's Martial Ancestor's Imperial Rambles to Hunt for Beauties and Their Cultural Meaning]. *Tianzhong xuekan* 天中学刊 31 (1): 31–35.

Li Xianfang 李献芳. 1999. "*Zengbu Xingyun qu* shuolüe" 增补幸云曲说略 [A Brief Discussion of *Zengbu Xingyun qu*]. *Pu Songling yanjiu* 蒲松龄研究 1999 (3): 102–107, 117.

Lin Xiaoshuang 李晓爽. 2015. "*Liaozhai liqu* yuyanxue yanjiu zongshu" 聊斋俚曲语言学研究综述 [A General Description of Linguistic Studies of the Rustic Songs of Pu Songling]. *Pu Songling yanjiu* 蒲松龄研究 2015 (3): 100–110.

Liu Jieping 劉階平. 1950. *Pu Liuxian yizhu kaolüe yu Zhiyi yigao* 蒲柳先遗著考略與志異遺稿 [A Brief Inquiry into the Preserved Works of Pu Songling and the Preserved Drafts of *Strange Stories*]. Zhengzhong shuju.

Liu Jieping 劉階平. 1970. *Liaozhai tongsu xiqu xuanzhu* 聊齋通俗戲曲選注 [An Annotated Selection of Popular Plays by Pu Songling]. Taiwan Zhonghua shuju.

Liu Ruiming 刘瑞明. 2006. "Lun *Zengbu Xingyun qu*" 论增补幸云曲 [On *Zengbu Xingyun qu*]. *Pu Songling yanjiu* 蒲松龄研究 2006 (1): 92–101.

Liu Ruiming 刘瑞明. 2014. "*Zengbu Xingyun qu* jiaoshi" 增补幸云曲校释 [Notes on *Zengbu Xingyun qu*]. *Pu Songling yanjiu* 蒲松龄研究 2014 (1): 98–109.

Liu Shiyi 刘士义. 2018. *Mingdai qinglou wenhua yu wenxue* 明代青楼文化与文学 [Ming Dynasty Bordello Culture and Literature]. Zhongguo shehui kexue chubanshe.

Liu Shuiyun 刘水云 and Che Xilun 车锡伦. 2003. "Liaozhai liqu yu *daola*" 聊斋俚曲与倒喇 [Pu Songling's Rustic Songs and Rhymed Declamation Pieces]. *Pu Songling yanjiu* 蒲松龄研究 2003 (3): 89–96.

Liu Xiaojing 刘晓静. 2002. *Sanbai nian yixiang: Pu Songling liqu yinyue yanjiu* 三百年遗响——蒲松龄俚曲音乐研究 [Lingering Echoes after Three Hundred Years: A Study of the Music of the Rustic Songs of Pu Songling]. Shanghai Sanlian shudian.

Liu Xiurong 刘秀荣 and Liu Tingting 刘婷婷. 2016. *Liaozhai liqu lungang* 聊斋俚曲论纲 [An Outline Discussion of the Rustic Songs of Pu Songling]. Qi Lu shushe.

Liu Yan 刘燕. 2020. "Guanyu Liaozhai liqu chuangxin chuancheng de wenti yanjiu" 关于聊斋俚曲创新传承的问题研究 [A Study of the Problem of the Creative Continuity of the Rustic Songs of Pu Songling]. *Pu Songling yanjiu* 蒲松龄研究 2020 (3): 286–291.

Liu Yuansheng 刘元声. 2001. "Daya bu sui cao mo: chongdu *Zengbu Xingyun qu*" 大雅不随草没——重读增补幸云曲 [Great Elegance Is Not Suppressed by Weeds: Rereading *Zengbu Xingyun qu*]. *Xiju* 戏剧 2001 (2): 89–97.

Lu Dahuang 路大荒. 1980. *Pu Songling nianpu* 蒲松龄年谱 [An Annalistic Biography of Pu Songling]. Qi Lu shushe.

Lu Zhenzhen. 2014. "*Scrounging for a School (Naoguan)*, a Play by Pu Songling." *Chinoperl: Journal of Oral and Performing Literature* 33 (1): 60–81.

Lu, Zhenzhen. 2017. "The Vernacular World of Pu Songling." PhD diss., University of Pennsylvania.

Luo Dianhong 罗殿宏 and Tian Cuiying 田翠英. 2006. "Mingdai kuxing sanli kaolüe" 明代酷刑三例考略 [A Brief Inquiry into Three Cruel Punishments of the Ming Period]. *Lantai shijie* 兰台世界, March 2006: 71–72.

Miao Huaiming 苗怀明. 2021. *Shuochang wenxue wenxianxue shulüe* 说唱文学文献学述略 [A Summary Introduction to the Sources of Prosimetric Literature]. Zhongguo shehui kexue chubanshe.

Nienhauser, William H., Jr., ed. 2010. *Tang Dynasty Tales: A Guided Reader*. World Scientific.

Ōki Yasushi 大木康. 2002. *Chūgoku yūri kūkan: Min Shin Shinwai gijo no sekai* 中国遊里空間——明清秦淮妓女の世界 [The Space of China's Red-Light Districts: The World of the Qinhuai Courtesans of the Ming and Qing Dynasties]. Seidosha.

Ōki Yasushi 大木康. 2017. *Soshū hanamichi sanpo: Shantōkai no monogatari* 蘇州花街散步——山塘街の物語 [Strolling the Pleasure Quarters in Suzhou: A Story of Shantang Street]. Kyuko shoin.

Pu Songling. Li-ching Chang and Victor Mair, trans. 1986. "The Wall, a Folk Opera." *Chinoperl Papers* 14: 97–152.

Pu Songling. Rick Yuan, trans. 2001. "Two Stories from *Liaozhai zhiyi*: 'The Wall Painting,' 'The Fourteenth Daughter of the Xin family.'" *Renditions* 55: 26–41.

Pu Songling. C. D. Alison Bailey and Bonnie S. McDougall, trans. 2008. "The Cold and the Dark: Extracts." *Renditions* 70: 65–88.

Pu Songling. Wilt L. Idema, trans. 2022a. "A Pleasant Song." *Renditions* 97: 7–52.

Pu Songling. Wilt L. Idema, trans. 2022b. "The Union of Beast and Beauty." *Chinoperl, Journal of Chinese Oral and Performing Literature* 41 (2): 182–190.

Pu Xizhang 蒲喜章 and Cao Juetian 曹厥田. 2007. "Liaozhai yizhu sanzhong" 聊斋佚著三种 [Three Surviving Works by Pu Songling]. *Pu Songling yanjiu* 蒲松龄研究 2007 (4): 105–133.

Pu Xianhe 蒲先和. 2017. "*Zengbu Xingyun qu* jiaoshi bianwu" 增补幸云曲校释辩误 [Mistakes in "Notes on *Zengbu Xingyun qu*"]. *Pu Songling yanjiu* 蒲松龄研究 2017 (4): 88–93, 13.

Pu Ze 蒲泽. 2016. "Xianhua Liaozhai liqu de chuanbo" 闲话聊斋俚曲的传播 [Some Comments on the Transmission of the Rustic Songs of Pu Songling]. *Pu Songling yanjiu* 蒲松龄研究 2016 (1): 105–114.

Robinson, David. 2001. *Bandits, Eunuchs, and the Son of Heaven: Rebellion and the Economy of Violence in Mid-Ming China.* University of Hawai'i Press.

Shao Jizhi 邵吉志. 2005. "Liushi duo nian lai Pu Songling liqu yanjiu gaishu" 六十多年来蒲松龄俚曲研究的概述 [More than Sixty Years of Research on Pu Songling's Rustic Songs: A General Description]. *Pu Songling yanjiu* 蒲松龄研究 2005 (1): 109–122.

Shao Jizhi 邵吉志. 2008. *Cong "Zhiyi" dao "liqu": Pu Songling xinjie* 从志异到俚曲——蒲松龄新解 [From *Strange Tales* to Rustic Songs: A New Interpretation of Pu Songling]. Qi Lu shushe.

Shen Defu 沈德符. 1980. *Wanli yehuo bian* 萬歷野獲編 [Rumors of the Wanli Reign]. Zhonghua shuju.

Sheng Wei 盛伟. 1997. "Pu shi beiyin liqu shisizhong shunxu kao" 蒲氏碑阴俚曲十四种顺序考 [An Inquiry into the Sequence of the Fourteen Rustic Songs Mentioned on the Backside of the Stele for Pu Songling]. *Pu Songling yanjiu* 蒲松龄研究 1997 (4): 34–50.

Sheng Wei 盛伟. 2012. "Pu Songling xie *Liaozhai liqu* xintan" 蒲松龄写聊斋俚曲新探 [A New Analysis of the Rustic Songs Written by Pu Songling]. *Pu Songling yanjiu* 蒲松龄研究 2012 (4): 113–117.

Starr, Chloë F. 2007. *Red-light novels of the late Qing.* Brill.

Tsai, Shih-san Henry. 1996. *The Eunuchs in the Ming Dynasty.* State University of New York Press.

Tao Muning 陶慕宁. 2006. *Qinglou wenxue yu Zhongguo wenhua* 青楼文学与中国文化 [Bordello Literature and Chinese Culture]. Dongfang chubanshe.

Wang Boyun, Zhou Liang, Luo Yang et al. 王波云周良罗扬. 2002. *Zhongguo quyi zhi, Shandong juan* 中国曲艺志山东卷 [A Compendium of the Performative Arts of China, Shandong Province]. Xinhua chubanshe.

Wang Fengling 汪玢玲. 1985. *Pu Songling yu minjianwenxue* 蒲松龄与民间文学 [Pu Songling and Folk Literature]. Shanghai wenyi chubanshe.

Wang Qingping 王清平, ed. 2020. *Liaozhai liqu lunji* 聊斋俚曲论集 [A Collection of Articles on the Rustic Songs of Pu Songling]. Qi Lu shushe.

Wang, Xing. 2020. *Physiognomy in Ming China: Fortune and the Body*. Brill.

Wang Yanyong 王延永 and Chen Yuchen 陈玉琛. 2020. "Wu Zhao: Liaozhai liqu lilun yanjiu de dianjiren" 吴钊——聊斋俚曲理论研究的奠基人 [Wu Zhao: The Foundational Figure in the Study of Pu Songling's Rustic Songs]. *Pu Songling yanjiu* 蒲松龄研究 2020 (3): 279–285.

Wang Yanyong 王延永 and Chen Yuchen 陈玉琛. 2021. "Lun Liaozhai liqu de renminxing" [On the Popular Nature of Pu Songling's Rustic Songs]. *Pu Songling yanjiu* 蒲松龄研究 2021 (6): 99–106.

Weightman, Frances. 2004. "Milestones on the Road to Maturity: Growing up with the Civil Service Examinations." *Sungkyun Journal of East Asian Studies* 4 (2): 113–135.

Wu Zhao 吴钊. 1983. "Tan Pu Songling de liqu" 谈蒲松龄的俚曲 [Comments on the Rustic Songs of Pu Songling]. *Zhongguo yinyue* 中国音乐 1983 (1): 25–26.

Yang Hairu 杨海儒. 1991. "Liaozhai liqu ji qi yanjiu" 聊斋俚曲及其研究 [Pu Songling's Rustic Songs and Their Study]. *Wenxue yichan* 文学遗产 1991 (3): 135–139.

Yang Hairu 杨海儒. 1994. *Pu Songling shengping zhushu kaobian* 蒲松龄生平著述考辩 [An Inquiry into the Life and Works of Pu Songling]. Zhongguo shuji chubanshe.

Yuan Shishuo 袁世硕. 1988. *Pu Songling shiji zhushu xinkao* 蒲松龄事迹著述新考 [A New Inquiry into the Facts of Pu Songling's Life and Works]. Qi Lu shushe.

Yuan Shishuo 袁世硕, ed. 2009. *Pu Songling zhi* 蒲松龄志 [A Compendium on Pu Songling]. Shandong renmin chubanshe.

Zamperini, Paola. 2010. *Lost Bodies: Prostitution and Masculinity in China*. Brill.

Zeitlin, Judith T. 1993. *Historian of the Strange: Pu Songling and the Chinese Classical Tale*. Stanford University Press.

Zhang Ningbo 张宁波. 2015. "Ming Taizu yu Qing Shizong fanfu bijiao ji qishi" 明太祖与清世宗反腐比较及启示 [A Comparison of the Struggle Against Corruption of the Hongwu Emperor of the Ming and the Kangxi Emperor of the Qing and Its Lessons]. *Hubei jingji xueyuan xuebao* 湖北经济学院学报 12 (9): 72–73.

Zhang Tai 张泰. 2011. "*Liaozhai liqu ji* yinshi wenhua fenxi" 聊斋俚曲集饮食文化分析 [An Analysis of the Food and Drink Culture in the Rustic Songs of Pu Songling]. *Pu Songli yanjiu* 蒲松龄研究 2011 (4): 90–99.

Zhou Yibai 周贻白. 1986. "Pu Songling de *Liaozhai liqu*" 蒲松龄的聊斋俚曲 [Pu Songling's *Rustic Songs of Liaozhai*]. In *Zhou Yibai xiaoshuo xiqu lunji* 周贻白小说戏曲论集 [Collected Articles by Zhou Yibai on Vernacular Fiction and Drama], edited by Shen Xieyuan 沈燮元, 646–650. Qi Lu shushe.

Zou Zongliang 邹宗良. 2021. "Tianshange ben *Qinsele qu* weituo Pu Songling kao: *Qinsele zuozhe kaobian zhi yi*" 天山阁本琴瑟乐曲伪托蒲松龄考——琴瑟乐作者考辩之一 [An Inquiry into the False Ascription of *Qinsele qu* to Pu Songling: A First Inquiry into the Authorship of *Qinsele*]. *Pu Songling yanjiu* 蒲松龄研究 2021 (3): 102–122.